Saru eyed Burnham. "You talk about following the letter of the regulations, but that isn't what you said in the mess hall. You ignored protocol by having the buoy beamed aboard the ship."

"That was different," she replied.

"How so? You advocate following regulations in one case but not another? It seems very arbitrary to me." They were falling into their familiar, combative rhythm once more, but Saru didn't care to halt it. At times he felt he understood Michael Burnham best when they were disagreeing.

"We're trained to interpret a situation based on the unfolding circumstances," Burnham shot back. "This is the frontier, Saru. The nearest starbase is days away at high warp; the same for the closest Starfleet vessel. We have to be ready to bend the regulations if the moment demands it. That's the thing that separates a good officer from a great one, knowing when to bend and when to be firm." She cocked her head. "If you want to command a starship one day, you need to learn when to make those calls. When to show boldness and when to use restraint."

A retort was forming in his mind when something in Saru made him halt. The human had a point, as irritating as it might have been to admit it. *Perhaps I should consider things from her viewpoint*, he thought. *What would Burnham do if our situations were reversed?*

Don't miss these other exciting books in the world of

STAR TREK®
DISCOVERY

DESPERATE HOURS

by David Mack

DRASTIC MEASURES

by Dayton Ward

STAR TREK®

DISCOVERY

FEAR ITSELF

JAMES SWALLOW

Based upon *Star Trek*®
created by Gene Roddenberry
and
Star Trek: Discovery
created by Bryan Fuller & Alex Kurtzman

GALLERY BOOKS
New York London Toronto Sydney New Delhi

G

Gallery Books
An Imprint of Simon & Schuster, Inc.
1230 Avenue of the Americas
New York, NY 10020

This book is a work of fiction. Any references to historical events, real people, or real places are used fictitiously. Other names, characters, places, and events are products of the author's imagination, and any resemblance to actual events or places or persons, living or dead, is entirely coincidental.

This book is published by Gallery Books, an imprint of Simon & Schuster, Inc., under exclusive license from CBS Studios Inc.

First Gallery Books trade paperback edition June 2018

GALLERY BOOKS and colophon are registered trademarks of Simon & Schuster, Inc.

Manufactured in the United States of America

10 9 8 7 6 5 4 3 2 1

ISBN 978-1-5011-6659-4
ISBN 978-1-5011-6660-0 (ebook)

For Bryan Fuller, with thanks for all the advice

Historian's Note

This story takes place in 2252. It is four years before a day in May 2256 when a fateful meeting between the *U.S.S. Shenzhou* and T'Kuvma's followers will spark a war with the Klingon Empire (*Star Trek: Discovery*—"Battle of the Binary Stars").

Nothing routs us but the villainy of our fears.

—William Shakespeare
Cymbeline, Act 5, Scene II

1

Out in the darkness, unseen and unheard, the danger was waiting for Saru.

He crouched low to the floor, his long arms and legs folded up close to his slim torso. He kept his head bowed and his eyes closed, extending his senses into the room, seeking the presence of the threat.

The aural channels of the Kelpien's lobeless ears and pits on the surface of his scalp channeled every last fraction of sound into his awareness. Electrosensitive nerve clusters beneath the skin of his face and along the backs of his thin fingers tasted the constant background hum of the vessel around him. He instinctively sifted the wash of sense-noise for anything untoward and found . . . *nothing*.

Slowly, Saru opened his eyes. His vision instantly adjusted to the dimness of the unlit compartment. He unfolded to his full height, rising with his back to the corner of the room, and the only doorway in or out in front of him. Shadowy shapes crowded the edges of his vision: his sleeping pallet, a desk and computer unit, a table upon which stood a careworn box made of carved wood, a three-dimensional chess set, and a data pad. The objects were benign, unthreatening. Or at least, that was what he was *meant* to think.

He stood there for a full two minutes without expelling

a breath. To an outside observer, he would have appeared totally inert, a strange statue in the still life of the cabin.

Then he moved, in quick and economical motions. It was exactly five hoof steps from the far corner of the room to the door, and Saru could cover it in an instant if he chose to, but today he stepped evenly, carefully. It was the pace of one passive and harmless, one who did not wish to upset the equilibrium of whatever might be waiting in the gloom.

He was taking his third step when he noticed a pair of identical cups sitting on the disposal tray of the cabin's food slot.

There was no need for there to be two. Saru had no company in these quarters. As a Starfleet lieutenant, his rank was of sufficient level and the *U.S.S. Shenzhou* was a ship of enough tonnage to afford him the advantage of privacy in his billet. And he was too fastidious to needlessly fabricate a second drinking container when one already existed. The metallic shape of the cup rippled with an oily light and he turned toward it, instinctively drawn by motion where none should have followed.

The cup *changed*. The cylindrical shape transformed into something between a gel and a powder, dropping into a pool of itself. It rebounded into a spiny form that resembled a cluster of skittering crustacean legs, a knot of shiny limbs that had no hub to them. The creature exploded into motion, its greasy sensor palps detecting the change in air density as Saru moved past it.

The tips of its legs hardened into a density near that of tempered steel. Once it found a victim, the creature would seek the softest tissues through which to force its limbs, and after dermal penetration had occurred, it would eat.

This was a process in three stages. Paralysis of the target life-form caused by an extruded neurotoxin; then systematic liquefaction of all nerve tissue, as agonizing as it was horrific; and finally consumption of internal organs from within. The victim would, mercifully, be dead by the time the third stage occurred. If the meal was of sufficient richness, the engorged attacker would enter a budding cycle and reproduce. One well-fed creature could spawn many times, given adequate sustenance. Saru's tall corpse would provide more than enough for a dozen generations.

He froze as it landed on his shoulder, and the cluster of legs halted, the needle-tips hesitating. It moved around the nape of his neck, across the back of his head, and then down his arm, palps twitching at the air. Its behavior suggested it was confused. The movement it had detected now ceased. In the creature's primitive, predatory brain, it could not understand how a prey-thing of such mass could be in motion one instant and still in the next. It was used to the thrashing and panicked frenzy of a target, the confirmation that it had found its next meal.

Saru remained immobile as the thing picked its way down the length of his dark blue uniform, plucking at the cloth. Presently, it became disinterested and dropped off, clattering to the deck. He watched it wander across the floor before finally reconfiguring itself. The simple little polymorph reverted back to the last form it had adopted, once again becoming a passable copy of the ceramic cup. Sitting on the deck in front of the door, it looked odd and out of place.

Saru took a breath and surged forward, bringing one heavy hoofed boot to stamp on the creature before it could revert. It glittered as it died, not through organic means but in transformation as it became a flash of fading holographic pixels.

"Simulation concluded," said a feminine voice from a computer panel on the far wall. *"Do you wish to reset?"*

"What was that?" Saru said to the air, refreshed with the rush of adrenaline tingling through his body.

"The holoprojection was a mature example of the species Salazinus metamorphii, *colloquial name Salazar's Feign. A type-two hazardous mimetic life-form native to a Class-Y world in the Lembatta Cluster. Do you wish to reset?"*

Again, he ignored the question and posed one of his own. "That felt slow to me. Was I slow? Would it have killed me in reality?"

"Negative. Your reaction time was sufficient to avoid a fatality. However, you were one point three milliseconds slower than your previous recorded instance."

"Ah. Yes, of course." Saru glanced up at the holographic projector module he had mounted on the ceiling of his quarters. That previous time, the simulation program had randomly generated a Denebian slime devil lurking in the waste disposal slot, and the thing had almost scored a bite that, if it had been real, would have taken off two of his fingers at the second joint. "Reason?" he demanded.

"Authorization required to access medical scans in order to generate conjecture," said the computer.

"Yes, yes," he said tersely, gesturing at the air. "Authorization Kappa-Saru-Seven."

"Working."

He glanced out of the cabin's port, observing an unmoving field of alien stars framed against a fathomless reach of night. Off the *Shenzhou*'s port bow, Saru's keen eyesight picked out a smooth-sided slab of gray metal, its surface marred by heavy carbon scoring. He studied it, then looked away.

By rights, Saru should have already been on his way to his duty station, but this was something he didn't want to put off. He'd been feeling sluggish and ill at ease for a few days, and if something was slowing him down, it was important he knew now. Before anyone else did.

"Analysis complete," announced the computer. *"Blood sugar levels are below recommended margins."*

Saru blew out a breath. "Ah." Twice in the last three days he had missed a meal in the mess hall and filled the gap with a ration bar. That, combined with the stress of his current assignment, explained it. "I cannot afford to be slow," he said to the air. "The slow and the weak are as good as dead."

"Please restate command."

"Suspend program!" Saru snapped irritably, then added, "For now."

The whole purpose of the hologram predators and the randomizing software that generated them was to keep him sharp, he reminded himself. Left to exist on only the baseline level of response stimuli that his crewmates took for granted, Saru found himself "climbing the walls," as Ensign Januzzi had once colorfully described it. The simulation helped to keep Saru focused and, more importantly, it was a constant reminder of the singular truth that he believed above all others—the universe was an inherently dangerous place, which would kill the unwary and the unprepared in a heartbeat.

Brushing lint off the silver tabs on the flanks of his uniform, Saru drew himself up and picked up the data pad from the table before stepping quickly out into the corridor beyond—

—And directly into the path of Chief Petty Officer Zuzub. The Kaferian security guard made a click-clacking noise with his wide mandibles and stepped back, apologetically raising his arms. "Pardon, pardon, Lieutenant," murmured the insectoid's shoulder-mounted vocoder unit. "Bridge has us on a drill, sir, in a hurry."

"Hmm," Saru managed, pushing away the flash of instant terror that had briefly come over him at the sight of a massive predatory arthropod looming in the corridor. "C-carry on."

Zuzub's large head bobbed and he went on his way. The Kaferian was actually a friendly sort, but his species had a fearsome aspect that belied their gentler nature. Saru considered this as he set off in the other direction. He had met many sentients since joining Starfleet and had visited several alien worlds. On an intellectual level, he understood that the outward appearance of most beings bore no connection to their inner natures. But it was hard to get past a lifetime of instinctive, ingrained reactions and a physiology like his, one attuned toward the triggering of a fight-or-flight reflex at the slightest impetus.

Saru continued on, having decided to postpone reporting to the secondary systems laboratory on deck three in favor of attending to a baser need: *a decent breakfast.* He could use the time to go over his notes on the data pad and prepare for the day's work. Moving along the corridor in loping, long steps, he nodded in passing as two human ensigns from the astrogeology department crossed his path.

Humans always seemed so relaxed to Saru—dangerously so, in fact. He wondered if they, like him, felt the pull of their primitive natures dragging against their evolved selves. Their open, smooth faces bereft of attractive striation and the blank regularity of their sensory aura-fields made it hard for Saru to parse the more subtle emotional states of their species. It required careful observation and evaluation on his part, and that could be tiring. Not for the first time, he wondered what it would be like going through life without being able to hear the ghost hum of electromagnetic energy emitted by everything around him. It would be no different from living without a sense of taste or smell.

For Saru, the *Shenzhou* purred to itself as the starship's systems operated in synchrony, the engines for now on standby as the vessel drifted at station-keeping. Had they been moving at impulse power, he would have known it the moment he stepped out of his cabin. There was a distinct resonance of the EM field that he felt somewhere near the crown of his scalp when they cruised at sublight, and a sharper timbre created by the bleed effect of warp travel that gathered at the base of his neck. After years in Starfleet, the Kelpien had become habituated to the effects, but there were still times—usually when he was fatigued—when they made it hard for him to concentrate. The captain had graciously allowed Saru to have a layer of baffle plating fitted around the walls of his quarters to aid his sleep, a fact that he was forever grateful for.

He sensed another human approaching just before *Shenzhou*'s chief engineer, deep in thought, came around a corner in the corridor and strode briskly past him. Lieutenant Commander Saladin Johar took a couple of steps, and then executed a swift about-face to stare up at Saru. "Science officer," he began, as if framing a question.

"Yes, sir?" Saru rocked to a halt, balancing on the tips of his hooves.

"I was on my way down to the bridge. Maybe you can save me the turbolift ride." Most humans were shorter than the gangly Kelpien, and Saru found that many of them exhibited an unconscious defensiveness when forced to look *up* at someone, just as Johar did now. He resisted the urge to hunch forward as the chief engineer went on. "My team is ready to deploy the replacement buoy as soon as you give us the green light. I'm wondering why you're making us wait."

"There are questions that still need to be answered," said Saru, his hands finding each other around the data pad.

"Lieutenant Burnham and I are in the process of a full investigation of the damaged unit. . . . It would be unwise to launch a replacement until we are certain what caused the previous buoy to malfunction."

"That's what you told me in the last staff meeting. Twenty hours ago." Johar eyed him, his tawny face creasing in a frown. The engineer had been pulling double duty over the last week, filling in for Lieutenant Commander Itzel García while the *Shenzhou*'s second officer was away on Pacifica, but that didn't mean he was about to let anything slip by on his watch.

Saru experimented with a shrug. "My explanation remains the same, sir. The damage was extensive. The cause is unclear. It's taking us a while to analyze." He didn't add that his disagreements with Michael Burnham over exactly *how* to handle the analysis had put a noticeable strain on the process.

To say that Saru and the human woman did not see eye to eye was something of an understatement. Burnham's tendency to become hyperfocused on certain details frequently clashed with Saru's innate desire to seek a more reductionist solution to problems—a disposition that stemmed from her education among Vulcans, he imagined—and while he was firmly a by-the-book analyst, her disinclination to consider other approaches was at times stifling.

Johar's expression didn't change. The chief engineer wasn't happy with the answer. "Speed things along, Lieutenant," he said, walking away. "Otherwise cobwebs will start forming on the warp nacelles."

Saru nodded, not quite following the idiom, and continued on toward the mess hall as the problem at hand pushed its way to the front of his thoughts.

The remote monitoring buoy the *Shenzhou* had located two days earlier was one of a wide network of autonomous, self-sufficient devices seeded throughout this sector of space by Starfleet Command. Dozens of identical units, cylindrical modules the size of photon torpedoes, drifted out here on the frontier of the United Federation of Planets. Each contained a compact fusion reactor, an ion drive, a suite of high-acuity sensors, and a long-range subspace transceiver array slaved to an expert computer system. Under ideal conditions, the buoys could operate for up to twenty standard years before requiring replacement. They would listen for energy patterns or communications from out beyond the edge of Federation space. Endlessly watchful, ready to sound a warning if a threat made its presence known, they were Starfleet's silent sentinels.

And they were stationed here with good cause. A few light-years distant lay the borders of another interstellar power, the maddeningly vague edges of the Tholian Assembly. Saru recalled what he had learned about the antagonistic crystalline species during his years at Starfleet Academy. They had an unpredictable, bellicose nature and a tendency toward punctuality and hostile actions. The Kelpien had never seen one of their dart-shaped "spinner" ships outside of blurry data-tape images, and he had no desire to do so. Everyone on board the *Shenzhou* knew that the Tholians would be out there somewhere, watching the Starfleet ship's every move from the extreme edge of sensor range. Saru imagined them like the *ba'ul*, the apex predators from his homeworld, which would lie in wait until they struck out at their prey.

The logical assumption, at least by Saru's lights, was that the monitor buoy had fallen victim to Tholian aggression, but if that were proven true, it would invite a whole new raft of problems for the *Shenzhou* and Starfleet to deal with. Burnham had raised an eyebrow at Saru's leap of reasoning, noting that proximity to the Assembly didn't automatically make the Tholians the culprits. Quite rightly, she pointed out that there were other sentient species in the nonaligned border space between the two larger states, as well as stellar phenomena and other possible causes for the damage that the unit had suffered. Saru knew she was correct, but the Kelpien had lived this long only because of his species' unerring sense for the dangerous, and right now that pragmatic streak was telling him to prepare for the worst.

The junior science officer was thinking of how he would explain that to Burnham when he stepped through the doors into the mess hall and found the dark-skinned human female seated at a table in front of him.

She was young and intense. Burnham's gaze had a searching quality to it, and Saru always felt like she was on the verge of action even as her more moderated manner reeled her back in. She paused with her spoon in the bowl of food in front of her and saw the data pad in his hand. Burnham nodded at her own pad, propped up on the table. Like Saru's, it showed blocks of dense text from the preliminary, close-range analysis of the buoy.

"Lieutenant. It appears we had the same idea this morning."

"Lieutenant," he repeated. "It would seem so." Resigned to the way this would now play out, Saru got himself some muesli and yogurt from the food synthesizer, seasoned it with a generous amount of Aldebaran paprika, then took the seat across the table from Burnham.

She didn't give him time to start eating. "I've reviewed the sensor readings . . . *again*. A physical tear-down of the damaged unit in the lab is the next logical step. Remote analysis simply isn't giving us the answers we need."

Saru doggedly chewed a large spoonful before replying. "Captain Georgiou's orders were clear. *Proceed with caution.* If we bring the buoy on board before we know for certain that it does not pose a risk to the ship, we will be negligent in our duties—"

"It's inert," insisted Burnham. "I am sure of that."

"I know *you* are sure," he countered.

"There comes a point where a degree of risk has to be accepted," she went on. "This ship wouldn't be out here if that wasn't true. Starfleet wouldn't exist. You would still be living on Kaminar."

"It could be booby-trapped," said Saru, cutting off her train of thought. "The Tholians have been known to use such tactics."

"There's no proof they're responsible." The ghost of a smile played over her lips. "But . . . that is a fair point. All right. If you won't let me bring it to us, we'll go to it."

"What?" Saru blinked.

"You and I can go out in thruster suits. With the work we need to do, I don't estimate the EVA operation lasting more than . . . say, ten or twelve hours?"

Saru's skin prickled. The notion of floating around in deep space with only a few layers of flex-mesh and a bubble helmet between him and an instant freeze-boiling death did not appeal to the Kelpien. "It has been a while since my last zero-g refresher course," he admitted.

"Really?" Burnham arched her eyebrow in a very Vulcan fashion. "Perhaps you'd like to reconsider my previous suggestion."

Her tone made him bristle, and irritation flared in Saru's eyes. His jaw dropped open slightly in an instinctive reaction, exposing the sensing surface in the roof of his mouth. Back on Kaminar, the action would allow his species to taste the air and pick up traces of predators, but here and now it was a signifier of his annoyance at Burnham's attempt to take charge of their shared assignment.

It would have been easy to give in to complete dislike of the human, if it wasn't for the fact that she was good at what she did. Saru couldn't deny that she had a sharp, incisive mind, and that only made things worse. It was no secret aboard the *Shenzhou* that Lieutenant Michael Burnham was a rising star, charting an ascent through the ranks that was positively meteoric. Saru had heard other officers talking about her as the front-runner for the post of ship's exec, in a few years when the time came for the current first officer Commander ch'Theloh to go on to a ship of his own. That sat poorly with the Kelpien.

Saru's own career arc was tracing a much flatter trajectory, a slow-and-steady path he had built through hard work and careful deliberation. He was a scientist, that was his first and truest impulse, but the role of XO, and the road that led to command of a starship, beckoned to Saru in a way that nothing in his life ever had. He didn't believe in concepts like destiny, but after leaving his homeworld for Starfleet Academy, Saru believed that there was a true vocation he was best suited for. Captain of a starship, exploring the unknown, keeping the Federation safe. That was a future he dared to aspire to.

But Burnham would get there first. He could sense the inevitability of it. She would eclipse him and race ahead, and on some level the human knew so. In his more pessimistic moments, Saru wondered if Burnham saw him as an obstacle in her path toward the center seat. He couldn't read her, and anything Saru could not read, he automatically considered to be a danger.

Before he could stop himself, he was returning to the pattern of argumentative discourse that seemed to color every conversation between the two lieutenants.

"The act of beaming the unit aboard could trigger a concealed weapon," he said quickly. "A protective force field would need to be set up around the lab to contain any possible discharge—"

Burnham tapped her pad. "I programmed a suitable containment-field macro earlier this morning."

"Of course you did," he muttered. "I find it difficult to understand why someone raised in the Vulcan doctrines fails to grasp the logic of being careful."

Her eyes narrowed. "Just as I fail to understand how a being who grew up around lethal predators can't make a value judgment between a real danger and an illusory one. Only so much can be achieved by watching from the sidelines, Saru."

He drew back and fixed her with an arch look. "I recall a human aphorism about *fools rushing in . . .*"

Burnham's lip curled. "We've been at this for days. There's no rushing of any kind going on." She let out a breath. "Which is why I chose to proceed with the transport before I started my breakfast."

"What?" Saru shot to his feet and took a step toward the ports along the length of the mess hall. He immediately looked out toward the bow, where he had seen the buoy adrift from his cabin. The object was no longer visible.

Burnham got up and walked over. "We're all still here. So I guess that means the buoy wasn't booby-trapped after all."

"You had no right to proceed without me." Saru's words were tight with annoyance, and he glared out at the stars. "We may share the same rank, but I have served longer, I have seniority!"

She stood beside him, looking at the void. "This isn't about that. I'm not trying to undermine you, I'm trying to complete our assignment."

"By ignoring regulations?"

"By interpreting them," Burnham shot back. "To best effect."

"Then what was the point of that comment about the EVA?"

She shrugged. "I was interested to see how you would reply."

Saru turned to face her, raising a finger, belatedly becoming aware that someone was standing behind the two of them. "Your assignment is to analyze the buoy, not my response to . . ." He trailed off as he realized that the new arrival was *Shenzhou*'s commanding officer, Captain Philippa Georgiou. Burnham, too, reacted with surprise at the other woman's appearance.

The captain had an unerring ability to approach out of nowhere that even Saru's acute senses sometimes missed, and a mentor's seemingly bottomless patience for the quirks of her crew. A wry smile played on Georgiou's face as she sipped at a mug of tea. "Oh, Mister Saru," she began, "don't stop on my account. It's fascinating to watch my officers bickering in their natural habitat."

"It isn't . . ." Saru stiffened in embarrassment. "We were not . . ."

To her credit, Burnham had the honesty to look as contrite as Saru felt. "We weren't *bickering*, Captain. It was more of a . . . a spirited . . ."

"Spirited discussion," Saru added. "Between two differing . . ."

"Scientific methods," concluded Burnham as the pair of them patched together a shared explanation.

"Was it?" Georgiou said mildly, and with those words Saru briefly felt like an errant child called to account by an elder. At his side, Burnham stood as stiffly as he did. "While I approve of competing schools of thought aboard my ship, I do draw the line at outright disagreement." The captain took another sip and eyed them both. "You are two of my best officers. Your skills are meant to complement each other, not create friction." Another commander might have made those words an admonishment, but not Philippa Georgiou. She made it sound like a challenge, like a request. Her smile deepened. "Well. Not too much."

"Lieutenant Saru and I will have an updated report by the end of the shift," said Burnham. "I'll inform the chief engineer he can deploy the replacement buoy." She gave Saru a questioning look that asked *Do you agree?*

"Of course." Saru was going to add more, but then a flicker of faint light at the corner of his vision drew the Kelpien's attention back to the mess hall's windows. For a brief instant, out in the darkness a needle-sharp glint of hard-white color flashed and then faded.

"Saru, what is it?" Burnham looked in the same direction, her brow creasing in concern.

"Did you see that?" It was possible that Burnham and the captain had not, as human optical ranges did not venture as far into the ultraviolet as that of Kelpiens. "A flash of light, like a distant supernova . . ." Saru paused. Had he been mistaken?

He was still wondering when the strident tones of a bosun's whistle sounded as the *Shenzhou*'s intraship activated, and the stern, uncompromising voice of the first officer issued out of the air. *"Captain and senior science officers, report to the bridge immediately."*

A chill crawled up the base of Saru's spine as he stared out in the direction of the flicker, and the brief instance of curiosity he felt began to shade toward fear.

Burnham followed her captain onto the *Shenzhou*'s bridge, with Saru loping along a pace behind. In the middle of the command deck, the captain's chair swiveled toward them and Commander ch'Theloh stepped smartly out of it, drawing up to full attention. "Captain on the bridge!" he snapped briskly, and the Andorian's antennae arched.

Ch'Theloh had an open face at odds with his rigid manner. His adherence to military protocol sometimes seemed overly ceremonial to Burnham, but the first officer's razor-like efficiency was without question, as was his ability to marshal the bridge crew in a time of crisis. Surveying the other stations, Burnham saw that every duty officer was hard at work. She moved to the science console, with Saru still shadowing her, and cast a glance toward Ensign Troke at secondary scanner control. The pale blue Tulian shot her a wary look as he tapped the wireless data implant on his neck. *Something is up.*

Captain Georgiou took her seat and turned back to the main viewer, studying the display projected on the inner surface of the bowl-like observation dome that formed the lowest deck of the *Shenzhou*'s spaceframe. Ch'Theloh already had a tactical plot overlaid across the starscape, the few scattered suns and dust clouds in the nearby region highlighted in glowing blue and green. "Report," ordered the captain.

As always, the first officer wasted no time with preamble. "Anomalous energy discharge at extreme range. Subspace frequencies, diffuse at this distance but enough to trip our sensors."

As ch'Theloh spoke, Burnham brought up the pattern of the energy effect that Troke had fed to the console and scrutinized it. Saru peered over her shoulder to follow the analysis. "Phase-wave pulse," he offered, his skull-like aspect creasing in thought. "Artificial?"

She nodded, pointing at the smooth peaks and troughs of the wave pattern. "Agreed. The high-order regularity would make that likely. A natural phenomenon would be more random."

"Engineer Johar was calling down almost the instant it reached us," continued the first officer. "Said the discharge was registering on his board in engineering."

"From this far away?" Georgiou pivoted to look in Burnham and Saru's direction. "Lieutenants, what's your take on this?"

Burnham inclined her head, letting Saru take the lead. He cleared his throat. "The flash of light I saw from the mess hall appears to be the visual component of a subspace energy shock. I believe we are looking at a localized, high-intensity quantum effect generated by an artificial source."

"It's a nadion pulse," added Burnham.

"Captain, nadion particles are generated by directed-energy weapons." Kamran Gant, *Shenzhou*'s senior tactical officer, spoke up. "The Romulans use that technology."

"Noted. But we're a long way from the Star Empire," said Georgiou, quashing that line of speculation before it could begin. "What else could be responsible?"

"A polaric-ion power matrix," offered Saru. "Certain varieties of contra-field warp drives use nadion injection primers . . ."

Burnham was listening with half an ear as she worked the console in front of her, assembling a virtual model of what the epicenter of the pulse would look like, based on the readings, the distance, and the particle decay rate. What formed on the holographic screen in front of her was alarming. "Captain, the initial source of the pulse was very strong. The fact that the UV radiation flare was visible to Saru means that this was a catastrophic release. I think we may have just witnessed the destruction of a starship . . ."

"Not the destruction," Saru corrected. He leaned in to tap out a command string on the panel, and a blurry quadrant of the viewer shimmered as it refocused. "If that were so, we would be picking up a broad field of irradiated wreckage."

"Confirming," said Troke, staring into the middle distance as his data implant beamed new readings directly into his cerebral cortex. "I have a high-probability detection of two discrete objects at the origin point of the pulse. Ships."

The captain shot a look toward Ensign Fan at the communications station. "Mary, are you receiving any signals from those vessels?"

Fan held a wireless transceiver to her ear and gave a slow shake of the head. "Nothing, Captain." Her catlike expression tightened in concentration. "But local subspace is so heavy with static from the pulse, they could be broadcasting Denobulan opera at full blast and we wouldn't hear it."

"Um, Captain?" The young officer at the rear of the bridge, where *Shenzhou*'s engineering monitor station was located, raised his voice. "I want to add, nadion pulse? Not good."

"Agreed, Ensign Weeton," said Georgiou. "Go on."

"Lieutenant Saru is right about some warp-matrix designs using that tech, but it's flaky as hell." Weeton made a complex shape in the air in front of him, trying to illustrate a point of quantum physics with just his fingers. "A particle release of this magnitude is enough to blow any passing ship out of warp. If we hadn't been at station-keeping, it would have thrown us out of warp. And anyone right in the middle of it would be staring down the barrel of a core breach."

Burnham watched the shift in the captain's expression and she knew where Georgiou's thoughts were going. And so did Commander ch'Theloh, the Andorian's antennae drooping slightly as he gave a grave shake of the head.

"Before you say it," warned the first officer, "take another look at the tac-map. Detmer, zoom out on that." The woman at the helm tapped a control and the tactical graphic dropped back to a larger scale, showing a wide swath of the border space. "I don't have to tell you we're on the edge of a danger zone here." The location of the pulse's epicenter glowed in the middle of two overlapping patches of color. "The phenomenon is located inside an area declared as a buffer region by both the Tholians and a nonaligned post-contact race called the Peliar. By any interpretation, it's outside of our jurisdiction."

"But it's not outside our *responsibility*, Number One." Georgiou sat back in her chair, and her eyes briefly met Burnham's. "Lieutenant, any indications that the pulse may reoccur and damage *Shenzhou*?"

"Unknown," Burnham replied. She hated not having more information to give, but the scans were vague and conflicted.

"If we approach, we will be going in blind," insisted Saru, and he felt Burnham tense by his side. She was thinking the same thing.

"Noted." Georgiou turned back to face the main viewer. "Ensign Detmer, plot an intercept course. Note in the ship's log we're departing our station and transiting from Federation space."

"Captain!" Saru blurted out the word, his hand flicking up to the back of his head as a set of fine feelers emerged out of the skin there. Burnham had seen this reaction from the Kelpien before, the appearance of his "threat ganglia," a pure reflexive response that occurred whenever Saru's species sensed the presence of an imminent threat. "The Tholians! They will consider any transgression into their space as an invasion!"

"I am well aware," said Georgiou, "but we've seen no sign of them in all the time we've been here, Mister Saru, and technically the buffer zone isn't actually *theirs*. I'm not going to let the possibility of their displeasure prevent us from rendering assistance to beings in grave danger. We're going."

"Course laid in," reported Detmer.

"Engage engines," ordered the captain.

Out beyond the viewer, the static pattern of stars leaped closer, transforming into warped streaks of light as the *Shenzhou* plunged through the barriers of relativistic motion.

Saru made a quiet, negative noise as he massaged the back of his scalp, unconsciously retreating a step from the science console. "I hope we don't regret this," he muttered.

Commander ch'Theloh crossed to the science console and made a show of looking at the display in front of Burnham. "I need you watching the sensors like a Tarkalean hawk, Lieutenant. The first inkling you have that the pulse might reoccur, I want to know about it."

"Aye, sir." She gave a nod as the Andorian turned to Saru and put a hand on his shoulder.

The *Shenzhou*'s executive officer was the only one on the ship close to Saru's near-two-meter height, and he gave the Kelpien a hard look. "Caution is useful," noted the commander, "but there's such a thing as worrying too much. Don't expend your energy dealing with problems we don't have yet."

"I understand, sir," Saru replied, glancing at Burnham, "but several ships have been lost without a trace in this sector over the years. Only a few weeks ago, a J-class transport belonging to the Evans Charter went missing—"

"Fret not, Mister Saru," said the captain, speaking loudly enough for the whole bridge to hear her. "I'm not about to let the *Shenzhou* . . . or those ships out there . . . become another statistic."

Saru's reply was glum. "Unfortunately, Captain, my species is genetically predisposed toward fretting."

2

The warp jump went from a smooth transit via non-Einsteinian space to a juddering, shaking race against invisible lines of spatial scission.

Shenzhou was an old ship, a *Walker* class in the light-cruiser range, and she had weathered more than her fair share of hard journeys since the day she came off the orbital slips. Still, the hull creaked alarmingly as feedback from the structural integrity fields resonated back down her forward saucer section and along the pylons of her underslung warp nacelles.

The concentrated particles of the fading nadion pulse had the effect of destabilizing any conventional starship's warp matrix, to the point that passing through a dense pocket of them would make the faster-than-light bubble evaporate and send any vessel that fell victim crashing back toward sublight velocity. A ship without adequate protection would crumple instantly from the sheer force of unplanned deceleration. But *Shenzhou* was an old war-horse, and she was tough. It would take much more than this to bring her down.

Space thickened around the starship as it closed in on the epicenter of the effect, and the vessel described a looping spiral to cross the distance. A head-on approach would have been like steering through mud; this way, *Shenzhou* skated across the top of the decaying nadion field and kept up her momentum.

Ahead of the Starfleet vessel, two alien craft drifted in a flickering haze of ice-blue Cherenkov radiation. The first was just over twice the size of a shuttlecraft, its core fuselage resembling a bulbous projectile with a pair of solar-array "wings" and a single-engine nacelle emerging from a ventral mount. The wings hung limply, incorrectly deployed as the smaller craft had reverted out of warp speed. It drifted in a nose-down attitude relative to the *Shenzhou*'s line of approach, and a tail of ejected coolant extended out behind it, ice crystals glittering in the dark.

The second ship was a giant. Nearly a kilometer long, the forward quarter of the hull was a heavy ingot of metal dotted with a few illuminated viewports. A collar of pylons at the rear of this forward section sported four large warp nacelles, the intercoolers along the flanks of each one flickering with uncontrolled discharges. The rest of the huge vessel's mass was made up of a skeletal frame like the bones of a fish, upon which were mounted countless numbers of massive modular containers, all interlinked. It bore a vague likeness to the design of the old "Boomer"-type warp freighters once in use all across the Federation, but the similarity ended there. Both of the craft had sculpted, decorative fascia over their superstructures, an aesthetic layer suggesting the organic shapes of bulbous plants.

Random patterns of green lightning crawled over the hulls of the alien vessels, the telltale signs of power cores bleeding off excess energy in the desperate attempt to forestall a critical overload. Any experienced spacer would only need to look at them to know that the life expectancy of the ships was running out.

They slowed to impulse power, and Saru surveyed the scene through the clear sections on the deck of the bridge as

Ensign Detmer brought the *Shenzhou* around. "Structure and configuration match known designs," he explained. "These vessels belong to the natives of Peliar Zel."

"No communications," Ensign Fan spoke up, anticipating the captain's next question.

Her gaze fixed on the same view, Georgiou called out to the duty engineer. "Weeton. That lightning effect on the hulls, is that what I think it is?"

"If you think it's sublimated warp plasma, then yes, Captain." The ensign gave a grave nod.

"I read identical fluctuation events in the warp cores of both ships," said Saru, studying his panel. "They're in a lot of trouble." His first instinct was to draw back, as if he were standing too close to a fire, and he ignored the urge.

"Are you sure?" Commander ch'Theloh leaned over to see the readings for himself. "There's a lot of interference on the sensors."

"Yes, sir," Saru allowed, "but the bleed from the warp cores is so strong it's cutting right through it. That in itself is a very bad sign."

"How long do they have?" said Georgiou.

"Minutes at best," offered Weeton.

"Send this in all known common protocols." The captain took a breath. "Attention, Peliar vessels. This is the Federation *Starship Shenzhou*. We stand ready to assist. Respond if you can." Transmitting the message was standard operating procedure, but no one on the bridge expected to receive a reply.

"They won't answer," Burnham said quietly, her voice so low that only Saru heard her speak. "They can't."

The inhabitants of the Peliar Zel star system were citizens of an independent sovereign state that for many decades had eschewed interaction with off-worlders, preferring to maintain their own planets and a handful of regional colony holdings. But recently, their government had made overtures toward the United Federation of Planets, and they were exploring the possibility of UFP membership. As a xenoanthropologist by training, Burnham would have been the one to know more about the Peliar culture than he, but Saru guessed that the most likely reason for the aliens reaching out to the Federation was the fear of ongoing Tholian expansion. With that thought preying on his mind, he eyed the long-range sensors warily, looking for anything out on the periphery that might have been a lurking spinner ship.

Georgiou leaned forward in her chair, as if she were pulling against restraints holding her in place. "Any clue as to the origin of the nadion pulse that crippled them?"

"The particle density is much higher around the bigger ship, the freighter," said Ensign Troke. "Best guess, the pulse originated inside the big one and knocked them both out of warp."

"I'd concur with that," said Weeton. "They were probably moving in close formation, the other ship acting as an escort."

"An engine malfunction, then?" Ch'Theloh considered the possibility. "Not the result of an attack."

"We can worry about cause after we deal with the effect," said the captain. "All right, if we can't communicate with them, what *can* we do? Is it possible to tractor them away from the denser areas of the particle field?"

"Tractors are operable." At the ops station, Ensign Troy Januzzi unconsciously ran a hand over his bald scalp, and glanced at the woman in the seat next to him. "It's up to Kayla if she thinks we can drag them out."

Detmer's face soured. "I'm not sure that's the best solution. The mass ratio isn't in our favor."

"You're right," said Georgiou, thinking it through. "That'll take too long. And we won't be able to use the transporters, not while the radiation still lingers."

Saru glanced at the display in front of Burnham, a live

feed from the forward sensor array tuned to detect life signs. The readout fluctuated wildly; one moment it showed the ship's complement as fewer than a dozen, and in the next it was giving out numbers akin to the population of a large town. "I can't stabilize this," she said irritably. "The interference is too strong."

"Anything from the smaller craft?" he prompted.

She frowned. "A consistent negative life-sign reading. I think it's an automated drone of some sort."

"Captain!" Troke called out in alarm, cutting through their conversation. "The escort ship! Readings from its warp core are spiking. Captain, I think it's going to explode!"

"Shields to maximum!" Ch'Theloh barked out the command, and all eyes turned toward the quadrant of the screen where the winged craft was adrift.

Georgiou raised her hand to cover her eyes just as the smaller Peliar ship blossomed into a tiny sun. The *Shenzhou*'s bridge was briefly drenched in white and hard-edged shadows as a fatal collision of matter and antimatter engulfed the escort craft. A rolling, thundering tremor ran through the starship as the shockwave from the escort's destruction battered at the shields, and her ship reeled beneath the impact.

"Status?" Georgiou's first officer reacted quickly, striding toward the damage control station.

"Minor damage, no hull breaches," reported Weeton. "But the Peliar escort . . . It's vapor, sir."

The captain turned toward Troke's station and saw that the Tulian's normally healthy sky-blue skin tone had turned a sickly pale green. She knew what he was going to say next before he uttered the words. "The larger ship's warp core is exhibiting identical breach precursors. The same thing is going to happen to them unless they can stop it."

"Why don't they eject the core and get the hell out of there?" said Detmer through clenched teeth, almost as if she could send her demand through the void to the other vessel.

"Won't matter," said Weeton bleakly. "They wouldn't be able to get far enough away to avoid the blast effect."

And even at full power, the Shenzhou *won't be able to drag them out of the way.* That grim realization presented itself to Georgiou, and a heartbeat behind it came the prospect of a terrible choice. There were hundreds of lives aboard her ship and she could save them all right now if she gave the order to warp out to a safe distance. She was in command and her first responsibility was to her crew.

But if they backed off, the runaway destabilization of the Peliar ship's warp core would certainly claim every life on that other vessel, and Philippa Georgiou would have to live with the knowledge that she let it happen.

The captain drew herself up and began speaking, not so much for the sake of her officers, but once again for the record. "We have received no distress call. We are unable to interpret the intentions of the Peliar crew. Nevertheless, these are my orders. We are going to render all possible assistance to those people. If we wait for an invitation, it will be too late." She glanced toward her first officer. "Commander, prep a shuttle for immediate takeoff."

"Aye, Captain." Ch'Theloh set to work.

Georgiou tapped a key on the arm of her chair. "Engineering. Commander Johar?"

"Here, Captain."

"Get yourself a pilot, a medic, and a couple of your best technicians, then double-time it to the shuttlebay. You're about to take part in an unsolicited boarding action."

"Right. I'll pack a Jolly Roger." Johar paused. *"Can I take Weeton? He's good on the stick, and he knows his way around a hyperspanner."*

"He's on his way. Bridge out." Georgiou threw the ensign a nod and the junior officer stood up, masking a flash of anxiety as he did so.

"Captain, I'd like to volunteer to join the rescue party." Burnham stepped away from her panel, coming stiffly to attention. "They could use a science officer over there."

"And it has to be you?" The barbed comment fell from Saru's lips before the Kelpien was even aware he had voiced it.

Burnham gave him a sharp look, and Georgiou saw the rekindling of the same argument she had interrupted in the mess hall. The two of them were both excellent at their jobs, but the ongoing issue of getting Saru and Burnham to work together had a habit of flaring up into conflict at inopportune times. And right now, the captain had no time to waste.

Michael Burnham was always the one to go into harm's way, and Saru was always ready with a reason to play it safe. Despite the grave seriousness of the situation, Georgiou suddenly saw a way to defuse the tension between the science officers and hopefully solve the larger dilemma at hand. "A good suggestion, and your offer is appreciated, Lieutenant Burnham . . . but stand to and hold your station." The other woman couldn't mask her disappointment, but that turned to surprise when Georgiou glanced at the Kelpien. "Lieutenant Saru, join the team in the shuttlebay."

"Me?" Saru's pale blue eyes blinked in shock.

"You," said the captain, nodding toward the turbolift. "Now snap to it."

The turbolift ran on priority pathing, speeding straight to the shuttlebay at the aft of the *Shenzhou*'s primary hull without stopping, and Saru's thoughts were racing to keep up as he spilled out of the lift with Ensign Weeton leading the way.

What just happened? He had spoken without thinking,

opening his mouth to criticize Burnham's eagerness to impress without stopping to consider the alternative, and now he was going to pay for it. Captain Georgiou had put him on the spot, and Saru had no choice but to obey orders and accept the assignment.

"I guess you weren't expecting that," said Weeton as the two of them approached the shuttle *Yang*. The ensign handed him a gear vest and an operations kit from a rack, then grabbed one of his own. "Time to get your hands dirty, huh, Lieutenant?"

Saru couldn't be sure if he was reading sarcasm in the ensign's tone, so he ignored it. He clamped his mouth shut and silenced the misgivings that echoed in his thoughts as he shrugged on the vest. *Don't see this as a perilous situation*, he told himself, *see it as an opportunity to show your mettle to the crew.*

"Faster would be better," called the chief engineer, hanging out of the hatch at the back of the *Yang*'s lozenge-shaped hull. "Weeton, get in here and get us moving, while we still have someone to rescue!"

The two of them scrambled aboard and Saru found a seat across from Johar in the rear compartment as Weeton vaulted into the pilot's chair and powered up the impulse engines. The hatch clanged shut and Saru shot a look out of the forward canopy. The shuttlebay was already open, a glittering wall of force separating the atmosphere inside from the vacuum. Out beyond the *Shenzhou*, he could see the still-expanding cloud of radioactive debris that had been the Peliar escort drone.

The *Yang* lifted off, light blurring as the interior of its mothership fell away and they rushed into space. Saru double-checked his gear as Johar launched into a brisk briefing.

"All right, everyone. We're on the clock here, so I need

you all to work fast and smart. A nadion pulse most likely means an overload in the secondary injector modules of the warp core, so we get in and we provide whatever help we can to stabilize it." He pointed to the straw-pale female Vok'sha seated next to Saru, a petty officer with the bronze tabs of an engineering specialist. "Yashae, you know this stuff like the back of your hand, so I want you running point. Crewman Subin, do what she tells you, understood?" The thin Mazarite woman across the cabin gave an emphatic nod in reply.

"What about me?" Nurse Zoxom was dressed in medical division whites beneath his gear vest, and the husky Xanno seemed eager to get started.

"There are going to be injured people over there, count on that," Johar told him. "You're going to have your hands full."

Zoxom held up a heavy medical pack. "I've got plenty of hyronalin to go around. Speaking of which . . . time for a booster shot." He loaded a hypospray with a vial of the anti-radiation drug and proceeded to work his way around the shuttle, injecting each person in turn.

"Lieutenant Saru," concluded Johar. "We only have a rough idea of what we're going to find over there, so I need your head on a swivel."

Saru touched his neck, wondering if the human literally meant what he said, then decided just to nod and not question it. "Aye, sir."

"Approaching the target vessel," called Weeton from the cockpit. "It's big all right."

Johar moved forward and Saru followed, peering over the pilot's shoulder. Ahead of the *Yang*'s prow, a wall of tan-colored metal filled the windows. The shuttle was closing on the rear of the forward section, toward the ring of warp nacelles. If the massive transport ship followed usual design logic, then the main engineering deck would be close by.

"Anyone see a hatch?" said Weeton.

"There." Saru spotted a hexagonal port in the hull and pointed it out.

With a few bursts from the shuttle's maneuvering thrusters, Weeton positioned the *Yang* over the hatch and settled them down in place. "Activating magnetic clamps."

In the crew bay, Subin and Yashae had already retracted the deck plates as the shuttle made a hard seal, revealing the hatch below them. Subin drew her phaser and adjusted the setting. "I can burn us through . . ."

"Wait!" Saru bounded back into the rear cabin and dropped into a crouch. "Peliar technology has a high degree of automation. I think I may be able to access the airlock control remotely." He pulled the tricorder from his belt and quickly programmed a tight-beam transmission that would mimic the mechanism's control signals.

"Tick-tock," noted Johar.

Saru sent the transmission, and the hatch popped open with such rapidity that everyone in the shuttle flinched. Searing hot air wafted into the shuttle, bringing with it the acrid stench of burnt polymers and the braying hoots of what could only be an alarm siren.

"Go!" said the chief engineer, and one by one they vaulted through the open hatchway—

—And into a scene of chaos.

Saru landed in a cat-fall on a curved service gantry. The platform extended away in both directions around the equator of a thrumming column of hardware built in an hourglass shape. The alien design was markedly different from the system aboard the *Shenzhou*. Two massive injector arrays pulsed with bright light as matter and antimatter were channeled into a central chamber at the nexus—but rather than the steady, rhythmic heartbeat they should have been exhibiting, the pulses were coming at conflicting intervals, colliding out of sequence. The entire framework of the warp core was vibrating against its support structure, sending sparks flying in great orange-red gushes from the connector points. Plasma vents on the upper levels spat gaseous plumes of vapor as the system spiraled toward a critical overload.

Beside him, Johar cursed softly in Arabic as he cast an eye over the situation. "This is very bad." He took a breath, then raised his voice to be heard over the alert sirens. "Someone find me a command console, right now!"

The team scrambled to obey and Saru found himself a step behind Zoxom as the nurse came across a member of the Peliar crew. A female of the species in a metallic crimson shipsuit with a simple headdress around her scalp, the Peliar woman was slumped next to an auto-valve control that appeared to be part of the ship's deuterium conduits. Saru scanned it with his tricorder as Zoxom got to work.

"Just unconscious," said the nurse as he applied an injector to her neck. "I think she fell and struck her head."

Saru glanced down at the Peliar. She was hairless, with skin the color of dry earth and a high, ridged forehead bisected by a long nasal rib. Like all Peliars, she had dual sets of nostrils and they twitched in unison as she started to come around. Saru checked his universal translator and held his breath.

"What . . . happened?" Her eyes fluttered open and tried to focus.

"You are all right. Please don't make any sudden moves," began Zoxom, in as soothing a tone as he could manage over the howl of the sirens.

His request was ignored as the Peliar woman reacted in shock to the sight of the intruders aboard her ship. She jerked backward, snatching a beam cutter from the tool belt around her waist and brandishing it like a dagger. "Who are you? Keep back!"

"I am Lieutenant Saru of the Federation *Starship Shenzhou*, this is Nurse Zoxom." Saru raised his hands and tried to look nonthreatening. "We've come to help you."

"Nathal said there was another ship on sensors . . ." She blinked, distrust written across her face. "Did you do this to us?"

"We are here to help," reiterated Saru. "When we could not reach you via subspace radio, we boarded your ship." He gestured upward to where the *Yang* had force-docked. "We mean you no harm."

"Get away from her!" The shout came from close at hand, and Saru spun to see more of the Peliar crew emerging from the smoke. Another female, this one in a similar uniform and headdress but pale green in color, led from the front. She drew a spindly pistol from a belt holster and aimed it in Saru's direction. "Touch her and you'll regret it!"

"Commander Nathal . . ." The other Peliar spoke as she struggled to get to her feet, and Saru ignored the threat, helping her regain her footing. "I am all right."

"You are intruders on my vessel," said Nathal, disregarding her subordinate's words. "I have every right to shoot you where you stand!"

"Your ship is malfunctioning and that's your first thought?" Johar appeared behind Zoxom, holding his engineering kit tightly in one hand. "Shoot first, accept help later?"

"What did you say to me?" Nathal's face darkened.

"I'm saying, don't ignore the chance to save your vessel!" Saru had never seen Johar this angry about anything. "We don't have time for niceties, so put that damned gun away and help us stop that core from breaching, or else we all die!"

The chief engineer's words were stark and cutting, and

Saru found himself nodding. "Please," he began, "I'm sure none of us wish to perish today."

"We can solve our own problems," Nathal shot back, glaring at the other Peliar woman. "Hekan, you fell silent! I need your report!"

"With respect," said Hekan as she detached herself from Saru, "this is not a time to choose obstinacy over survival. We could use more hands."

Saru counted only a half-dozen Peliars on the platform. "Where are the rest of your engineering staff?"

"This is everyone," Nathal growled, finally jamming her weapon back into its holster. "The rest are injured."

"I can help with that," said Zoxom. "Take me to your injured."

Nathal's quadripartite nostrils flared, but then she relented, barking an order to another of her crew. "Dakas, take the alien to the infirmary." Then she glared at Saru and the chief engineer. "Very well. You may assist us here. But if you try anything—"

"Sure, whatever." Johar was already turning his back on her, jabbing a finger at a sandy-faced Peliar in a blue outfit. "You! Where are the injectors?" The alien crewman pointed and led the engineer away.

"Do all Federation officers speak that way to their superiors?" muttered Hekan.

"Some more than others," Saru admitted. "Is there a monitoring station I can access?"

"This way." Hekan led him to a U-shaped console with an interface of sliding control rods. "I was attempting to avert a photon surge when the deck shifted . . ." She touched her head where Zoxom had applied a dressing. "You have to forgive my commander, she's quite protective of her crew."

Saru scanned the system. "Understandable." A worrying number of warning flags blinked across the screen of his tricorder. "If you only have a small complement on board, perhaps we should consider evacuating all of you to our shuttle—"

"No," Hekan cut him off before he could finish. "We're not abandoning this ship, there are . . . there's too much at stake." Her stubby fingers pushed and pulled at the sliders, but to no avail. "Curse this! The decay rate in the core isn't slowing."

"Lieutenant Commander!" Saru heard Yashae shout through the haze, her voice coming from somewhere back toward the hatchway. "I think we can save this barge, but it's not going to be easy! We need to bleed off the energy buildup and take the warp core offline, but the safety interlocks won't disengage! It's caught in a loop!"

Saru peered at his tricorder and saw the problem. "The sensors governing the interlocks are malfunctioning." He looked down the length of the shuddering core stack, picking out a broken section of the framework. The system that would normally have allowed the crew to attempt this risky override was unable to release, the computer doubtless still operating with false readings from damaged sensors telling it everything was working well.

"I can't switch off the interlocks from here," said Hekan, her face creasing in annoyance. "They keep rejecting the commands!"

"You must have a secondary reset control." Saru cast around, looking for a manual switch.

"We do." Hekan pointed upward, to a narrow, enclosed catwalk that ran the length of the chamber and down toward the central spinal frame of the starship. "It's inside the maintenance crawlway, a set of two levers behind a blue panel."

"Ah." Saru belatedly realized that he had just volunteered himself to climb up there and throw the switches. He couldn't stop himself from looking down, through the mesh plate of the decking beneath his feet, right into the black abyss of the engine spaces beneath.

"You'll need a gravity belt to get up there," Hekan was saying.

"I won't," Saru told her, slinging his tricorder over his arm and rolling his shoulders. *This is a poor survival choice*, said a voice in the back of his head. It sounded worryingly like one of the elders from his youth, admonishing him for venturing out after curfew. *It could kill you.*

"Yes," Saru said to himself. "If in doubt, assume everything will kill you." The Kelpien crouched and coiled the muscles in his long, whipcord legs; and then, from a dead start, he leaped upward to grab the bottom of the catwalk dangling three meters over their heads.

The next few moments passed in a fear-charged blur for Saru. Acting on instinct, he hauled himself up onto the walkway and scuttled down the length of it toward the enclosed section. He didn't allow himself to think about the empty space below his hooves, how one random shudder from the Peliar ship's spaceframe could fling him off and send him down to be dashed apart on the machinery below. He only thought about one step after another and a set of levers behind a blue panel.

The scorching thermal release coming off the damaged warp core rose past him in shimmering waves, and the spiracles in his bare skin itched as they bled off the heat. Saru ducked low and squeezed himself into the catwalk proper, bumping his head on the curved ceiling.

"Do you see it?" Hekan shouted up at him.

"Not yet," he called back.

An unpleasant electrostatic hum resonated through the frame of the metal, oscillating at a frequency that to Kelpien senses was like having a needle driven through one's skull. That, and the heat, and the churning terror he was barely keeping under control, made it hard for Saru to concentrate. He screwed up his courage and pushed on, the access conduit widening into a small chamber ringed with varicolored panels.

Saru swept around and found the blue one, wrenching it off with a quick twist. Behind it there were the two levers, and he allowed himself the briefest flash of relief. He gripped them both and was about to pull when he heard a noise below him.

The Kelpien looked down. Crouching there, beneath the mesh of the deck plate under his boots, sandwiched between the lower section of the catwalk and another crawlway, was a humanoid that was most certainly *not* a native of Peliar Zel. Heavyset and stocky, the being was likely from a high-gravity world. It wore ragged, unkempt clothing, and the alien had six limbs, a pair of thick legs, and two sets of muscular arms. Their eyes met. He glimpsed the mirror of his own fear in the other being's gaunt features, the certain knowledge of imminent death only heartbeats away. The alien looked up at him imploringly, and Saru saw that one of the being's arms was trapped beneath a baffle plate that had dropped into place when the overload began.

The other being's circumstances would be meaningless if Saru did not complete his task here. He braced himself against the deck and pulled hard on the reset levers.

The warp core gave off a sound like an animal in agony, and Saladin Johar winced in sympathy with the machine.

Some of the junior ratings aboard the *Shenzhou* joked about him when they thought he didn't hear it, suggesting the chief engineer was actually part Betazoid—but that

Johar's empathic sense worked only on mechanical objects and not organic life-forms. Perhaps there was some truth to it, he reflected. A good engineer could almost *feel* the stresses on their hardware like it was an extension of their own body. This might not have been his vessel, but still he could sense the strain as it resonated across the span of the Peliar ship's hull.

"Saru?" he shouted. "Did he do it?"

"Reset is active!" called Subin, from a nearby control podium. "Emergency core shutdown cycle in progress!"

"Everyone brace for the outage!" Johar grabbed at a safety rail as the throbbing glow inside the warp core slowed to a gradual stop and then went dark. He felt his body briefly grow lighter as the big ship's gravity generators went through a power dip, before that passed and the core lit up once again.

"Cycle complete," Nathal said grudgingly, her hard gaze boring into a holographic display. "Hopefully the restart won't kill us all."

The Peliar engineer in the blue jumpsuit ran his hands over a gestural interface, and Johar used his tricorder to remotely manipulate the firing sequence of the injector modules. He could see where the problem had originated; a misalignment had set up a destructive cascade effect inside the system that had built and built until it was self-sustaining. Part of his analytical mind-set was dismantling that revelation in the back of his thoughts, trying to understand why such a thing had occurred. But for now, it was more important to get the warp core up into standby mode. Without the power it supplied, other vital systems like life-support would fail and kick off a whole raft of other problems to deal with.

The pulsing glow began a sluggish ascent from the lower section of the core, a twin band of light descending from the upper array to meet it in the middle. A wave of relief broke over Johar as the pulses moved in unison and collided in synch. The telltale vibration from the alignment error was absent. "Well, there we are," he said, putting aside a burst of joy at the thought of not perishing. "A little teamwork, and a grisly death for all is averted."

"You can go on your way now," said Nathal, turning her gaze on him. "The problem has been dealt with."

"You're welcome," Subin replied, with a snort.

Johar shot the Mazarite a warning look, then glanced at Nathal. "Seriously? You don't actually believe that we *fixed* this, do you?" He shook his head. "Commander, what just happened was an act of survival, not a solution."

"The human is correct." The Peliar engineer offered the comment, but quickly wilted under Nathal's stare and went back to his console.

"I want you off my ship," said the alien captain.

"You have made that abundantly clear," Johar replied. "But I do my job right, Commander. And I tell you now, if I leave this vessel with my people and you run this warp core back up to operating power, it'd be like I pulled a phaser and shot you myself." He pointed up toward the injector array. "We need to track down and eliminate the cause of that nadion pulse, because if we don't, it'll happen again." Johar met Nathal's look. "And next time you come crashing to a halt, help might not be so close at hand."

"Or worse . . ." Hekan, the other Peliar woman who seemed to be the ship's second-in-command, approached from across the platform. "What if it were the Tholians who came to investigate?"

Invoking the specter of the quarrelsome crystalline beings gave everyone pause. Both the crews knew what kind of threat they represented, and certainly for the Peliars, who lived close to the Assembly's borders, the danger was all too real.

Johar released a sigh and raised his hand. "Starfleet respects the sovereignty of Peliar Zel and your authority on this ship, Commander Nathal . . ."

"You have an unusual way of showing it," said the captain, ice forming on the words.

"But I cannot in good conscience leave this vessel until your crew is safe," Johar went on. "I'm sure you have no desire to risk their lives."

Nathal glanced at Hekan, and then to her engineer. Both of them made a gesture with the flat of their hand that Johar guessed was their equivalent of a nod. At length, she spoke again. "When this is over, I will have some words with your commanding officer."

"I am sure she will be very happy to listen," he replied, catching sight of Petty Officer Yashae as the other engineer came through the fading haze.

"All systems are in low power mode and read stable," she reported. "The lieutenant did us proud."

Johar's eyes narrowed. "Where is Saru?" He looked around. The Kelpien was nowhere to be seen.

"He went into the central maintenance channel," said Hekan. "He didn't come back out?" Her face fell. "I didn't think . . ."

Nathal's expression turned stormy and she barked out an order to her crew. "Find him!"

Curiosity kills.

There was a story that Saru had heard many times as a youth, a cautionary tale designed to instruct. It was a sorry narrative about a young Kelpien who disregarded the rules of his society. This fictitious youth, whose name changed depending on whoever was most deserving of admonition that day, grew curious about the prohibited places, to the point that he foolishly ventured into dark and unknown territory. It did not end well for him. For no matter what wonders he saw, the youth would ultimately suffer some terrible fate. And all because he became too inquisitive for his own good.

Curiosity kills, the elders would say, nodding sagely.

Now, as Saru carefully picked his way along the length of the curving, enclosed walkway, he wondered why he had never learned the lesson the story had been trying to impart.

The act of pulling the manual reset levers had also caused the mechanism in the baffle plate to retract, freeing the trapped being beneath the decking. Before Saru could call out to him, the six-limbed alien scrambled away and vanished into the shadowed depths of the long catwalk, the clatter of his feet fading as Saru descended toward the aft spaces of the vessel.

Saru should have turned back, returned to the gantry and the rest of the damage control party. But curiosity, that old fascination, pulled on him. Holding out his tricorder, Saru took one step, then another, following the non-Peliar into the bowels of the massive transport ship.

In the dimness, it was difficult for him to estimate the distance he had traveled, but it felt like a long way. More than once, he halted and deliberated about turning around. Each time, curiosity drew him on, but with every step it was at war with his fear.

The catwalk extended into the first of many cavernous cargo modules, huge pods that were large enough to encompass an entire city block. Saru wasn't certain what he expected to see in there—stacks of freight, storage tanks and the like, perhaps—but it wasn't *this.*

Ranged out beneath him, the interior of the module was a chaotic mess of cables strung from every available support, and between them were thick sheets of flexible metal or heavy sailcloth like one might expect to find on a wind-powered watercraft. Tents and enclosures hung from every corner, and bioluminescent lights cast soft, weak color into the darkness. The heavy warmth and earthy scent of living beings in close proximity wafted up to him, and as his eyes adjusted to the low light level, Saru became aware of figures moving around the suspended structures. There were a lot of them, dozens—no, *hundreds or more.*

The tricorder in his hand chimed, and he studied the device's display. He saw the same confused patterns of myriad life signs that Burnham had glimpsed on the *Shenzhou*'s sensors when they first arrived. What he had thought to be a scanner glitch was nothing of the kind. The cargo module was filled with people.

Curiosity kills. The words echoed in his thoughts once more, but Saru shook his head to banish them and reached out to grab hold of one of the cables. The alien construct beneath him seemed threatening and gloomy, but Saru had come too far now to draw back from what he had discovered.

Who are these beings and what are they doing here? He could not return without knowing the answer.

Slowly and carefully, he descended into the shadows.

3

The suspended cables and flexible floors formed a makeshift encampment in the middle of the cargo module. Stitched together out of mismatched materials, discarded storage crates, polymer shrouds, and more, there was a kind of threadbare ingenuity to the haphazard structure of it. As Saru worked his way down the cable to what was the "roof" of the settlement, he picked out sections that appeared to be dormitories, and others packed with barrels of some fast-growing fungal matter. Moving along the upper surface, he passed over inverted conical ducts that acted as dew catchers, collecting ambient moisture from the air, harvested from the ship's life-support system and the exhalations of the people inside the module.

The shadowed, dim space had its own microclimate, as warm as blood and with a spicy tang to the air that made the Kelpien's nostril pits twitch. There was something else he could sense, too . . . an ambient ebb and flow, like distant waves breaking upon a far-off shoreline. The feel of it came through the striations in his skull as Saru's innate electrosensitivity picked up the impression from all around him. In a peculiar way that he couldn't articulate, it reminded him of *home*.

Setting his tricorder to continuous scan mode, Saru pressed on, spreading his weight so he could move without drawing attention to himself. He saw no sign of the being that had met his gaze back on the maintenance catwalk, but there were many others of the same species, some exhibiting differing genders, some clearly at the younger or older ranges of age. By their activities, these did not appear to be members of the transport ship's crew. Saru guessed they were passengers of a sort, but if that were so, the crude and basic living conditions they were in did not speak well of Peliar generosity.

He looked up again, considering the size of the module. *Shenzhou*'s scans had shown eight containers of this dimension mounted on the spinal frame of the big ship. Were there other gatherings of these beings in each one, similarly clustering side by side in the belly of an alien vessel?

Saru pulled his communicator from his belt, but the dull chirp it emitted when he flicked up the antenna grid told him it would be impossible to signal Johar, Weeton, or the *Shenzhou*. The local particle density was still extremely high, smothering all the frequencies he could access.

He paused, considering his next move. His desire to know more conflicted with his instinct for self-preservation. It would be possible for him to retreat, perhaps, climb the support cables and eventually retrace his path back to the engine chamber. But that would leave too many unanswered questions, and Saru could imagine Captain Georgiou's steady gaze on him, pressing him for an explanation he didn't have. He pictured ch'Theloh and Burnham and the rest of the crew. *They would expect me to retreat*, he told himself. *They would expect me to flee.*

Saru rejected that option. He was a Starfleet officer. This was a first contact situation. He was obliged to reveal himself and attempt a meaningful interaction with these beings . . . and besides, he had already "met" one of them.

He continued on, looking for a clearing, for a place

where he could show himself without engendering a negative reaction from the humanoids. Ahead, the wash of the invisible electrostatic field grew more intense and Saru was drawn to it, picking up the sounds of multiple, overlapping voices.

He came across a space like a courtyard, a set of interlinked metal decks beneath a web of cables where dozens of the aliens were gathering. Their language was quick, full of sibilants and harsh glottal noises that went back and forth in rapid chugs. Saru's universal translator was having difficulty interpreting the speech, continually stopping and restarting its program as it failed to find a key into the alien tongue. It was rare to find a linguistic framework that the UT's expert system couldn't quickly configure into Federation Standard, but so far the device could only render the most basic of concepts from the conversation happening below. *Anxiety. Waiting. Conflict.* The translator gave no more detail than that.

The key component was *fear*, and Saru gave a rueful nod. That was something he could appreciate. He took a deep breath and gathered himself. There was an open spot at the back of the courtyard. He would lower himself down, raise his hands in a gesture of friendship, and—

A change passed over the crowd in the blink of an eye, every single one of the aliens falling silent. Saru spotted movement on the far side of the open area. A trio of the four-armed beings in close order moved through the group, and he noticed they each wore a dusty band of red cloth around their four wrists. By the way the others stepped back to let them pass, it was clear they had a kind of authority among the aliens. Looking more carefully, Saru noted that others in the gathered crowd wore bands of their own in different colors, some with two or three on their wrists but none with four.

Then the red-bands stepped apart and Saru realized that they had been shielding a fourth figure from sight. Not an adult, he guessed, a younger female of the species. She wore white robes that were grubby with age and use, and her stance was off-kilter. As she walked forward, Saru saw why. One of her legs was severely deformed, and each step she took was an effort. But as she passed by the others in the crowd, they reached out to touch her and in turn she ran her hands over them. Where the white-robe moved, the humanoids seemed to grow calmer and more assured.

A spiritual leader? The thought crossed Saru's mind. Although she seemed too young to be considered any kind of elder, the effect the robed female had on her fellow beings was immediate and undeniable.

She was just a short distance away when the hobbled young female stopped suddenly and looked straight up, directly at Saru. He blinked in shock, tensing for a shout of alarm, but instead her gaze was full of interest, of *curiosity*.

Not so that of her escorts, however. Two of the red-bands followed the female's gaze and saw the Kelpien hiding in the shadows overhead, and they showed the reaction he *had* expected. Angry shouts boiled up from the courtyard and the assembled crowd below closed ranks to shield the white-robed figure from whatever threat Saru represented, others squaring off in a manner that clearly promised violence.

"No, no . . ." Saru raised his hands and tilted back his head in an attempt to look harmless. Empty hands proved he carried no weapons and showing his throat was a signifier among many species of a passive intent, but it did little to calm the mood.

Anger. Panic. Distress. The UT tonelessly reported the temper of the aliens to Saru, but without specifics it was of little use.

With care, he climbed down into the courtyard, and the aliens drew back to give him space. The tallest of them only came to the level of Saru's sternum, and he could feel the ripple of raw terror his appearance generated in the assembly. It was a strange experience for the Kelpien to be the *feared* rather than the *fearful.*

There was no means of escape for him. The humanoids surrounded him on all sides, and some of them had produced heavy cudgels or stubby blades. Saru knew without doubt that if he made one wrong move, they would interpret it as an attack and react accordingly.

If it came to that, could he fight his way out? There was a type-2 phaser on his belt set for stun, and he knew how to use it, but the last thing Saru wanted to do was to start shooting at a race of beings who were perfectly within their rights to consider him an invader.

The situation was slipping out of control, and he knew he had to navigate a way through it. *They are afraid. You know how that feels. Use that.* Saru took a breath and silenced his own anxieties; he felt the ephemeral pressure on his senses once more, the phantom crackle of electromagnetic energy in the air.

The subtle play of sensory fields was a part of how Saru's kind communicated intimately with one another, and with each passing second he became more certain that these beings shared a similar trait, but on a different level.

Moderating his breathing, drawing his own electrostatic pattern into quiescence, Saru opened his arms once again and showed the humanoids that he was defenseless. "I come in peace," he intoned. "I ask you to forgive my intrusion. I mean no disrespect."

Anger ebbed, turning to *suspicion* and *doubt.* It wasn't much of an improvement, but it was a step in the right direction. The weapons he had seen were lowered, but still the humanoids kept their distance.

Then from the far edge of the group came the female in the white robe, pressing awkwardly through the ranks of her red-banded companions despite their obvious displeasure. She cocked her head to study Saru, her wide, dark eyes taking him in. He mimicked the motion, then tapped a finger on his chest. "I am Saru." It was the most basic, most elementary communication in the universe. "Sah-roo," he repeated, sounding it out. The Kelpien hoped that his name didn't translate to some terrible insult in their language.

"Sah. Roo." The female in white echoed his words. Her voice had a soft, musical quality to it.

"Yes." He pointed at her. "You? Who are you?"

She was reaching up to touch her chest, in the same place Saru had touched his, when the crowd around them erupted in a new wave of fear. Before he could react, the three males with the red bands had shot forward and enveloped the female in white, dragging her away. She vanished into the depths of the crowd with a gasp, and in a blink it was as if she had never been there.

Saru thought that the humanoids were reacting to something he had done, some cultural taboo he had inadvertently transgressed. But then he realized they were drawing back from an area to the rear of the courtyard, forming into a ragged defensive line. He turned on his hooves to see four Peliars in steel-gray shipsuits advancing into the light from the biolumes. Each of them carried a particle-beam carbine and they threw wary, uneasy glares at the crowd surrounding them.

One of them—a stern-faced male with tattoo markings across his cheek—pointed at Saru. "At last! There's the offworlder."

Another of them, wearing a sensor monocle, made an exasperated noise. "What in the name of the suns are you doing down here? They could have killed you!"

"Who are these beings?" Saru demanded, drawing himself up to his full height. "Why are they on board this ship?"

"Come with us, now!" said the tattooed male. "You can't be here. They don't like outsiders!"

"Who?" demanded Saru once more. "They aren't from Peliar Zel."

"They're Gorlans," said one of the other Peliars, as if that answered all possible questions. "Come on! We don't want to provoke them any more than you already have!"

Saru turned back, searching the faces of the crowd for any sign of the female in the white robes, but he saw no trace of her. "I was communicating with them . . ."

"No you weren't," said the Peliar with the monocle. "Their language is impossible to translate."

"Like talking to the rocks," said another, with a derisive snort.

The crewman with the tattoos put a firm hand on Saru's shoulder and pulled him away. "Come with us," he insisted. "Don't worry. They won't follow." Reluctantly, the Kelpien allowed himself to be led off.

"They're here because they want to be," said the other Peliar. "Everything is fine as long as nobody does anything stupid . . ." He glared at Saru. "Such as disturbing one of their gatherings!"

They walked through a connecting tunnel and out of the cargo module, into a corridor that went back toward the bow of the ship. A hatch rolled shut behind them, sealing off the passage.

The Peliar with the tattoos eyed Saru coldly. "Is this all you Starfleet officers do, go where you aren't wanted?" He didn't wait for Saru to reply. "It's a wonder your Federation still exists!"

"I will freely admit, this is not the sort of complication I was expecting to encounter out here," said Captain Georgiou as she rested against the side of the desk in her ready room. "Now it appears we have stumbled across not one group of beings in need of assistance, but two?"

"That is . . . unclear," said Lieutenant Commander Johar.

Burnham's gaze shifted to the holographic images sharing the room with them, the grainy virtual versions of the chief engineer and Lieutenant Saru being transmitted from the cockpit area of the shuttle *Yang*. The images were laced with static and of low definition, but she could clearly read their expressions. The engineer had that tight-lipped look he got whenever something wasn't working exactly as it was supposed to, and for his part, Saru's face was the very definition of *hangdog*.

"The Peliars have told us that the Gorlans are on board the ship of their own volition, and we've yet to see anything that—" Johar's words suddenly became a jumble of grating hisses, and the image disintegrated into random pixels.

At Burnham's side, Commander ch'Theloh scowled and tapped an intercom panel. "Boost the gain on the signal."

There was a pause and then Johar's image returned. *"*Shenzhou*, do you hear us? You dropped out for a second."* With the wake of nadion particles still interfering with subspace communications, it had been Ensign Fan who came up with the idea of using a low-powered, line-of-sight laser as a means of keeping in touch with the rescue party. The only problem was, the beam worked point to point, meaning it had to be constantly aimed at a receptor panel on the shuttlecraft's hull to work.

"Please repeat your last," said Georgiou.

"I said, we've yet to see anything that contradicts the Peliars' assertions."

"Lieutenant Saru doesn't agree," said ch'Theloh, studying the science officer's expression.

"I am . . . still forming a hypothesis," ventured the Kelpien, returning to a phrase Burnham had heard him utter more than once during their analysis of the damaged monitor buoy.

"Burnham." Abruptly, the Andorian first officer turned his piercing gaze on her. "The Peliars and the Gorlans. What do we know about them?"

"As we're aware, the cargo craft is a Peliar vessel," she began, drawing up recall from her years of studies on Vulcan. "They are a small but highly technological civilization, rated at type two on the Kardashev scale. If you prefer, I can provide the Richter classification—"

"Generalities will do for now," said Georgiou.

"I would characterize the Peliars as thinkers rather than doers," she went on, shifting to a more colloquial vernacular. "They are carbon-based bipedal humanoids comparable to standard norms from a Class-M planet. They use robotic drones to perform most of their manual labor or hazardous tasks."

"There was that autonomous ship we saw on arrival," noted ch'Theloh.

Burnham nodded. "Peliar culture is broadly divided into two discrete but cooperative factions, the Alphans and the Betans, who live on the respective moons of their homeworld. They have recently approached the Federation Council to discuss the possibility of membership."

"And the Gorlans?" Georgiou picked up a data pad from her desk and studied the ethnological charts of the humanoids displayed there. "I have to admit, I'm not at all familiar with that species."

"It would be true to say they are the polar opposite of the Peliars, Captain." Burnham gestured at the pad. "They originate from a high-gravity environment, so they exhibit greater muscle mass and bone density. They have a reputation for being . . ." She searched for the right adjectives. "Roughhewn. Hardscrabble types. In the past, they are what some would have called 'frontiersmen.' "

"I've heard of them," offered Johar. *"Well, secondhand. My CO on the* Stonewall *once told me about encountering one of their ships. They have a wanderlust, Captain. They range far and wide from their home system, looking for planets where they can set up subsistence colonies."*

"Correct," agreed Burnham. "Gorlan culture is based around tenets of self-reliance and a strong theological belief system. But they are an introspective race, largely private. . . . We really know comparatively little about them."

"Lieutenant Saru, in your report you mentioned issues with the universal translator," said Georgiou. "More detail, please."

Saru sighed. *"The Gorlan speech patterns are very malleable and nuanced in ways that are hard for the UT software to parse. Extracting anything other than the simplest concepts was not possible."*

"It could be that the UT needs a larger sample to work from," said ch'Theloh. "With time and exposure to their language, we might be able to program a better solution."

"With respect, sir," Burnham broke in, "there may be nonverbal elements of communication that our systems can't pick up on." The prospect of learning more about a little-known race of sentients was compelling, and she wished once again that the captain had sent her instead of the Kelpien.

The Andorian's cranial antennae arched slightly. "Do tell," he said firmly.

"Lieutenant Burnham is right," said Saru. *"I sensed an extant electromagnetic field effect while I was in close proximity to the Gorlans. I believe it was directly linked to their group emotional state."*

Georgiou raised an eyebrow. "Can you . . . read that?"

"At present? Only in a crude fashion. As the commander suggested, I would need time to observe and interact with the Gorlans over a longer period to gain a greater understanding."

"And the Peliars don't want to let us do that." Ch'Theloh folded his arms across his chest. "Commander, what's the status of the transport ship at this time?"

"There's no immediate danger to the vessel or the Shenzhou,*"* said the engineer. *"I've got Ensign Weeton working with Yashae and the rest of the team on the final elements of the warp-core repairs. Sir, I have to tell you, tensions are running pretty high over here."* He paused and gave an uncomfortable frown. *"It's not just Saru's walkabout that they didn't like. I have to take the blame for some of it. . . . I didn't exactly get off on the right foot with Commander Nathal. I wasn't as delicate with my opinions as I should have been."*

"That is putting it mildly, sir," noted Saru.

The captain gave a low chuckle. "Saladin, if this situation was about playing nice with people, I would have sent a diplomat and left you in engineering." Then the levity was gone and Georgiou focused on Saru. "Mister Saru, when you were down in the hold with the Gorlans . . . tell me what you *felt*. I want your emotional take on this."

Saru looked away. Burnham sensed the Kelpien was struggling to find the right words. *"There was a very real fear among them, Captain. But I cannot be certain if* I *was the source of that, or if there is more going on here we are unaware of."* He went on, talking about the gathering he had witnessed and the apparent presence of some kind of venerated figure among the Gorlans. *"I believe there was an avenue of communication to be opened there . . . but because of the Peliar intervention, we may have missed our opportunity."*

"I want more than that," said Georgiou.

Johar looked away, at something out of the hologram's visual field. *"You may get it, Captain. Commander Nathal and her XO are here."*

Burnham saw the unmistakable stiffening of Saru's body as the Peliars arrived.

"This way, if you please." Ensign Weeton gestured up through the hexagonal hatch toward the interior of the docked shuttle, and Nathal's expression soured.

At her side, the Peliar officer called Hekan waited patiently for her commander to climb up into the Starfleet craft, and Saru watched them closely as they surveyed the interior of the *Yang*. Hekan's obvious interest in the technology was tempered only by the formality of her role as Nathal's second, and he imagined that if she had been alone, the Peliar woman would have been looking at everything. Nathal, however, glanced around with a haughty and dismissive glare, finding the holographic images of the officers in the *Shenzhou*'s ready room.

"Which of you is in command?" she demanded, wasting no time with preamble.

Georgiou leaned forward slightly. *"I'm Captain Philippa Georgiou of the* Starship Shenzhou, *and—"*

"Do you make a habit of illegally boarding other people's vessels, Captain?" Nathal didn't wait for her to reply. "You acted without authority or permission!"

"I regret that was necessary." The captain inclined her head, letting the comment roll off her. *"I am pleased to hear that your ship and your crew are now safe."* She didn't need to add that that state of affairs only existed because of the *Shenzhou*'s intervention.

Nathal's hands clasped each other and held rigid. "I have a recovery operation to attend to, Georgiou. This conversation is cutting into my time, so can we be quick about it?"

"Of course." Saru heard the captain's tone harden. *"I really only have one point that requires clarification. I would like to understand why there is a large population of Gorlans on board your ship. As our sensors return to full capacity, we're detecting quite a lot of them."*

"How is that relevant?" Nathal looked to Hekan for support, but the other Peliar offered nothing.

"Starfleet's mission includes safeguarding the welfare of all life-forms we encounter," added Commander ch'Theloh. *"We're simply inquiring after their well-being."*

"The Gorlans are not in any distress," Hekan said quickly. "They're not prisoners." She seemed affronted by the possibility.

"They are refugees," Nathal corrected, with a frown.

"From where?" Saru couldn't stop himself from asking the question. "The coordinates of their homeworld are clear across the quadrant."

"From a colony planet, of course." The Peliar commander shot him a sideways look. "They were settlers, or some such. Their outpost was attacked by a Tholian patrol. . . . They obviously didn't realize how territorial the Assembly is."

"The displaced Gorlans were forced to flee into space," said Hekan. "But their vessels barely made it to the nearest habitable worlds."

"*Our* worlds," Nathal broke in, her tone clipped and accusatory. "They limped into orbit around Peliar Zel, begging us to help them. And now we are doing so, taking them to a safe place."

"Our government has found the Gorlans a new planet to colonize," added the other woman.

"I see." Captain Georgiou seemed to consider this. *"And where is this planet?"*

"A few light-years distant," said Hekan. "Most of them are already there. We are the last of the transports."

Saru became aware of Nathal watching him intently. "I can see why your officer might have come to some erroneous conclusions about the Gorlans. Their ritualistic ways are strange to outsiders. It would be easy to observe them and make the wrong assumptions. But as my second stated, we're not depriving them of anything."

"Then why are they afraid?" Saru bristled at the Peliar commander's dismissive tone, blurting out the questions. "Why are their living conditions so basic?"

"Don't mistake their lack of sophistication for anything other than what it is," Nathal replied. "The way the Gorlans choose to live is up to them."

"And yet you think less of them for that." Saru spoke without thinking, and the moment the words had left his mouth he knew he had been wrong to voice them—even if it was what he believed.

"That'll be quite enough, Lieutenant," said ch'Theloh, silencing him with a look.

Nathal went on without any indication that Saru had uttered a sound. "You must understand that the satellites of Peliar Zel could not accommodate such large numbers of displaced aliens. The ecologies of our Alpha and Beta Moons are delicate, they are strictly organized. Our solution is the best for all parties involved."

"I'll make that clear in my report," Georgiou said neutrally. Saru waited for her to challenge the Peliar commander, but she didn't. *"As well as detailing the circumstances around your warp-drive malfunction."*

"We only wish to complete our mission," said Nathal, and then she straightened her shipsuit, putting on a formal air. "On behalf of my crew and the Peliar Cohort, I would like to thank the crew of the *Shenzhou* for their altruism." Her words had the rote diction of something rehearsed, and Saru wondered if Hekan had coached her commander. "But we do not require any further assistance." Nathal looked around at Johar, Weeton, and Saru, as if she expected them to leave immediately.

"Respectfully," added Hekan, "the situation aboard this ship is an internal matter, and Peliar Zel is not yet a member of the United Federation of Planets."

"Or bound by its rules." Nathal had the last word.

"Quite so," agreed Georgiou. *"I apologize if you feel that I"*—she looked at Saru and Johar, and then away—*"or any of my officers overstepped our bounds. I assure you we had only the best of intentions."* The captain took a breath, and Saru saw a flicker of steel in her eyes. *"But I would remind you that if Peliar Zel does wish to join the Federation, showing cooperation with Starfleet would work in your planet's favor."* She glanced back.

Burnham took this as her cue to speak. *"For full clarity . . . for our report to Starfleet Command . . . it would be useful to speak to a representative from the Gorlan colonists. To be sure they do not require any specific assistance of their own."*

Belatedly, Saru realized that Georgiou's tactic throughout this conversation had been to lead Nathal to this point, so that any refusal from the Peliar commander would make it clear she had something to hide. If she kicked them off her vessel in the next ten seconds, that would give the lie to her assertion that all was well.

Nathal's cheeks darkened, and at length she gave a tight reply. "They have a designated speaker to communicate with other species. Hekan will arrange the meeting with him. Then you can leave." She got up and pushed past Saru, climbing out through the shuttle's hatch without another word.

Burnham entered the lab and crossed the room in quick steps, approaching the workspace against the far bulkhead where the monitor buoy lay in a line of deconstructed parts. The alert from the ship's computer had brought her down here, an automated message in her work queue informing her that the first-stage analysis of the unit was complete. In all the excitement of the rescue operations and the discoveries aboard the Peliar transport ship, she had pushed aside working on the buoy.

"What do you have to tell me?" she asked the air, taking in the dismantled device. In working condition, the unit would have resembled an oblate silver cylinder ringed by a curved solar array, with a sensing head at one end and a cluster of comm antennae at the other. But now it was an orderly set of stripped component parts, the outer surfaces bleached by solar radiation in some places, or pitted with micrometeorites in others.

The sections had been broken down by a set of automated manipulator arms and arranged for examination according to guidelines put in place by the Starfleet Corps of Engineers, but Burnham ignored that, instead gravitating straight toward the midsection, where the buoy's memory banks were situated—and, she hoped, the answers as to why it fell silent. Programming a macroprobe, she retracted the casing and surveyed the interior of the module.

Dozens of duotronic data cores were arranged in rows within it, each one capable of holding gigaquads of stored information. The memory bank should have contained months of recorded sensor scans and subspace telemetry, but the buoy's subsystems had refused to transmit any of it back to the *Shenzhou*. Burnham would need to physically unplug the cores and reset them, one by one, in a reader array that could recover the data.

She had the first core detached when the lab door hissed open and Commander ch'Theloh strode in. "Lieutenant."

"Sir." Burnham didn't look up, her eyes on the delicate duotronic core held in the macroprobe's grip. "Forgive me if I don't rise. This needs steady hands."

"Can't you just use a micro–tractor beam?" said the Andorian, coming over.

Burnham held her breath as she slowly moved the core to the reader. "These components show signs of particle bombardment. I don't want to project any other energy at them unless I have to." The core dropped into the reader with a soft click. "One down, twenty-three more to go." She exhaled and glanced up. "Can I help you, Commander?"

"Checking in," he explained. "This business with the Peliar ship is the captain's main concern, but we can't neglect our mission." He aimed a long blue finger at the dismantled unit. "There's a one hundred light-day gap in Starfleet's early-warning net. The other buoys can compensate somewhat, but the loss in acuity is noticeable. We need to solve why this happened." He frowned and his antennae arched forward. "The last thing we need is someone . . . something sneaking through a hole in the fence."

Burnham's eyes narrowed. "Sir, do you suspect the Tholians?"

"I never *suspect* anything, Lieutenant," he pointed out. "I make predictions and educated tactical evaluations. Have you ever seen one of their ships?"

She shook her head. "Just simulations."

As ch'Theloh spoke, he started to pace. "They're fast. Agile. Extremely dangerous. We'd have our work cut out for us." Then he shook off the grim thought and studied her anew. "The quicker this is done, the better it will be. And I imagine you would prefer to have the analysis completed before Lieutenant Saru returns from the rescue mission."

"Sir?" Burnham had an uncomfortable feeling about where this conversation was going. The first officer and Saru had never really gotten along, not in all the time that Burnham had been serving on board the *Shenzhou*. The Kelpien's stiff manner didn't mesh well with the Andorian's own brand of martial discipline, while conversely, Burnham had always felt that ch'Theloh's cool restraint was admirable. Almost Vulcan in its way, a rare sentiment considering that the people of Andoria and of Burnham's adoptive homeworld were once bitter enemies, at opposite ends of the emotional spectrum.

"I know you beamed the buoy on board over Saru's objections," he went on. "Therefore, you are invested in proving that was the right decision. For the record, I agree with you, Lieutenant. Perhaps this will go some way toward convincing our Kelpien crewmate that his default conservative take on every situation isn't always the most *practical* approach."

Burnham gave a nod, but still, she felt a little bad for Saru. For all his experience, she couldn't shake the feeling that he was in over his head on board the alien ship, and that realization would not be easy for him. Saru had an ego that often expressed itself in an impulse to try too hard, and getting shut down by the Peliars *and* his senior officers over his conduct would smart.

"You are wondering how you would have handled things over there, had Captain Georgiou sent you instead of Saru." Ch'Theloh's penetrating, ice-cold gaze met hers and Burnham gave nothing away. The first officer had an uncanny knack of seeing right into the thought process of his juniors.

Would I have dealt with it differently? She considered the question as she examined the reader array. "I would have gone looking too." As a science officer, Saru was a generalist, but Burnham's specialty was the study of alien cultures, and the chance to peel back the layers on a little-known society like the Gorlans was an enticing prospect. She said as much to the commander.

"We can reach out to them. This situation could offer us a greater insight into the Gorlan race, even on a basic level." The first officer paused. "I've heard they have a strong warrior spirit. It would be interesting to know more." His gaze shifted to the analysis rig. "But one step at a time." Then ch'Theloh pointed at a dark band of crimson unfolding on the display. "Correct me if I am wrong, Lieutenant, but that does not appear to be a positive result."

"Oh, no." Burnham leaned in to the readout and her heart sank. The reader showed the content of the duotronic core as a mass of corrupted files, millions of fragmented shards of data in complete disarray. "That should not be possible. The memory banks are triple shielded, hardened against solar flares and transient subspace phenomena."

"It may only be this single core."

"I don't think I am that lucky," Burnham said with a sigh. She pointed at the display. "Look at the pattern of corruption, sir. It's asymmetrical. Like a localized effect, centralized on a point . . . right *here*." Estimating the scope of the pattern, she realized that the damage would be spread not just through this core, but across the entire memory bank.

The commander folded his arms across his chest. "Are you telling me this was done deliberately?"

"I . . ." Burnham took a breath and hesitated. Suddenly, she wished that Saru were here with her. Just to have the Kelpien looking over her shoulder and double-checking her work would have helped. Then, at length, she nodded. "I will need to run diagnostics on all of the duotronic cores to be certain, but that would be my preliminary conclusion, sir." She gestured at the screen. "The collimation of the effect is just too regular to be the result of a natural phenomenon."

"Theorize," said ch'Theloh, making it an order. "How could it be done?"

Her mind raced as she considered and disregarded a handful of possibilities in short order. "A coherent energy beam, sent from long range. Something attuned to the correct frequency could do this. But it would need to penetrate the monitor buoy's deflectors. If it was . . ." She stopped herself from saying *the Tholians.* "If it was the influence of a hostile actor, why would they not just destroy the unit and be done with it?"

"That question is the one you're going to answer for us," said the first officer. "If we can't figure out what happened here, the next thing to go silent could be the *Shenzhou.*"

4

"Hatch secured," Weeton reported from the pilot's chair. "Ready to disengage."

"Understood." Lieutenant Commander Johar's voice cut through the air in the cabin, but Saru was only half listening. He was too busy trying not to stare at the Gorlan interpreter sitting across from him. *"Tell the captain we'll be finishing up soon over here, Britch. By the time you come back, we should be almost done."*

"Affirmative," replied the ensign. "Shuttle *Yang* cutting loose . . . now."

A dull thud echoed through the hull, and the small auxiliary craft floated away from the hull of the massive Peliar transport. Lines of light cast through the windows shifted as they oriented around toward the *Shenzhou* drifting nearby.

The Gorlan drew himself up onto the seat to get a better look at the Federation starship as they crossed the distance. He had introduced himself as Vetch, speaking a halting, broken version of a basic Peliar Zel dialect that Saru's universal translator could parse. At first, he seemed disturbed by the idea of leaving the cargo ship to visit the *Shenzhou*, but now that he was looking at the Starfleet vessel, he appeared resigned to it. Saru concentrated on the Gorlan, trying to feel the boundaries of the alien's electrosensitive aura, but it was feeble, deliberately muted.

Vetch held himself up with three of his hands, the fourth pressed to the transparent aluminum of the viewport. He was muttering something, too quietly to be heard over the hum of the shuttle's impulse engines.

Saru considered him. Like many of the other Gorlans he had seen in the cargo module, Vetch was dressed in shabby, handspun clothes in a dusty, red-orange hue. His hair was long and streaked with gray, matching a salt-and-pepper beard coiled into crude braids, and he wore two ribbons of soiled green cloth around the biceps of his upper right arm. Saru noticed that the interpreter—*the speaker*, as he had been introduced—walked with a slight limp, and he thought of the female in the white robes.

Saru's curiosity about her rolled around in his thoughts, but he held off asking any questions. Now was not the time.

At Vetch's side, the Peliar woman named Hekan sat quietly, her gaze turned inward. From the skills and status she exhibited, Saru hypothesized that Hekan served in a combination role, equivalent to that of an executive officer and chief engineer, and the deference the other Peliar crewmembers gave her seemed to bear that out.

She was accompanied by one of them now, a male in an orange shipsuit with a silver vest affair over his chest. Judging by the hawkish manner displayed by the other Peliar, Saru believed that he was a security officer of some kind, although he carried no visible weapons. Still, the crewman's presence spoke volumes about Commander Nathal's trust level where the *Shenzhou* was concerned. She was no longer making herself available to talk to any of the Starfleet team, and it fell to Hekan to explain that away. Saru guessed Nathal's unwillingness to continue a dialogue was more about personal dislike than it was anything related to her duties, despite claims to the contrary.

"Many?" Vetch looked down at Hekan to ask the question, nodding in the direction of the *Shenzhou* as the ship grew larger.

Hekan glanced at Saru. "The Federation's Starfleet is quite large, is it not?"

"Yes." Saru nodded and looked to Vetch. "Many, indeed. The *Shenzhou* is an older craft, but it is only one vessel in a fleet that operates across several sectors."

"More come here?"

Saru wasn't sure what the question was leading toward. "If they are needed."

Vetch pursed his lips and said nothing.

Weeton brought them around and into the starship's open hangar bay in a smooth, gentle turn, and the ensign deftly dropped the *Yang* back into the very same spot it had left several hours before.

As the shuttle settled to the deck, Saru saw three figures waiting on the flight apron—Captain Georgiou, Lieutenant Burnham, and the captain's yeoman, Ensign Danby Connor. Inwardly, he winced. Saru's actions aboard the Peliar ship had crossed a line of due comportment that would earn him censure from his commander, but it would be worse if he was forced to suffer it in front of Burnham and Connor.

He shook off the thought. If the captain was going to give him a dressing-down, it wouldn't be now. *No*, he thought, *that is something I will have to look forward to.*

The *Yang*'s aft hatch dropped open and Saru led the way, followed in order by the Peliar security guard, Hekan, Vetch, and finally Ensign Weeton. Georgiou caught Saru's eye as he drew himself up to attention, and he knew his earlier thoughts were correct. *At least the first officer isn't present.* Saru doubted that Commander ch'Theloh would be discreet about pointing out his shortcomings.

Captain Georgiou gave Vetch an official greeting in line with his status as the representative of the Gorlan, but he appeared distracted, warily peering into the far corners of the cavernous landing bay as if looking for something.

"I asked for you to be brought here because I have some questions," Georgiou went on. "I wanted to converse with you face-to-face. And please understand, you're under no duress here. You may speak freely and make any request you require."

Saru was aware of Hekan and the other Peliar shifting nervously as the captain concluded her opening statement. If there was a moment for this to all become even more complicated, then it was now. The Kelpien ran through possible scenarios in his head. *What if he asks for asylum? What if there is violence? What if someone produces a weapon?*

It was a fact of life for Saru that he entertained such worst-case scenarios every minute of every day.

He glanced at Burnham, recalling something she had said to him a few months ago. *You always expect the worst, Saru.*

Yes, he had replied, *but I always hope for the best.*

"Ask what is to be asked," said Vetch, making a beckoning motion. "Will reply."

Georgiou exchanged glances with Burnham and Connor, then returned her attention to the speaker. "Are the Gorlans aboard the transport vessel in any distress?"

"Distress?" Vetch's face wrinkled.

"Is anyone . . . is anything hurting your people?" offered Saru. From the corner of his eye, he saw that Connor was discreetly conducting a tricorder scan of the group.

"Gorlan-kind are hardy. Spirited," replied Vetch. "Little hurts us. We endure."

"She wants to know if *we* have harmed you," said Hekan, shooting Georgiou a look. "That's it, isn't it? You're afraid we've enslaved these people, or something equally heinous? You just don't want to say it out loud."

"We're looking for some clarity," offered Burnham. "That's all."

"You're judging us," Hekan shot back, "and them, on a matter you know next to nothing about!" She made a terse, negative gesture at her throat. "Does the Federation think so little of Peliar Zel's people? I swear to you, on Beta's lands, I would not be party to such a thing."

Hekan spoke with honesty and passion, enough that Saru was willing to believe her. But she was only one person, he reminded himself, and the Kelpien wondered how Nathal would have responded in her place.

Vetch's head bobbed. "Peliar-kind have . . . not harmed Gorlan-kind. All is calm between us on the journey to the new place. Have no concern for us."

"Uh, pardon me . . ." Connor cleared his throat. "Sorry. I couldn't help but notice, the scans . . ." He held up the tricorder. "I'm detecting below-average biometrics compared to the Gorlan norms we have on record. Although admittedly, those are pretty vague."

"Ah." Vetch ran a hand down his beard. "Is nothing. Only fatigue caused by extended travel. Affects all of us, but it is inconsequential. We do not speak of minor thing." He frowned. "Gorlan-kind do not live at their best under metal skies," he admitted, pointing at the ceiling above them. "We need earth beneath feet. True air in breath."

"Are you talking about a vitamin deficiency?" said Burnham.

"That's about right," agreed Connor. "Noticeable but not life-threatening."

"We can help with that," said the captain, seeing an opportunity. "My chief medical officer, Doctor Nambue, can offer the Gorlans a medicine that will alleviate your fatigue. If you wish it."

"That would be of use," said Vetch, and the air of bluff inscrutability he affected dropped away, revealing genuine appreciation. But still, his eyes darted, watching the angles, and Saru realized he was seeing another emotion in the alien. The *fear* again, the same fear Saru had sensed back in the gathering space.

He let his other senses lessen and concentrated again on the aura-field of the Gorlan. Vetch was agitated, but he concealed it well.

"We are glad to assist," Georgiou was saying. "That's why we are out here."

But Hekan had more to say. "I believe you have good intentions," she began. "However, I must tell you that my commander considers your presence in this sector to be more interference than assistance. This space is beyond the boundary of your Federation. You cannot enforce your values here."

Saru had the immediate sense that the words Hekan was speaking were really Nathal's. "Would you prefer that we left you all to perish?"

"What my lieutenant means," interjected Georgiou, "is that Starfleet has a duty to protect all life. That goes beyond lines on a map."

"And I thank you." Hekan gave a small bow. "But I have my orders, and I must relay a message." She stiffened and her manner became formal. "Commander Nathal will be filing an official complaint with the Federation Diplomatic Corps over the *Shenzhou*'s conduct in this situation. Now that your demand to meet the Gorlans has been fulfilled, she asks that you withdraw your crew members from our ship and leave us to our mission."

The captain glanced at Saru and Weeton. "Are the repairs complete?"

"Almost done, Captain," replied the ensign.

"We will respect the wishes of our Peliar neighbors." Georgiou nodded. "My chief engineer will certify your warp drives are safe to operate." Hekan opened her mouth to protest, but the captain continued on. "It's the very least we can do for prospective members of the United Federation of Planets."

At length, the Peliar woman made the affirmative gesture at her throat and relented. "Of course."

"Yeoman." Georgiou looked to Connor. "Escort our guests to sickbay and see that Speaker Vetch is provided with medicines from ship's stocks."

"Aye, Captain." Connor stepped forward to meet the group and gestured toward the turbolift across the shuttlebay. "If you'll follow me, sir?"

Saru watch Vetch and the Peliars walk away, noting that the Gorlan moved slowly and carefully, as if he were unused to the gravity level on board the starship. When Saru turned back, he found the captain's hard look boring right up at him.

"I know I have a reputation for giving my people a lot of leeway," she began, holding Saru's gaze. "Is that a mistake on my part?"

The Kelpien squirmed a little, and she let it happen. "No, Captain. I admit I allowed my interest to get the better of me." He sighed, and Georgiou knew he was already beating himself up about it. "I couldn't ignore what I saw," concluded Saru.

"Sure made things a lot more complicated," muttered Weeton, and then he caught himself. "Did I say that out loud?"

"Lieutenant Burnham was right," she went on, letting

the ensign's comment pass. "Clarity is what we need here. Despite your methods, Saru, it's important that we learned about the presence of the Gorlans on that ship, and their circumstances."

"Given their attitude toward us, I very much doubt Commander Nathal would have freely volunteered that information," noted Saru.

"Is she hiding something else?" As ever, Michael was first to cut to the core of things. "Or is this just resentment directed toward us as outsiders?" Burnham cocked her head in that Vulcan way of hers as she analyzed her own questions.

"Uncertain," Saru said ruefully. Then he took a step forward and lowered his voice. "However, Captain, I do feel that there is more to this than we know. The speaker, Vetch?" He jutted his chin in the direction of the turbolift. "Who was it that provided him for us to converse with?"

"The Peliars," said Weeton.

"You don't trust him?" said Burnham. "What are you basing that on?"

"Instinct." As soon as he said the word, Georgiou saw the Kelpien's shoulders slump. "I know. It's hardly the most solid basis for scientific scrutiny."

"Weeton." She shifted her attention to the junior officer. "You were over there too. Do you share Lieutenant Saru's opinion?"

The ensign frowned. "Nathal doesn't like us and she doesn't want us around, that's as plain as the nose . . . I mean, *the noses* on her face. But, I mean, we might feel the same way if things were reversed, right?"

"Commander Nathal could perceive our intervention as a threat to her authority," said Burnham, mirroring Weeton's frown. "Admittedly, it's an illogical reaction."

"Not everyone is as rational as you, Michael," said Georgiou, letting some mild reproach into her tone.

"Are we going to just . . . let them leave?" Saru fixed her with those searching eyes of his. "We can't do that. There are too many unanswered questions."

The captain saw a look pass between Weeton and Burnham. The other officers were thinking the same thing she was. Georgiou had rarely seen Saru push the point, as he was doing now. It was out of character for the Kelpien to react in this fashion. "Lieutenant, that's all we *can* do. We don't have a right or due cause to restrict the passage of a Peliar Zel starship. Frankly, I've already overstepped my remit by sending the rescue team in blind. We can't risk causing an interstellar incident by involving ourselves in the affairs of non-Federation worlds."

"This isn't a Prime Directive issue, Captain," Saru insisted, his tone rising.

"I know the regulations," she said firmly, shutting him down. "And that's why we're going to abide by them."

"There's also another danger to consider," offered Burnham. "The Tholian Assembly is an ever-present threat to the Peliars. Commander Nathal and her crew have to deal with that potentiality every day. An increased Starfleet presence in this area, even one ship, risks an escalation of Tholian involvement."

"They want us gone," said Weeton, echoing his earlier statement.

"And we're going to oblige. Let's not forget, we have a mission of our own to get back to." Georgiou nodded toward the *Yang*. "Be ready for immediate departure, Ensign. Let's not outstay our welcome any more than we already have." She turned away and threw Burnham a glance. "I'll be on the bridge. In the meantime, Michael, bring Saru up to speed on the buoy situation."

The captain's last look was toward the Kelpien, but Saru was staring out and away, through the shimmering force field over the open shuttlebay door, toward the massive alien freighter floating beyond.

"The buoy," began Burnham. "I've uploaded the data from the preliminary tear-down into your queue."

Saru nodded, but it was difficult for him to focus on the thought of the analysis. His mind kept drifting back to the face of the Gorlan female in the white robes. There was something compelling about her, and he felt a growing sense of incompleteness at the prospect of never learning what she might have said to him.

"The memory cores were affected by an outside energy source," Burnham went on. "I'm not sure of the origin, but we have to consider that the Tholians may be behind it."

Saru nodded absently. "They have been known to interfere with attempts to scan their domains in the past. They utilize radiation baffles to conceal sections of their ships from close-range sensor sweeps." He watched Weeton through the open hatch of the shuttle as the ensign ran the *Yang* through a prelaunch checklist.

"That's a passive measure. We're talking about an active one, a deliberate denial operation." Her lips thinned, and Burnham moved to step in front of him, blocking his view. "Saru, do I have your full attention?"

"Not really," he confessed. "Perhaps a third of it?"

"What's going on?" Burnham looked him over. "This morning you were fixed on the idea of running the analysis by the book from start to finish, now you're barely listening to me . . ." Her tone softened. "What happened to you over there? What did you see?"

"I don't have a good answer for that question," he admitted. For the most part, Saru was a stickler for process and protocol, a firm believer in scientific rigor. But there was also a side of him that was pure Kelpien, a throwback to the reactive, primitive nature of the prey species his kind had once been. That conflict was pressing on him, the responsive elements versus the rational, both trying to make sense of the emotions that his venture into the Gorlan gathering had brought up. "I believe . . . this situation has affected me more deeply than I was aware of."

"Do you need to see Doctor Nambue?"

He waved the comment away irritably. "I am not unwell, Lieutenant. I am . . . *disquieted.*" Saru saw the questions in her expression. "You don't understand. But you would, if you had been there."

"Maybe," she allowed. "Perhaps then *you* would be the one asking *me* if I was okay."

"I think the captain is wrong to disengage from this situation." Normally, Saru would think twice about voicing such a comment, but it fell from him and he didn't try to walk it back.

"You made that clear enough," said Burnham. "But there are regulations that have to be followed. Captain Georgiou knows that, and it appears that Commander Nathal has read the same rulebook."

He eyed her. "You talk about following the letter of the regulations, but that isn't what you said in the mess hall. You ignored protocol by having the buoy beamed aboard the ship."

"That was different," she replied.

"How so? You advocate following the regulations in one case but not another? It seems very arbitrary to me." They were falling into their familiar, combative rhythm once more, but Saru didn't care to halt it. At times he felt he understood Michael Burnham best when they were disagreeing.

"We're trained to interpret a situation based on the

unfolding circumstances," Burnham shot back. "This is the frontier, Saru. The nearest starbase is days away at high warp; the same for the closest Starfleet vessel. We have to be ready to bend the regulations if the moment demands it. That's the thing that separates a good officer from a great one, knowing when to bend and when to be firm." She cocked her head. "If you want to command a starship one day, you need to learn when to make those calls. When to show boldness and when to use restraint."

A retort was forming in his mind when something in Saru made him halt. The human had a point, as irritating as it might have been to admit it. *Perhaps I should consider things from her viewpoint*, he thought. *What would Burnham do if our situations were reversed?*

"You appear to have things in hand with the monitor analysis, Lieutenant." He pulled the tricorder from his belt and moved off. "I'm happy to follow your lead."

"You are?" Burnham raised an eyebrow.

"Yes," he said distractedly, spooling through the tricorder's memory files for the data recorded by his universal translator. "Carry on. I want to review these scans and upload them to the *Shenzhou*'s computer . . ."

A plan of action was starting to form in his thoughts, each element building on the next.

"That's it, sir," said Yashae as she pulled a hand across her brow. "I think we're all good."

Johar didn't say anything, instead making a *give it here* gesture. The chief petty officer handed him the data tablet she had been using, and he tabbed through the display, holding up the device so he could look at it and the Peliar warp core side by side.

On the portable screen, green status flags illuminated

in a line to signify that all the systems inside the alien machinery were now operating normally. The repairs were complete, and they were ready to give the word to Nathal, up on the command deck, to begin the cold-start sequence that would spin up the big cargo ship's warp nacelles.

But Johar hesitated. "Did Subin report back to you about the pulse-wake scan I wanted?"

Yashae nodded, blinking her long-lashed eyes. "She ran the checks, sir. No detection of any lingering nadion particles in any of the emitter coils or injector mechanisms. Whatever caused the pulse effect they encountered, there's no trace of it now."

"Yes," he agreed, "and that annoys the hell out of me." Johar waved at the warp core. "I mean, we know it wasn't a transient subspace effect they passed through; that would have left a different decay signature. We know it wasn't an imbalance in the warp field. Again, that would have been obvious." The engineer started to pace. "So what made this happen? I want a conclusive answer, mister. Otherwise, we're leaving the job half done, and you know how I feel about sloppy workmanship."

"Sir . . ." Yashae broke in, but Johar kept speaking.

"They rev up to warp speed, and that nadion pulse reoccurs, the next time it could cause a supercritical failure. It might invert the Cochrane bubble, or worse! Makes my skin crawl just thinking about it. We need to know for sure if this was a random anomaly, a systemic glitch, deliberate sabotage, or—"

"*Sir*," Yashae repeated, this time with force, at the same time inclining her head in the direction of the hatchway across the compartment. "Company is coming."

Johar turned to find Nathal advancing toward him as if she meant to start a fight, with Riden, the senior Peliar engineer, rushing to keep up with her. "Commander," he began, unconsciously hiding the data tablet behind his back. "Here you are. I was just about to contact you."

"You have worn out whatever small measure of welcome you had on my ship, human," she began. Her tone was ice cold. "I've tolerated you for long enough."

"I was out of line before," Johar said apologetically. "I am very sorry. Heat of the moment and all that." He looked to Riden for some shared understanding. "You know how it can be! Engineers are overly candid at times, and—"

"Insolent?" offered Nathal. "Disrespectful?"

"That's fair." He swallowed hard.

"In our fleet, you would be broken down to the rank of deckhand for talking to a superior officer in such a way." Nathal glared up at the warp core. "Riden informs me the drives are fully repaired. It's time for you to go back to your own vessel."

"That is sort of true," Johar replied. "But the work isn't finished." Again, he looked to the Peliar engineer for support. "Did Mister Riden also tell you that we don't have a definitive cause for the nadion pulse that crippled your ship and destroyed the escort drone?"

"The malfunction has been corrected," Riden said firmly.

"No, the damage has been fixed," said Johar, and he felt his deferential manner starting to slip again. "That's not the same thing." He took a chance and pressed on, before he lost control of the situation. "We're currently running a final diagnostic protocol on your warp subsystems, isn't that correct, Chief Yashae?"

He handed back the tablet to the Vok'sha and gave her a hard look. "Yes, we are," Yashae agreed smoothly, and stepped away before anyone could see that she hadn't actually started any such diagnostic. "I'll go check on it right now."

Nathal came right up to Johar, and her voice dropped to a low growl. "If I believe that you are making an attempt at subterfuge . . . it won't matter if you are an engineer, or Starfleet, or Federation. I will have you put out of an airlock and Captain Georgiou can fish you from the void. Is that statement candid enough?"

"Very much so," managed Johar, "Captain."

The Peliar captain stalked away, with her engineer following closely at her heels. As soon as she was out of earshot, Johar sought out Yashae, who stood with Subin at one of the control podiums.

"Where's Zoxom?" He looked around. There was no sign of the Xanno nurse.

"He's on the tier above," explained Subin. "Apparently, a few of the Peliar technicians took a low dose of delta rays during the incident. He's handing out shots to everyone who was affected."

"Get him back down here when he's done," Johar told them. "I don't want any of our people out of my sight." Then he tapped the data tablet in Yashae's hand. "And get that diagnostic completed. *Quickly.*"

There was an unattended workstation in an alcove off the *Shenzhou*'s landing bay, and Saru secreted himself there, out of sight where he could work at a console and keep one eye on the shuttlecraft on the launch cradle.

He loaded the contents of his universal translator's memory into the ship's computer via his tricorder, and called up a linguistic program to evaluate the dialogue he had recorded while among the Gorlans. Saru was convinced there was more nuance to mine from the data, if only he could find a way to frame it. These were, after all, complex beings with their own spacefaring culture, not some primitive semisentients with little concept of the larger universe—even if that was how some of the Peliars appeared to think of them.

He didn't trust Vetch. Something about the speaker made his threat ganglia itch. Saru was certain, if he could just converse with the Gorlans on the same level, all the questions and the uncertainties Captain Georgiou was being forced to overlook would snap into hard focus. They would know for sure what was happening on board the transport ship.

Leaving that question hanging made Saru despair. He imagined the Gorlans facing some terrible fate, and felt a sting of guilt. He could not stand by and allow those beings to go to an uncertain future, not if there was still a chance to prevent it. "This is not a time for restraint," he said aloud, recalling Burnham's comment as he worked through the data. "This is a time for boldness."

Saru reviewed the tapes, observing how the translator's learning software assembled and reassembled the syntax and sounds it recorded into something approximating linguistic communication.

Anxiety. Waiting. Conflict.

Basic concepts like these were decoded quickly, but the deeper streams of meaning were harder to reveal.

Fear. Curiosity. Anger. Panic. Distress.

He closed his eyes and struggled to recall how he had felt, reaching back to the feel of the air about him, the sub-sensory crackle of the electrostatic fields generated by the press of the gathered Gorlans.

Anger. Suspicion. Doubt.

"It's not enough," he told himself, shaking his head. Saru brought up visual representations of word clusters and clouds of possible meaning, watching as the ship's computer offered up conflicting potentials.

This alignment of sounds here could mean "friendship" or "group" but it could also be "temperature" or "sustenance." The Kelpien scowled at the readouts. *This one here equates to either the size of a living creature or the age of an inanimate object.* Either one of the translations could be correct, he realized, their context modified by location, tone of voice, or the invisible pattern of a neuroelectric field.

Toward the end of the recorded data, he noted that a single phrasing was repeated several times by many different Gorlan voices. Saru zeroed in on it and highlighted the word cluster. "Computer, concentrate on this particular grouping. Based on all available data, theorize as to the most likely meaning."

"Working," said the synthetic voice. Unhelpfully, the display erupted with a dozen different potential answers. *"In descending order: Writing implement. Doorway. Carrier. Mother. Liquid. Grouping. Central. Heart organ. Nexus—"*

"Stop." Saru waved the computer into silence. "None of those are correct. There's something more, something missing . . ." His brow furrowed as he struggled to remember what he had sensed when those words had been spoken. How had they made him *feel*? "That's close, but it's not . . . not *central*, not a *nexus* . . . a . . ."

He could feel the concept was almost within his grasp, if only he could visualize it. And then suddenly he understood.

"*Hub.* That's the term. A figurative central point to which all others connect. The Gorlans were talking about *a hub.*" Saru experienced a rush of excitement at the discovery, an instant of pure enthusiasm as a piece of the alien puzzle locked into place.

But was this a literal idea or something more symbolic? Again he thought of the female in the grubby white robes and the open curiosity in her eyes when she had seen him. Was he seeing in her what he wanted to see, projecting his own feelings onto an alien being? Or was she what he thought she might be, someone who was willing to communicate outside the boundaries of Peliar oversight?

Contact with other life-forms and other cultures was always fraught with the possibility of critical misapprehension, of imposing one's ingrained prejudices on outsiders. The only way to comprehend was to attempt to bridge that gap, and if the *Shenzhou* left now, Saru would be tormented by the possibility of what had gone unsaid.

He looked out at the shuttle, seeing Ensign Connor returning with Hekan, Vetch, and the other Peliar crewman trailing behind carrying medical pods. Saru drew himself up and strode purposefully back across the landing bay, smoothly intercepting Connor as the captain's yeoman gave the aliens a formal send-off.

"On behalf of Captain Philippa Georgiou and the crew of the *Shenzhou*," Connor was saying, "it was our pleasure to host you aboard our ship, and we hope that the Federation can continue to maintain cordial relations with the peoples of Gorlan and Peliar Zel."

"Indeed," said Saru, interposing himself in the conversation. "I'll take it from here, Mister Connor."

"Sir?" The yeoman was going to protest, so Saru cut him off swiftly.

"You're dismissed." He made an *after you* gesture to the group of visitors, directing them back aboard the *Yang*. "Allow me to help." Saru took the medical containers and carried them the rest of the way into the shuttle, securing the hatch behind him as he boarded last.

Up in the cockpit, Ensign Weeton was talking to the hangar operations officer. "*Shenzhou*, this is shuttle *Yang*. Passengers are secure, we are good to go."

"We read you, Yang. *Cleared for launch."*

"Thank you . . ." Weeton trailed off as Saru climbed into the copilot's seat next to him and ran a hand over the controls. "Lieutenant? You're . . . coming back with us?"

"That's right." Saru said it firmly, as if the answer to the question was obvious. "I will assist Lieutenant Commander Johar with a final check on the repairs before we return with the rescue team." Weeton hesitated, and Saru pressed on, pulling rank. "In your own time, Ensign." He nodded at the open launch bay ahead of them.

"Aye, sir," Weeton replied warily, and with a slight bump, the shuttle lifted off.

"Is this really necessary, sir?" said Zoxom, his face creasing in a frown. "I'm sure there won't be any physical danger to any of us."

"You didn't see the look in her eye," muttered Johar, glancing up at the hatch as the *Yang* made a hard seal with the Peliar ship's hull. "I know you think the best of people, Nurse, but I'll be more comfortable with you waiting in the shuttle."

"As you wish, sir." Zoxom sighed. "But you should know, not all the crew are as . . . prickly . . . as Commander Nathal. Some of them are very personable, in fact."

"I'll keep that in mind," said Johar. Back in the engine chamber, he had seen two of Nathal's crewmen, both of them wearing the silver vests that seemed to designate security officers. Neither of the Peliars had spoken to him, but it was abundantly clear they were there to keep watch over the warp core.

Above, the hatch slid back into the ceiling and a ladder dropped down. Hekan was the first to come through, and she gave Johar a loaded look that seemed half sympathy and half irritation. "We talked to your captain," she told him. "Vetch explained things to her."

Johar watched the diminutive, four-armed Gorlan scramble easily down the ladder and slide to the deck. "Did he? And what was that?"

"We are all going our separate ways," Hekan replied neutrally as her crewman emerged from the shuttle and stood aside.

"My technicians, Subin and Yashae, they're almost done." Johar decided to play a hunch and made one last attempt to get his point across. "But look, I have to say this, as one engineer to another. The origin of the pulse effect still isn't clear. With some more time, if we can work together—"

"I have my orders and so do you," Hekan cut him off in midsentence. "Don't make me say it again." She didn't seem happy about it, but she walked away before he could press the point.

"Stand by below, cargo coming down," said another voice. Johar turned to see Saru's gangly form descending the ladder with two medical pods balanced awkwardly across his arms. As his hoofed boots hit the deck, Vetch reached up and took one of the containers, feeling the weight.

"What are you doing back here?" Johar took a step closer to the Kelpien. "I didn't request you."

"I'm here to . . . assist," Saru offered. "The captain provided the Gorlans with some supplies they requested."

Something in the science officer's reply rang a wrong note with the chief engineer, but he held off on it, glancing back at the Xanno nurse. "Zoxom, get in the shuttle and tell Weeton to be ready to undock."

Meanwhile, Saru was already stepping after Vetch along the corridor, carrying the second medical pod with him.

"Lieutenant!" Johar caught up to him. "You drop that stuff off with the Gorlans and you get back up here on the double, is that clear? Don't stop to smell the roses."

"The Gorlans grow fungus, sir, not flowers. But I will act with alacrity," he replied, stepping into the cradle of an elevator platform that would descend into the main cargo module.

As the lift fell away, Johar heard Zoxom calling out to him from the hatchway. "Sir! Is Saru there?"

"He's gone below." The engineer walked back toward the hatch. "Why?"

Zoxom made a guttural noise that Johar knew was a Xanno curse word, and threw a wary look toward the two Peliar security guards. "Better if we talk in the shuttle, sir."

"What now?" Johar grimaced and hauled himself up the ladder, emerging in the *Yang*'s crew cabin.

Weeton was waiting for him, and he jerked a thumb at the shuttle's control console. "As soon as we docked, I re-established the line-of-sight laser comms with the *Shenzhou*. The XO wants to talk to you."

Johar dropped into the pilot's chair and saw Commander ch'Theloh's face on a small holoscreen projected over the control yoke. The Andorian's usual sky-blue features were a darker cerulean shade, and that did not bode well. His gut sank as Johar opened the channel. "Commander?"

"Weeton says Saru was on that shuttle," snapped ch'Theloh. *"He wasn't ordered to return to the Peliar ship. I need to speak to him, right this second."*

"Ah." Johar shot a look over his shoulder. "Sir, he just went below. Down to the decks where the Gorlans are living."

"And you let him?"

"I didn't see any—"

"Never mind," the first officer cut him off. *"The lieutenant's actions are both uncharacteristic and unauthorized."* The Andorian leaned into the visual pickup, his face filling the small screen. *"Find him, and reel him back in before whatever misguided impulse he has surrendered to causes a diplomatic crisis!"*

5

The elevator platform rattled as it continued its descent into the heart of the massive freighter, and Saru quickly lost count of the levels as they flashed past.

At his side, Vetch put down the crate he had been carrying and sat upon it, looking up at the lofty Kelpien. “Why you here, alien?” His deep-set eyes fixed Saru with a distrustful glare. “What you hope to grow?”

“I hope to understand you better,” he said truthfully.

“Should go home,” Vetch replied. The words were lazy, almost offhand. But Saru couldn’t miss the warning buried beneath them. “You get trouble.”

“Yes, well . . .” Saru frowned and pulled absently at his uniform. “I’m afraid that I’ve already generated enough of that.”

The lift rocked and began to slow. Vetch made a spitting noise and rose from the crate. “Say not Vetch warned you.”

The elevator shaft opened up for the last few meters, and Saru got a glimpse of another area of the cargo-module interior as they came to a halt. Like the other spaces he had seen earlier, it was busy with makeshift dwellings remade from whatever was at hand, all built from surplus plating, suspended cables, and flexible materials. It was one more district in the contained but sprawling bivouac township.

A group of Gorlans were waiting for them in a small

court area near the loading apron in front of the platform, most of them dressed in clothes similar to Vetch's. *Does that make them part of a subgroup, perhaps a tribe within the greater whole?* Once again, Saru wished he had Burnham's eye for the study of alien cultures.

With a few quick-fire grunts, too fast for Saru's universal translator to pick up, Vetch directed one of his kinsmen to take the other crate of medical supplies. He handed off his own to a second male wearing a yellow band around two of his biceps.

"What does that mean?" Saru ventured the question, pointing toward the colored band. "Does it designate status or position in your society?"

The Gorlan speaker gave him an odd look, and Saru guessed his translator hadn't clearly rendered the inquiry. Vetch walked away, and he seemed surprised when the Kelpien took a step after him. "Where you go?" He raised all four of his arms, palms flat.

"I wish to speak to your people," said Saru. He had his tricorder set in constant scan mode again, recording everything going on around him—not just his interactions with Vetch, but the hushed conversations and furtive glances of the other Gorlans loitering nearby. They milled around, looking up at him and exchanging hushed comments. Saru was very likely the tallest being any of them had ever seen, at his full height towering over even the Peliars with their elaborate headdresses.

"They not speak you." Vetch made a dismissive gesture.

Saru saw an opening and took it. "We can learn to. With this device." He showed him the universal translator. "I only require time to . . . to *grow* the knowledge."

Vetch made a shaking motion, like a shrug. "Nothing for you here. Better back on *Shen-zoo*."

"Respectfully, I would prefer to stay a while."

The Gorlan repeated the shake-shrug again. "Choice yours." He moved away, and Saru watched him cross the open atrium to a yurt-like enclosure, disappearing inside with the crates.

As the entrance flap flicked open, he thought he saw figures inside with red bands on their arms. Then Saru realized he was alone again among these beings, once more surrounded by the aura of their anxieties and suspicions.

Behind him, the elevator platform that had brought Saru here began its ascent back toward the upper tiers. *That settles it,* he thought. *I am here. I have come this far. I am going to do this.*

He regulated his breathing and opened his hands to present the most neutral, unthreatening aspect possible. Around the Kelpien, a ring of Gorlans was slowly gathering, all of them chattering and sizing him up. They stared at him with mistrust and interest in equal measure.

"Sah. Roo," said one of them. He turned to see the speaker; it was a young Gorlan male, the patina of hair on his arms shaved into lines and dyed a dusty white. He rocked on his heels and grew bolder, saying the name again. "Sah-Roo."

"Were you there before, in the gathering place?" Saru took a careful step toward the youth. "Yes. That is my name. I am Saru." He tapped his chest and then pointed at the Gorlan. "Who are you?"

"Nahah." The Gorlan eyed him, and Saru felt the prickle of a soft electrostatic aura emanating from the youth. "Am Nahah."

Progress! Saru shot a look at his tricorder. With every second that passed, the device was soaking up data like a sponge, incrementally improving the UT's ability to parse the Gorlan language and relaying it back to him. *A few days of this,* he thought, *and we could have a complete lexicon . . .*

"I greet you in peace, Nahah." Saru bowed slightly. "I wish to learn."

His words sent a ripple of consternation through the group, and the aura became prickly and irregular. Saru took a deep breath and concentrated on evening out his own electrostatic energy—and that wasn't easy, given the racing of his own pulse. He was experiencing a peculiar mix of excitement and trepidation. *One mistake, and I will ruin any chance I have to make a connection with these beings.*

He took it slowly, recalling his Academy classes on First Contact Protocols. Saru asked Nahah leading questions based around simple concepts, and little by little the Gorlan relaxed, supplying him with fragmented, monosyllabic answers. The problem was, the translator software was still struggling to keep up, so asking the youth to describe his planet of origin gave a reply of *land sky open close counting remote area.*

Saru sensed Nahah's aura as it flickered and waned with each utterance. His jaw stiffened in frustration. Without being able to factor in the Gorlans' naturally generated EM fields into the communication methodology, there would be no way to machine-translate their language fully and completely.

But I don't need to be able to craft a sonnet, Saru reminded himself. *I just need to be able to ask them one question: Are you in danger?*

"Are you friends with the Peliars?" He waited for what he thought was the right opportunity, and then dropped the question into the mix.

The prickle in the EM aura briefly became an itch that made Saru reflexively scratch the sensing spiracles on his temple, but the impression faded just as quickly.

Nahah toyed with a patch of discolored fur-like hair on his bare forearm and rolled his shoulders. "You ask," said the Gorlan. "You know?"

"I don't understand," said Saru, and he felt the conversation starting to drift away from him.

What why seen hurting sleeping curling unless. The translator momentarily lost the meaning of the exchange and spat out a string of seemingly random concepts. It was all on the verge of falling apart.

Saru decided to reach for a shared experience as a way of keeping the tenuous connection he had made with the Gorlan youth. "Before, we were in the gathering place. There was a female of your kind there, dressed in robes of white." He indicated his own clothes, pulling at them with his long fingers. "I want to learn more about that . . ." Saru struggled to find the right word. "That ceremony?"

In an instant, the motile, shifting resonance of the invisible aura faded away to nothing. It reminded Saru of a cloud passing in front of a sun, a pleasant warmth instantly becoming chills and shadow.

That was a mistake, he told himself, watching as the body language of Nahah and the other Gorlans became stiff and defensive. *Did that question transgress some sort of cultural boundary?*

"I am sorry," he began, instinctively crouching, drawing low to minimize his size. "I meant no disrespect . . ."

Nahah rocked on the balls of his feet, and the Kelpien thought the young male would respond. But the crowd began to break apart, drawing away. The elevator platform was coming back down, and Saru's heart sank as he saw a familiar figure riding it, a figure in a dark blue uniform with flashes of bronze down the flanks.

The platform clanked to a halt, and Lieutenant Commander Johar stepped off, his eyes wide. Saru couldn't help but notice the engineer had one hand very close to the grip of the phaser on his belt. "Lieutenant!" he snapped. "You've got some explaining to do."

"Sir." Saru's fingers curled in the air. "I have a very good reason—"

"Not to me," Johar retorted, and beckoned him closer. "Come on, neither of us are supposed to be here. Let's not complicate this any more than you already have."

Irritation flared in the Kelpien's eyes. Just as before, he was in danger of being dragged away before he could make a breakthrough. "Sir," he said more forcefully, "I am trying to fulfill our mission."

Johar lowered his voice so that only Saru could hear him, keeping one eye on the silent Gorlans gathered around them. "Look, I know this situation is a complex one. And I don't disagree with your intentions. Your methods are ill considered, but I get what you're trying to do here." Saru opened his mouth to speak, but Johar kept talking. "None of that has any bearing on our orders. We have to *go*."

"There's more happening here than what we are aware of," Saru insisted.

"I don't doubt it," Johar shot back. "But we have stuck our noses in far enough." He jerked his head toward the elevator and put his hand on his weapon. "Do I need to make it an order . . . or do I have to stun you and drag you back unconscious? I'd prefer the former; it'd be a pain in the backside hauling you into the shuttle."

"You would do that?" Saru guessed that Johar was only half joking about that last statement. At length, he gave a weary nod, feeling a great weight press down on him. *I have failed*. A sting of inward-directed anger followed. *What was I thinking? I am not Burnham. This isn't my way.*

"What's this?" Johar's question drew Saru's attention back. The chief engineer was looking over the Kelpien's shoulder, toward the enclosure where Vetch had gone. The speaker had emerged again, this time with a group of five

Gorlan males walking in lockstep behind him. All of them wore the red bands Saru had seen before.

Vetch ignored him and wandered over to Johar, invading the human's personal space. The Gorlan made no attempt to hide his interest in the phaser on the other officer's belt. He peered at it and licked his lips.

"Excuse us. We'll be going now," said Johar, backing off toward the elevator. He threw Saru a look. The human didn't need to be able to feel aura-fields to sense the sudden sense of threat in the air.

"Agreed." Saru took a last look over his shoulder and saw one of the red-bands share a word with Nahah. The older Gorlan had some similarities in skin tone and hair color with the youth, and Saru wondered if they were related. Nahah reacted sharply to whatever was said to him and stepped away, never meeting Saru's questioning gaze as he melted into the crowd.

Saru felt a sudden tension in the flesh at the back of his skull, and his threat ganglia distended as the danger made itself apparent.

Something is wrong. The ghostly electrostatic aura scratched at the skin of the Kelpien's bare hands, and that was when he saw the weapon in the other Gorlan's grip. An energy pistol of some kind, with the fluted emitter characteristic of a disruptor.

The universal translator spat out a garbled, unreadable noise as the armed Gorlan shouted a word, the sound hard and sharp with the unmistakable timbre of a command. The other red-bands produced weapons of their own, some of them like the disruptor, others more rudimentary blades that were no less lethal.

Vetch moved in a flash, snatching Johar's phaser from his belt and dancing back out of his reach. Saru spun to find a wicked-looking dagger up at his throat, held by a muscular red-band who stood as tall as the gangly Kelpien's chest. The other Gorlan, the one that had spoken to Nahah and given the command, came over and took Saru's gear, removing his weapon and his communicator.

It was only when he reached for the rodlike universal translator and Saru's tricorder that the Kelpien attempted to block him. "Please do not take those. They are very complex." Saru made a motion at his mouth. "We need them to converse, do you understand?"

Vetch made no effort to intervene and the red-band took the devices regardless. "You get trouble," the speaker said, walking toward Saru. "I told you." Vetch took the rodlike translator and turned it over in his stubby fingers, examining the function controls. "I keep this."

"Return our equipment and step aside." Johar spoke slowly and clearly. "We just want to leave."

"Not happen," Vetch replied, and he gestured to one of the red-bands holding a disruptor pistol. The Gorlan moved in and pointed the weapon at the engineer's chest. "You help Peliars. Now you help Gorlans."

Saru shook his head. "We have done so, and there was no need to threaten us. My captain gave you medicines!"

"That's not the kind of thing he's talking about, Lieutenant," Johar said gravely.

"Walk." Vetch pointed back at the elevator platform. "Or there will be pain for you."

The Gorlans forced their two hostages to stand in front of them as the platform rose once again, swiftly climbing out of the cargo modules and through the hull spaces of the freighter.

Twice, Johar tried to turn his head for a sideways look at Vetch and the red-bands, but on each occasion they noticed him watching and jabbed him in the back with Saru's phaser. All he got a glimpse of was one of them pulling an access panel off the side of the elevator's control podium, exposing the glowing wires within. He understood why when the lift rattled past the level where he had first boarded it and continued to rise at a fast clip, bypassing the ship's engineering spaces and ascending on toward the bow.

Johar's thoughts raced. From the piecemeal scans the *Shenzhou* had made of the Peliar cargo carrier, he knew that the massive vessel's command and control decks were situated in the forward sections of the craft—and the prospect of an armed assault with him and Saru as living shields led inexorably to one conclusion. Vetch and his red-band companions were on their way to take over the ship.

The way the Gorlans moved, the speed and the purpose behind their actions, all of it told him that this was something that they had planned and prepared for. Perhaps they had always meant to involve the Starfleet team, or perhaps the rescue party from the *Shenzhou* had accidentally walked into their scheme and forced them to trigger it early. . . . It didn't matter now. The chief engineer and the junior science officer were caught up in the unfolding events, and their chances of getting out unharmed diminished with each passing second.

Johar kept his gaze fixed on the bulkheads flashing past on the other side of the elevator platform's mesh-screen doors, but from the corner of his eye he could see Saru shifting nervously from foot to foot, his hooved boots scraping on the deck plates.

"Calm down," whispered Johar, out of the side of his mouth.

"Do you think they are going to kill us?" Saru hissed back, reaching up gingerly to massage his ganglia into the back of his head.

"If they wanted us dead, they would have dealt with us down in the cargo compartment." Johar shook his head. "Besides, our phasers are set for stun."

"Do they know that?" Saru eyed him. "Disruptors and daggers don't have that functionality, sir." The Kelpien let out a weak sigh. "This is my fault. I should never have come back here."

Johar decided there was little to be gained right now by apportioning blame and ignored the comment. "Nothing has happened yet that can't be taken back." He spoke loudly enough for Vetch to hear him. "There's still time to talk about this like reasonable beings."

The words had barely left his mouth before Vetch was prodding him in the shoulder with the flat head of his stolen weapon. "Human say reason? Reason gone far ago."

Saru glared at the Gorlan. "When you came to our ship, you told Captain Georgiou that everything was calm between your kind and the Peliars. Was that a lie?"

"Words for them, not you," Vetch said dismissively. "Now I make use." The elevator began to slow. "Interfere and there will be pain," he added.

Saru looked to Johar. "Sir?"

"Follow my lead," he told him as the platform finally emerged in the middle of the freighter's command tier.

The engineer only got a quick glimpse of things, barely getting his bearings before the mesh slid back and the Gorlans shoved the two Starfleet officers out in front of them. The bridge of the Peliar star-freighter was a windowless oval chamber with a curved ceiling, and at one end there was a raised platform where Nathal stood, her face a picture of shock at the sight of the unexpected arrivals. Hekan and the other senior crew were all in front of their podiums, working haptic control interfaces for the big ship's primary systems. Many of the consoles were unmanned, suggesting that the vessels were constructed with a far larger crew in mind.

"No move!" Vetch shouted the words at the top of his voice, waving the phaser in the air. "Back, go back! Resist and pain comes!"

The Gorlans spilled out of the elevator shaft, each of them menacing a different member of the crew. Most of the Peliars did as they were told to, but Commander Nathal was not cowed by the naked display of aggression. She strode down to the lower level, ignoring the red-band who threatened her and fixing Vetch with a venomous glare.

"You dare to do this? After all we have done for you?" She came at the Gorlan speaker. "Ungrateful creatures—"

"Back!" As Vetch shouted the word at her, the red-band who had taken Saru's phaser fired a shot into the deck at Nathal's feet. She staggered back, as if she had never expected them to go that far.

"You better do as they say," said Johar, playing for time.

Nathal turned her ire on the two Starfleet officers. "You are the cause of this! Did we not tell you to stay away from them? Do you see now? Your interference has stirred them to violence!"

"We did not make this happen," Saru blurted out. "We came to help you, all of you!"

"And that has been of such benefit," Nathal spat back. "Aid us now, then. Rid my ship of these criminals."

"No Gorlan crime," barked Vetch, baring his teeth. "You, Peliar. Your crime!"

"I never wanted this mission," said Nathal. "But I accepted it, because I do my duty. I overlooked my dislike of these outworlders." She cut the air with the blade of her hand. "I was wrong to ignore my instincts."

"You always hate." Vetch glared back at her. "Gorlan see. Gorlan know."

Johar took a step forward, trying to interpose himself between the two beings. "Listen to me. Whatever ill feelings you both have toward each other, it doesn't need to be debated at the barrel of a gun!"

Nathal gave a sneering grunt. "You're wasting your breath on these primitives. Look at them! Violence is all they know!"

"You made us!" Vetch clasped two of his hands around his stolen phaser, the other pair bunching into fists. "Drove us to this!"

"Animals!" The shout came from one of Nathal's men, the crewman named Dakas, and Johar saw him pull something from a storage locker in the base of one of the podiums. Dakas's hand came back up with a clutch-grip needle laser in his fist and he fired, stitching a fine thread of brilliant red light through the air.

The beam sliced through the upper biceps of one of the red-bands, and the Gorlan let out a piercing scream; then all hell broke loose as the would-be hijackers hit back.

The emerald crackle of disruptor bolts spat from multiple weapons, striking down two of the Peliar crew in the first salvo. Johar dove forward, desperately trying to find cover behind a console, aware that Saru was close by. But the lanky Kelpien was just over two meters tall, and he presented a large, obvious target.

The engineer saw the injured red-band turn, the heavy shape of an energy weapon cradled in three of his hands swinging to point at the science officer's back.

"Saru!" Johar reacted without thinking, throwing himself at his crewmate, shoving him out of the way as the Gorlan pulled the trigger. Green fire filled his vision, and suddenly Johar's entire body was an inferno as the nerve-shredding discharge of the disruptor hit rippled across him.

The horrific, heart-stopping agony engulfed the engineer, and he sank into it, swallowed by darkness.

Saru was not a stranger to death. His people were born with an innate sense of it, an almost preternatural capacity for sensing the immediacy of the end of life.

Death is the shadow at the heels of every Kelpien-born. It was an old axiom, taught to him from childhood as he listened to elders tell cautionary tales of those who died of foolishness, of inattention, of curiosity. Saru had never forgotten those words, even though time had taken him far from his home, countless light-years distant from the hunter-beasts upon it.

Some among his crewmates on the *Shenzhou* thought him to be morbid, even fatalistic, in the way in which a shadow lurked behind his every waking moment, his every thought and action. They didn't understand that the reverse was true. Saru's certainty that danger and death awaited him did not shade his life in morose tones. It made him all the more determined to *live* it, down to the very last second.

The grotesque odor of seared skin entered his olfactory slits, and he grimaced as he turned over Lieutenant Commander Johar's body. An ugly wound had melted together flesh and fabric across the engineer's torso, the shock effect of the near hit from the weapon leaving a spider web of damaged blood vessels over the man's dark skin. Had the bolt struck him squarely, his end would have been instant. Johar was alive, but the shadow of death was passing over him. He would not last long without medical attention.

He saved my life. The realization was stark and harsh, a blinding light in Saru's thoughts. *I didn't think he liked me.*

"Move! Move now!"

The shouted command brought him crashing back, and

Saru looked up to see the red-band with the white-streaked hair pointing a weapon at him. At his side, Vetch was jabbing his fists in the air, crowing over their victory.

The brief firefight had ended as quickly as it began. Johar and another of Nathal's officers were the only wounded but Saru now saw there had been deaths as well—two Peliar crewmen in the silver vests of their security detail.

Vetch sniffed, giving Johar's bloodless face a brisk once-over. "Unfortunate. This one is ended."

"Not yet!" A burst of indignant anger propelled Saru to his full height, and he hauled Johar off the deck. "Where are the others from our shuttle? What have you done with them?"

Around him, the Gorlans were herding the remaining Peliar command crew into a tight cluster, backing Nathal and the others against the far wall. Vetch watched them work, then made an idle nod. "Below. Unharmed. There is value to them."

"But not to this man?" Saru glared at the Gorlan as he held Johar up. "Not to me?"

"Unfortunate," repeated Vetch, throwing a sideways look at the injured red-band who had almost killed the engineer.

"I need to take the commander to our medic," Saru went on. "Otherwise he *will* die and you will personally be responsible!"

The white-haired Gorlan orbited close to the conversation and snarled something quick and forceful. Vetch chattered back at him, and Saru guessed he was translating for his comrade. Another of the Gorlans went to a nearby control podium and activated an exterior scanner display.

"This agreed," said Vetch. "Take Sah-roo's man below . . . after you help."

Saru's blood chilled as the other Gorlan came over and

took Johar from him. "I will not assist you in endangering any more of this ship's crew!"

"Not this ship." Vetch waved toward the Gorlan at the console, and the holographic panel above it illuminated with an image of the *Shenzhou*, the vessel floating at station-keeping a few thousand meters off the Peliar freighter's bow.

Indicators that could only be the targeting cues for the freighter's weapons array danced over the length of the *Shenzhou*, moving back and forth, ready to lock on and fire.

"No," said Saru, feeling the color drain from his face.

"We leave now. But no chase, not to be followed." Vetch pointed at the *Shenzhou*. "Help us stop this following." Where his finger met the hologram, the weapons chose a target. The aiming cues flicked across the crew decks, the underslung bridge, the main deflector. "You choose best. Or we choose *all*." Vetch opened his hand and the entire length of the *Shenzhou* lit up with potential hit points.

Saru felt sick inside as a terrible choice unfolded before him. An unexpected strike on any one of those locations would result in massive loss of life. But a carefully targeted shot could be sent somewhere that might cripple the ship and injure no one.

"You help," grunted the white-haired Gorlan, aping Vetch's earlier words.

His hand trembling, Saru slowly reached up to touch the display.

"What the . . . ?" The half-formed question fell from Kamran Gant's mouth and his brow furrowed as the blip on tactical display panel appeared and disappeared in the space of an indrawn breath.

"Problem, Lieutenant?" The *Shenzhou*'s first officer

caught the muttered words from halfway across the bridge and in two quick strides the Andorian was at Gant's station.

How does he do that? Gant wondered. *Has to be those antennae of his. Or maybe it's like Connor says, he really does have eyes in the back of his head.* "I'm not sure, sir." He ran a quick scanning macro to check the starship's tactical systems for any kind of anomalous readings. "For a second, I thought there was a low-power sensor beam out there."

Ch'Theloh glanced at the wallowing Peliar transport through the main viewport. "From them?"

"It's—" Gant started to explain when the blip suddenly returned, once more blinking on and then off. "There it is again!"

"I saw." The commander leaned over the console. "Could the sensors be picking up a radiation artifact, something left over from the nadion pulse?"

"Possible." Gant looked up, across the bridge to Ensign Troke at the science station. "Are you seeing this too?"

"Gentlemen . . . ?" Captain Georgiou put down the cup of tea she had been drinking and gave her crew a sideways look.

"Potential sensor anomaly, Captain," said ch'Theloh.

"Ah, no it isn't," corrected Troke, tapping the neural implant at his neck. "It's coming from the Peliar vessel. But not powerful enough for a full-blown scanner emission."

The Andorian threw the Tulian a brisk nod. "Thank you for the clarification, Mister Troke."

"Could it be a communication?" said the captain. "Like the line-of-sight laser we've been using with the *Yang*?"

"Why would it be bouncing all over the hull?" said ch'Theloh.

"They're bad at aiming?" Gant said the words without thinking, and his breath stuck in his throat as his mind caught up with his mouth, the solution to the mystery abruptly revealing itself. "It's not sensors! It's a targeting sweep!"

As he spoke, a flicker of warning icons appeared down the length of the *Shenzhou*'s twin warp nacelles, zeroing in on the intercoolers and magnetomic flux arrays that were vital to the vessel's faster-than-light drive system.

"Confirmed, alien ship is locking on to us!" Ensign Detmer called out from the helm console in alarm.

"They're charging weapons . . ." Gant heard himself give the report.

"Red alert!" ordered Georgiou. "Tactical, raise the—"

Blood-crimson light doused the chamber, and Gant's hand was already on the activation control for the *Shenzhou*'s deflector shields when the attack came, but it was too late. A blinding storm of phase cannon bolts ripped past the lower tier of the ship's primary hull and the crew reacted, turning away from the firestorm. An instant later, the precisely aimed salvo cut into the starship's engines and blew through the nacelles, sending a cascade shock down through the warp coils in stormy flashes of vented plasma.

Gant shook against his station as a rumble of tormented metal vibrated back up the engine pylons and through the *Shenzhou*'s saucer-like fuselage. Across his alert board, impact markers bloomed in a line of orange and yellow icons. Power, light, and gravity briefly dropped away as the vessel rolled with the blow, like a streetfighter shaking off a sucker-punch.

He tried to tap into the auxiliary power, desperate to route energy to the shields. If the surprise attack was the opening blow in a sustained assault, they had to be ready for another hit. The light-headedness from the low-g surge went away and the red lights glowed once more.

"Warp drive is offline." Lieutenant Oliveira had taken an early shift to cover the bridge's engineering station, and

Gant had to wonder if the young Brazilian woman was now regretting it. "Captain, that attack was *surgical.* They knew exactly where to hit us."

"Fan, can you reach our people on the shuttle?" Georgiou shot a look toward the communications officer, but the young woman could only shake her head.

"Shields? Weapons?" The first officer stalked back toward Gant's panel, his face like thunder. "Can we return fire?"

Gant stifled a curse. "Power is intermittent . . . I've got thirty percent on the forward deflector array. But it's that or phasers, sir, I can't give you both."

"Helm, back us off, one-quarter impulse," said the captain.

Detmer scowled. "Impulse drive is not responding. Thrusters only, Captain."

"Do your best, Kayla."

"Yes, Captain." The ensign complied, using the maneuvering jets to extend the distance between the Starfleet vessel and the bigger ship.

"Why did they shoot at us?" At Detmer's side stood Ensign Januzzi, his dark face a mask of confusion. "We were no threat to them . . ."

"They hit us while we were looking the other way," ch'Theloh said grimly. "Because that is the only way they could wound us. *Cowards.*"

Gant nodded to himself. The Andorian was right. The Peliar ship's weapons systems were basic, even compared to those of an older class of cruiser like the *Shenzhou.* Had they been at combat readiness, the shots that knocked out the nacelles would have been repulsed. But now none of that meant a damned thing. As well as phase cannon turrets, the Peliar ship carried a cluster of merculite rocket pods that would make short work of the *Shenzhou*'s hull plating if they decided to go for a coup de grace.

"Lieutenant, are we still being targeted?" Gant looked up as his captain spoke.

"Negative," he replied. "At least, as far as I can tell." He glanced out of the main screen. Dust and flecks of wreckage from the damaged engines swirled around the bridge's bowl-like windows as they continued to draw back. "I think I can give you a photon torpedo spread."

"They shoot at us, we shoot back at them . . ." Georgiou shook her head. "I didn't bring us across the border for a firefight." She trailed off as the turbolift at the back of the bridge hissed open and Lieutenant Burnham rushed out.

"Captain!" Burnham sprinted over to the second officer's station. "I thought I could help."

Georgiou nodded and glanced at ch'Theloh, still processing Oliveira's earlier statement. "The Peliars never had access to our systems while they were on board," she said, and the Andorian shook his head.

"We would have known about it. Those were more than lucky shots."

"What about Saru and Johar, the rescue team . . . ?" Burnham couldn't bring herself to voice the question that Gant and everyone else on the bridge was thinking.

Are they still alive? His brow furrowing, the lieutenant peered at the tactical scan coming in from the *Shenzhou*'s sensor grid. "I'm reading the shuttle's mass attached to the outer hull of the Peliar ship. Whatever's going on over there, the *Yang* is still intact."

"Captain." Ch'Theloh drew himself up. "How do you wish to proceed?"

"They're not giving us a lot of options," said Georgiou. "Lieutenant Gant, can we return the favor and knock out their warp drives? Level the playing field?"

"Not with photons," he replied. "The destructive yield of our torpedoes is too high; we'd blow holes in their spaceframe if we hit the nacelles. Tight-beam phaser strikes could do it, but I'd need to transfer power from the shields for that."

"The instant we do so, we give them an opening to fire on us again," said the first officer. "If you ask me, they hit us, we should hit back harder."

"There are civilians on that ship," said Burnham.

"And our own people too," noted the Andorian. "I haven't forgotten."

"Preliminary damage report coming in," called Oliveira. "Confirming . . . we are dead in the water." She couldn't keep a sigh from her words.

Burnham shot her a worried look. "Any casualties?"

"Doctor Nambue says no fatalities, minor injuries only."

"Something to be thankful for, then," said the captain.

"Small mercies," ch'Theloh countered. "I have little time for those."

A new flicker of light blossomed on Gant's console and his head jerked up in shock. Across the compartment, he saw Troke reacting to the same sensor reading.

"Power flux detected!" snapped the Tulian. "Reading an energy buildup on the Peliar freighter!"

"The phase cannons? The missiles?" Ch'Theloh glared at Gant, demanding an answer. "Are they going to fire?"

"They're not charging weapons," he reported, seeing the juddering returns from the still-fogged sensors. The power flow was too regular to be going into a distributed offensive system. Gant thought the Peliar ship was bringing its shields online, but then he realized what the crew was actually doing. "They're powering up their engines."

Out past the bow of the *Shenzhou* and the halo of splintered metals from the damage she had suffered, the massive hull of the bulky transport ship was moving, gathering momentum as it came about. Gant and the rest of the bridge crew could only watch as the star-freighter presented its stern to them and accelerated away at high impulse. The engine nacelles clustered around the forward section of the big vessel's hull glowed purple green as they came to full potentiality, and then with a shudder of twisted light and distorted space, the Peliar ship threw itself into warp speed and left them adrift behind it.

For a long moment, no one spoke; then Captain Georgiou stood up, breaking the silence with her words of command. "Track that ship. Assign every able hand to repair details immediately." She turned to study the faces of her crew, briefly making eye contact with Gant. He saw the steel there beneath the softness.

"This will not stand. No one takes our people from us."

6

The makeshift prison where the Gorlans had placed their hostages was what remained of the star-freighter's long, narrow mess hall. Food fabricators, water purification modules, and raw ration bins from the storage compartments along the longest axis of the room had been removed, dragged away to the lower decks and the refugees in their tent-city communities. All but one hatch had been welded shut to keep the captives inside, and a pair of red-bands armed with disruptors stood guard outside.

Commander Nathal and the Peliar Zel crew clustered together and talked amongst themselves in low tones, ignoring the Starfleet team from the *Shenzhou*. There were very few of them, the small skeleton staff that had been running the big vessel now all crammed into this chamber.

For his part, Saru had been able to convince Vetch to let him recover some equipment from the shuttle—some survival packs, a medical kit, and another universal translator—but anything that looked like a weapon had been confiscated. He hoped that wouldn't matter. Right now, the very last thing on Saru's mind was armed conflict. He sat on one of the hall's steel benches, staring across at a table opposite where Zoxom was working to make sure Saladin Johar did not die. The Gorlan had refused to let them use the freighter's own meager infirmary, so the task had to be done here, under these crude circumstances. Subin worked with Zoxom, handing over loaded hyposprays, anabolic protoplaser tools, and other items as they were required.

The Xanno nurse's wrinkled face was filmed with sweat. He had been at this for a few hours now, refusing to step away until Johar was stabilized. The chief engineer lay across a survival blanket on the metal table, his breathing shallow and his chest rising and falling in stutters.

Saru sensed someone at his side and glanced up. Chief Petty Officer Yashae stood there, and she offered him an emergency ration pack. The Kelpien waved it away. "Later," he managed.

"We all need to keep our strength up, sir," said Yashae, and she dropped the pack in Saru's lap. Then her expression clouded. "What happened back there?"

"I have already explained," Saru said quietly. "They took control of the ship. Fired on the *Shenzhou*. The rest you know."

"How the hell did they neutralize a starship?" The question came from behind them. Ensign Weeton looked as worn out as all the rest of them, but he was turning that fatigue into anger. Anger that wanted a target. He glared at Nathal and the other Peliars. "Who's responsible for this mess?"

I am. Saru stiffened, and for a terrible moment he thought he had said the words out loud. *I helped them cripple our ship.* The inner voice went on, refusing to fall silent. *I delivered us into the hands of the desperate and the violent.*

He couldn't look away from Johar, couldn't move. A great weight of guilt was pinning him in place.

At length, Zoxom stepped back from the table and pulled up the survival blanket to cover Johar's torso. The nurse dosed him with another hypospray and the injured man grew still.

"How is he?" said Yashae.

Zoxom dropped onto the bench across from Saru's and hung his head as he cleaned off his hands. "Stable. I did what I could to stanch any internal bleeding, but the halo effect from the disruptor did a lot of damage to the organs down one side of his body. Kidney function, one of his lungs . . . all badly affected. Nothing we couldn't deal with in the *Shenzhou*'s sickbay, but—"

"We're not on the *Shenzhou*," snapped Weeton.

The nurse's head bobbed, and then he glanced at Saru. "Sir, the commander is unconscious, and I intend to keep him that way. His body needs to rest."

"That makes you the ranking officer, sir," Yashae said quietly.

"I know." Saru's bleak mood threatened to engulf him, and he tried to force it away. He had made a stark choice in order to preserve the lives of his crewmates, and if one were to consider it in the light of pure, exacting logic, his decision had been the right one. Somehow he doubted that Weeton, Yashae, and the others would see it that way.

"Lieutenant," said Subin, a warning in her voice.

Saru turned to see Nathal approaching with her second-in-command Hekan and a few other Peliars. Nathal's default grimace was, if anything, even more deeply ingrained on her face. "He lives?" She jerked her head at Johar.

"He does," Saru replied, without getting up.

"Two of *my* crew were not so lucky." She waved in the direction of her officers at the far side of the compartment. "Their deaths are at your feet, Federation."

"I was not the one who drew a weapon." His reply was flat and toneless. Saru could not find the energy to fight. "Your crewman did that. You should have ordered your men to surrender peacefully. Then *no one* would have been hurt."

"Weakling!" Nathal spat the curse at him. "The children of Peliar Zel are proud. We fight to defend what is ours." She stared into his eyes. "You are the cause behind all of this! Why could you not have just gone on your way? Instead Starfleet had to meddle in the affairs of others, and now we pay the price!"

Saru looked up at her. "Shout at me if it will make you feel better. But know that it does nothing to help our shared circumstances." He waited for Nathal to berate him further. Had the Peliar captain seen him assisting the Gorlans to fire on the *Shenzhou*? If she had, there was nothing he could do to prevent her from revealing it to everyone.

"Some things about this whole sorry mess are starting to make sense to me," said Yashae, breaking the tension.

"What do you mean?" Hekan's nostrils flared.

Yashae jerked her thumb over her shoulder, in the general direction of the transport ship's warp core. "Lieutenant Commander Johar and I, we both knew there was a stink off that whole nadion pulse. That kind of event doesn't come on accidentally. A hundred things have to go wrong for it to just *happen*."

"Clarify," said Saru. He had a bad feeling where the Vok'sha's explanation was going to lead, but he let her get to it on her own.

"We're at warp. We've been at warp for hours now, but there's been no sign of that pulse effect reoccurring. I admit, we're not familiar with Peliar tech, but a warp drive is a warp drive. The basic mechanisms are all the same. At the time I wasn't certain, but after all the guns coming out?" Yashae's lips thinned. "I am now."

"You're saying the nadion pulse was deliberately triggered?" Subin paled. "A person would have to be utterly reckless or extremely desperate to do something like that."

"As desperate as the Gorlans?" said Yashae, glancing at the other technician.

Saru kept his eyes on Nathal. "It was most likely their first attempt to waylay this ship, but they failed to account for the full effects of their sabotage."

Nathal's face darkened with new rage. "Vetch. He betrayed us. He could have killed us all!"

"And when your starship arrived, they saw another opportunity to move against us." Hekan glanced at Saru. "Dragging the Federation into their plans along the way."

"We should never have brought those savages on board." Nathal stalked away a few steps, her hands tightening into fists. "How could we ever believe they would accept our goodwill? It is true what is said about them, the Gorlans only respect violence."

"Is that so?" Saru studied Hekan. Of the Peliars he had encountered so far, the second officer seemed the most moderate.

"Many of my kind consider the Gorlan people to be a threat to our safety and our resources on the Alpha and Beta Moons." Hekan broke eye contact. "When the time came to decide their future, those beliefs were the core motivation. So we decided to find them a home . . . away from ours."

"There is proof we were right," snapped Nathal, jabbing a finger toward Johar. "Our gravest fears about those stunted barbarians, borne out! They lie, kill, and steal, even when we offer aid! It is all they know!" She summoned Hekan back to her side with a sharp gesture. "I won't allow it. We are going to take our ship back by force." Nathal turned a hard look toward the Starfleet group. "Do not get in our way when that happens."

Saru could feel the conversation slipping away from him again, the same empty feeling that had torn at him when he was among the Gorlans. "No . . . no." He rose to his feet, his hands curling in the air. "Be careful, Commander. Rash actions brought us to this juncture, and more of the same will only send us down a dangerous path."

Nathal made a derisive snorting noise through her quadripartite nostrils, and strode away with Hekan at her heels.

He let out a long, exhausted breath. "This is not how I wanted my first command scenario to unfold," Saru said quietly.

"I'm just going to come right out with this and say what we all are thinking," Weeton began. "She's right."

"That's not what *I* was thinking," muttered Zoxom.

Weeton went on. "These Gorlans are dangerous, and they clearly have little regard for anyone's lives. They've put everyone on this freighter in serious jeopardy, at least twice over. And every minute we're not doing something about them, we're putting more distance between us and the *Shenzhou*. We don't know what state our ship is in, we don't know who is alive or dead back there."

"The *Shenzhou* was rendered immobile, it was not destroyed," insisted Saru.

"Right, Lieutenant, you saw what went down, so you more than anyone should see the sense in what I'm saying." Weeton didn't pause for breath. "We have no idea where the Gorlans are taking us. What if they're going to execute us when this is all over, or worse? They could wind up selling us to the Orions or even the Klingons . . ."

Saru raised his hand in a *halt* gesture. "We must hold back and evaluate the situation before we do anything." He dug deep to find some of the same steel he always saw in Captain Georgiou. "Rash actions, ill conceived, will result in more errors." Saru drew a deep breath. "I have made that mistake once already," he admitted.

But Weeton was up to speed now, and he barely acknowledged the Kelpien's attempt to slow his train of thought. "But we don't have the luxury of waiting around, am I right? The longer we delay, the more the Gorlans solidify their position. What I'm saying is, we have to be proactive! We have to do something, somebody has to make a command decision here . . ." He looked over at the table where the chief engineer lay. "What do you think Lieutenant Commander Johar would say? I think he'd agree with me, can we ask him? We can ask him, right?" Weeton turned his attention on Zoxom. "You could wake him."

"Yes," replied the nurse, "but waking him is not a good idea."

"I think he'd want to be a part of this conversation, don't you?" Weeton scanned the faces of the others, ending with Saru. "Don't you?"

"I will not be responsible for putting anyone else in undue danger," Saru blurted, trying to maintain control of the exchange.

"So you agree," said Weeton, misreading Saru's reply. "The chief engineer is a command-level officer, he has the rank to make those kind of choices."

"Lieutenant Saru is the ranking officer," began Yashae.

"Yes, but he's . . ." Weeton faltered, and Saru got the immediate sense that the ensign had barely prevented himself from saying something disparaging. "I mean, no offense, but the lieutenant is not—" He came to an abrupt halt. "You know what I mean."

I am not what? Saru's thoughts echoed with the question. *Not strong enough? Not respected enough?*

And what if he is correct?

Saru drew himself up and looked down at the ensign, marshaling all the firmness he could muster, hiding how hollow it made him feel. "I assure you, Ensign Weeton, I am capable of making whatever 'command decision' is required. Am I clear, mister?"

"Okay, maybe I should have worded that better," said the ensign. "My point is, I was just thinking of the team, sir. I mean, after what you just had to deal with on the bridge, with the hijacking and all, I thought maybe you would—"

"That I would wish to abrogate my responsibilities? You are mistaken." They were all watching him now, and Saru knew that how he handled the next few seconds would set the tone for whatever would come next.

Weeton carried his thoughts close to the surface, saying what he meant and meaning what he said, but the others—Yashae, the taciturn Mazarite Subin, and Zoxom—were harder to read. If Saru couldn't prove to them that he was a leader worth following, when the time came to follow an order they might hesitate and make the situation worse.

But how could Saru instill that respect in them if he doubted himself the most? The ghost of the choice he had made up on the bridge of the freighter clouded every thought in his head. With effort, he forced himself to push that aside.

"I am the senior officer," he told them. "The decision is mine, and mine alone to make." Saru met Weeton's gaze, searching it for the ensign's true thoughts, but finding nothing he could be certain of.

"Aye, sir," said the human.

Without warning, the hatch on the far side of the chamber shuddered open, and there were three more red-banded Gorlans crowding at the doorway. Saru recognized one of them as the male with the white-streaked hair along his arms and head, and they briefly locked eyes before his gaze raked over the hostages.

The Kelpien knew a hunter when he saw one. The Gorlans entered the chamber and went to the Peliar group, gesturing for them to stand up. The warrior with the white hair looked from one resentful face to another, before finally settling on the second officer, Hekan. He barked out an order in his native tongue, and from across the room, Saru felt the invisible flare of his electrostatic aura, a silent flash of anger-analog.

Hekan was marched out of the group and forced to stand to one side, much to the consternation of her comrades. Then two of the Gorlans crossed to the Starfleet team and the same study was made of them. The white-haired warrior settled on Yashae, for reasons Saru couldn't be sure of, and made a sharp *come here* gesture, his aura-flash rippling silently in its wake.

"No." Saru raised a hand and held her back. "You are not going anywhere." He faced the Gorlans and stepped forward in the engineer's place. "You want someone to go with you?" he asked, even as he knew they would only barely be able to understand him. "Take me, not her."

Yashae shook her head. "Lieutenant, it's all right . . ."

"No," Saru repeated. "I will not see anyone else put at risk. I will go."

The Gorlans seemed to grasp what was going on, and accepted the substitution without further action.

Saru took a step toward the hatch, then looked back toward his crewmates. "Ensign Weeton, you're in charge until I return. Keep our people safe."

Weeton accepted the order without further comment. "Will do, sir."

Hekan threw him a worried look as the two of them were marched away, through the hatch and down the corridor beyond. "You may have just volunteered for death," she told him.

"I refuse to believe that," he said. Of its own accord, Saru's hand went up to the back of his scalp and touched the subdermal sacs where his threat ganglia lay. For now, they remained quiescent.

No matter what the circumstances, before she entered the captain's office, there was always a similar flash of emotional recall for Michael Burnham. A fragment of memory from her childhood, of each and every time she was summoned to her adoptive father's study for a "discussion," whether it was to address her academic progress or her continued assimilation into Vulcan culture.

In each instance, try as she might to moderate it, there was always an ember of emotion that years of learning logic and control could never fully conceal. Sarek had been a patient teacher, but he had never allowed her to falter, and even now Burnham felt that same need to show stoicism before her mentor, to resist the corrosion of any doubts.

Of course, Philippa Georgiou was not Sarek of Vulcan—the two of them were poles apart—but the approval of the *Shenzhou*'s captain was as important to Michael Burnham now as Sarek's had been to her young self all those years ago.

Her commanding officer rose from the chair behind her desk and gave Burnham a brief smile, but it was forced. Almost a day had passed since the surprise attack from the Peliar transport ship had crippled the *Shenzhou*, and if the captain had rested in that time, Burnham wasn't aware of it.

Standing as rock-rigid as he always did, Commander ch'Theloh was at a port, peering out into the blackness. His antennae quirked at her arrival, and he picked up a data pad lying on the desk before Burnham could see what was on it. Still, she caught a quick glimpse of an image. *Was that the face of a Kelpien? Saru?* She couldn't be sure.

"Reporting as ordered," she began.

"Any new data from the long-range scans?" The Andorian went straight to business.

Burnham shook her head. In the aftermath of the incident, she had been paired to work with Jira Narwani, teaming up with the ensign to repair and enhance the sensors. With the ship adrift and vulnerable, it was vitally important for the crew to be aware of any potential threats while they were still at a distance. Enclosed inside a virtual-environment helmet, Jira extended her senses out to watch for alien vessels while Burnham had worked to interpret the ion trail left behind by the fleeing Peliar transport ship. "The Tholians haven't taken any interest in us yet, sir."

"Oh yes they have," Georgiou gently corrected. "They just want us to think they haven't." She shot ch'Theloh a look and then went on. "That's not why I asked you to report. We need your opinion on something."

The first officer picked up the thread of the conversation. "You work closely with Lieutenant Saru. You've done so for some time, yes?"

"Yes, sir." Burnham frowned. Jira had told her that Saru had gone back to the Peliar ship shortly before it had attacked them, but no one seemed to know why. "Is he—?"

"We do not know the status of any members of the rescue team," ch'Theloh said bluntly. "But certain facts are coming to light, and given your close association with Lieutenant Saru, the captain thought your input would be valuable."

"I don't follow." She frowned. "I wouldn't say Saru and I are *close*. I mean he's . . ." Burnham found herself unconsciously imitating the Kelpien's hand gestures. "You know how he is."

"No," said the first officer, "I really don't. I believe your human term is, he's a closed book."

"Saru is a private being," said the captain. "And I've

respected that about him. But the commander is right." Georgiou tapped a keypad on her desk. "And you were the last person to speak to him before he left the ship." A holoscreen blinked into being, showing a monitor's view of the interior of the *Shenzhou*'s shuttlebay. In the corner of the frame, Burnham saw a tiny version of herself in conversation with Saru. "Do you recall what he said?"

"Did he seem agitated?" added ch'Theloh. "Was his behavior uncharacteristic in any way?"

I believe this situation has affected me more deeply than I was aware of. Saru's words came back to her in a rush. "He was . . . distracted." Burnham paused, thinking about it. "No, actually the word he used was *disquieted*. We talked about the situation, we disagreed about some of it."

"Be specific," said the Andorian.

"The difference between following regulations to the letter and understanding when to bend them." As the words left her mouth, she stiffened.

"I think Lieutenant Saru may have taken your point too literally," said the captain. "He was not authorized to return to the Peliar ship. He deliberately went back, I believe to make contact with the Gorlans once again."

"You think Saru's actions had something to do with the attack on us?" Burnham blinked, trying to frame that. She knew better than most that navigating the complexities of interactions with an alien culture was difficult, but she couldn't accept that someone like Saru could provoke a violent response, accidentally or otherwise.

Ch'Theloh waved the data pad in his hand. "We've been going over our sensor scans of the ship, just before the attack. Numerous Gorlan life signs were detected on the upper decks of the ship, along with energy signatures that could be weapons discharges. It's possible that, for whatever reason, Lieutenant Saru's attempts to converse with the Gorlans were the catalyst for them to act in an aggressive fashion."

"With all due respect, sir, that's a reach. Do we have proof that the Gorlans were behind the attack? It could have been the Peliars." Burnham met the first officer's gaze, and neither the captain nor the commander challenged her comment.

Ch'Theloh had always been dismissive of Saru's prim, aloof manner, and now she found herself seeing the seed of genuine distrust in the Andorian. He was looking to her to cement that point of view, she realized, and if anything, that made Michael all the more determined to stand up for her absent crewmate. She had her own issues with Saru, that was true—but it didn't seem fair to lay this all at his feet.

"Saru isn't reckless," she went on. "He's the absolute antithesis of reckless. It's just not in his nature."

"Fair point," allowed the first officer, and he wandered back to the port, resting one hand on the old optical telescope positioned before it on a tripod. "We are attempting to form a picture of what may have transpired on the Peliar ship. And we must accept that Mister Saru was an unexpected variable in the mix."

"It's not like him to disobey an order," said Georgiou, her gaze briefly turning inward.

"Did he?" Burnham looked at the captain. "You didn't literally order him not to go back. I don't believe Saru would return to the freighter without a solid reason."

"Perhaps so. But there is another troubling piece of data to consider." Ch'Theloh turned and studied Burnham carefully. "Just before we were fired upon, Lieutenant Gant detected what appeared to be multiple, intermittent weapon locks coming from the Peliar ship. They briefly targeted sections of the *Shenzhou* such as the bridge, the crew quarters, infirmary, and mess hall." He let that sink in. With their shields down, any hits in those areas would have incurred grave loss of life. "Then, at the last second, the weapon locks shifted to direct fire against our warp nacelles. At very specific components of the drive."

Burnham felt her skin chill. "What are you suggesting, sir?"

"Unless the Gorlans or the Peliars had precise technical readouts for a *Walker*-class cruiser in their data banks, there's no way they would have known where to aim in order to hobble us so effectively." Captain Georgiou grimly laid out the reality of it. "A Starfleet officer would have known."

"Saru isn't the only one on the rescue team with that knowledge," insisted Burnham. "Any engineer would have it too."

"True," admitted the captain, "but none of them ran off on their own to undertake an unauthorized mission. None of them showed a serious lapse in judgment. The niceties aside, Saru knew what was expected of him, and he chose to proceed despite that." She shook her head. "I don't like this line of reasoning any more than you do, Michael. Saru has served under me for a long time, and he is a valued member of this crew . . ."

"But no matter how unpalatable, we have to consider all the possibilities," concluded the first officer. "He may be under duress. He may be compromised in some way. Captain, I think security should check out Lieutenant Saru's quarters. Look for anything unusual, anything amiss."

"I'll do it," Burnham broke in. "You're right, Commander. If anyone knows Saru best on this ship, it's me." That might not have been true, but again she felt compelled to defend the absent Kelpien. "I don't need security to accompany me. I can do it alone." She looked to the captain. "I'll be . . . discreet."

At length, Georgiou gave a nod. "All right, Michael. See that you are."

"Do you have family?" Hekan asked the question as she stared down at the floor of the elevator. The Peliar engineer looked up and met Saru's gaze. "Is that something your species possess?"

"Yes," he replied, and clicked his tongue. It was a uniquely Kelpien action, a way to fill an awkward pause rather than give a direct answer. "I have been away from my homeworld for quite some time."

Hekan blinked. "All I want is to see my daughters again. Do you think, when they do it, it will be quick?"

All at once, he realized that the engineer believed they were being taken to their execution. "No! I mean . . . Hekan, they're not going to kill us."

"How do you know that?" She threw a worried glance at the red-bands, and the weapons they carried. "The things I have heard about them . . . I dismissed it all as rumors spun by the narrow-minded, but now I can't help wondering. What if those stories are true?"

"What stories?"

"That the Gorlan tribalist society is inherently aggressive. They actually have a culture that believes in ephemeral deities, and some people say those beliefs direct them to violent behavior against all outsiders, all aliens." Hekan spoke as if she was sharing a secret with him.

"Who says that?" asked Saru. "People from your planet?"

"No." Hekan seemed taken aback by the suggestion. "Betans try not to prejudge, it's how we are raised. I meant people from Alpha Moon. They're more forthright in their views."

"Like Commander Nathal?"

Hekan nodded. "Most command cadre are from Alphan nobility. Nathal comes from a long line of starship officers."

"Were the Alphans the ones responsible for the Gorlan . . . ?" Saru searched for the right word. "The Gorlan relocation?"

The flash of guilt on Hekan's face told him that they were not. "Peliar Zel only wanted to help them!"

"Did you think to ask the Gorlans what they wanted?" said Saru, without weight to the question.

"We did our best. But they make it so difficult to communicate with them. Sometimes I think they can understand us but they choose not to. I have tried myself, but it never seems to bridge the gap, and we do not have the advanced universal translator systems as you do in Starfleet, and . . ." She caught herself and trailed off. "I apologize. I am afraid. It makes me talkative."

"I am afraid," Saru agreed with a sigh, "most of the time. But I've learned to live with it. And I am still learning to understand when a threat is truly apparent, and when it is not."

She studied him. "You are an unusual being, Saru."

"I am told that quite often," he noted as the elevator slowed to a halt.

Once again, Saru was marched onto the command deck of the Peliar freighter, and it struck him how sparse it seemed. Only a handful of the operations consoles and podiums dotted around the chamber were online and active, the rest of them in some form of standby mode. He cast around, observing the few Gorlans standing sentinel there. One element of his mind was considering what function each podium control performed, while another more basic part of him looked for potential avenues of escape.

Lieutenant Saru never enters a room without knowing at least three ways out of it, Commander ch'Theloh had once said of him, and the Andorian had been mocking him. But he was right, and Saru saw nothing unwise about it.

The speaker Vetch disengaged from a hushed conversation with the white-haired Gorlan and approached. He produced the universal translator that had been taken from Saru what seemed like a lifetime ago, and the Kelpien saw immediately that the device had been half dismantled and then reassembled with an ugly clutter of new components fitted to it.

His heart sank. "What did you do?" Without a fully functioning UT, communicating with the Gorlans would become a hundred times more difficult.

Vetch slapped the rodlike device into his open palm. "We improved upon it. The unit functions far more efficiently now."

Saru blinked. Rendered through the translator, Vetch's previously broken, stilted speech pattern was now an order of magnitude more precise. He held up the UT and saw that among the new components rigged to it were a complex sensor antenna and a signal processor. As Vetch spoke, Saru felt the tingle of the ever-present Gorlan aura-field, and it seemed that the modified translator now had the capacity to pick up on that energy and merge it with vocal patterns, tones, and inflections.

"Our species may have the appearance of simplicity," Vetch went on, showing his teeth in a smug grin, "but as you can see, we too have a mastery of technology. But we do not choose to let it dominate every aspect of our life, unlike some cultures." The speaker eyed Hekan.

Saru studied the translator closely. "If you could do this, why wait until now? You had the chance to speak directly to us when you were on board the *Shenzhou*."

"Sometimes, it is better to be underestimated by those around you," said Vetch. "It reveals the truth of things far sooner."

"And we have learned not to trust those who have mouths full of promises," said the white-haired Gorlan, coming closer. "It is our way to find a path through adversity without relying on the charity of others. All too often, gifts come with a price." He glared at the Peliar engineer. "She knows."

"Madoh, if you will?" Vetch addressed the other Gorlan. "Let me deal with this. I am speaker, after all. It is my role."

"I will help you make them understand," Madoh replied, and made no move to leave.

"That is what we want," said Saru, seeing an opening. "To understand." He weighed the translator rod in his hand. "Thank you for this. Now that we can speak more clearly to one another, I hope there will be no more need for conflict between us."

"Are you not angry that your companion was injured?" said Madoh. "Do you not want recompense?"

"This . . . is not the time for that," Saru said warily.

Madoh made a guttural noise accompanied by brief, hard jolts of invisible aura-static. The translator rendered it as derisive amusement.

Undaunted, Saru pressed on. "Before, when we used only the vocal component to converse, much was unclear. But I understand there is a more ephemeral element to your communications." He gestured at the air. "An electromagnetic aura. My species has a similar sense."

"The Peliar and the humans are dead to it," Vetch replied dismissively. "We know it as—" The translator struggled with the term, briefly unable to parse the name into something Saru could grasp. Eventually, the device rendered the term as *the circle.*

That makes sense, Saru thought. *The collective aura-field of a Gorlan community is a circle, a unity that encloses them all.* It wasn't that they were a group consciousness or a mass-mind like some hive species the Federation had documented. What the Gorlans seemed to possess was something simpler than that. A connection that existed beyond words, a shared, almost tangible sense of *harmony*.

"I do not understand," ventured Hekan.

"Of course not," said Vetch, a little sadly. "How could you?"

Saru turned to the Peliar. "You must have seen avians flying in a flock on your world. Have you ever wondered how it is they can move and turn in unison? The Gorlan 'circle' is their equivalent of that group connection. I believe it is the basis of their higher communication, and a core component of their societal structure."

"You do not speak like an engineer," said Madoh, looking the Kelpien up and down. One of the Gorlan's hands drifted toward the disruptor pistol clipped to his vest.

The Kelpien hesitated. "You are correct. I am Lieutenant Saru, I am a scientist."

"I told you to bring us engineers!" Vetch shot a hard look at the Gorlans that had escorted Hekan and Saru to the command deck.

"I insisted they take me instead," Saru continued. "I am the senior officer. I will not send my people into any danger I am not willing to face myself." The words were paraphrased from a page of the *Starfleet Officer's Leadership Manual*, and he could not help thinking they sounded a little hollow as he repeated them.

"You want to show courage, is that it?" Madoh came uncomfortably close. "I think you have little experience of such things."

"Nevertheless, I am here." Saru stood his ground. "What do you want with us? You already have control of this ship."

"No, they don't," Hekan said quietly.

Vetch made a spitting noise. "The female is right. The Peliars are devious."

Saru was about to ask what the speaker meant by that, but Madoh interposed himself and continued to stare at the Kelpien. "You think you know what is going on here. You are mistaken." Madoh's hooded gaze reminded Saru all too much of a hungry predator considering its next meal. "Do you know why my kind are on this ship?"

"The government of Peliar Zel is relocating you on another planet," said Saru. "Although I believe there may be more to that action than is apparent to me."

"Good answer, outworlder." Madoh showed his teeth. "The reality of this was hidden from you and your *Starship Shenzhou*."

"Hidden from all beyond Peliar Zel, I do not doubt," added Vetch.

"We are here because the Peliars *forced* us onto these ships!" Madoh's temper darkened. "They withheld food and shelter, they told us this was the only way for us to survive! We made planetfall on their Alpha Moon, but they would not allow us to remain there."

"He omits the fact that they landed on Alpha without permission," retorted Hekan.

"We had no choice," Vetch told her. "Our vessels were overloaded. Damaged and failing. We had to abandon them."

"Some of her kind accused us of being the vanguard of an invasion force," Madoh told Saru, pointing at the engineer. "As if we could have done such a thing. A few hundred thousand of us, desperate and clinging to life."

"We helped them!" Hekan said hotly, looking to Saru. "I know for a fact Beta Moon donated a huge amount of supplies to the relief effort!"

"We did not want your pity and charity," Madoh said coldly. "A measure of trust would have been enough."

Saru held his silence. Where was the truth in all of this? He felt out of his depth here. It was one thing to attempt to better communicate with an alien race, but quite another to be drawn into a hijacking and armed revolt. Finally, he came to the question he knew would have to be answered. "You had Hekan and me brought up here for a reason. What is it?"

"Show him," growled Madoh.

Vetch led Saru to what appeared to be the freighter's main helm. Although the iconographic Peliar text was foreign to him, Saru soon grasped the layout of the panel, finding the equivalent of an astrogator display and the ship's course-correction controls.

Aside from the navigation screen, where a dot representing the freighter made slow progress along a curving line, every other control was totally inert. Vetch made a show of tapping several controls, each time rewarded by a sour bleating tone from the console. "This ship is fixed on a preprogrammed course to its final destination," said the Gorlan. "It appears to be a fail-safe measure triggered automatically in the event the crew are neutralized."

"They want us to unlock it for them," said Hekan.

"We want full control of this vessel," Madoh insisted. "The freedom to go wherever we wish."

Saru studied the command screen closely. "Deactivating this system is a complex task. It would involve decompiling the entire helm control matrix. That is a lengthy process at best." He paused, studying the astrogator. "The final destination point is an M-class planet in a star system two days distant from our present location."

"The *sanctuary*," Vetch said with a snort. "The world where the Peliars decided to dump us."

"We prefer to seek our own destiny." One of Madoh's hands dropped to his pistol once more. "You will unlock the helm, Lieutenant Saru. If you refuse, I will be forced to compel you."

"For beings who think little of charity, you ask for a great deal of assistance," said Saru, and his comment earned him a narrow-eyed glare in return. "Even from a cursory examination, I can see this system is protected by a multi-modal recursive encryption algorithm. Breaking the code through brute-force means would take until the heat death of the universe."

"You lie," Vetch snapped. "We are right to distrust you. You are in alliance with the Peliars, as suspected."

"I am telling you the truth," Saru replied defiantly.

Madoh's gun came out of its holster and he aimed it at Hekan's chest. "Are you certain of that?"

The sound of the disruptor discharge that had struck Johar echoed in Saru's thoughts, and he tensed. He thought of the terrible wound that even a glancing miss from that weapon had left in its wake. A direct hit would mean instant death for the Peliar engineer.

What should I do? The stated policy of Starfleet Command was not to negotiate with terrorists, but Saru had already compromised once on that point to prevent deaths aboard the *Shenzhou*. Now he was backed into the same corner. *If I refuse, will they kill Hekan and bring someone else up here? Make the same threat again until I comply? Or will I be the next to perish?*

He met Madoh's gaze. It was hard and unreadable.

At length, Saru turned back to the helm console. "I can give you no guarantees. But I will make the attempt."

7

A low tremor resonated through the *Shenzhou*'s deck, and Burnham felt it rise through the soles of her boots. She paused by a viewport and glanced out, watching the star field slip past as the ship began to pick up speed. The engineering team had worked flat out over the last day to repair the damage to the vessel, and although there was still much to be done, the cruiser's impulse drives were finally back on line. At last, they were moving again, and if they were moving, then they were doing something to save their missing crewmates.

A couple of noncoms farther down the corridor gave a ragged whoop of triumph, but then they caught sight of Burnham and stiffened. She waved away the moment and gave them a tired smile. If ch'Theloh had seen it happen, the first officer might have given them a talking-to about decorum, but Michael could relate.

The past hours had dragged on everyone; the impotent sense of being hobbled and left for dead by the sneak attack was a weight bearing down on the entire crew. Little was worse than feeling like you could do nothing to help, she thought, passing the two technicians as she made her way toward the senior crew quarters.

Now that they were on their way, the crew's focus would be renewed.

Burnham imagined that Lieutenant Commander Johar would have been proud to see how hard his engineers had worked to get *Shenzhou* mobile again, many of them putting in double or even triple shifts. Still, they were a long way from being warp capable, and at interstellar distances it would take forever for them to catch up with the missing Peliar freighter. But this wasn't about the cold facts; it was about belief.

Thinking of the chief engineer made her dwell on the fate of the rest of the rescue party. *Were they still alive? Johar, Saru, Weeton, and the others?* Burnham had lost friends and crewmates in the line of duty before, but each time she felt the pain of it anew. For all her embrace of Vulcan stoicism, there was an undeniable kernel of human empathy in her that never went away. *Perhaps once upon a time, I would have wanted to silence it. But not now.*

Burnham halted outside the door to Lieutenant Saru's cabin, pausing to check the setting on the tricorder hanging on the strap over her shoulder. Setting the device into scan mode, she pulled a data card from her pocket and inserted it in a hidden slot near the door's locking mechanism. An override code provided by Commander ch'Theloh did the rest, granting her entry into the Kelpien's quarters.

She hesitated on the threshold, self-consciously looking left and right down the corridor to see if anyone else was observing. Burnham wanted to tell herself that this was in Saru's best interest, and that she would be proving he wasn't under any kind of malign influence. But any way you looked at it, entering his quarters without permission was a violation. Being here alone might be an attempt to protect his privacy, but if she was honest with herself, Burnham's own curiosity as a xenoanthropologist was piqued by the opportunity to learn more about her standoffish crewmate.

The door hissed closed behind her as she stepped through and Burnham took a breath, committing to the act. “Okay,” she said aloud. “What do you have to tell me, Saru?” She cleared her mind and tried to take everything in, attempting to get a sense of the being who lived here.

On a basic level, the layout of Saru’s quarters was little different from Burnham’s own, a single-occupancy cabin for a junior bridge officer with a bed in one section and an open living area in the other. But the lighting level was much lower than the brighter setting she preferred, the air slightly cooler. The atmosphere in Burnham’s cabin was a temperate near-analog to the Vulcan norms she was familiar with, while Saru seemed to favor gloom and shadows. She waited to let her eyes adjust.

It didn’t surprise her that the fastidious Kelpien’s quarters were neat and tidy. Spare uniforms hung near the fabricator alcove, meticulously folded so that their longer legs wouldn’t drag on the floor. The automated ’fresher unit was spotless, and if it hadn’t been for the single empty mug resting on the disposal pad of the cabin’s food slot, she might have been forgiven for thinking the device had never been used. There was a box of herbal tea bags on a shelf close by, next to a container of what she first thought was sugar, but turned out to be table salt.

Burnham made a slow orbit of the room, leading with the tricorder, scanning for anything that might be an anomaly. She detected the additional layer of acoustic shielding in the walls—it seemed to be functioning normally—but there was a peak appearing at the lowest levels of the sensor bands.

She retuned the tricorder to focus on the discovery. There was something on the walls, flecks of an inorganic compound scattered here and there in what seemed to be a random manner. When she asked the device to analyze it, the conclusion it presented seemed incongruous.

"Ink?" Burnham raised an eyebrow and spoke to the air, "Computer, acknowledge."

"Waking from standby mode," said a synthetic voice from a console on the far wall. *"Do you wish to reset?"*

She wasn't sure what that meant, and glossed over the question. "Yes, I suppose so. I want to access environmental control for this compartment. Specifically, please re-attune the local light frequency to . . ." Burnham studied the analysis. "This setting." She sent the data to the ship's computer and waited.

"Working." If Burnham was correct, then the alteration of the lighting would allow her to perceive the interior of the cabin as if she were looking at it through Kelpien eyes—*Saru's eyes.*

There was a brief blink of blue-shifted color and the landscape of the room suddenly changed. The effect was like night and day; one moment, Burnham had been staring at blank, polymer-coated walls and the next she was seeing a matrix of glyphs written across the floors, the walls, the ceiling. She dropped into a crouch to take a closer look.

This is . . . the Kelpien language? Did Saru write all this? Burnham was aware that some species in Starfleet altered their quarters in subtle ways to accommodate their personal or cultural needs, but she had never come across something like this. Tiny, tightly packed script in Saru's careful hand moved in long lines from the doorway, up and around, and back again. "What does it say?"

She scanned a short section and ran it through a translation program. It was a part of what appeared to be a poem. Perhaps this was how his people recorded their history, honored their culture, by scribing it onto every available surface in an ink that could be perceived only at extreme ultraviolet-light frequencies.

The glow that illuminated the text also gave light to something else—a rectangular box sitting next to Saru's desktop console. At first glance, Burnham had thought it unimportant, but under the changed illumination it was bright with subtle striations and intricate carving.

The box was as long as her forearm and carved from a dark, dense wood. The smoothness of the shape suggested it was old and careworn. She couldn't help but run her fingers over the surface of the lid, feeling a regular grid of indentations and symbols impressed upon it.

Burnham hesitated at the thought of opening it. Aside from the glyphs, the cabin contained nothing else that she would have considered to be a personal item. Everything else was standard Starfleet issue. Peering inside the box felt like a step too far. Instead, she scanned it with the tricorder. The device registered small objects inside made of metal, glass, and bone, but nothing that seemed unusual.

It was then that she saw the motion of the shadow from the corner of her eye. A deep-black shape made of hard angles, the surface of it glassy like obsidian. It advanced slowly, and she realized that it had used the change in light levels to move silently around behind her.

The questions of what this intruder was or how it came to be in Lieutenant Saru's quarters were pushed aside. The shape moved like a threat, and she found herself emulating the Kelpien, tensing for the danger to approach.

But where Saru's instinct might have been to draw back and escape, Michael Burnham's was rooted in a very different impulse. There was a lamp on the end of the desk, and she slipped her hand toward it, fingers gripping the heavy base. It would serve as a makeshift weapon.

The shadow seemed to discern her intentions, and it came across the remaining distance in a flurry of silent movement. Drawing on the *Suus Mahna* defensive training she had learned in her youth, Burnham pivoted away and got her first good look at the intruder.

Tholian!

It could be nothing else. The distinctive crystalline shape, in this form with the six spindly legs clustered together into a tripedal configuration. The arms like scimitar blades, slicing toward her. The two smoldering eye spots glaring out of the gloom at Burnham.

It was impossible for the alien to be here, and yet it was. The surface of its faceted skin was night black instead of the hot orange red Burnham knew from Starfleet visual records, a signifier that this intruder was one of the rumored stealth aspects, the Tholian equivalent of an elite covert-soldier class.

The bladelike arms stabbed toward her, and she jolted back out of the way. Something was wrong—*it all seemed illogical!*—but Burnham couldn't bring herself to stop and reason it through.

She should have run for the door, should have screamed for security as loudly as she could, but in that instant Michael Burnham was caught in her pure, emotional reaction.

She swung the lamp around in a hard arc, and the weighted end connected with the "brow" of the Tholian's head—

—And passed right through it, encountering nothing.

She was so shocked by the reaction that she didn't avoid the counterblow coming the other way. The ink-dark intruder stabbed her through the chest with its right arm, the glassy length of it piercing her sternum.

But there was no pain, no sensation. Nothing at all. The Tholian stood there, frozen in time.

"Failure condition," said the computer. *"Your reaction time was insufficient to avoid a fatality. Simulation concluded. Do you wish to reset?"*

"No!" snapped Burnham, and the phantom intruder vanished in a glitter of holographic pixels. She drew in a shaky breath and muttered an ancient word in Low Vulcanian, self-consciously rubbing at the spot on her chest where the crystalline being would have stabbed her. "*Tviokh.*" The Vulcans didn't have many ways to curse, but Burnham remembered that one, and she said it with feeling.

"Please restate command," said the synthetic voice.

"What was that?" she demanded. "That . . . Tholian? Why did it attack me?"

"Personal holographic program designated Saru-Six. Automated aggressor simulation keyed to trigger at random intervals."

"Purpose?"

"Controlled stimulation and moderation of Kelpien fight-or-flight response, to facilitate continued emotional stability."

"Oh." Suddenly it made sense to her. Burnham's first thought had been that the hologram was some kind of alarm system, a trap for the uninvited entering Saru's quarters just as she had. But it was nothing of the kind. It was a test.

Just as Burnham would regularly engage in workouts down in the *Shenzhou*'s gym or sparring matches with an automated opponent, Saru had his own version of that exercise in the form of this program. "He can't exist without some kind of danger at hand," she said aloud, carefully putting the lamp back where she had found it. "Even if it's just a simulated one."

The words brought her thoughts into sharp focus. Saru had never made it easy to serve alongside him, his fussy, often prickly manner causing friction over the most trivial of things. But she respected his skills, even if she would rarely tell him so. The Kelpien had a keen analytical mind and a strong intuitive manner that would have served him better, had he not been so inward looking. For all his distance, his aloofness, Saru was a driven being, and the hologram program showed it. *He's always pushing himself,* thought Burnham, *even if the rest of us don't see it.* That Saru was competing with her had never been in doubt, but now she wondered how much it cost him to do that.

She felt a twinge of empathy for him. Burnham understood all too well what it was to be driven, to be constantly tested, and to be secretly afraid of faltering and failing those around her. *If there's anything wrong with Saru, it's that. He went back to the Peliar ship because he was pushing . . . and he got in over his head.*

"You didn't see what you were walking into, did you?" She asked the question to the air. "You looked, but you couldn't see . . ." Burnham trailed off as her own words echoed around the empty room. "Couldn't see," she repeated, and a sudden head rush came over her, the realization of something she had missed. "Because I was looking at it with the wrong eyes . . ."

She rocked off her heels, abruptly propelled by her new flash of insight. *Have to get to the lab. The monitor buoy . . . I know what to do!*

Burnham hesitated at the door, remembering ch'Theloh's orders about checking Saru's quarters. She tapped the intercom panel on the wall. "Lieutenant Burnham to XO."

"Go ahead, Lieutenant," the Andorian answered immediately.

"I've completed my survey as requested," she said briskly. "No anomalies found. Saru is still Saru. That's the problem as much as it is the solution. Burnham out." She cut the channel before the first officer could reply, and set off at a rapid pace toward the lab decks. If ch'Theloh wanted to find a way to place some blame on the Kelpien's shoulders, he would have to do it without her help.

The Gorlans left Saru to work on the helm control podium, and when it was clear that the Peliar engineer was unable to assist him, Vetch had two of the red-bands escort her below.

He watched the speaker closely, trying to gauge his intentions. Would Vetch or his people be so callous as to take Hekan away to be killed? What purpose would that serve? It was difficult to remain focused on the problem at hand when his thoughts continually drifted off toward worries about the fate of the rescue party and the Peliars.

One of the other Gorlans, a female named Kijoh, was assigned to give Saru whatever he needed to do the job, but he suspected she was there to act as his watcher. Kijoh had tightly cropped, sand-yellow hair that fell into a stubby queue down her back, and her round face bore a recent scar below one eye. She told him she had been a pilot aboard one of the ships that had borne the Gorlans to the Peliar Zel system, and that she understood the helm system of the star-freighter. Saru took that as a subtle warning from Kijoh, that she would know if he was trying to interfere with the controls, or stall the work in any way.

Saru managed to get the control podium to switch into a self-diagnostic mode, and as he watched, a seemingly endless stream of computer code fell through a display readout on the illuminated panel. His tricorder dutifully scanned it line by line, attempting to find a loophole in the lockout software, but the task was slow and tedious. Not only did the data need to be translated from the Peliar language into Federation Standard, but the alien operating system had to be rendered into something Starfleet tech could interface with.

Saru sighed and gave Kijoh a sideways glance, feeling the need to fill the wary silence between them. "If I may ask . . . The colony your people left, were you present when the Tholians attacked it?"

The Gorlan's severe green eyes fixed him with a glare. "Are you saying we lied about that?"

"No." He held up his hand. "Why would you assume so?"

"How do you think I got this scar?" Kijoh countered, then let out a breath. "I have been questioned a hundred times by Peliars, from the first day we fell into orbit around their Alpha Moon. *Did the Tholians really attack you? Did you provoke the situation? How many ships were there? What did you do to antagonize them? Did you fire first?*" Her jaw worked, as if she were chewing on something tough and unpalatable. "I was on the surface when they came in their spinner ships. That saved my life. They put their energy webs around our orbital station and dragged it away. . . . The cargo lighter I crewed for was lost then."

"They attacked your planet without a reason?" Saru studied the Gorlan carefully, watching as her four hands clasped over one another.

"Oh, they had a reason," corrected Kijoh. "They didn't care that it made no sense to us. The Tholians said that our colony was inside the borders of their Assembly, and it belonged to them. They gave us one rotation to leave. *One!*" She spat out the word. "We'd been there for twenty-two full solar cycles, you understand? Over four hundred thousand of us. Built lives and towns and chapels. Bonded there, had litters of young there. It was a home. And then overnight, these aliens came and told us to abandon it!"

"But you were aware of the existence of the Tholians," Saru pressed. "This sector of space borders their territory. You could not be ignorant of that."

"We knew what they were," she snapped. "We always

respected their boundaries. We kept our distance. We were no threat to them!"

Saru gave a solemn nod. "In some circumstances, that is not enough. The Tholian Assembly are extremely aggressive in maintaining their borders." He paused, reading the Gorlan's stiff expression. "Your people refused to go."

"We drew together to protect the . . . to protect ourselves." Kijoh made a growling noise in the back of her throat. "They had no interest in listening to us. When their deadline passed, they started bombarding the colony from space. We had no choice then. We had to flee, or die." She told him how the panicked rout of the Gorlans had claimed almost as many lives as the Tholian beam blasts. A shadow passed over the pilot's face as she recalled their desperate flight to escape the star system, fearful that the dagger-shaped spinners would come after them. "Our vessels were overloaded and under supplied. Some went cold out there in the void. We prayed to the Creator for safe harbor, and when we stumbled on Peliar Zel, we thought we had found it."

Saru framed his next words very carefully. "You must have known they would be wary. The Peliars would have been as afraid of you as you were of the Tholians."

"Of course. That is why we threw ourselves on their mercy. One sentient to another. And at first, the Peliars seemed to welcome us. But that changed when they realized our ships had spent themselves reaching their shores. When they understood we were not going to leave anytime soon." She made the growling noise again. "We didn't want to be there. We wanted to be on our colony, living the lives we had built! Then the Peliars told us there was no room for us on their moons, just as the Tholians had told us there was no room on the planet we had made our home." Kijoh eyed him. "What would you have done, Saru? If your life was torn away from you?"

The question hit the Kelpien with a force he hadn't expected. Saru experienced a sudden and very powerful sense of distance from the world that *he* had once called home.

Taking a breath, he silenced the thought. "I would have run," he answered honestly.

"That is what we are doing," said another voice. Saru turned to see Madoh, the bigger red-band, walking toward them with a weary swagger, one hand forever on his gun. "What we have been forced into." He glared at the console. "It's been several hours and you do not appear to be making any progress."

Saru knew full well what would come next: the threats. He deliberately stayed where he was, crouched low but raised up enough that he was at eye level with the shorter Gorlan, rather than towering over him in a way that would unconsciously trigger an aggressive response. "From what I have been able to determine, the only way to halt this vessel's progress would be to directly interfere with the power train from the warp core."

Madoh's lips curled. "We can do that. We did it before." He nodded at Kijoh. "You agree with the alien?"

"I agree that we cannot divert this ship from its automated heading, not without breaking something vital," said the pilot.

It wasn't the answer Saru or Madoh was expecting. The Gorlan red-band flexed his hands irritably, jabbing two of them at the Kelpien. "He said it is possible."

"Possible, and very dangerous," Saru broke in. "I believe that if you attempt to force this ship out of warp again, the cascade effect that threatened to destroy it last time will reoccur. This time, the nadion pulse will be much more severe."

"You prevented it then. You can do so again." Madoh dismissed his concerns with a snort.

"*No, I cannot!*" Saru's exasperation finally broke its banks and he almost shouted. "Please tell him!" He implored Kijoh.

"The alien is right," said the pilot flatly. "Interfere with the drive and it will kill us all."

Madoh's sneer grew. "Has the Federation's timidity tainted you, Kijoh? Where's the boldness you showed when we broke through the Tholian blockade?" He made a point of studying her scar.

"You are confusing bravery with desperation," Kijoh replied. "We are on this journey to the end, like it or not."

Belatedly, Saru realized that the Gorlan pilot had been observing his work on the helm controls more closely than he had thought.

"That is unacceptable!" spat Madoh. "If we cannot break this chain, then we need to find another way to stop the vessel." He raised his voice so that all the other Gorlans on the command deck could hear him. Saru watched them pause and listen to their leader. "I do not wish to kill in cold blood," he went on. "It is not our way. But our prayers go unanswered and for the Creator's sake, we cannot stand with hands bound while the Peliars continue to control us!" Madoh marched to the helm console. "We have them as our captives, and yet still they are in command of this vessel! How much longer must we march to the demands of outworlders?" His angry words drew affirming nods from many of the other Gorlans.

Saru saw what was coming. "Violence will not change the facts. You cannot coerce reality into re-forming itself to your needs with a destructive act."

"So ending your life would make no difference?" Madoh's voice dropped to a low, threatening register.

"It would not," he managed, tensing his muscles. Saru's

threat ganglia stirred at the back of his skull, and it took a physical effort to stop them from emerging. He did not want to give the Gorlan the satisfaction of knowing how afraid he was.

"We can't shoot our way through this, Madoh," said Kijoh. "Haven't you realized that yet?"

"Then what *should* we do?" Madoh's hand dropped away from his weapon and he snarled at the other Gorlan. "You and the alien here have more intellect than I, so please . . . educate me."

"You are frustrated," began Saru. "And that expresses itself in anger. I know how that feels."

"You do?" Madoh cocked his head, his tone half-amused, half-insulting.

Saru went on. "It accomplishes nothing."

"I disagree." Madoh's words became icy cold. "Violence stole my home from me. Threats drove me onto this rusting, Creator-forsaken hulk. Those things have worked well against me, so now I see no fault in directing the same toward others."

"You are so desperate that you would kill another sentient being." Saru made it a statement, not a question, but Madoh took it as the latter.

"Yes!" he retorted. "If that is the act that must be committed, I will not shrink from it, no matter what words you use to bar the way. I will do what must be done to ensure the survival of our colony and our—" Madoh's rage almost carried him to the end of the sentence, but he caught himself in time and clamped his jaw shut.

It was the second time that Saru had witnessed one of the Gorlans trying to conceal something, and his eyes narrowed as he pieced together what those silenced words might be. He remembered what the translation matrix had rendered out of the voices he captured after first encountering the Gorlans. *What was it they had spoken of? What was the name?*

"The hub." Saru drew up the words and spoke them quietly, but the response from the Gorlans was as if they had been hit by an electric shock. Madoh actually flinched, reacting like he had suffered a physical blow.

At his side, Kijoh gave Saru a long and measuring look. "The alien needs to know. If we want any of them to understand how important it is . . . to know why we are so desperate to act . . . we must show him."

Madoh's bellicose behavior had shifted in an instant, to a more reverent manner. "Outworlders are not permitted to approach the hub."

"These are extreme times," said Kijoh, spreading all four of her hands. "The old strictures count for nothing."

Saru was aware that every Gorlan on the command deck was staring at him, and he felt more threatened than he had since first boarding the Peliar ship.

Slowly, Madoh's simmering anger returned. "Very well." He beckoned the Kelpien toward him. "You want to see? To *know* us? Then follow."

Saru cautiously walked after the red-band, with Kijoh trailing a step behind him. A cold sense of foreboding made his skin prickle. He knew that in speaking those words, he had crossed a line with the Gorlans that could never be taken back.

It had been hard work, hauling the isophotonic emitter unit up from the *Shenzhou*'s engineering decks to the analysis lab on her own, with only one semifunctional antigrav, but with all the starship's technicians engaged in repairs, there was no other way to carry the rig. She managed it, though, keeping out of the way as Johar's people tried their best to put the starship's warp drive back together.

They were fighting an uphill battle. The surprise attack from the Peliar ship's particle weapons had destroyed a key component of the warp field coil, something called an "axis control" that Burnham recalled vaguely from her elective classes in space-warp theory. Without it, the *Shenzhou*'s warp bubble would become unstable when it tried to exceed the speed of light, with catastrophic results. The engineers were in the process of fabricating a replacement, but the component was extremely intricate and would take days to manufacture.

Days of traveling at impulse power. In the infinite void of space, even that incredible velocity was glacially slow. At such a rate, it would take decades to reach the current endpoint of the freighter's ion trail, and the Peliar ship was still moving away from them.

Burnham considered the thought with clinical logic and then discarded it. There was no point dwelling on a problem that she could not fix. Instead, she would focus on a matter she *could* solve.

She set up the isophotonic rig around the opened spaceframe of the monitor buoy they had recovered days earlier, and aimed the emitter head at the solid-state memory bank inside. The buoy's data storage device was corrupted by the backwash of whatever energy shock had struck it, and to most observers, that would have been evidence enough that it had been wiped clean.

But digital information never really went away, and inside complex storage systems like the duotronic components of the buoy, the phantom imprint of the data was still there. Pieces of it, jumbled together, but perhaps still readable. Burnham imagined her well-thumbed copy of *Alice's Adventures in Wonderland*, but with the paper book's pages cut up, shredded, and tossed into a pile. The data in the damaged memory bank was the same, a *découpe* of broken pieces that she might be able to reassemble, given time.

"The key," she said out loud, "is to look at things with different eyes." The emitter threw a beam into the metallic-crystal structure of the memory module and Burnham pulled up a real-time display on a nearby monitor. As the beam sought out and bounced back off tiny fragments of intact code, they flashed up on the screen. If enough of them were intact, it was possible that she might be able to reconstruct the last few seconds of the buoy's operational life.

Hours passed in a blur, and Burnham was drawn into the slow action of the scanner device, watching it assemble vague shapes and half-formed images by raking through the digital ashes of the damaged memory.

She was so intent on the screen that it took her a moment to notice that the door had hissed open behind her.

Captain Georgiou entered the compartment with a purposeful stride, but her gait slowed as she caught sight of the jury-rigged engineering tool Burnham had set up in the lab. "Michael, whatever are you doing with this?"

"A lightbulb went off, Captain," she said, making a vague shape over her head. "I was in Saru's cabin, and it came to me from out of nowhere." She pointed at the monitor. "We're looking at this the wrong way, like peering into a room through a tiny hole in the wall. But if we adjust the spectrum of perception, suddenly there's no wall in the way. And all the pieces are laid out in front of us. Before, we couldn't even see the pieces."

"Yes, about Saru," said Georgiou, pulling on the conversation before Burnham could lead it away. "Your report to Commander ch'Theloh on what you learned from his quarters was, shall we say, rather brisk?"

Burnham faltered. "Yes, Captain. I guess it was, I'm

sorry. I was just distracted." She paused, considering. "And to be honest, I thought that *terse* and *snappy* was his entire thing."

"Sonny likes it when *he's* terse and snappy," Georgiou allowed, using the diminutive for the XO's first name that only she could get away with. "Junior officers? Not so much. He expressed concern that you might not be wholly objective when it came to Lieutenant Saru's mental state."

She stopped and raised an eyebrow. "Captain, if the first officer is intimating that my relationship with Saru is anything other than professional—"

Georgiou chuckled. "It's not that at all. You two quarrel like troublesome siblings." The smile faded. "And sometimes siblings cover for each other."

Burnham framed her reply. "You know me better than that, Captain."

"I do," she admitted. "Sonny is a good exec, but sometimes he sees problems that aren't there. He's more like our Kelpien lieutenant in that way than he'd probably like to admit." The captain paused. "I just want to hear you tell me what you really think Saru was doing on that ship."

"Saru isn't unbalanced. He isn't under any kind of malign influence. I don't think it is stress or anything like that." Burnham took a breath. "I believe he's just trying to do what he has always tried to do: *the right thing*. He strives to be a better Starfleet officer, and uphold the same oaths and ideals we all do. But that may get him killed."

"That's the risk that comes with the job," said Georgiou, reaching up to trace the arc of the delta shield on the breast of her uniform. "But it's one we're supposed to share, not carry alone."

Was that directed at me, or at Saru? Burnham was still weighing the question when an alert chime sounded from the computer, drawing the attention of both women. Her pulse jumped at the possibility. If she was right, if this had actually worked . . .

The captain came closer, peering at the flickering image on the screen. "What are we looking at here?"

The display was messy and full of disruption artifacts, but it was discernible as a visual feed from one of the monitor buoy's sensor masts. There was only a half second or so of material that could be considered usable, but Burnham's unorthodox recovery process had definitely caught something.

"Let me try to compensate for the visual distortion." She ran the imagery through a software filter to sharpen it up, but it did little to help. The footage appeared to show a smooth-edged, regular object crossing the edge of the buoy's locked visual field. Then the object seemed to change shape, compacting its long axis and then expanding in diameter. Radiation effects grew as the images replayed until a whiteout smothered everything, and the playback started again.

Georgiou shook her head, looking at the other data streams from the memory bank. "This doesn't help. If we had readings from the mass spectrometer, gravity sensor, particle counter, anything, it would help to interpret what we're looking at."

"It's not a piece of debris, a comet, or an asteroid," said Burnham. "Look. It very distinctly changes aspect and course." She slowed down the footage.

"That's why it appears to alter its shape," said the captain, reasoning it out. "It's an artificial construct. A ship. And it's turning." Georgiou made a motion in the air with the flat of her hand, like a vessel moving through space. "Turning toward the buoy, coming at it head-on."

"That's an attack posture."

"Yes, it is." Georgiou's expression became grim.

"Computer?" Burnham leaned close to the touch-sensitive screen and used her finger to highlight the object on the display.

"Working," came the synthetic reply.

"Analyze this shape and extrapolate a complete form for it, based on available data. Then project a three-dimensional holographic model of the findings."

"Stand by."

"If the buoy was deliberately destroyed, that throws up a whole other set of problems for us," said the captain. "Not the least of which is, could the *Shenzhou* be in danger as well?"

Burnham nodded, unwilling to give voice to the answer she suspected was about to be confirmed.

"Rendering complete."

A shadow appeared in midair over the computer console, a long and tapering form that resembled polished black stone. Burnham reached for it, and haptic sensors responded, allowing her to turn the object around in her hands. The shape had a cross-section like an elongated diamond, thick at one end, coming to a sharp point at the other. It instantly suggested the shape of a blade, *a weapon*. Burnham thought of the ink-dark hologram she had encountered in Saru's quarters and suppressed a shudder.

"Is that what I think it is?" Georgiou asked.

"Computer," Burnham went on. "Generate a holographic model of a Tholian spinner-type starship, match scale with unknown object, and display."

"Working." A second image, this one a metallic-crystalline form that was all edges and implied threat, materialized next to the shadow. The similarity in mass and shape was obvious.

"Computer, what is the probability that the unknown object is a match for the vessel?" said Georgiou.

"Probability estimated at 84.3 percent."

"The Tholian Assembly took out the monitor, and they did it in a way so we wouldn't know it was them." Burnham laid out the plain facts of it. "Saru was right all along."

"We need to contact Starfleet Command. If the Tholians are on the move again, if they're testing our resolve, this could be the precursor to an expansion of their borders. We have to be cautious and—" Georgiou was cut off as a warning tone sounded over the *Shenzhou*'s intercom system. "What now?"

"All hands, yellow alert," called the first officer's voice. *"Captain report to the bridge."*

Burnham and Georgiou exchanged a grave look as the captain crossed to the intercom panel. "Report, Number One."

"Long-range sensors have picked up a large vessel on an intercept course," said the Andorian. *"It will be within weapons range in nine minutes."*

Georgiou looked away. "Is it Tholian?"

"Unknown. But whatever it is, it's coming in fast."

8

When they reentered the cargo modules, Saru sensed immediately that something had changed.

Before, the prickle of the Gorlan sensory fields had washed over him like the current of a river, moving about the Kelpien as if he were a stone in their path around which they had to flow. Now it was different. The auras were shaded toward more subtle nuance and finer detail. There was less of the brute-force emotional content he had sensed before, and in its place there was a kind of strange anticipatory air. *Like the world around me is holding its breath,* he thought.

Saru frowned, walking slowly to keep pace with Vetch and the others, thinking back to what he had said before to Captain Georgiou about the Gorlan aura-field. It was difficult to put it into words for a being who had never experienced such a thing. *How would one explain colors to someone whose eyes could only perceive in monochrome?* Saru could think of it as music, or as the rush of wind through trees. An effect that lay beneath everything, on which dialogue and unity could rise or fall.

The Gorlans walking with him seemed to be aware of it too, on some level. As they moved closer to their destination, Saru was sure that he saw them walk a little straighter, unconsciously reflecting the emotional timbre of the atmosphere. *This is the circle,* he thought. *Little wonder their bonds of community are so strong.*

But part of the Kelpien was fearful as well as fascinated. If this was how the Gorlans were, if their collective, gathered will had a common focus, what might happen if it was turned to a darker end? The Peliar engineer Hekan had spoken of those who called the Gorlans violent and primitive. Did those rumors have a grain of truth in them?

A thought formed as Saru examined the prospect. There was another possibility, and the more he considered it, the more it seemed to fit the facts at hand. Saru could actively sense the aura-fields of the Gorlans, and he imagined that given enough time and cooperation, it might even have been possible for the Kelpien to learn to communicate with the aliens *without* the use of a universal translator device. A species like humans would never be able to bridge that gap without a technological aid, their more limited senses forever deaf to the ephemeral, additional component to the Gorlan language. Saru could sense the aura and be fully aware of it.

But what if the Peliars sensed it too? Their physiology is certainly comparable, he thought. Saru would need to conduct a full tricorder scan to be sure, but even a cursory visual examination could pick out the telltale cranial structures on the Peliars where clusters of epithelial cells existed, suggesting that they were beings with a very basic, instinctive electroreceptivity.

Saru's theory snapped into sharp focus. *What if the Peliars unconsciously sense the auras of the Gorlans, but on a level so subtle they are unaware of it?* He thought about the unease that Hekan had shown toward them, the anger exhibited by Nathal. *Could those be emotional reactions stirred by proximity? All their biases and fears, quietly magnified . . .* He tried to put himself in the place of the insular, defensive Peliars. If his theory was right, it would go a long way toward understanding why they instinctively felt the need to reject the Gorlans.

Finally, the group reached the gathering place where Saru had made his first, unplanned contact, and they halted. The small open square emptied as they approached, the few Gorlans milling around in it immediately dissipating as Saru drew nearer. No one spoke, no one made a sound or a sign to tell the others to leave; they simply departed of their own accord, melting into shadows, disappearing through tent flaps or around makeshift walls. It was disconcerting.

"Wait here," Kijoh told him, breaking the silence. "If she wishes to know you, she will come to you. If not . . . then this will go no further." The pilot bowed her head and walked away. She had only taken a few steps when she stopped suddenly and looked back. "Did you bring a token?"

"A what?" He blinked at the question.

Kijoh sighed. "It doesn't matter. You don't know our ways. Perhaps it won't be expected of you." She turned and left.

Saru watched the other Gorlans move away, unsure what would happen next. Madoh was the last to go, and before he did, he pointed at Saru with one hand and up into the gloomy hull spaces above with another. "Look there. Do you see?"

The Kelpien squinted, his eyes adjusting swiftly. He could make out a shape, a small figure crouching in the dark where a nexus of support cables came together in a heavy bundle.

"She doesn't know," Madoh went on, his voice dropping to a whisper. "Not everything. Not about all of the steps we take to protect her. It is better that way."

Up there, Saru saw that the crouching figure was holding something. Light glittered off the keen edge of an arrowhead, nocked and ready to be released. The tip moved as he moved, tracking him.

"Understand?" said Madoh. "If you try to hurt her. Threaten her. If you make any sudden moves, anything that marks you as a danger . . ." The Gorlan reached up and put a thick finger on the flesh of Saru's throat.

"That is not my intention," Saru said stiffly.

"Good." The Gorlan took a deep breath and looked around. The gruff, bellicose manner he had exhibited up on the command deck was gone. He seemed calmer, almost sorrowful. "What you are being granted is an honor. Prove you are worthy of it, outworlder." Then, at length, Madoh turned and walked off, vanishing in the half dark like all the rest of them.

Saru waited patiently, shifting from hoof to hoof, unsure if he should remain in the same spot. Time passed—an hour, perhaps?—and at last he dared to take a few steps, peering up into the gloom. No swift arrow came whistling out of the blackness to bury itself in his neck, so he decided to take that as a sign he was free to move around.

A faint, floral odor reached his nostrils and Saru cautiously followed it to its source. In the center of the open area was a repurposed thermal radiator, casting out a low simmer of warmth.

He hadn't noticed it before. Atop it was a metal flask, with a wispy pennant of pale steam escaping from a vent in the lid. Saru moved closer. The flask appeared to be brewing a heated solution of tisane, and unconsciously his mouth watered.

Odd, he thought. The smell was totally new to him, and yet Saru's first compulsion was to want to drink some of the brew.

"I have brought cups," said a musical voice. He heard her footsteps, the shuffling gait of the distorted leg as she stepped and half dragged it.

Saru shifted to face the Gorlan female in the white robes. She seemed very small to him, hardly larger than an immature humanoid child. Her face, though, her eyes—there was an age to them, and a gracefulness that reminded the Kelpien of Philippa Georgiou.

At once, he felt a sense of trust move through him. "Are you doing that?" he asked, waving a hand in the air as if trying to catch a handful of the aura-sense. "Are you trying to set me at ease?"

The question seemed to confuse her. "You may as well ask me if I am breathing, if I am living." The moment passed, and she smiled. "Saru. Welcome back." She nodded at the modified UT clipped to his uniform. "It's good we finally have a way to talk without the barriers of our diverse natures falling between us."

Gathering her white robes up, she picked her way across the makeshift decking to the radiator pad and found a place to sit. She seemed so delicate, her limbs thin, her body stiff. Saru watched her, let her take her time about it. "You are what the others think of as the hub," he ventured.

She sighed. "The center of the circle. It does sound so very serious, doesn't it?" She gestured to the flask. "Could you get that? Do be careful, it's hot."

Saru did as she asked, bringing the steaming container down to her level. He placed it within arm's reach and backed off. "What do I call you?"

"Ejah was the name I was born with," she said as she poured out two generous measures into the battered metal cups she held in one hand. "You're welcome to use it. I don't have much call to. After I was lifted, it wasn't important anymore."

"Lifted?" The term seemed out of place.

Her head bobbed. "Yes. The ones like me, we have a role to play." She patted her twisted leg with one hand and tapped her brow with another. "The Creator withers us in one way, empowers us in another. As in all things, there has to be balance."

"I think I understand." Again, Saru wanted very badly to submit Ejah to a deep biomedical scan with a tricorder. *What are the odds I would see a loss in bodily mobility combined with a marked increase in the size of her brain's electroreceptive organs?*

She sat back and studied the two cups, but made no move to offer him one. "So. Did you bring me a token?"

"Uh . . ." He swallowed hard. "Is that your custom? I am sorry, I don't have . . ." Saru trailed off. He didn't want to offend the Gorlans; and then an idea occurred to him. "Wait, no. Yes, I do." He reached up and took off his Starfleet insignia. "This?"

She held out a hand, and he dropped the badge into her palm. Ejah seemed delighted by the offering, running her fingers along the curves of the silver delta shield. "I like it. What do these things mean?" She touched the raised dots indicating Saru's rank, then the etching on the reverse side, showing his name and serial number.

He explained the significance, and she seemed pleased, the insignia vanishing into the folds of her grubby white robes. In return, she pushed a cup of tisane toward him. Saru waited for Ejah to drink first, and then he followed suit. The flavor was bittersweet. Not unpleasant, but lacking something.

"You don't like the taste?" she asked.

"It needs salt," he said.

"Ah. I will remember for next time." Ejah mirrored his careful sip and gave him a solemn look. "And so with this sharing of my vital fluids, you and I are now betrothed, Saru of Starfleet."

"What?" All the color drained from the Kelpien's face in a cold rush. He raised his hand questioningly. "I don't . . ."

"I am very fertile, so I will bear a large brood from our copulation," she went on. "Afterward, our children and I will consume your flesh, as is our way."

"What?" he repeated, shocked rigid. Saru's threat ganglia crawled at the back of his head, squirming so much they seemed to be trying to break off and escape.

In the next second, Ejah was making the same rough chugging noise that Saru had recognized earlier from Madoh—she was *laughing*, but in this case the sound was warm and inclusive instead of harsh and mocking.

She held up the cup and gave him a wide, toothy smile. "Forgive me! I am teasing you. It's just a drink, nothing more." Ejah leaned in to share a confidence. "I have heard there are beings who serve in Starfleet that have no sense of humor. At all!" Two of her hands came up and made the shapes of points at the tips of her ears. "Is that true?"

"It is," he agreed, an unashamed relief flooding through him. "They are called Vulcans."

"*Vul-Kans.*" Ejah tried out the word. "I'd like to meet one. Have you met one?"

Saru recalled Michael Burnham's face, and the telltale arch of her eyebrow when she posed a challenge to him. "In a way."

"It is a strange concept for me to process," admitted Ejah. "My life would be desolate without laughter. But I imagine these Vulcans are like us, Saru, yes? We are the sum of our natures. We're all on the path that our birthright sets out for us."

"I'm not sure if I agree," he replied, taking another sip of tisane. "I took a different path from the one I was born into."

"Did you?" Ejah smiled again. "Or did you just find the way to the path that had been right for you all along?" She paused. "I am Gorlan. What form are you, Saru?"

"My species is known as Kelpien. The others who came with me to this ship are humans, a Mazarite, Vok'sha, and a Xanno."

"So many." Ejah's eyes widened. "Is it difficult for you to be united, on your ship and in your Federation?"

"We disagree on some things," he admitted, and he saw she was opening a door for him. "But what we agree on far outweighs those concerns. I hope we can do the same with your people."

"And the Peliars?"

"All of us."

Ejah sighed. "I wanted that too. But they haven't made it easy." She shook her head. "They don't see what is coming."

Saru's brow furrowed as he considered the words. *Was she speaking about the hijacking of the freighter, or something else?* "The Federation and Starfleet . . . our duty is to the preservation of life."

"Mine is to my people," she replied. "Do you understand what I am to them?" Ejah nodded in the direction of the silent dwellings all around the open atrium. "My people believe my gifts are the embodiment of our Creator's will. I am a living conduit to that faith."

Do you see?

The words were in Ejah's voice, but she did not speak them aloud. The shape of them was abruptly present in the front of Saru's thoughts, forming out of nothing.

He couldn't help himself. He jerked back in shock, and knocked over the metal cup, sending what was left of the tisane across the metal decking. Too late to stop himself, Saru flicked his head up, searching for the archer above, fearful of what would come next.

Ejah raised one hand in the direction of the shadows overhead.

No.

"Oh, you've spilled it. Let me pour you some more." She gave a brittle smile and set the cup upright, before carefully refilling it. "I am sorry, Saru. I didn't mean to frighten you."

"You're a telepath."

"Is that your word for my gift?" She made a shrugging motion and handed him back his cup. "I've never been able to define it. I've always thought I was just more aware of things than others around me."

Saru worked to contain his reaction, gripping the cup firmly. *Is there something in this,* he wondered, *something affecting my mind?*

He was well aware of the existence of psionic ability in some species, but he had never encountered it directly. The communication Ejah had sent to him was so strong, so clear, he couldn't help but wonder what else she was capable of.

She became sad. "Ah. I have overstepped. Now you don't trust me."

"It isn't that . . ." He took a breath. "It was unexpected." Saru looked around. "Is that why Madoh seemed different when we came down here? Are you affecting him?"

"Yes," she admitted, "but not in the way you think. I can only project, I cannot read others. And what I do is not coercion, not something I can force on you."

"You spoke to me."

"That is only possible when I am very near to a person, and if they are open to it. If you don't wish to hear me, you won't." Ejah gave a long sigh. "It is a great effort to communicate that way. But my mind is unfettered, Saru, even as my body is a withered thing. This is the Creator's will, so that I am kept humble. I do not question it."

Saru's thoughts raced. "They call you 'the hub' because you bring unity, am I correct?"

"I was lifted after my birth. In every community, those like me come once in a generation, and we are brought into being to guide our brothers and sisters." She tapped a finger on the middle of her brow. "I . . . bring them clarity. I help them work as one."

"Does every Gorlan colony have a hub?"

"Yes. There are old stories of a before-time, when the Creator's face was turned from us and the Gorlans had little harmony with one another. There was no circle then, only discord."

Saru considered that. "You command them, is that it?"

"No. If that were possible, I would never have allowed Madoh to take up arms against the Peliars." Ejah looked into her cup. "I provide focus. And insight." She looked up, and one of her hands clasped Saru's. "That is why it is important we speak. I have to warn you about what is coming. The Peliars do not hear me, but I think you will."

There are things I have seen.

The silent voice pressed into his thoughts again, and Saru instinctively resisted it. He forced himself to relax and allow it to continue.

When I dream, I see pathways. Futures.

"How . . . ?"

"Everyone around me is moving in different ways, cutting paths, making ripples . . ." Ejah swirled the tisane in her cup. "When you exist at the center of all that, you begin to see patterns. They vary, but as time passes, they collapse toward a single eventuality. I've dreamed things, Saru."

A world made of ash. Destruction falling on threads of fire.

The form of the words and the imagery propelled them into Saru's awareness with an almost physical force. He reeled, struggling to process it.

He gasped and held up his hands. They were shaking. "Please, stop. It's overwhelming!"

"I am sorry," repeated Ejah, reaching up to wipe tears from her eyes. "But I need you to understand. This is why they protect me with such desperate dedication, Saru. And this is my attempt to protect *them*."

The Kelpien was still trying to comprehend what he had just experienced when he became aware of figures approaching from the shadows. Madoh, Kijoh, and the other Gorlans drew to a reverent distance and waited there.

"You have to go," said Ejah, rising unsteadily to her feet. Despite himself, Saru automatically reached out and helped her up. "We are here," she added.

"Where is—?" He began to ask the question but fell silent as a rumbling tone echoed through the hull of the massive starship. The constant mutter of the vessel's drives faded. They were dropping out of warp.

"The sanctuary world designated by the Peliars." She turned her back on him. Other Gorlans appeared to crowd around Ejah and spirit her away.

You will see.

Saru turned as Madoh approached. His gaze trailed after the hub as she vanished behind the flaps of a darkened yurt. "It seems she thought you were worthy," he muttered.

"Few are," added Kijoh. She carried a glassy data pad in one hand, and held it up. "This is a relay from the sensors up on the command tier. We have reverted to impulse drives and the autonomic navigation is vectoring us to a nearby planet." She offered it to him, and he took it.

"You spoke to her," Madoh grated. "So now you know what is at stake. She is precious to us." He jabbed a fist at the Kelpien. "I need you to do what you promised!"

But Saru did not reply. He stared at the image on the data pad, a long-range visual of the star-freighter's final destination. It was a dark and uninviting sphere wreathed in streams of gray-white cloud, broken up by small, colorless oceans surrounding pallid, barren landmasses.

A world made of ash, he thought.

Burnham dashed onto the *Shenzhou*'s bridge and into a carefully controlled maelstrom of activity. At every station, the starship's command crew were fully engaged in preparations to meet the unidentified alien vessel. From the corner of her eye, she saw Kamran Gant running through the available offensive and defensive systems, and he briefly met her gaze.

Gant didn't need to say it. With the damage *Shenzhou* had suffered still being repaired, they were in no shape for a fight.

Let's hope it doesn't come to that, Burnham told herself as Captain Georgiou took the center seat.

"Lieutenant, take science station two," said her commander, indicating the console with a nod of her head. As Burnham followed the order, Georgiou glanced up at her first officer, who stood nearby. "Give me the count, Number One."

"Target vessel will be on us in less than two minutes," said the Andorian. "They show no signs of slowing, Captain. It looks like a combative approach."

"Are they trying to make us flinch?" Georgiou straightened in her seat. "Ensign Fan, any contact on subspace?"

"Negative," reported the communications officer. "Captain, we've been hailing them on all channels since they entered range. They're not responding. There's no way they're not hearing us."

"Rude," noted Georgiou. She looked back at Burnham. "Sweep the craft, tell me what we have."

Burnham had anticipated the captain's orders and already started a comparative analysis of the incoming ship against known designs in the Federation's database. Her first answer was the one she imagined everybody on the bridge was waiting for. "It's not a Tholian design. Power curves, warp matrix emissions are all way off that baseline."

"We need to know what it *is*, not what it *isn't*," snapped ch'Theloh. "Details, Lieutenant."

"Yes, sir." Her hands danced over the controls, and in seconds the potential origins of the craft narrowed down to a single high-percentile probability.

"I want to see what we're dealing with," Georgiou was saying. "Januzzi, give me a visual and magnify."

The ops officer tapped in a command and part of the main bridge port rippled, becoming a viewscreen. The other vessel lurched closer as the view stabilized, and the craft was revealed. A crescent-moon shape, approaching them on a vertically oriented plane, it rose up like the blade of a vast, curved sword ready to be dropped in a swift executioner's blow. Four warp nacelles—two at either end of the structure—glowed purple-white as it started to bleed off its approach speed.

"Tonnage has to be at least twice, maybe three times ours," offered Ensign Detmer.

"We don't have this design in our memory bank," Burnham reported, shaking off the grim mental image of the ship as weapon. "But sensors are picking out emission vectors from on-board systems that match those of the Peliar Zel freighter."

"A warship," said ch'Theloh. "Come looking for its lost compatriot?"

"Still bearing down on us," called Gant. "Slowing now, but with a very aggressive posture . . ."

"Captain, we should go to red alert," said the first officer. "We can't afford to be hit again."

"No one is clearer on that than I am," Georgiou said briskly. "We hold." Then she threw a look toward the tactical station. "But be ready, Mister Gant."

"Count on it, Captain," said the lieutenant. Burnham guessed that after the surprise attack they had suffered earlier, Kamran would not let the *Shenzhou* be caught unprotected for a second time.

Her panel chimed a warning tone and Burnham's attention switched back to it. "Sensors are reading an aspect change on the target. . . . It's shifting attitude . . ." She halted. That wasn't all there was to it, though. All down the length of the craft, new blooms of energy were appearing beneath the outer hull.

On the screen, the still-slowing vessel performed a ninety-degree roll into a horizontal position, and across its surface, multiple hatches irised open one after another.

"What is it doing?" Burnham heard Ensign Troke ask, from the other science station.

"They're deploying something," she said. "Thrusters are firing."

As one, a dozen bullet-shaped objects burst out of the open silos along the length of the other ship's hull, and swarmed together into a geometric formation. Ensign Januzzi tracked one of the objects with the visual feed, and it grew distinct.

Burnham recognized it at once. The same projectile-like fuselage, ventral engine nacelle, and twin solar array of a Peliar escort drone.

"The, uh, carrier has come to a dead stop," reported Gant. "Drones are moving to intercept us."

"Detmer, put some distance between us and them," said the captain.

"Trying," replied the helmswoman, "but they're gaining on us!"

"If we had warp drive, we could leave them eating our ion wake . . ." The first officer didn't bother to finish the sentence.

On her panel, Burnham saw the same thing the Andorian did. The drones were splitting apart, spreading wide. "Captain, I think they're trying to surround us."

"All right, we've been polite enough," said Georgiou. "Red alert! Battle stations!"

"Battle stations, aye!" repeated Gant, and across the bridge, the illuminator panels in the walls flashed to a stark crimson shade.

"Comm," continued the captain, "warn them that if they don't back off, we will consider it an act of open aggression and defend ourselves." She looked back at the helm. "Detmer, evasive maneuvers."

"Evasive, aye," said the ensign, and the starscape outside shifted as they went into a hard impulse turn.

"We can't outrun them." The thought escaped Burnham's lips as she watched the drones breaking into smaller packs, attempting to position themselves at all points around the *Shenzhou*. One or two of the smaller robotic ships, each armed with a single phase cannon, would have been an easy win for the cruiser in a head-to-head conflict. But this many, acting in concert, represented a grave danger. *A cloud of dune hornets can bring down a* le-matya, she thought.

"Options," said the captain. "And quickly, we're running out of room here."

"Wide-angle phaser salvo," said ch'Theloh. "We take out a few of the drones, the others might think twice. That or photon torpedoes set to proximity detonation, could be enough to blast a hole through the swarm—" He broke off and grabbed the back of the captain's chair to steady himself as the *Shenzhou* pivoted sharply, faster than the gravity control could compensate.

Burnham gripped the sides of her console and rode out the turn. Her eyes were fixed on the screen in front of her. "They're tightening the noose."

"Thank you for that cheerful analogy, Lieutenant," said Georgiou. "Detmer?"

"She has a point, Captain," said the helmswoman, through gritted teeth. "There's too many of them. It's only a matter of time before they run us down."

"Then we do this another way. *All stop.*" The captain stood up. "Lieutenant Oliveira, divert all available power to shields, if you please."

"Aye, Captain," came the reply.

"Let's look them right in the eye." Burnham watched her commander stride into the middle of the bridge and glare out of the main viewport, past the shifting formation of the drones to where the carrier craft floated in the darkness. "We're done playing the role of the hunted."

"All stop," said Detmer. "No forward momentum."

"We're having a staring contest now?" Ch'Theloh glanced at Burnham, looking for a reply.

"Somehow, sir, I don't think we'll have long to wait." Burnham had barely finished speaking when a chime sounded from Mary Fan's console.

"Incoming hail from the Peliar carrier," she reported.

"And suddenly they're in the mood for a conversation," Georgiou said lightly. "Now that they think they have us right where they want us." She stiffened and pulled her uniform straight. "All right, Ensign. Put them on."

A holographic form shimmered into being in front of the main viewport. An older Peliar male, clad in a dark-red shipsuit with a silver tunic and an austerely patterned headdress, stepped forward and gave the *Shenzhou*'s crew a withering, chilly once-over.

"Federation vessel," he boomed, *"lower your shields and*

prepare to be boarded. Your craft and your crew are deemed in violation of Peliar Zel Cohort star-law. Defy us and we will use force."

"I'll do nothing until you identify yourself," the captain said mildly, refusing to match his tone. "I'll show you how it is done. I am Captain Philippa Georgiou, commander of the Federation *Starship Shenzhou.* We are unaware of any violations."

"I am Admiral Tauh, of the Alphan Defensive Primary. And I will be the arbiter of what you will or will not do, Captain Georgiou." Tauh motioned to someone out of range of his holo-transmitter.

Burnham saw the sensor sweeps react. "Captain, the drones are targeting us."

Georgiou acknowledged with a nod. "Admiral, you appear to be laboring under a misapprehension. We've done nothing to break any Peliar laws."

"We found the wreckage of the escort," Tauh seethed. *"An automated distress call drew us to those coordinates before it was cut off. Did you silence it?"*

"You're talking about the star-freighter," said the captain.

"Our escort obliterated, our ship missing. And what else do I discover? An ion trail leading to a rogue Starfleet vessel disrespecting our borders. I will have the truth from you." Cold, stony anger radiated from the Peliar admiral's manner, enough that Burnham felt it like frost in the air.

"I'm happy to provide it, sir," replied the captain. "But not at gunpoint."

"You are aliens here. You are in no position to make demands." He leaned in until his dark, stormy aspect was almost filling the bridge. *"My daughter was aboard that transport. Do not doubt I will take any measure in order to ensure her safety."*

"My people are aboard your missing ship as well, Admiral," said Georgiou. It was a risk to reveal that, thought Burnham, but it might also be the only chance she had to establish a rapport with the stone-faced Peliar commander. "Why don't we take our hands off our weapons and talk about how we can get them back?"

Tauh's silence seemed to stretch forever, but then the admiral flicked a hand toward his subordinates once more, and on her screen, Burnham saw the targeting sweeps from the drone blink out.

"I warn you, Captain Georgiou," growled Tauh. *"If you have answers I find lacking, it will not go well for you. And no agreements between politicians on your worlds or mine will temper my response."*

The hologram vanished and no one spoke. Finally, Troy Januzzi broke the silence. "Can I stop holding my breath now?"

Georgiou turned away, catching Burnham's eye as she did. "I'm afraid, Ensign, that we're just getting started."

In silence, they gathered around the captain's station on the upper level of the Peliar freighter's command deck, watching the images streaming to the curved screens suspended from frames overhead.

Saru stood at the back of the group of Gorlans, conscious of his own presence among them. He felt like an interloper at a wake, at once able to understand the emotions churning around him and disconnected from the ones they affected. But Madoh and his red-bands, Kijoh and the others, all of them were looking down at the dark end point to the lies they had been told about the so-called sanctuary world.

As the freighter's autonavigator began to settle it into a stable geostationary orbit, the nature of the planet beneath was revealed in full. Saru used the tricorder the Gorlans had allowed him to keep to parse the feed from the ship's sensor array, rendering the data into Federation Standard. What he saw reflected there gave him pause.

The planet was just barely on the right side of habitable, clinging to the definition of a Class-M world. The atmosphere was thin but breathable, the gravity high but tolerable. But few could look upon it and not see a harsh, desolate place bereft of any kind of comfort. Much of the surface registered as composed of black metallic sand, broken up by high mountainous regions and the thin oceans. Native flora and fauna were sparse, and powerful storm cells swept with alarming regularity from pole to pole.

Perhaps, with time and the application of advanced technology to terraform the surface, this planet might have been able to bloom. But as it was right now, Saru could only see a bleak wilderness where long-term survival would be a constant challenge, even to a species as hardy as the Gorlans.

"This is where they chose to abandon us," said one of the red-bands, quiet shock in his words.

"Are there any other ships in the system?" Madoh shot Kijoh a questioning glance, and in turn she looked toward Saru.

The Kelpien frowned, tapping into the sensors once again. "Scanning range is limited. As far as I can see, this is the only craft in near-orbital space." A cluster of blips flickered into existence as the sensor sweep passed over the surface of the sanctuary world, and he studied them closely. "Curious. I am detecting evidence of starship-grade metals on the planet. Tritanium and other alloys."

Kijoh moved to one of the vacant consoles and mirrored the same data to it. "Saru is correct. Several clusters on the southern continent, here and here." She pointed out groups of signals in an area of flatlands close to the foot of a mountain range.

"Something crashed?" said Madoh.

"No. Those are cargo modules." Saru ran a quick comparison to the container pods fitted to the spine of the star-freighter. "They are of Peliar origin. It looks like they soft-landed."

"Life signs," said Kijoh, switching the sensor view over to a different scan filter. A myriad of data points filled the zones around the downed pods, each one indicating a living being down on the surface. The closer he looked, the more Saru could pick out elements of what appeared to be a shantytown settlement built up around the grounded cargo modules. "All Gorlan," added Kijoh. "No Peliars detected."

"How many?" Madoh bit out the words.

"Approximately two hundred thousand." Kijoh went pale. "Thank the Creator, we have found our people."

"What is left of them," said Madoh. He glared at Saru. "You see, Kelpien? Here is the truth! The ships the Peliars sent before this one, coming to this barren ember to cast us away. This is the reality of their false promises."

"How could we live in such desolation?" Kijoh asked the question to the air. "The weakest of us could never survive down there."

Saru thought of Ejah, the hub, and her delicate form. *That place would end her,* he realized. And then another, more troubling thought rose to eclipse that one. If this was the "world of ash" that she had predicted, then what of her other warning? Could Ejah's extranormal abilities encompass something as incredible as precognition? As a being of rational and scientific thought, Saru found the concept difficult to process, but still the Kelpien's blood ran cold at the dark possibilities her words represented. *Destruction, on threads of fire.*

Across the command deck, the elevator platform clanked open and the speaker Vetch emerged, along with a pack of armed Gorlans and a handful of the Peliar crew. Saru saw Commander Nathal among them, and at her side the second officer Hekan and the engineer named Riden.

"What do you want with us now?" demanded Nathal. "I swear to you, we will die before we help you!"

"I want you to answer for your deceit!" said Madoh, shoving Saru aside as he strode across to meet the Peliar captain. He waved two arms toward the gray-black, ashen planet on the viewscreen. "Peliar Zel promised us a refuge! You gave us no choice but to leave, and we agreed!"

"We agreed because you Alphans and Betans told us the sanctuary would support our people." Kijoh's voice was thick with emotion, and Saru sensed a powerful wave of abject despair radiating from her. "Look at it."

"Look at it!" bellowed Madoh, and he grabbed Nathal, shoving her violently toward the scanner screen.

Nathal shook him off and glared at the monitor. "What is this? This isn't the sanctuary, you fools!"

"The commander does not lie," Hekan called out. "I've seen the colonial reports for the refuge world. It's a verdant, abundant place!"

"You did something to my ship, you did something wrong!" snarled Nathal, and she turned her ire on Saru. "You helped them, Starfleet? We came out of warp in the wrong place!"

"I assure you, I did nothing," Saru said stiffly. "And no alterations to your vessel's course were made." He showed her the control console. "Even as we speak, this ship is still acting under the autonomic controls that your crew activated." Saru nodded toward Riden, who watched silently from across the compartment.

"That is not possible . . ." Nathal pushed past the Kelpien to see for herself. She jabbed at the console, bringing up the navigation subsystem.

The freighter's line of transit redrew itself across the local star map for Nathal, and as Saru watched the realization dawning on the Peliar commander, he saw the fight drain out of her.

"This is wrong," she repeated, but now her words were hollow and distant. "They told us where we were taking you, there would be a fair chance."

"Lies. And lies. And lies," hissed Madoh. "Is that all your kind know, Peliar?"

Without warning, a bright-blue alert sigil flashed into life across all of the command deck's visual displays. Saru heard a strident, echoing bell tone, very different from the warning siren that had met him when he first boarded the transport ship. "What is that?"

A long, lingering groan of metal on metal sounded through the hull of the huge vessel, and on the screens, preprogrammed thruster controls were coming on line to adjust the ship's orbital attitude. It entered a slow roll, shifting to present its ventral hull to the planet.

"The cargo modules," said Hekan in a dead voice. "That's the release cycle. When it is complete, they will be ejected from the ship."

"Down to the planet," said Saru, looking back at the cluttered surface scan.

9

The humming cascade of rematerialization rippled over Burnham's skin as it dissipated, and she experienced that familiar, abrupt shift in location that was peculiar to beaming. The octagonal panels of the Peliar transporter pad glowed brightly beneath her feet, and it took a second for her eyes to adjust.

The Starfleet-standard gravity and environment of the *Shenzhou* was replaced by the atmosphere of the Peliar carrier's interior space, and she attuned quickly, shifting her weight. The air in the alien ship had a faintly spicy quality to it, and she wondered if that was unique to the vessel, or something to remind the crew of their homeworlds.

Burnham filed the thought away. Each time she encountered a species she had never met before, her curiosity to learn more about them pushed to the fore. But this was not the time to conduct a survey, obviously or not. She was, and her captain with her, very much in harm's way.

"Thank you for allowing us to board your vessel, Admiral Tauh." At Burnham's side, Captain Georgiou described a shallow bow of greeting. "I hope we can settle this matter amicably." She went to step off the pad, but Tauh raised his hand.

"Remain where you are. This conversation will be a short one." Tauh had been waiting for them in the large, open compartment the Peliars had set up for the meeting. Burnham guessed it was a storage bay of some kind, a wide chamber with a raised, ring-shaped catwalk overhead. A couple of his crew—most likely officers, judging by the headdresses they wore—flanked Tauh silently, and above on the walkway, she saw armed security guards cradling stubby disruptor weapons. The admiral was taking no chances with them.

"Who is this?" Tauh asked, pointing at her.

"Lieutenant Michael Burnham, one of my junior officers," explained Georgiou. "My second-in-command insisted that I not come over here alone."

The captain, as usual, was downplaying things. Commander ch'Theloh had turned ocean dark when Georgiou told him she was going to beam over to meet with the admiral, and in the end she had made it an order for the XO to remain where he was. Burnham could picture him pacing the *Shenzhou*'s bridge, ready for even the slightest sign of duplicity from the Peliars.

"You allow your subordinates to influence you that much," sniffed the Peliar, glancing at his own executive officer. "My adjutant Craea here suggested I meet you with all the formality and warmth of a diplomatic welcome. But then, he is from Beta Moon, and our Betan cousins are sometimes soft-hearted. I rejected such a show of obvious sycophancy."

The captain gave the lieutenant a brief look. Back in the ship, Burnham had asked her why she was taking her along instead of someone like Zuzub or one of the more imposing-looking security officers. *This situation doesn't need someone who's quick with a phaser*, she replied, *it needs someone observant.*

Burnham took a breath of the spiced air and resolved to see everything and ignore nothing.

"I owe you an explanation," Georgiou went on. "My ship is outside of its patrol zone, that is true. We are within a sector of space that is claimed by a number of stellar powers. But I have good reason."

"Your missing crew," said Tauh with a grimace. "If we are to believe you." He cocked his head, examining the *Shenzhou*'s commander. "I will tell you now, in the interests of clarity. I have reason to suspect you entered our space on a mission of provocation."

"Our purpose here is altruistic," Georgiou countered. "But I will admit, it has pulled us into a situation that we did not anticipate."

"Where is my daughter's vessel?" Tauh's patience was thinning, but both the captain and the lieutenant caught the reveal.

Does he mean Nathal? Burnham considered the possibility. Now that she thought about it, there was some familial similarity between the admiral and the acerbic commander of the star-freighter.

"We don't know for certain," began Georgiou. "Our first inkling that something was amiss came when my ship detected a subspace pulse effect at long range . . ." The captain provided a quick but thorough précis of the events that had transpired over the last few days; the nadion pulse, the rescue operation, the suspected hijacking of the transport, the surprise attack on the *Shenzhou* and resulting damage to its warp drives. She made no mention of Saru's behavior, or her own terse conversation with Nathal.

Like father, like daughter, thought Burnham, recalling the commander's manner. She could see where Nathal had learned her brisk and uncompromising methods.

Once or twice during her explanation, Tauh's subordinate Craea had reacted to Georgiou's statements and tried to interrupt, but the admiral silenced him with a hard jerk of the wrist each time. Still, by the time the captain was done, Tauh's expression has turned thunderous.

"This would not have happened if you had not interfered," he said, cold fury seething beneath the words. "What gives you the right?"

"Lives were in danger." Burnham said it without thinking, and then it was too late to take it back. "We had to act."

Tauh turned his full attention on the lieutenant for the first time. "Your officer speaks out of turn," he said.

"She does," Georgiou admitted. "I encourage it."

"And now this situation is spiraling out of control," he went on. "Your ill-considered good intentions have escalated a problem that was ours to deal with! Do you understand that, Captain?"

Georgiou's tone cooled. "Your daughter, her crew, and the Gorlan refugees aboard that vessel are alive because of Starfleet intentions, sir. I won't apologize for that."

Tauh advanced a step toward them, glaring at Georgiou. "Of course not. The Federation's arrogance is legendary. You think you can do no wrong, and it galls me that some foolish Betans believe we are better off under your banner than on our own." He made a negative noise in the back of his throat, shooting a brief, withering look at his own officer. "You come here, to our space, with little understanding of the delicate balance of things. And you *interfere*."

A brittle note entered the admiral's voice, and Burnham caught it. She got the sense that there was more to this than just the Peliar's wounded pride and a father's concern for his child. *Step back,* she told herself. *Consider the whole. Think of what you know of these people and ask yourself . . . what is he* really *afraid of*?

"You do not live in this place," Tauh was saying. "You and the other outworlders, you pass through. And Peliar Zel must deal with what comes in your wake."

She had it then, the element that she had been missing. Burnham gave her captain a sideways look and Georgiou inclined her head, granting permission.

"Admiral, if I may ask . . . When was the last time the Peliar Cohort encountered a Tholian ship in this area?"

It was as if the temperature in the compartment had instantly dropped ten degrees. Burnham saw Tauh stiffen at the mention of the alien threat, and his mask of belligerence briefly slipped. Beneath it, she glimpsed someone on edge, fearful of what unknown dangers the Tholian Assembly represented.

"We stay out of their way," he said, at length. "Only a fool would draw their attention."

"And you are afraid that the presence of a Starfleet vessel will do that." She made it a statement, not a question.

"I was not granted command of a ship like this because I blunder into battles that cannot be won," Tauh retorted, covering his lapse. "I understand the realities of the situation. Unlike *you*."

"If that is so," said Georgiou, "then you know that the Tholians are always watching. And whatever they choose to do, neither Peliar Zel nor the Federation will get a say in it."

"My standing orders, Captain, are to ensure we give them no pretext, and to maintain the security of my people." He aimed a thick, gloved finger at her. "Your presence risks both of those things." Tauh took a breath. "You said you were following the freighter. Where was it heading?"

"Their course was taking them toward an uncharted system near Dimorus." Georgiou folded her arms across her chest. "We tracked the ship's ion trail, but without warp drive we couldn't catch up to them."

Tauh exchanged glances with Craea. "No matter how we try to solve it, the Gorlan problem continues to waylay us. This time they have gone too far." He turned away.

"Go back to your ship, Captain, and return to your Federation."

"We are in nonaligned space, sir," replied the *Shenzhou*'s commander. "Peliar Zel does not have sole right of authority here."

He ignored her, speaking directly to his men. "Adjutant! Recall the drones and ready the ship. There can be only one place they are heading. . . . Set a course for the sanctuary."

"As you order, Admiral," said Craea, and he tapped a button on a wrist-mounted control device.

"Let us come with you!" Burnham blurted out the words, and Tauh turned on her.

"What do you ask of me now?"

"Take us with you," she repeated. "There are Starfleet officers on your missing ship, it's in our interests to help you find it and deal with this crisis."

"I do intend to deal with it," Tauh said firmly.

"If not that, then help us complete the repairs on our warp drive," said Georgiou, sensing an opportunity. "The *Shenzhou* will join you. Our two ships together can bring this matter to a close, peacefully."

"Again, you are arrogant enough to assume we are of the same mind. I do not seek a peaceful resolution." He paused, letting that sink in, then gave his subordinates another order. "Leave a pair of drone units behind. They will escort the *Shenzhou* to the Federation border. By force, if necessary."

"What about our officers on the freighter?" demanded Burnham.

"We will repatriate whatever we recover," Tauh said distantly. He jutted his chin toward the Peliar technician at the transporter controls. "Send them back."

"No!" As the word formed, Burnham felt the humming in her ears, and emerald light washed over her.

The metallic mesh panels enclosing the elevator platform drew back, and Britch Weeton was shoved unceremoniously onto the command deck of the Peliar star-freighter.

He tried to look in every direction at once. This was his first ever hostage situation, and he wasn't really sure of how things were supposed to play out. Starfleet's broad guidelines on this kind of thing took the position that negotiating was the first and best way to defuse a dangerous situation; anything that prevented loss of life was to be considered, and a violent response was warranted only under the most serious of conditions.

But it was one thing for an instructor in Weeton's Academy class on Comparative Ethics to talk about those things in a calm and rational manner, and quite another to be in the thick of it, with angry four-armed aliens pointing guns in your face and snarling at you in a language your UT can barely process.

When they pulled him out of the mess hall, his first thought was that they were going to make an example of him. Lieutenant Saru had been gone for hours, and just before the Gorlans had come for Weeton, they'd taken away a bunch of the Peliars as well.

Are they flushing people out the airlock one at a time? He'd heard scuttlebutt about Nausicaan pirates doing that to their victims, and his skin crawled with the grim possibility. But they went right past the docking ring and headed up to the command level.

Weeton and the others had felt the change when the big ship had dropped out of warp, and for a while he had dared to hope that meant this ordeal was nearing its end. For all Nurse Zoxom's hard work, Lieutenant Commander Johar was still unconscious, and Weeton feared that the chief engineer would never awaken if they couldn't get him to a proper medical facility. Watching Johar's face turn the color of tilled earth and his breath come in gasps made Weeton's hands clench. He hated not being able to do something to help.

Now he was here, and there were lights and screaming sirens, and he had no idea what the hell was going on.

"Ensign!" He spun toward the sound of the voice and there was Saru, gesticulating wildly with those big, long Kelpien arms of his, frantically beckoning him toward one of the consoles. "Get over here!"

"Sir?" As he approached, he saw a Gorlan female working another panel, and the Peliar engineer Riden at a control rig. Riden very clearly didn't want to be doing whatever it was he was doing.

"This ship is counting down to an ejection sequence that will detach all of the cargo pods," snapped Saru, waving his hand at a screen that showed a graphic of the transport vessel and the container modules attached to its spinal hull frame. "We have to stop it, now!"

"Drop sequence will start at the stern." Standing close by, the Peliar second officer Hekan studied the same screen. "It's all automated. Once started, it can't be stopped."

"For the Creator's sake, pray you are mistaken," growled the Gorlan female, and she looked to Saru. "We are moving everyone forward, but it may not be enough . . ."

"I can understand what the Gorlans are saying," said Weeton, his mind racing as he tried to take everything in. "I mean, better than before. How is that?"

"Not relevant!" Saru said sharply. "You're here because I told them to bring you! Get on that console and block the activation sequences on the release mechanisms."

"Okay . . ." Weeton went to the panel and immediately saw the problem. The automated controls had multiple redundancies that meant no single operator could override them alone. To force the module ejection sequence into a null mode needed at least four pairs of hands. *Lucky we have a Gorlan here,* he thought.

Weeton brought up the main control and made an attempt to put the command system into a feedback loop, but it bifurcated the order string to the other consoles and worked around him. "Oh, this is a tricky one . . ."

"Try to put the release gears into a maintenance mode," said the Gorlan woman. "It won't stop the drop sequence, but it will delay it . . ."

"Why is this happening . . . ?" Weeton asked the question out loud, but then he pushed it aside. *Those pods are full of people. We have to keep them alive.* That was all that was important for now. The young engineer put out of his mind all thought of the armed, angry Gorlans crowding around him. He didn't dwell on whose lives he was being asked to save. He set to the task, just as he had been trained to.

"I can't stop it!" cried the Gorlan. "Oh, Creator, grant mercy . . ."

Weeton looked up as the rearmost cargo module on the display changed to a blinking blue white. On an inset screen, he saw huge hatches dropping closed to seal the container off from the rest of the vessel. Tiny figures scrambled to get through to the far side before the gap closed. Dozens of terrified Gorlans clawed at the deck as they tried desperately to escape.

Then the timbre of the warning siren changed and the screen went blank. Weeton heard a distant thudding of magnetic bolts and couldn't stop himself from stealing a glance out of the main viewport. A dark, slab-sided shape was drifting away from the star-freighter's stern, trailing crystals of frozen atmosphere. "Did . . . did they all get out in time?"

"Unclear," said Saru grimly.

On Weeton's panel, he saw the same process repeating itself in the next module as the mechanisms of a second container prepared to detach. He made a decision and switched off the visual feed showing the chaos and panic unfolding at the hatches. *I can't look. Can't lose myself in that. What would Johar say? Do the work, Britch,* he told himself, repeating it like a mantra. *Do the work.*

He looked back at the failed loop program and frowned. "Okay, wait, I think I see what I did wrong." Weeton looked to Saru. "Can we both try this together? Two inputs at the same time might slow the function cycle . . ." He glanced at Riden and the Gorlan woman. "At the same time, if you try the maintenance-mode thing?"

"That might work." Saru saw the way Weeton was thinking. "Kijoh, can you do it?"

"I will try," said the Gorlan woman, and she gave Riden a pointed look.

The Peliar engineer glanced at Hekan, seeking her permission. She gave it, and he made an affirmative gesture.

"Do it now," Saru ordered, and Weeton committed the program once again. It was awkward working on the unfamiliar Peliar console, with their splayed-out keypad setup and curved screens, but he got around it.

"Done!" he shouted, his heart pounding in his chest.

"Done," echoed Saru.

Riden and Kijoh both did their part, and there was a moment where no one moved or spoke. Then a new and more strident alarm began to bray, loud enough that it gave Weeton a start.

"What? No! Did we screw it up?" He looked back through the viewport, afraid that he would see more modules coming adrift, more debris clouding the space around the big ship.

But then Kijoh gave him a double slap on the back that almost knocked him over. “The alarm is the shutdown warning! We stopped it!”

“For now,” muttered Riden, stepping back from his console. He gave Hekan a poisonous glare and let himself be led back to where his commander was watching from across the compartment.

“I’m missing something,” said Weeton. “Little help, Lieutenant?”

“We have just saved thousands of lives,” Saru told him. The Kelpien looked washed out and fatigued. “That is all that matters.”

That wasn’t in doubt, but there was more going on here, and the ensign wasn’t about to be brushed off. “So we’re working with *them* now?” He nodded toward the Gorlan hijackers.

“It’s . . . complicated,” sighed the lieutenant.

“Yeah, no kidding,” Weeton replied.

“You failed again,” shouted a hard, angry voice. The Gorlan with the white hair strode forward and menaced the captive Peliars. “You have underestimated us, denigrated us from the start . . . but we endured!”

“He looks *really* pissed off,” the ensign said quietly.

“You have no idea,” Saru offered.

“No more lies!” hissed the Gorlan leader. “Peliar Zel will be called to account!” The red-band reached for the disruptor holstered on his crossbelt, and Saru saw it too.

“Madoh! Stop . . . !” The Kelpien rose up and waved his hands, and he looked to Weeton like a scarecrow trying to hold back a thunderstorm. “What good does it do to take out your frustration on them?”

“Perhaps you are a better target?” The alien called

Madoh cast a threatening glare in Saru and Weeton's direction.

"Those cargo modules down on the planet's surface." Saru gestured at the gloomy ball of cinders they were orbiting, and Weeton started to piece things together. Suddenly, the automated drop sequence made sense. This wasn't the first time this had happened. "Your people are alive, surviving," the lieutenant was saying. "We can find a way to communicate with them, and those modules are still intact and whole. It might even be possible to bring them back up into orbit . . ."

"Evacuate them?" Kijoh came closer, running a single hand over her sweating brow. "Yes. It might work . . . if I can remote-program the thrusters on the modules, tie in to the freighter's tractor beam arrays . . ."

"You see?" Saru was animated by the possibility. "Aggression wins you nothing." The lieutenant looked toward the ensign for support, but all Weeton could do was give him a wooden nod.

"Will you do *anything* to prevent bloodshed?" Madoh said coldly, and Saru didn't seem to pick up on the menacing subtext in his words.

"The *Shenzhou* will come looking for its people. For us," Saru went on. "And when they do, I will speak for you. I will put your case to my captain and the Federation, there will be an appeal—"

Rough, harsh laughter rolled around the command deck and the lieutenant fell silent. Weeton had been in rooms with hard-faced, hate-filled people like this before, in darker times of his life, and despite the fact he was on the bridge of an alien starship light-years from home, it felt horribly familiar. "I don't think he's interested in that, sir," he said.

"I am tired of promises," Madoh said slowly, weighing

every word. "I have heard too many of them. They are all made of dust." He crossed the chamber toward the Starfleet officers. "Our patience is at an end." The Gorlan leaned in, and he fixed Saru with a pitiless gaze. "Yes, your ship will come for you."

What he said next made Weeton's blood run cold.

"I am *counting* on it."

"The carrier passed beyond the edge of our sensor range three minutes ago," said ch'Theloh as he entered Captain Georgiou's ready room. "The drones they left behind are crowding us." He made a dismissive gesture toward the window on the aft bulkhead.

Burnham leaned forward and looked out through the portal. She could see one of the automated escort craft cruising uncomfortably close to the *Shenzhou*, off the ship's stern. There was a weapons turret protruding from the prow of the vessel, and the muzzles of the high-energy phase cannons mounted there were tracking them.

"Admiral Tauh left us with an ultimatum," added the first officer. "If we don't start moving back toward the border within the hour, the escorts will open fire on us. We try to raise shields, they open fire. We power up our weapons . . ."

"I get the picture. Can we neutralize them?" Georgiou sat on the edge of her desk as she shrugged out of the tactical vest over her duty uniform.

The Andorian's expression soured. "Yes, but not without taking some hits ourselves. Phasers are still not up to optimal status." He paused. "Our engineering team is good, but they're not . . ."

"Not Saladin Johar or Britch Weeton, no," she agreed. "Next time, Number One, remind me not to send our two best engineers off on any landing parties at the same time." She paused, thinking. "What about our warp drive? Are they done building that replacement axis control?"

Ch'Theloh's grim expression hardened. "There's been an issue with the fabricator. The first replacement didn't meet spec. . . . It's a very delicate piece of equipment. It has to be flawless."

"We have warp engines in our shuttlecraft, they use axis control units," said Burnham, breaking her silence. "Can't we pull the same component from the *Fei* or the *Liu*, modify it somehow?"

"That was the first thing we tried," he told her. "They burned out immediately. Something about comparative mass versus size of the warp shell. We'd need a unit from a vessel with a larger tonnage to have any chance of making it work."

Burnham's eyebrow rose. "How *much* larger, sir?"

"I know that look," said Georgiou.

"If you have a suggestion, Lieutenant, let's hear it." Ch'Theloh folded his arms. "At this point, we're open to all counsel."

She raised her hand and pointed out of the window, toward the escort drone.

With the situation on the command deck stable, the redbands crowded around Saru and Weeton, and under Madoh's orders they were again led down through the lower decks, this time into a section of the ship they had not visited before.

Here, the transport's artificial gravity was set to replicate a zero-g environment, and the hatchway opened to allow access to a spherical chamber crisscrossed by metal bars studded with handholds. The Gorlans, with their additional limbs, moved through the space with speed and ease, pushing themselves off the walls and slipping from grip to grip. The Kelpien and the Terran were forced to take things slower, floating in toward the construct in the middle of the space.

"Computer core?" suggested Weeton, taking in the thick trunks of data cables that emerged from the walls to converge with the tetrahedral unit.

Saru nodded, watching the to-and-fro pulses of white light moving along the lines. The compartment had the same shabby, hard-working air as the rest of the vessel, but it was a functional space. "Why have you brought us here?" he asked, searching for Madoh.

"This ship is still fighting us," said the Gorlan. "The control software in its systems must be completely purged. Then, and only then, will we be sure that the Peliars can no longer affect it."

"And you'll release them? And us?" Saru pressed.

"When this is done," Madoh continued, "we will do as you said. Bring our people up from where they were abandoned. Kijoh says the additional cargo modules can be docked to this ship's exterior." He made a *coming together* motion with his hands, then looked back at them. "Can you delete the programs working against us, or not?"

"It is possible," admitted Saru. "But the Peliars would be better equipped to do it."

"They won't help us anymore." Madoh dismissed the suggestion. "But you, Saru. You'll help me again. Won't you?"

"Again?" Weeton shot him a questioning look. "Lieutenant, what is he talking about?"

Saru's threat ganglia squirmed and the skin across the Kelpien's face tightened into a grimace as he fought the reaction. "I will help you recover those people on the surface, if that is what it takes to save lives."

"It will," said Madoh. "Starting with those of your people and the Peliars."

The weight of the endless, circular argument came pressing down on Saru once again. "You do not need to threaten me," he said.

"That is untrue," Madoh shot back. "We need to prove our resolve. The Tholians and the Peliars taught us a lesson. If all you do is run, then you are nothing more than prey." He showed a mouthful of teeth. "I see something in you, Saru. I think you know better than anyone on this ship what it is to be that. On some level, you understand."

And the terrible truth was, *he did*. Saru had lived a life under threat from predators, and a part of him would always resent those creatures. *There is no prey that does not dream of becoming the hunter.* He could feel Madoh's powerful aura-field, the invisible crackle of the Gorlan's barely chained anger and his rebellious will.

"Do not . . . keep pushing," Saru managed, finding an iota of defiance. "The Federation offers the hand of peace but do not think that we are weak. It would be a grave mistake for you to make an enemy of Starfleet."

"You're trying to intimidate me? *Now*?" Madoh shared a callous chuckle with his red-bands. "Too late for that."

"He's not making a threat," Weeton blurted. "He's stating a fact! You heard him before, we can help your people! Find you a world to colonize, a better one than some half-dead ball of rock! Why wouldn't you want that?" He gave Saru that questioning look again. "Why can't he trust us?"

"The answer is simple," said Madoh. "The Gorlans have no more of that commodity to spare to outworlders. From now on, things will be on our terms." Hand by hand, he pulled himself along a support pillar until he was floating in front of Saru and the ensign. "We will take back our people. And when the *Shenzhou* comes, we will take that as well."

The statement was so unexpected that Saru took a second to be sure of what he had heard. *Impossible!*

"With your ship and this one, we will be free to go wherever we want, and the Federation, the Peliars, the Tholians . . . the Creator can damn them all." Madoh's cold rage had crystallized into an iron-hard certainty.

"That's not going to happen," retorted Weeton. "Captain Georgiou will never let you have her ship!"

"You will show us how to take it," said Madoh, staring at the Kelpien.

"No," said Saru. His voice sounded small and weak.

"If you do not do as I say, I will kill the prisoners. I will start with the Peliar captain and your wounded engineer. Or perhaps this one." He pointed in Weeton's direction. "Do you see, Saru? Your only value is what you can do for me. Aid us and you live, you have worth. Or do not, and become worthless. This is the reality we inhabit now." He drew back and began making his way toward the hatch. "But one step at a time. Purge the computer. Begin the recovery process."

The other red-bands drifted toward them, some drawing their weapons. Weeton pulled close to Saru and his eyes were wide. "Sir, we can't do this—"

"You can," Madoh called from the hatch. "Tell him, Saru. You did it before. Once the line is crossed . . . once you have bowed the first time, it becomes easier to do it again." He left them behind in the silence that followed.

"What did he mean, before?" The question in Weeton's expression shaded toward confusion and then anger. "Lieutenant! Is he talking about our ship? When they attacked them? Did you—?"

"I am giving you a direct order, Ensign," Saru said in a toneless, dead voice. "Full responsibility for whatever follows is mine and mine alone. Purge the control software from the Peliar computer core."

The shock on Weeton's face was raw and bitter. "I won't collaborate with them," he began, but Saru didn't let him finish.

"Do it!" he barked.

There was a long pause, and Saru was afraid that Weeton would defy him again and that would cost the ensign his life; but then the junior officer's face became a stony mask. "Lieutenant Burnham would never have done this."

"I know," Saru sighed. "Carry out my orders."

The interlaced communications between the two escort drones flashed back and forth between them at speeds most organic brains would have been unable to follow. Second by second, the automated craft shared data on the most optimal targeting solutions to maintain on the Federation starship they were flanking, their phase cannon turrets constantly adjusting and readjusting to account for drift and course corrections. So far, the attack criteria they had been programmed with had not arisen. The target ship was following the determined course, its weapons were inactive, its deflector shields down.

Constant sensor sweeps pulsing in tandem kept the *Shenzhou* firmly in their crosshairs. The synthetic combat intelligences running each craft were ready to open fire if their target deviated from the predetermined behavior pattern.

But the automated ships were only as good as their programmers could make them. Even with the advanced heuristic learning algorithms that Peliar Zel gave their autonomous machines, they lacked the ability of an organic being to anticipate, to become suspicious, or to make an intuitive leap based on partial data.

Thus, when both drone brains detected the activation of the *Shenzhou*'s matter transporter system, there was a pause as the craft collaborated over the problem of what to do about it. Their masters hadn't provided a specific retaliation program for such an occurrence. It would be up to the drones to decide how best to proceed.

All of this transpired in a matter of heartbeats, and given the martial nature of their standing orders, it was no surprise that the drones decided in unison to default to their most basic command. *If in doubt, attack.*

But the delay in processing that conclusion was a fraction longer than the *Shenzhou*'s transporter cycle.

Both drones registered two sets of rematerialization events in very close proximity to them, and the immediate activation of electromagnetic clamps on their outer hulls.

The unit following the *Shenzhou* from behind reacted by spinning its turret around, so that the visual sensors mounted beneath its gun cluster could see what was now attached to the outside of its fuselage.

The sensors fixed on two figures, each one clad in a protective EVA suit. The closer of the pair—a dark-skinned humanoid female, whose face was visible through the transparent shell of a helmet—held a phaser rifle in her hands. The weapon was aimed directly at the turret.

"Surprise," said Burnham, and she squeezed the trigger.

The pulse bursts blasted through the swivel ring at the base of the phase cannon turret, and the whole upper section of the weapon array was blown free. Trailing bright orange sparks, the neutered guns drifted away into the *Shenzhou*'s impulse wake.

Burnham was aware of another phaser blast going off at the periphery of her vision, back where the second drone was ahead of the starship's bow, but she had no time to dwell on it.

"Shanahan, go!" she called out to the engineer standing behind her, similarly affixed to the drone's hull via magnetic boots. The chief petty officer had a cutting torch ready to go, and she quickly set to burning through a panel in order to gain access to the vessel's interior.

Puffs of ion thrust shot from ports on the side of the drone and it started to move. Burnham looked for and found clusters of sensor antennae on the craft's bow and shot them off, blinding it.

"We're in!" said the engineer. She let the cutter drift free on the end of the lanyard securing it to her arm and crouched over the hole she had cut in the hull. *"Okay. Let me see . . ."*

"No time!" Burnham retorted. "We can't allow this thing to self-destruct."

"I got it, Lieutenant. Forget the finesse." Shanahan's face screwed up with effort as she plunged both hands into the spaces where the drone's central processor was located, and ripped out whatever she could grab hold of. Glowing cables came free in her hands and a shudder ran down the length of the craft.

The ion thrusters went dead and Burnham felt the drone starting to drift. "I think that may have done it."

"Let's not wait around to find out," said the engineer, grabbing the cutter once again. *"Give me two minutes, and I'll have the axis control chopped out of there."*

Burnham let out the breath she had been holding in. "Team two, this is team one." She turned to look out toward the other drone. It was in a slow tumble, and she could make out two suited forms still attached to its hull. "Ensign Harewood, report!"

"Target neutralized," came the reply. One of the figures threw a wave in her direction. *"We got it, Lieutenant! Chief Guymer's doing the extraction right now."*

"All right." She allowed herself a smile of relief. "*Shenzhou*, did you copy that?"

"We did," said Captain Georgiou. *"Good call, Michael. You've just solved both of our problems at once."*

She started back toward the aft of the drone, her mag boots thudding as she walked. Ahead of her, Shanahan was slowly pulling a large, cube-shaped module from the escort's warp nacelle. "The Peliars won't agree." Burnham didn't want to think that what she had set in motion could technically be considered an act of piracy.

"We don't answer to them," said Georgiou. *"And if Starfleet Command has a problem with this . . . well, I'll burn that bridge when I come to it."* She became brisk and businesslike. *"All EVA teams, get what we need and beam back. We have a lot of lost time to make up."*

10

"Warp one," said Detmer as she slowly eased the *Shenzhou*'s throttle control forward, increment by increment. "Two. Three."

A worrying vibration rang through the length of the decking and a low alarm chimed at the engineering station. Burnham looked toward Belin Oliveira, who stood at temporary duty before Britch Weeton's usual post. The dark-haired junior lieutenant didn't look up, her attention buried in the display screen in front of her. She raised a hand and signaled with a half-hearted thumbs-up.

"Proceed," ordered Commander ch'Theloh. He stood at parade-ground attention behind the helm-ops console, looking out over Detmer's head at the coruscating colors of the distorted stars flashing past them.

"Warp factor four." Detmer pushed the throttle up one more detent, but the vibration didn't ease out. "Warp five—"

The alarm at the engineering panel went up a pitch, and the shuddering in the deck matched it. "Captain, I am getting a lot of red flags here," said Oliveira. "We're outside acceptable parameters. We can't maintain this speed for more than a few minutes."

Ch'Theloh made a soft growling noise and turned back to the center seat. "We knew this might happen. Peliar technology is close to Federation standard, but not close enough. If the *Shenzhou* were a newer ship, we might be able to better synchronize the axis controls, but—"

"We'll make do," Georgiou broke in. "We may not have the clean lines of those new *Constitution*-class boats, but we're built tough."

The Andorian shrugged. "To be honest, I don't really like that new-minimalist look."

"Ensign Detmer," continued the captain, "ease us back to three point five and hold there. We're at warp and that's better than where we were an hour ago."

Burnham glanced at data readouts on her screen at the science station, a telemetry feed from the warp core where one of the "recovered" Peliar axis-control units struggled to do the job of its Starfleet equivalent. It was a jury-rigged repair, what Chief Petty Officer Shanahan had called "a bloody lash-up," but it was working.

Hang on, Saru, she said silently. *We're on the way.* But that thought was immediately followed by the shadow of a doubt. *Will we catch up to that ship before something worse happens?* Burnham brought up a different display, this one a navigation plot from Troy Januzzi's station. It showed *Shenzhou* following the decaying ion wake of the star-freighter and the fresher trail left behind by Tauh's carrier ship, twin arcs of faint color that curved around nearby nebulae and back toward what the Peliar admiral had called "the sanctuary," a nondescript star system designated in the galactic catalog as DRL-559-G.

"At best speed, just under two days," said a quiet voice behind her. Captain Georgiou looked over Burnham's shoulder at the star map. "Not good enough."

"Forty-seven hours, seventeen minutes," Burnham said automatically, the calculation coming to her by reflex. "Avoiding that nebula formation virtually doubles our point-to-point transit time."

"It's laced with reactive metreon gas pockets, so we can't warp through it. We take that route and we're back to impulse power, no shields again," Georgiou said with a nod. "I've had enough of that for one day."

Burnham turned as the first officer crossed over to her console. His antennae arched forward in the way they always did when he was frustrated over something. "There's another option," he said, in a low voice. "I am loath to even voice it, but I am this ship's executive officer, and it is my duty to point out alternatives."

Burnham suspected she knew what ch'Theloh was going to say, and she stepped back to allow him to use her console. He manipulated the star map, zooming out to show a larger slice of the local region. DRL-559-G, the nebula, and the Peliar Zel and Dimorus systems appeared on the visual, along with a patch of space that was marked out in a stark crimson. The color designated a Starfleet-mandated danger zone: stellar hazards or enemy territory.

Beware the Jabberwock, she thought, the line from the old poem coming to mind unbidden.

"There is a course that will get us there a lot faster," ch'Theloh said as he plotted a new path. "And in my opinion it is an extremely bad idea."

The adjusted course projection took a different heading, away from the route around the nebula and directly over the red line, cutting across the corner of the danger zone. Into space formally annexed and controlled by the forces of the Tholian Assembly.

"We'd be inside the Tholian borders for around ten hours," he went on.

"Nine hours, thirty-one minutes," said Burnham.

"As I said, an extremely bad idea."

"That could stir up the hornets' nest," admitted Georgiou. "It's fairly certain they've been keeping tabs on us.

We know for sure they blasted our monitor buoy. If we cross into their space . . ."

"We're giving them what they want," finished Burnham. "But if we don't, and we arrive too late for Saru and the others . . ." She trailed off.

"Have we detected any activity on the Tholian side of the border?" said Georgiou.

"Negative," noted the first officer. "In fact, it's been unusually quiet over there. Odd, considering recent events. If I had to hazard a guess, I would reason their ships are elsewhere. Either that or deliberately lying dormant."

"I know what Starfleet Command would say," said the captain. "Do you think we need their guidance, Number One?"

A wry smile pulled at the corner of ch'Theloh's mouth. "We haven't up until now."

Georgiou nodded to herself. "Roll the dice, Commander. With any luck, the irregular warp field emissions we're putting out with that replacement axis unit will confuse the hell out of them."

"Captain!" Burnham reached out to Georgiou before she could move away. "There's something I have to ask you."

Georgiou exchanged a look with the first officer. "Go on."

"I believe we should transmit an encrypted subspace message to the *Yang*. Our people need to know that Admiral Tauh is on his way." Her tone rose, becoming insistent. "You heard what he said. He doesn't want to end this situation peacefully. If we can warn Saru and the others, it might give them an advantage. If we don't, they'll be looking the other way when Tauh's ship arrives with a squadron of attack drones."

"You *were* paying attention?" ch'Theloh said firmly. "To the parts of the conversation we just had about Tholians, and nests of deadly stinging insects, yes?"

"Yes, sir, but—"

He spoke over her, in a low hiss that didn't travel. "To get through this, we need to keep our emissions as low as possible, Lieutenant. Avoid detection. Sending out a subspace signal would be the very opposite of that!" Ch'Theloh's antennae stiffened. "We don't even know if any of our people are still alive to hear it."

"Then why are we going after them?" Burnham matched his tone. "Just to pick up the bodies of our dead? Tauh already promised to do that for us."

"Commander, Lieutenant." Georgiou raised a hand to end the discussion. "We're doing this thing, and I say we go all in." She gave Burnham a nod. "Send the message, Michael. Work with Ensign Fan to mask the signal as much as possible."

"I don't like it," said ch'Theloh.

"You don't like anything, Sonny," the captain told him, patting the Andorian on the shoulder. "That's your job."

Saru sat alone in the familiar silence of the shuttle's cockpit and stared mournfully through the canopy.

Out past the *Yang*'s nose and the acres of curved hull metal it rested upon, he had a view that extended away toward the distant aft impulse-drive cluster, which formed the end of the star-freighter's "spine." Large, dark shapes cluttered the space around the flanks of the vessel, each one the asymmetrical, wedge-like form of a massive cargo module. As the Kelpien watched, he saw flashes of ion fire flare at the corners of some units, nudging them closer to the transport ship. In turn, fans of glittering blue-green light spread from heavy-duty tractor beam emitters along the length of the vessel, capturing the modules and maneuvering them into position. The containers were stacking atop ones already in place, locking together to form one single structure. Over the past few hours, the mass of the Peliar ship had almost doubled with all the new additions.

He watched the silent motion and wondered about the beings inside the containers. The *Yang*'s sensors were reading a massive density of Gorlan life readings within them as the entire surviving population of their colony packed themselves into the last few functioning modules and evacuated their temporary home.

Saru had listened in on the messages Vetch had sent to the Gorlans on the surface. Even across the distance, he had sensed the powerful mix of raw anger, desperation, and elation at the possibility of a second chance. The refugees down on the sanctuary planet had been lost without their hub to guide them, and to know she was still alive gave them renewed hope.

But that would soon fade, he realized, and the Gorlans would turn to resentment for what they had been put through. *They are a proud and passionate people*, he thought. *I don't know if Ejah's guidance will be enough to temper their fury.*

Saru wanted to speak with her again, to implore her to turn Madoh away from his plan to mount another attack on the *Shenzhou*, but the red-bands had made it very clear to the Kelpien that would not be permitted. He had no way to know if Ejah was even aware of what her guardians were considering. He imagined not; Madoh and Vetch had both spoken of deeds they had done without her knowledge, of acts that were "necessary" to keep her safe. In their own way, they were protecting her, shielding the hub from the darker truths of their survival.

He considered trying to find a way back down into the cargo compartments, but the red-bands were watching him closely at all times. Even now, one of them was nearby, in the corridor below the hatch connecting to the shuttlecraft. Saru had told the Gorlan he needed to prepare a data card, using the *Yang*'s small mainframe, that would complete the work of deleting the control software from the freighter's subsystems, but that was a partial truth. He could have finished the work up on the transport's command deck or by using his tricorder.

The real reason he had come back to the shuttle was to find some brief isolation. Saru was worn down by the certainty that everyone around him was judging his behavior. Ensign Weeton made no secret of his aversion to Saru's orders, and the junior officer had practically called him a coward to his face. Despite their own shock at learning the truth about the sanctuary planet, he suspected Nathal and Hekan saw Saru as a Gorlan collaborator, and the Gorlans themselves thought him to be weak.

"How did this go so wrong?" he wondered aloud, peering morosely at the control console as the data card completed its upload. "My intentions were good. How have I ended up here?"

Down below, the red-band who had been shadowing him banged a cudgel on the bottom of the hatch. "Outworlder! How much longer is this going to take?"

"It will be a while," he lied. On a bleak impulse, Saru let his hands drop onto the shuttle's flight control yoke. He briefly considered closing the hatch and firing up the thrusters, tearing the *Yang* away and escaping.

Run, Saru. A voice in the back of his mind, a memory from his deep past, clawed its way up to the surface of his thoughts. *Run, Saru*, it said, *run and don't look back.*

"No." He bit out the word. The frightened, untested youth he had once been was long gone. It was one thing to embrace caution, but he was not a coward.

He wanted to get up out of the chair and march back

down there, demand Madoh's attention and another audience with the hub, the consequences be damned. But his self-doubt was corrosive, and with every moment he hesitated, the fear and anxiety second-guessed each thought that passed through his mind. It was like a horrible kind of paralysis, and if only he could see a way past it, he might overcome it.

A beeping tone sounded from the *Yang*'s subspace communicator grid, and it came as such a surprise that it shocked Saru rigid. In the next second, he shook off the reaction and snatched up a wireless receiver, pressing it to his ear. The communicator's system asked him for a personal security code to decrypt the incoming message. His eyes widened as he saw the origin of the narrow-band signal. *U.S.S. Shenzhou* NCC-1227.

"Authorization Kappa-Saru-Seven," he whispered, throwing a worried look back at the open hatch in the compartment behind him. If the Gorlan came up to see what was taking so long, if Saru was caught, it would not go well for the Kelpien.

A loud, buzzing crackle sounded in Saru's aural canal, and he winced at the noise. The communication had all the characteristics of a burst-transmission message, sent at high gain in the hopes that it would be picked out of the void by the *Yang*'s monitoring systems. As the shuttle's decryption subroutines rearranged the coded signal back into something discernable, Saru listened with increasing concern as the garbled sounds merged together into a familiar voice.

"This is Lieutenant Burnham aboard the Shenzhou, *to anyone aboard the shuttle* Yang. *This is a priority-one message. We've repaired the damage inflicted on our ship and are currently tracking the fugitive transport. Be advised, a drone-carrier warship from the Peliar Zel system is ahead of us and will arrive at your location before we can reach you. This vessel's intentions are aggressive, repeat aggressive."* Burnham

paused, and Saru could hear the dread in her voice. *"Do whatever you can to protect yourselves. We're on our way, but it may be a while. . . . We're taking a shortcut. Until then, hold fast.* Shenzhou *out."*

A torrent of reactions swept through Saru, and he had to steel himself to rein them all in. *Relief* that Burnham—and hopefully everyone else—aboard the *Shenzhou* was unhurt, *hope* that they would arrive in time to stop things from getting any worse, *trepidation* over this new reveal of the approaching warship, and finally *dismay* at the reckoning that would come from the choices he had been forced to make.

It took a physical effort on his part to take all of those conflicting emotions and push them down, seal them away. *I should have paid more attention to Burnham when she talked about those Vulcan meditation rituals of hers.* He sighed, drawing a deep breath, and then played back the message once again to make certain he had missed nothing.

Saru heard the clanking of heavy footfalls on the ladder frame beneath the hatch, and then the red-band's head and shoulders appeared through the open panel. He looked around suspiciously, finally finding Saru up at the shuttle's bow. "You have been in here for too long. What are you doing?" The Gorlan hauled himself the rest of the way inside and immediately swatted the open door of an armory locker on the wall, where the *Yang*'s small store of phasers was kept. All of the firearms had already been looted by Madoh and his comrades, but the red-band was clearly wondering if they might have missed some.

Saru deftly pocketed the wireless receiver before the Gorlan saw it and deactivated the communications grid. "I am finished."

"Then get moving," snapped the Gorlan.

"Of course . . ." Saru climbed out of the pilot's chair and stepped around the red-band. He considered his options. If he brought what he now knew to Madoh, if he forewarned him about the approaching Peliar warship, it might be enough to convince the militant leader to let him talk with Ejah.

That would mean surrendering the only advantage I have, Saru considered. *And to what gain? The hope that Madoh will show me trust?* He frowned. *No. I must approach this in a different way. But before I can do that, I must take ownership of the mistakes that I have made.*

"You," he said, drawing himself up to his full height. "You will take me back to the rest of the captives."

"No, Madoh said you need to complete your tasks for us, and then—"

"I need the rest of my team to complete the tasks," he shot back. "Do you want to be the one to tell Madoh that you stopped me from finishing what I started?"

The red-band scowled and kneaded the grip of the cudgel in one of his hands, enough that Saru thought he might strike him for daring to show defiance. But then the Gorlan gave a rough shrug and waved him away. "Go on, then. And do not waste any more time."

"I don't intend to," Saru replied, dropping back through the open airlock hatch.

"He's still the senior officer," said Yashae, blinking her large eyes. She looked up and met Weeton's gaze as he sat across from her, on the other side of the table bolted to the mess hall floor. "We can't just ignore his orders."

"Who said anything about *ignore*?" Weeton replied. "I'm talking about someone *countermanding* him." The ensign nodded toward the next table along, where Saladin Johar lay unconscious beneath a silvery survival blanket. "Saru is making one bad choice after another and it can't go on."

"We're not waking Johar," said Zoxom, and the words were stone hard. "I mean it. I don't care whose rank says what, you can write me up or whatever. The chief engineer is not well enough. I can't be sure what the shock to his system would do."

"No one is saying we need to do that," Weeton backtracked. "I'm just saying that Lieutenant Saru isn't who we need in charge right now." His argument picked up momentum as he went on. "I like the guy, kinda. I do, but he bends like the willow and we need an oak right now, you know what I mean?"

"I don't, sir." Subin ran a hand over her brow. "What are 'willow' and 'oak'?"

"They're both kinds of Terran animals," said Yashae.

"They're *trees*," Weeton corrected, with an exasperated snort. "Okay, listen, forget the analogies. I'll stick to facts. Saru is all about playing it safe, right? And so every time something has happened here, he's chosen not to put up a fight. So where does that leave us? As hostages, like them?" He jerked a thumb at the group of captive Peliars, keeping to themselves on the far side of the compartment. "No, worse than that. We're collaborating with terrorists. We've helped Madoh take full control of this ship from its rightful owners. And now he's demanding we help him take *our* ship next! How the hell does that square up to the chain of command?"

Yashae stared at the deck. "So what are you driving at, Ensign? Because this sounds a lot like mutiny talking."

"Don't be ridiculous, Chief," Weeton replied. "We're not using the m-word! But there's precedent for overruling an officer if he continually makes questionable decisions." He looked at Zoxom. "Fitness for command and that kind of thing, right?"

"I don't know if I could go along with that," said the nurse.

"Why not?" Subin glanced across at the broad-shouldered Xanno. "The ensign's not wrong."

"Because we don't know what Lieutenant Saru is thinking, and we don't get to second-guess our officers," Zoxom said firmly.

"Then maybe we need to know what he's thinking," said Yashae, looking up as the mess hall's doorway clanked open. "So let's ask him."

Weeton turned with the rest of them as Saru entered, and the Kelpien stiffened as he realized that he had been the subject of their now-silenced conversation.

"Lieutenant," said Yashae as he approached. "Sir. We've been talking . . ."

"I do not doubt it," Saru replied, and he glanced in Weeton's direction, then away again. "What is Mister Johar's condition?"

"Stable," said Zoxom. "But I honestly don't know how long he'll stay that way. He needs proper medical attention, and a full surgical suite. The sickbay on this tub isn't good enough. It's just a bunch of auto-doc robots, and they're only programmed with Peliar anatomy."

"I know you're doing your best, Nurse." Saru's head bobbed in a nodding motion, and he halted in front of the group, scanning their weary expressions. At length, he sat down on the bench so he could address them all. "Where are the Gorlan guards?"

Subin glanced over his shoulder. "Moving back to the hatch, sir. Out of earshot, I'd say."

"Good." He let out a sigh. "None of this is going the way we expected it to. I came back to this ship because I hoped I could help these people, but instead I dragged all of us into . . . this."

"No one . . ." Weeton started to speak, then paused, trying to frame his words correctly. "It's not your fault,

Lieutenant. You're just not the . . ." He faltered again. "I mean, uh . . ."

"I'm not up to it?" Saru met his gaze. "The Kelpien, who runs and hides every time someone drops a hyperspanner? I know what is said about me, Ensign, I am not deaf."

"Are you up to it?" Subin said softly. "Because I will follow your orders, sir. But I need to know. We all need to know."

"Yes," he agreed. "You do."

"In my officer training classes at Starfleet Academy, they told me that in order for a commander to lead, they must have the trust of their subordinates." Speaking in hushed tones that would not carry beyond the group, Saru leaned close, offering Subin, Weeton, and the others the only thing he could: his honesty. "I don't have yours, and the fault is mine alone."

None of them disagreed, and the silence was damning.

Saru went on. "I have acted rashly and without full consideration of my actions. I wasn't supposed to come back to this ship, I was expected to remain on board the *Shenzhou*. But I did so anyway, because I thought I knew better."

Weeton and Zoxom exchanged glances. "The XO said as much," noted the ensign. "He told Johar to go haul you back."

Saru nodded. "That man is badly wounded because of the choices I made. He took a disruptor blast meant for me. And if I dwell on that guilt for more than an instant, I fear it will become crippling." He shook off the thought. "The only way I know how to engender your trust is to be truthful. This is my truth." He looked to Subin. "I came back to this ship because I thought I could do something against my nature. Take a blind risk in the name of achieving something greater." Saru recalled that conversation in the *Shenzhou*'s shuttlebay, when he spoke to Burnham of rules and regulations. "I tried to emulate someone else, to be a person I am not, and it was a mistake." His gaze shifted to Zoxom. "Then we were here, and things started to fall apart. I told myself I could hold things together, if only I could find a way to prevent any more loss of life. So I made another choice. A compromise. I aided an aggressor in an attack against our own ship."

"You told Madoh where to hit the *Shenzhou*," said the nurse. "The engines, not the crew decks."

Saru nodded again. "It was . . . logical."

"I can't believe you did that . . ." Weeton's face hardened. "You should have refused point-blank!"

"And then what?" Zoxom looked to the ensign. "Madoh would have put a salvo into our ship anyway, killed who knows how many—"

"The captain would have fired back—"

"If she was still alive," the nurse countered. "And how many dead would there have been?" He shook his head. "It was an impossible decision to make. It was . . . triage."

"I did what I thought would save lives," said Saru, silencing them both. "And then again when Madoh threatened to kill Hekan. And again when he promised he would execute Johar and Nathal if I did not assist him."

"And what about now, sir?" Yashae said, her voice catching. "Are we really going to help these hijackers take control of the *Shenzhou* as well? Madoh thinks if he pulls a gun, you'll buckle. Are you going to keep on making compromises? Where do we draw the line?"

Saru marshaled his thoughts. *This is my only chance to make them comprehend*, he told himself. *If I can't convince them to stand with me, then my rank and commission mean nothing*. He looked down and glumly realized that his rank insignia was already gone, already sacrificed elsewhere for the vain hope of a peaceful resolution. "On my homeworld, our lives were an endless cycle of fear. We could never stand our ground, because the odds were always against us. Then things changed, and I left my world behind. I became part of *this*." He pulled at the blue metallic material of his uniform. "And I learned that there are always predators, and that they wear many skins. But I also learned what Madoh and Nathal and the angry, bitter people on both sides of this conflict have not." He looked toward Ensign Weeton. "Compassion is not weakness. Enduring is not living. And belligerence is not strength."

The phantom weight that had been bearing down on Saru seemed to lessen and fade. Saying the words out loud, meaning all of it. The sensation was *freeing*.

"This conflict we have been drawn into is about to get much worse," he told them. "And we have a duty to stop it from devolving into open battle."

"What are you talking about, Lieutenant?" Weeton paled.

Saru quietly explained the content of the troubling message Burnham had sent from the *Shenzhou*. He offered Weeton the earpiece, the decrypted signal still loaded into its internal memory, and one by one the ensign and the noncoms took turns to listen to her warning.

Saru watched the slow spread of realization across their faces. "I'm sharing this with you so that everyone here understands the stakes. This is not just about us and Lieutenant Commander Johar. There are people among the Gorlans and the Peliars who will be in grave danger if the shooting starts. I know you believe I am afraid to take a stand, but you have to see the reality of this. I am trying to prevent bloodshed. I can't do it alone. I need you, all of you, to work with me."

"Would the chief engineer agree?" said Weeton.

Saru's skin tightened around his skull-like aspect. "He can't answer that question, Ensign. Do you want to challenge my command? Go ahead. But it won't change what is coming."

Saru wondered if the ensign would oppose him; but then Weeton blew out a breath and shook his head. "What exactly is it you want us to do, sir?"

Saru reached for a tricorder resting on the table in front of him, and with the other hand he pulled the slim data card from a pocket. He offered both to the junior engineer. "I need you to program something for me." Then he looked at the rest of them. "And I need you to trust me with your lives."

The red-bands brought Saru before Madoh once again, marching the Kelpien onto the command tier before the leader of the Gorlan hijackers. After learning of his plan, Ensign Weeton had surprised Saru by insisting on coming with him, ignoring the lieutenant's protestations. *I've been thinking about being insubordinate all day, sir,* he said, *so I'm disregarding your orders to stay put.*

Saru felt strangely heartened by the ensign's company, and left Chief Petty Officer Yashae in charge of the remainder of the Starfleet team. He did not allow himself to dwell on the possibility that this might be the last he would see of them, or that those orders might be the last he would ever give.

"Not turning out how you expected, is it?" said Weeton, out of the side of his mouth.

Saru said nothing, catching sight of Nathal and Hekan across the compartment, both of the Peliars under the guns of Madoh's men. Commander Nathal gave Saru a hard, unreadable look.

"She blames you, outworlder," said Madoh as they approached the main control podium. "There might be something to that."

The Kelpien's shoulders slumped as he sighed deeply. "I've done what you asked. This will activate a purge protocol to clear this ship's systems of all automated command-and-control software." He offered up the slim data card and Vetch stepped forward, snatching it from his grip. The speaker flipped it from hand to hand, before slotting it into a port on the control panel.

"Purge is running," said Vetch, as he watched the progress of the program across the screen in front of him. "Soon this ship will finally be under our control."

"You've doomed us all!" Nathal called out.

Madoh eyed Saru with a mixture of arrogance and pity. "You serve well, Saru. Your Captain Georgiou clearly instilled a sense of discipline in her officers." He glanced at Weeton. "Do all you Starfleet types obey so readily?"

"Not really," admitted Saru, nodding at the ensign. "This one, certainly not."

"It does not matter." Madoh came closer. "I have a new order for you. You will tell me how and where I need to board the *Shenzhou* in order to take control of it. You have my word the crew will not be harmed, if you assist me." He paused. Saru could feel the pressure of Madoh's aggressive aura-field churning at the edges of his senses. "The Peliars already know the price of defiance. Must I teach it to you as well?"

"No."

"Good," Madoh went on, "now, do as I—"

"*No*," Saru repeated firmly. "I will not help you anymore. This is as far as I will go."

The compartment fell silent as Madoh turned back, one

of his hands rising up to rest on a holstered phaser stolen from the *Yang*. "Saru, you have sung this song before, and it failed then. Do you expect me to believe you have waited until now to grow a spine?" He looked around, finding Vetch and the others, playing to his audience. "Or is it that you doubt me? You don't think that I will take a life to get what I want?" He started to draw the phaser.

"I do not doubt you," said Saru. "I have seen what you did. I know you are more than capable. But my refusal stands." He continued as the Gorlan's face grew thunderous. "We will help you take this vessel away from the sanctuary planet, but that is all. We won't give up our ship or any more of our people to you."

Madoh removed a communicator disc from a pouch on his tunic and raised it to his lips. "Tayak, status?"

"Standing guard outside the mess hall," came the gruff reply. Saru recognized the voice as belonging to one of the red-bands who had been watching the hostages. *"Is something wrong?"*

"We'll see," Madoh replied. "Pick out one of the Starfleet captives. Be ready to execute them when I contact you again." He clicked the channel closed, and shot Saru a level look. "Do you want to reconsider your previous statement?"

Slowly, Saru drew up until he was standing at attention. "I am . . . ashamed that I allowed the situation to go this far."

"You should be," sneered the Gorlan, and with those words he offered up the opening that Saru had been hoping for.

"Like you?" he shot back.

"I have no regrets about the choices I have made," Madoh went on.

"You're lying," Saru said, refusing to back down. "You *are* ashamed of those choices. That's why you are hiding them from the rest of your people. The other Gorlans, the ones down in the cargo modules. They have no idea what you've done. You haven't told them the price of their safety, because you know they would be appalled by it!"

"Not as many as you might think," he replied coldly.

"Ejah would," Saru said firmly, and he saw Vetch and some of the others look away at the mention of her name. "That's why you are hiding this from her. The hub believes in unity and peace. What you are doing dishonors her."

"I do what is necessary for our people to survive!" Madoh's voice became a snarl. "I protect her from all this! She is not to be sullied!"

"You lie to her," Saru countered. "Tell me how that shows respect, Madoh. You lie to her because you know she would never agree to this!"

Madoh teetered on the edge of imminent violence, and Saru felt his threat ganglia writhing over the flesh of his scalp. Then the Gorlan spat on the deck and rocked back. "What happens next is on your head, outworlder," he said, bringing up his communicator. "I gave you a chance to stop it."

"No!" Saru's hand shot out and he snatched at Madoh's wrist. One of the Gorlan's arms grabbed his, another ripping the stolen phaser pistol from its holster. "Listen to me," he called out, ignoring the weapon, pitching his voice so that everyone on the command deck could heard him. "This vessel needs to leave here immediately. A Peliar warship is on its way, and their intentions are to attack! We are all at risk! We will help you leave, but it must be now."

"How do you know this?" demanded Vetch.

"A signal from the *Shenzhou.* Sent to our shuttle. A warning."

"You fool," said Madoh, tearing free of Saru's grip. "Is this weak ruse all you have left?"

"He's not lying," said Nathal, pushing forward. "I managed to transmit a distress signal to Peliar Zel when you launched your takeover. The Cohort will have received it and dispatched a warship to track us down. And when they come, it will not be with peaceful intent."

"How soon?" Vetch strode over to her, his hands slashing angrily at the air.

Nathal shot Saru a look. "I expected them to arrive hours ago."

"Computer, scan nearby space," Vetch addressed one of the control podiums. "Alert us to any incoming objects."

"Processing command," said a stilted, Peliar-accented voice. *"No detections. At this time."* The large scanner screens showed empty space and the planet below.

Madoh gave a dismissive grunt. "You are stalling," he concluded. "It will gain you nothing."

"You're not leaving me with any other option," said Saru. "Please reconsider."

"And if I will not?"

Saru took a deep breath, and when he spoke again, he pitched his voice toward the nearest console. "Computer, *the sun is getting low.*"

"What did he say—?" Vetch began.

"Processing command," replied the synthetic voice. A heartbeat later, all but one console in the compartment went dark, and the hatchways leading to the corridors slammed shut. The main screens winked out and ambient lighting slowly dimmed to less than a quarter of its standard levels.

"Computer, respond . . ." Madoh slammed his fist on the single illuminated console. "Respond, now!"

Across the way, Nathal gave a low, humorless chuckle. "Very clever, Lieutenant. The data card, yes? That's how you did it."

At her side, Nathal's second-in-command peered at another dead panel. "Voice-controlled shutdown command, linked to a specific key phrase. He reprogrammed one of our own security protocols."

"Actually, I did that," said Weeton, then reconsidered. "Well. Team effort. It started running when the data card was uploaded."

"Idiot!" Madoh glared at Vetch. Then he rounded on Saru, clutching the phaser in his hand. "What do you think you have achieved here?" he barked.

"Listen," said Saru, pointing a long finger up at a vent in the bulkhead above them. "The atmosphere processors have been deactivated. Along with every operational control matrix in this section of the ship. All hatches have been sealed. In a few minutes, life-support functionality will cease and it will get very cold in here, very quickly." He gestured to Weeton. "I instructed the ensign to isolate the forward section of the ship only. None of the cargo modules will be affected. The refugees will not be harmed. But everyone in this compartment, your men in the engine core, and those in the mess hall or elsewhere . . . we will either freeze or asphyxiate." He gave Nathal and Hekan a sorrowful look. "My apologies."

"Undo it!" said Vetch, his voice rising in alarm.

Madoh nodded slowly, and glared up at Saru. "Do as he says, or I will make your last few breaths agonizing."

"No," said Saru. "Have your men surrender their weapons and stand down. Relinquish control of this vessel and I'll deactivate the program. Or else we die here."

"I do not fear death!" Madoh retorted.

"I believe you," said the Kelpien. The next words he spoke were difficult for him, but he pressed on. "That is why I am threatening the one single thing I know you do care about. Ejah. *The hub.*" A ripple of consternation went through the chamber. "We will perish, and this ship will be left to drift with no one to keep her or the rest of your people safe."

"If the Cohort have declared this ship a renegade, when they arrive they may not even pause before destroying it." Nathal's bleak prediction only served to narrow the corner that Saru had backed Madoh into.

The Gorlan's fierce expression shifted, turning bitter. "I was wrong about you, Kelpien. There is some of the hunter in you after all. Without it, you could not be so callous."

"I asked you to reconsider," he said. "We're here now because of you, Madoh. But it's not too late to step back from the brink." In the dimness, a polar chill was spreading through the air, and Saru's words escaped in a puff of white exhalation.

Madoh became silent and still as the reality of Saru's threat became clear. He had been outmaneuvered, and he knew it. "Curse you," the Gorlan said stiffly, and then with an angry flick of the wrist, he tossed his stolen phaser to the deck. He raised the communication disc. "Kindred . . . this is over. Give up your weapons and stand down. We are returning control of this ship to the Peliars." His voice was thick with frustration, resignation, and remorse.

"Madoh, are you sure of this?" Even over the communicator link, Tayak's shock was palpable.

"The deed is done," Madoh told him. "Do as I say."

Weeton grabbed the phaser as Nathal and Hekan surged forward to disarm the other Gorlans. None of them resisted, but Saru could feel the resentment and dejection coming off them in waves as their aura-fields darkened along with their emotional states. When the weapons were gathered up, Weeton contacted Yashae, and the Vok'sha reported that all the hostages were free.

"They gave in quick," said the noncom. *"After all that happened, didn't think they would . . ."*

Saru shook his head. "It isn't that," he said. "I just didn't give them anywhere to go."

"You have what you want," Madoh called out, hugging himself as the cold grew deeper with each passing second. "Keep your promise, outworlder."

"Computer," said Saru, "*the moons have risen.*"

"Processing command." The console accepted the code phrase, and the systems cycled back to an operational state. One by one, the screens hanging over their heads blinked on, showing views of the space beyond the freighter's hull.

Out of the cold and the silence, a braying shriek of alarms shocked abruptly through the compartment as brilliant blue alert beacons flashed in unison. Several of the consoles switched to panic mode, warning of imminent danger close at hand.

Saru's threat ganglia opened in twitching fans as he felt the sudden and very real sense of *threat.*

On the closest screen, a scan return from the starfreighter's sensor array was alight with new detections.

Where there had been nothing before, now there were dozens of objects emerging from behind the sanctuary planet. A flotilla of attack drones were closing in on the transport in a swift, purposeful swarm. Trailing behind them was the wide arc of a carrier vessel, its particle beam turrets target-locking one after the other. Flickering globes of energy gathered at the tip of each cannon, holding in check enough firepower to rip the ship open with a single salvo.

11

The ship approached in an oblique trajectory, using the mass shadow of the sanctuary world to mask its approach from the star-freighter's sensor array. In the moments of blindness while the transport's central computer matrix was offline, the Peliar warship had crossed the day-night terminator and powered toward its target. The remaining complement of its autonomous drones were deployed, blasting out of their silos and into a widening attack formation.

By the time the transport's computer reawakened, the drones and their mothership were already inside optimum firing range for their weapons. Any avenues of escape the bigger, slower craft might have taken were closed off as the drones followed the same approach they had taken with the *Shenzhou*. They surrounded it, mimicking a tactic that the Peliar Cohort had learned from the spinners of the Tholian Assembly.

The transport ship possessed defensive screens and a network of short-range plasma turrets on its dorsal and ventral hull, but they were not military-grade weapons and the machine intelligences controlling the drones assessed them as being of middling lethality.

On the warship, heavy-gauge particle emitters designed to punch through the hulls of enemy craft readied firing solutions, targeting warp engines, power trains, and the dense clumps of interlocked cargo modules.

If battle were joined, it would be a massacre.

"What did you do?" Madoh's words were a gasp, a strangled cry. Some of his previous fire rekindled as he glared at Saru. "I was right! All your talk of equity, and it meant nothing! You gave us up to the Peliars!"

"No. . . . No!" Saru shook his head. "I warned you, I told you they were coming. *We* did not bring them here!"

"Those drones," said Weeton, half to himself. "Robotic combat units, same as the one we saw escorting this ship, back before all this kicked off. They're from Peliar Zel, all right."

A console to Saru's right let out a warning tone. An outside force was overriding the transport's shield controls, shutting them down. Then a humming whine rose from nothing, and rods of sparkling viridian light formed out of thin air in the middle of the command deck, drawing everyone's attention. The beaming effect dissipated to reveal the forms of several armored Peliar soldiers and two imperious-looking Peliar males in the high headdresses of ranking officers. The older of the two scanned the room with a glower, and Saru saw Commander Nathal physically react at the sight of him.

"Father," she whispered. Saru glimpsed a new, worrying vulnerability in Nathal that he hadn't thought her capable of.

"I am Admiral Tauh of the Peliar Cohort," began the older officer—and if he noticed his daughter among the assembled faces, he gave no indication of it. "This vessel will no longer be allowed to remain under the control of criminals." His soldiers raised their disruptors, finding the Gorlans and taking aim at them. "Tell your compatriots," he went on. "All resistance toward the directives of Peliar Zel is to halt immediately, or I will employ lethal force against you. Those responsible for acts of defiance will submit themselves for summary judgment. All remaining aliens in orbit are to deposit themselves on the designated sanctuary world. There will be no negotiation."

Vetch slumped against a support stanchion. "We've failed. We gave up our advantage and now we will perish . . . here in the void, or down there on that poisoned rock!"

Saru rounded on Nathal. "Commander, please. You must do something."

Nathal blinked, as if coming out of a daze. "Yes . . . of course." She straightened her tunic and stepped forward, giving a brisk salute at her shoulder. "Admiral, thank you for your intervention, but you may recall your escorts, sir. This ship is already under Peliar control. The Gorlans who took over the craft have surrendered. They are no longer a danger."

"I will be the arbiter of that," replied Tauh. "A grave series of events have occurred under your dominion, Commander. You bear the responsibility. The Cohort is dissatisfied with your performance."

Nathal's double nostrils flared. "I accept that. My crew did the best they could against superior numbers." She gestured at Saru. "These Federation officers helped us retake the ship without further violence." Nathal faltered. "But Admiral, this planet . . . What we were told about it . . ."

Tauh turned his attention to Saru, ignoring her. "Ah, yes. The meddlers from Starfleet." He gave Saru a dismissive once-over. "A Kelpien. I have heard of your species. Still alive, are you? Your Captain Georgiou was quite concerned about your well-being."

Saru couldn't stop himself from asking the question. "The *Shenzhou* . . . Are they all right?"

"If they did as they were told, they will be fine," Tauh said airily. "I ordered them to return to your side of the border zone. For their own safety."

The Kelpien considered that reply, thinking of how his captain would take that demand. It didn't square with what Lieutenant Burnham had said, but Saru decided to keep the discrepancy to himself and pressed on.

"Admiral, I am Lieutenant Saru. As you are the highest-ranking official of the Peliar Zel Cohort present here, I wish to offer my services to you as an independent third party to mediate for the Gorlan refugees aboard this ship, on behalf of the United Federation of . . ." Saru trailed off as he realized that Tauh was laughing at him. "You find my words amusing, sir?"

"I find your *arrogance* amusing, Lieutenant," he snapped, his chilly humor vanishing. "You have no authority here to offer anything, or expect anything. Perhaps you were not paying attention to my initial statement? Let me reiterate the relevant point: All aliens are to deposit themselves on the designated sanctuary world. That includes you and your Starfleet associates."

"This is the true face of Peliars' so-called altruism," said Madoh, glaring at Saru. "You see, yes? Now it is too late for any of us."

"It speaks?" Tauh gave an arch sniff, as if noticing the Gorlan red-band for the first time. "I have no need to hear what you have to say, criminal." He refocused his attention on his daughter. "Commander, repatriate these aliens aboard the cargo containers and deposit them on the surface. Or must I have my adjutant do it for you?" He gestured to the other Peliar officer accompanying him, who took a wary step forward.

"You're going to send them back there?" Nathal shot a glance at the desolate world on the main screen. "Father, look at it. The Alphan Council told us this place was verdant, that the Gorlans would have a fair chance at a new life. But that was never true, was it?"

"Child," he intoned, "I taught you to be smarter than this. In warfare, certain realities have to be accepted. Don't be naïve."

"We're not at war with the Gorlans," she countered.

Tauh's displeasure deepened. "You talk like a Betan. I expected more."

"Admiral! That world is a harsh and unforgiving wilderness," insisted Saru. "If you abandon these people there, you doom them."

"Then they can thank me for thinning the herd." Tauh was dismissive. "The Gorlans boast of their fortitude. This planet will give them ample opportunity to prove it, and Peliar Zel will be rid of a distraction our worlds never wanted."

"You *cannot* do this." Saru's voice rose with his ire. "Have you no empathy? Despite whatever violence a handful of these people may have committed in their desperation, you cannot sentence tens of thousands of innocents to a slow death!" The flesh of his face colored as indignant rage overwhelmed his innate instinct for self-preservation. "I won't allow it! The Federation will not allow it!"

"The Federation won't hear of it," Tauh sniffed, and the threat hung silently in the air.

"Sir . . ." Tauh's adjutant dared to speak for the first time. "I would counsel against any rash actions that might jeopardize Peliar Zel's future membership in the Federation."

"Be silent, Craea!" Tauh waved him away. "The chattering politicians of Alpha and Beta are light-years distant. *I* am the authority here."

"I will always serve Peliar Zel and the Cohort," Nathal began. "And I have no loyalty to these aliens . . ."

"As it should be," said Tauh.

She disregarded him and kept speaking. "But I do have a moral code! Those who acted against my crew must answer for what they have done, yes, but Lieutenant Saru is right. I won't be a party to this."

Tauh gave his daughter a withering stare. "I should have expected this. There is too much of your pair-mothers in you."

"I think now that they taught me better than you ever did," she shot back.

The admiral glanced around, finding Nathal's subordinate. "You, the second-in-command. Hekan, isn't it? Nathal is relieved of her captaincy. You're in charge now. Execute my orders."

Hekan folded her arms and stood fast. "I'm afraid you won't find anyone on this ship who will go against our commander, sir."

"Oh?" Tauh's gaze swept the chamber and zeroed in on Saru once more. "Is this your poisonous influence, alien? Bad enough that your sickly Federation moralizing has won over the Betans and the weak willed among my fellow Alphans, but now you think that I will swallow it too?" He clasped his hands together. "Very well. I'll make this clear for everyone concerned, one final time. Follow my orders now, to the letter, and I may be willing to consider this as a minor outbreak of insubordination, induced by the stress of recent events. But if anyone refuses, if the Gorlans do not return to the sanctuary of their own accord . . ."

From the corner of his eye, Saru saw the blink of indicators flashing on dozens of vacant consoles. Ensign Weeton stepped closer to one, his brow furrowing as he examined the screen.

"I will have my gunners disable this barge," Tauh continued, unware of what was going on. "And then blast those cargo modules free, and they will fall back to the surface where they belong! I don't imagine all of them would survive an uncontrolled descent, so consider the choice carefully."

But Saru's attention was fixed on the other Starfleet officer. Weeton had gone pale. "Lieutenant?" He beckoned the Kelpien over. "You really need to see this."

"Do not ignore me!" raged Tauh, but Saru did exactly that, crossing to the console in two loping steps. "My orders are all you need concern yourself with!"

As Saru studied the data on the panel, his threat ganglia pulled tight and he had to physically restrain himself from reaching up to press at the tiny dendrite-like fronds. "You are gravely mistaken, Admiral." The brief surge of anger that had buoyed Saru up beyond the reach of his deeper, fearful nature now fell away as a new and more lethal threat made itself apparent. "I would direct your attention to subspace frequency zero-one-one-four."

Tauh's adjutant Craea peered at a digital panel fixed to the forearm of his uniform, and he tapped a few keys on the device. The Peliar reacted with shock and whispered something that Saru didn't catch.

Tauh spun toward his officer. "What? What did you say?" All his bluster seemed to evaporate in an instant as he drew into a hissed, secretive conversation with Craea.

"Zero-one-one-four," said Hekan, thinking aloud, "that's a general frequency used by the . . . the Tholians."

Saru was already tapping at the panel. A holographic projection phased into being across from where they stood, and it resembled a piece of abstract art—against a twinkling background stood a diamond-shaped pillar cut from misty crystal, vanishing out of sight beneath the image pickup.

The upper facets of the form were broken by a pair of harsh eye spots that glowed with infernal light.

When it spoke, the Tholian's screeching, grating communication became a high-pitched, haughty voice rendered through a translator matrix. *"Attention, intruder vessels. We have determined that your craft represent a threat to the security of the Tholian Assembly. We have dispatched a defensive force to this star system. It will arrive presently. We expect your craft to be beyond the outer orbit of the system at that time. Any vessel remaining within that perimeter will be considered a threat and dealt with accordingly."* Its message delivered, the image of the Tholian blinked out.

"How soon is *presently*?" said Weeton as Saru pivoted over another of the podium consoles.

"Sensors are picking up unidentified readings at the edge of range," he said carefully. "Judging by motion and energy output . . . two, possibly three ships. They'll be here in . . . nine-point-seven minutes."

Hekan gasped. "Even if we go to warp right now, with the added mass of those cargo modules we won't make it past the outer orbit before they catch up with us!"

"They know that," said Madoh bitterly. "A potential threat? We are nothing of the kind, just as our colony was no danger to them."

"Were we meant to perish there?" Vetch muttered, his head bowed. "Is this fate catching up to us? Events repeat themselves. We are condemned."

"Not yet," Saru insisted, overlooking the hollow ring of his own words. His thoughts raced as he struggled to formulate a solution to the imminent problem. "Mister Weeton! Engineer Hekan! Would it be possible to modify the warp bubble generated by this ship, and merge it with that of the warship?"

"Uh . . . in theory . . ." The ensign gave the Peliar woman a questioning look.

"It could be done," admitted Hekan. "We have dozens of heavy-duty tractor beam emitters on our outer hull; they could be used to secure both ships together."

Weeton nodded rapidly, picking up Saru's idea and running with it. "Stresses would be high, and the spatial drag would slow down the carrier severely, but it could work." He paused, blinking as he tried to figure it out.

"Ensign, would we make the perimeter in time?" Saru pressed.

"I don't know," Weeton admitted. "But better we try."

Across the compartment, Admiral Tauh turned slowly back to face them. He seemed to have aged years in the space of a few seconds, briefly struck silent by the unexpected arrival of the new danger.

"Listen to me," he grated, his previously superior and languid manner now replaced with what Saru saw was genuine dread. "The Peliar Zel Cohort's standing orders are unequivocal in this situation! Under no circumstances are our ships to engage in any actions that will antagonize the Tholian Assembly." He turned to bark a command to his adjutant. "Recall all the drones immediately! Task the carrier's helm to put all power to the star drive!"

"Father . . ." Nathal approached him. "*Admiral.* What are you doing?"

"A tactical reevaluation," he snapped. "Come! I will have my transporter operator lock on to all Peliar life signs. . . . Prepare yourselves! We are leaving!"

"You're going to abandon this ship and everyone aboard it to the Tholians?" Saru said the words aloud and still he could hardly believe it. It was one thing to be ready to force the Gorlans to return to the desolate planet below, and quite another to leave them here, on a lightly armed cargo barge at the mercy of a Tholian attack force.

"The drones have disengaged and are falling back toward the carrier," reported Weeton. "He's gonna do it, Lieutenant."

Nathal was aghast at her father's actions. She looked to the adjutant for support. "Craea, say something! You cannot sanction this!"

"Don't make demands of him!" Tauh retorted, regaining some of his previous venom. "I am in command here! You will obey me!"

Saru could taste the raw terror crackling through the air of the compartment. He sensed it in the thrumming, silent pressure of the aura-fields cast out by the fearful Gorlans, saw it on the faces of the Peliars, and felt the acidic churn of his own anxieties threatening to rise up and engulf him.

The raw, potent power of the fear—his old, constant, and most-hated companion—seemed to come at the Kelpien from every angle at once. It took all of his will to hold it at bay.

"Admiral, if you run, what do you think will happen?" He fixed the Peliar officer with a grimace. "Do you believe the Tholians will stop here, if they are not challenged? It has always been in their nature to press the limits around them! If you take your ship and retreat, they will see you go, they will be able to track your ion trail."

"Maybe all the way back to Peliar Zel," Weeton added darkly.

"Perhaps," said Tauh. "Perhaps not. If they are on the move, then it is even more imperative to warn the Alpha and Beta Moons to prepare!" He tapped at his own wrist control. "I do not fight battles that cannot be won."

"You won't even try?" All of Nathal's flinty exterior was

suddenly gone, and Saru saw through to something of who she really was, and the conflict she was caught in.

"Activate—" Tauh raised his arm, speaking into the device—but his words were choked off as his daughter aimed a phaser at his chest.

"Sir!" One of the armored Peliar troopers called out. He and his men were uncertain where to aim their weapons. "What do we do?"

"Hold your fire," ordered the adjutant, before Tauh could respond.

"No, Father," Nathal told Tauh. "I won't run. My crew will not run. Saru is right. We must defy the Tholians."

"You're taking tactical advice from a being genetically programmed to be a coward?" retorted the admiral.

"I can overcome my instincts when the situation demands it," Saru said, with as much firmness as he could muster. "Can you say the same, sir?"

"Gorlans will fight!" shouted Madoh. "We have nothing left but our defiance!"

"For each other," Vetch said, with a resigned nod. "For our community and for the hub."

Tauh's fear built into fury as he glared at his daughter. "So be it! I hoped for better from you, but the truth is you have always been a disappointment to me, child! Stay here with these alien mongrels and die, then. I am leaving!"

"No," said Nathal, looking to Saru for a nod of support. "You're not. We must protect the Gorlans, just as we promised we would!"

Off her cue, the Kelpien stepped in and tore the control device from Tauh's wrist before he could use it. "The people of Peliar Zel looked the Gorlans in the eye and they promised them safety." Saru cast around, meeting the gazes of the Peliar soldiers one by one. "Was that a lie or was it the truth? Each of you has a choice to make, as Commander

Nathal did. Will you let other sentient beings die, or will you band together against a greater threat that can destroy us all?"

"Outworlder lives are not worth Peliar lives!" Tauh shouted.

"Who among you truly believes that?" Saru asked, in the stark silence that followed.

Craea gave a slow shake of the head. "We made a promise," he said, echoing Nathal's words. He raised his wrist unit and spoke into it. "Carrier control, belay previous orders. Go to battle status and configure the drones into a defensive screen."

"You too?" Tauh scowled at his subordinate. "But then this is what I get for elevating a Betan to a combat post!"

"Adjutant?" said a voice over the open channel. *"Where is Admiral Tauh?"*

"He has been relieved of duty," said the other Peliar. "We're staying to fight."

"Fools . . ." muttered Nathal's father. "Now we will all perish!"

Off that bleak prediction, the compartment's atmosphere was cut by a proximity alert that sounded from the console before Ensign Weeton. The engineer picked at the haptic keypad, and his eyes narrowed. "Huh. Nine-point-seven minutes, on the dot. The Tholians really are as punctual as everyone says."

"The fates watch over us," said Craea. "We will return to the carrier and prepare for battle." With another tap on his control, the Peliar boarding party were snatched back by their transporters.

Saru didn't miss the venomous glare Tauh spared for his daughter as he dematerialized. "You did the right thing," he told her.

"I don't need your platitudes, Saru," she retorted, turning stony once more. "I need a way to defeat *them.*" She pointed at the main viewscreen.

At the upper edge of the display, a trio of silver craft, sleek and sharp like arrowheads, were slipping into position.

The Tholian ships moved in swift, dashing motions akin to the way that fish would dart beneath the surface of a river, making it difficult for any weapons system or gunner to draw a bead on them. Shimmering crimson power grids on their trilobed hulls bled excess energy out into the darkness as they shed velocity, slowing to make a combat approach.

The formation dithered, then parted. Two ships rolled together into a new element, bringing their needle prows to bear on the Peliar warship. They moved front on, presenting the smallest possible target aspect to their opponent. The third vessel broke away in a hard power turn that became a spiraling course toward the slow-moving bulk of the star-freighter. Bubbles of glittering light briefly shimmered around both the Peliar craft as their crews put up their deflector shields, but the Tholians moved in undaunted.

There was no pause in their actions, no hint of hesitation. Weapons grids drew power from within and the prefire arrays of their particle beam cannons were readied. One way or another, conflict was coming to the skies above the sanctuary planet.

"Attention, intruder vessels." The screeching tone of the alien voice was like scraping two pieces of broken glass across each other, and the dissonant sound set Saru's teeth on edge. *"You have made no credible attempt to depart this area. Therefore, your craft have been designated as enemy combatants and will be treated as such. In the interest of amity,*

the Tholian Assembly will allow you to surrender unharmed. Depower all weapons, shields, and drive systems. Do it now."

The iridescent holograph of the alien being shimmered in the middle of the command deck as if being viewed through a heat haze. Saru recalled a xenobiology briefing suggesting that the interior temperature of Tholian craft was kept at several hundred degrees, and he tried to imagine what kind of life could have evolved to live at that extreme.

"We're not going to be doing any of that," said Nathal.

"It is as we expected," replied the Tholian.

Saru was startled; he hadn't realized that the transmission was live, expecting to get another self-contained statement as they had before. He took a step forward, a flash of hope stirring in him. If the Tholian was talking with them, then they were not fighting, and if they were not fighting, there was still a slim chance to stop this from escalating. "We have no wish for battle, but what you ask is unreasonable. Our presence here is in no way a threat to your species or its territories!"

"Untrue," came the harsh rejoinder. *"Your presence alone is the threat."*

"You're wasting your breath, Kelpien," said Vetch. "I said the same thing to them when they came to our colony, and received the same answers. They're not interested in compromise."

"Why not?" Saru looked back at the hologram, his mind racing. "Why are you doing this? Do you really wish to provoke an interstellar conflict?"

"The provocation is yours," grated the Tholian. *"We observe and evaluate. You build bases from which to conduct espionage operations against the Assembly."*

"It's talking about the Gorlan colony planet," said Weeton. "They think we had something to do with that?"

"You establish military alliances that imperil our borders," continued the hologram. *"We react to protect ourselves."*

"You mean the discussions with the Federation?" Hekan shot Saru a look. "How are they aware . . . ?"

"We observe and evaluate," repeated the Tholian.

Saru raised his hands in an unconscious gesture of appeasement. "You are mistaken. The Gorlans are not part of the United Federation of Planets, and we have no part in their colonial missions. They, like the beings of Peliar Zel and your species, are our neighbors. We seek only to coexist in peace."

"You are not like us," said the Tholian, and Saru could not deny the edge of menace in the words. *"Carbon-based forms are inherently inferior. Inherently dangerous. You will be removed."* The hologram dissipated, and in the next second Madoh was shouting out in alarm.

"They've opened fire!"

Bright shocks of coruscating light stabbed from the prows of the Tholian craft and lanced through a cluster of Peliar drones, puncturing their deflectors and reducing them to shrapnel. The attacker triad blasted past the defensive line erected by the warship without slowing, even as the remainder of the drone squadron reacted and tried to waylay them.

The Tholian spinners continued to power ahead on their attack vectors, ignoring the smaller automated craft in favor of the two larger targets. The battle pair moved as if an invisible tether were connecting both vessels, vectoring into a twisting barrel roll that brought them hurtling down toward the ship's flat, curved hull. Particle guns on the surface of the Peliar ship opened up, spewing jags of crimson fire into the path of the dart-like attackers, but they hit nothing but dead vacuum.

The agile Tholians suddenly broke formation and fired at the carrier's fuselage, cracking sectors of the shields and striking hard secondary hits that overloaded plasma conduits and liquefied hull metal into scattered gobs of flash-melted tritanium.

The drone force, acting on its networked commands, swarmed back toward its parent vessel, driven by preprogrammed directives that compelled them to protect their mothership. Controllers on board the carrier worked to retask them, but it was too late. A window of vulnerability had opened over the transport ship, and the remaining Tholian spinner shot toward it, becoming a hurled dagger.

"Incoming!" called Saru, watching the shape of the silver attacker grow larger on the main monitor.

In comparison to the transport ship, the Tholian craft was small, but the power curves it exhibited showed a deadly energy-to-mass ratio. Its internal systems were keyed to weapons functionality. Where the transport was built to shift vast amounts of cargo across star systems, the Tholian craft was constructed around the lethal particle cannon that ran the length of its core. It was, in every sense of the term, a *gunship*.

All around him, figures scrambled to man the command deck's empty stations—Peliar, Gorlan, and Starfleet alike—but there were not enough of them to operate all of the giant vessel's complex systems.

Saru saw the danger as it unfolded. *Too few to run the ship, too slow to get away, too weak to put up a real fight*. For all his earlier thoughts of defiance, the Kelpien wondered if at last he had gone too far for his own good.

"Thrusters!" Nathal called to him. "Roll the ship, Saru!"

"Yes!" He saw the commander's intention, and his long

fingers raced over the panel in front of him, bringing up the attitude control matrix. He fired the huge ship's clusters of ion jets in bursts of blue fire, and the view on the screen shifted.

Turning a hulk as big as the star-freighter was a difficult proposition at any time, and there was no way they would be able to avoid getting hit by the nimble spinner vectoring in on them. But rolling the vessel along the length of its primary axis would mean that incoming fire could not concentrate in any single location.

A streamer of brilliant flame connected the tip of the Tholian ship with the Peliar transport, and the huge vessel's shields buckled as gigawatts of destructive power poured into them.

Under Saru's deft control, the freighter spun, turning away from the crippling blow and spreading the incoming attack over a wider area. Flash-burn overspill from the particle beam drew an ugly scar of carbon scoring across the hull plates.

"Take the brunt of it on the forward section," ordered Nathal. She didn't need to explain that any hits aft of that part of the ship risked puncturing the cargo modules packed with terrified Gorlan refugees.

"I can't connect . . ." said Weeton. He called out to Hekan. "What's wrong with the targeting grids on these plasma turrets? Every time I try to draw a bead on that Tholian, the shots go wide!"

Hekan stabbed a finger at a vacant podium near where Weeton was standing. "The stabilizer system is out of harmony. Someone man that station, help him!"

"Which one of us?" Vetch took a half step away from his own panel, then faltered. "Should I, I don't know—"

The deck quaked as the Tholian attacker followed up its initial assault with a salvo of torpedo shots, and Vetch was thrown to the floor. Saru hung on to his own podium for dear life, but he couldn't miss the flash of orange discharge on one of the secondary viewscreens.

The torpedoes punched through the shields and struck one of the transport's warp nacelles. Saru gasped as the entire engine pod was ripped free of its support pylon, tumbling away end over end into the ship's impulse wake, to collide with an escort drone that had been racing to catch up with them.

"There's not enough of us to adequately operate this vessel under combat conditions," he said flatly, tearing his communicator from his belt. Saru flicked it open and spoke into the pickup. "Yashae, Subin! Get up to the command deck, on the double! Bring anyone you can!"

"Negative, Lieutenant, we have problems of our own!" replied the Vok'sha. *"That last hit blew out an EPS relay down here, we have fires in the corridor. I'm getting everyone out of the compartment, sir . . ."* There was a pause, and Saru heard the distant crunch of twisting metal. *"We'll get to you if we can."*

"Understood, Chief," he said. "If all else fails, fall back to the *Yang* and detach. We will attempt to do our best up here."

Saru looked up as Madoh drew his own communication device. "You need people? I can bring them!"

"Do it," said Saru, and he shot Nathal a look, heading off her complaint before she could voice it. "We don't have time to be choosy, Commander."

The Peliar woman scowled, and she resembled her father's severe bearing. "It won't matter if we can't work together."

"Something is happening!" called Vetch. "The other two Tholians, they're falling back."

"He's right," said Weeton. "Lieutenant, the sensors are

reading very strong energy surges aboard each ship. A new pattern. Something we haven't seen before."

In careful lockstep, the two spinners harrying the Peliar warship veered off and looped around as the bulk of the drone flotilla came powering across the dark toward them. Pulse bursts jetted from cannon maws on the automated craft as the escorts tried to lay down a wall of fire. The machine intelligences inside the drones networked with one another over their subspace links, coordinating their counterattack to place the maximum amount of lethality across the path of the Tholians.

The memory banks carried by the drones were filled with thousands of hours of long-range sensor scans, predictive models, and espionage data based on what Peliar Zel knew of the forces of Tholia—but for all that, what the drones lacked was the ability of a nonsynthetic intellect, the insight to make a choice that was truly random, truly unexpected.

Against reason, the Tholian two-ship formation turned *toward* the incoming fire and threaded the gaps in the salvo as bright glittering needles passing through the weft of spun cloth. The collective network of the drones detected the unusual energy pattern building up in both ships but could not recognize it. No scans or records of such a pattern existed in Peliar records.

The reason for that was a simple one. No ship from Peliar Zel had ever survived the weapon the Tholians were about to deploy.

The effect burst from the hulls of the two spinners in a crackling wave front, coruscating blue lightning expanding outward in milliseconds until it spread wide enough to pass through the drone force.

Each drone touched by the passing of the twin-lobed wave suffered the same catastrophic overload sequence. First, their meager deflectors collapsed, then their power systems were swamped by an incredible flood of energy that blasted through their surge protectors. The high-intensity energy-dampening field emitted by the Tholians faded after only a few thousand meters, but the drones had gathered so closely that the effect was devastating.

Thruster grids died and weapons arrays went dark, but the forward momentum of the Peliar escorts was unchecked, and the drones became a cloud of uncontrolled missiles. Several of the robotic craft collided with one another, some tumbling away into the gravity well of the planet below, others pitching into crash courses with their mothership, forcing the gunners on the carrier to destroy their own craft or risk a deadly impact. Most of the affected drones obliterated each other in short-lived fireballs, gutting the offensive capacity of the larger Peliar warship in less than a minute.

The use of the weapon was like the Tholians themselves. *Ruthless, precise, and unyielding.*

The most immediate threat to them neutered, the two spinners reversed their course and shot back toward the warship, once more weaving side to side as they passed smoothly through the expanding debris field their attack had created. Crimson beams flashed from the sharp prows of each ship, combining their fire to impact the same points on the carrier's outer hull.

Plates of metal across the exterior of the sickle-shaped craft boiled off in gaseous jets of sun-hot plasma, and a violent shuddering racked the Peliar warship as vital systems were burned out.

The warship's gunners had no way of knowing how long the energy-dampener weapon's recharge cycle would take, only that if their vessel was rendered inert, then the

Tholians would be free to cut them apart at their leisure—or worse, build one of their strange energy "webs" around the carrier and drag it back into their domain.

The Peliar crew fought with the terrified desperation of those facing an enemy they knew only through rumor and half-truths. Beam salvos cut the dark orbital space, slicing through vacuum as they tried to find their targets. With the melee happening in such close quarters, it was inevitable that some shot would make the mark, and a particle beam turret on the aft ventral quarter of the warship scored a direct hit that shredded part of the spinner's crystalline hull. Superheated atmospheric gases vented from the breach, and the craft veered off again. Its companion sought out the cannon that had landed the strike and melted it into blackened slag with a high-intensity burst of power.

The Tholians attacking the warship extended away and regrouped. Less than a kilometer distant, the third craft in their triad continued its savage assault on the bigger, slower star-freighter.

A storm of plasma bolts rained upward toward the twisting, turning shape of the Tholian spinner, but none of them connected with their attacker, and Saru felt his heart sink as the alien craft began to mimic the transport ship's roll-and-lurch escape course. Each hit from the Tholian's main gun was a hammer blow, making the decks tremble and the screens hanging from the ceiling flicker and fade.

Warning displays hinted at the unfolding horror taking place belowdecks and down in the cargo pods. Several levels of the forward module were torn open and naked to space, and there were sporadic damage readings trickling in from the container units to the aft. Sections of those modules were holed and losing life-support.

How many dead already? The horrible question made Saru sick as he contemplated it. *All those civilians back there. The old and the young. Ejah.*

He shook off the thought. There was no time to dwell on that. The Kelpien frantically tried to divide his attention between the control console in front of him and a secondary drive station to his right. It was hard work, dealing with a non-Starfleet interface and two sets of outputs, some of them in conflict, others in accord. Saru released a low gasp of exasperation as the ship rocked again and his head snapped up. He looked toward Weeton, and the ensign appeared every bit as beleaguered as Saru felt, trying to take in too much information at once, and run a cargo vessel never designed for combat through a deadly battle scenario.

There are too few of us up here. Half of the control podiums were unmanned, while Nathal, Hekan, and the others dashed from one to another, attempting to do the work of a full bridge crew. *And we are failing.*

That cold inevitability that always lurked in the back of Saru's thoughts crept forward. The sense of the coming of death, the fear that never left him, it was welling up. An old memory came with the sensation.

Saru remembered being a young child, cowering in a cave, still stiff legged and ropy of limb. He remembered seeing the fear in his mind's eye like a dark, glutinous mass of oil. Rising up to cover him, smother him. Until there was nothing left of the Kelpien called Saru, no intellect or reason or persona. The fear would drown him and fill every corner of his being. Then there would be nothing left but a terrified, quaking animal. He would be consumed.

His long fingers tightened into fists.

I. Will. Not. Submit.

Now, as he had then, he pushed back with all the

strength he could muster, struggling to free himself from the inexorable gravity of the terror. If he could just stop himself from giving in to the burning fear for a second more, for ten seconds more, a minute, then he could hold it back.

I am afraid, he told himself. *But it shall not rule me.*

"I can't hit him!" said Weeton, cursing under his breath. "Somebody give me a push on lateral control, and do it quickly!"

Vetch dithered over his panel. "Which one is that?"

"Red keypad, rotate through ninety degrees," Hekan called out from across the compartment.

"Red . . . ?" The Gorlan speaker faltered. He was out of his depth and he knew it. "I do not—"

"That one!" snarled Madoh, lurching over from the console he was using, stabbing a finger at the panel in front of Vetch.

"Too late," said the ensign, and he swore again as the ship weathered another shuddering impact. "That thing out there is going to carve us up like a turkey!"

"That would not be optimal," Saru replied, burying his darker emotions. The fear would come back—it always did—but not in this second, not in this minute. He would not allow it.

The Kelpien gripped the edges of the lectern-like podium in front of him and sucked in a breath over his tongue. The sense organs in the roof of his mouth tasted burnt plastic, perspiration, and the tang of ozone.

"We can't go on like this," he said. "Ensign Weeton is correct. We need to shift our strategy."

"Strategy?" echoed Nathal. "Did it escape your notice that this is a cargo barge, Lieutenant Saru, not a warship? The only tactics we have to hand are *run* and *run faster.*"

He raised a hand. "Respectfully, I disagree." Saru glanced

at Hekan. "Before, you talked about this ship's multiple tractor-beam arrays. Can you activate them?"

"You want me to channel power *away* from our shields and engines?"

"Yes." Saru gave a brisk nod. "And also, I am going to stop rolling the ship."

"You'll be handing that Tholian an easy target," said Nathal. "They can blow through the hull, target this deck! Kill us all with a single shot!"

"That is precisely what I hope they will attempt." He turned to Weeton. "Ensign, conserve your fire on all dorsal plasma turrets. Stand by to trigger them in unison on my order."

To his credit, Weeton didn't hesitate to follow the command. "Aye, sir. Reconfiguring."

"The Peliar makes a good point," snapped Madoh. "Have you suffered some kind of neural damage, outworlder?"

"Please, trust me." Saru took another deep breath and held it. "Here we go. Halting roll program . . . *now.*" He feathered the thruster controls to make it look like there had been a system failure, and the Tholian spinner took the bait.

The attacker bore down toward the bow, angling for a kill shot at the upper decks, just as Nathal had warned.

"He's coming in fast!" called Weeton.

"Hekan, the tractor beams," said Saru. "Calculate for the mass of the Tholian ship and snare it. Use every emitter you can!"

"That will overload our field coils," said Nathal.

"We don't need to hold it for long . . ." Saru looked back to Weeton. "Do we, Ensign?"

A wild grin broke out on the junior officer's face as he got what Saru was doing. "No, sir, we don't." His hands flashed over the weapons controls, copying Hekan's tractor target coordinates straight into the firing solutions for the plasma cannons.

"Brace for it," called Hekan as the Tholian ship dove at them. "Ready . . . ready . . . *now*!"

Bright emerald lines of light stabbed out from tractor beam emitters all along the upper fuselage of the starfreighter, converging on the slick silvery hull of the spinner and stopping it dead. The energy effect locked hard on to the crystalline vessel and the shock of momentum transfer resonated through the cargo ship's hull. Power regulators blew out in chugs of hot white smoke, and the bigger craft moaned.

Saru wondered what the Gorlans down in the cargo pods were thinking. Was the fear smothering them? Did they feel this, hear that, and believe that their end was at hand?

"Not today," Saru muttered.

On the main screen, the Tholian craft struggled against the pull of the tractors, the intercooler grids on its drives burning crimson as it tried to tear away.

Hekan coughed through the smoky air. "I can't hold it much longer!"

"Ensign," said Saru. "Fire all turrets."

"Firing!" Weeton slapped the flat of his palm over all the plasma-gun triggers, and they lit off in a bright ripple of light that converged on the shape of the Tholian attacker.

The alien craft splintered, and whole sections of the outer hull cleaved off, exposing glittering innards that resembled seams of glowing magma in a rock bed. It could have shrugged off one or two hits from the plasma cannons, but a strike from all of them at once, and with no way to avoid the impacts, doomed the spinner.

Hekan finally deactivated the tractors before their grids could overheat with the strain, but it had been enough. The

Tholian attacker fell away from the star-freighter, a trail of glassy pieces glittering behind it as it tumbled and spun. Saru heard a ragged cheer go up across the compartment as the other two spinners—one damaged and limping, the other still intact—swept past their companion ship and snagged the wreck with yellow web beams.

"They're breaking off . . ." said Nathal, stepping closer to his station. "Very impressive, Lieutenant Saru. I've never heard of the Tholians retreating before."

Saru tried to reach for a fraction of the elation that showed on the faces of Weeton, Vetch, and Hekan, but he found nothing but a grim certainty. "That is not a retreat." His hand drifted to the back of his scalp and the threat ganglia that still twitched there. "Have no doubt. They're coming back."

12

Saru's eyes widened as he studied the waveband readout on the shuttle's subspace radio panel. The message he attempted to send from the *Yang* was reflecting back at him in a shower of garbled echoes, his words broken up and distorted before the signal could even travel a few light-seconds.

He sighed and slumped back in the pilot's chair, looking out of the canopy but not really focusing on the view beyond. It was a near miracle that the shuttlecraft had survived the engagement with the Tholians and remained clamped, limpet-like, to the hull of the Peliar star-freighter. Close by, a particle cannon blast had ripped open a section of the transport ship's maintenance decks. Had it been aimed a few degrees to the starboard, the beam would have cut the *Yang* in half.

Still, the familiar confines of the shuttle were doing nothing to meter Saru's turbulent mood. He had not exaggerated when he told Commander Nathal that the Tholians would be back for another round. It was a known trait, a familiar battle tactic of their species, sending in a probing attack in the first instance to gain the measure of their enemy and following it up with a more heavily armed strike.

There *were* additional Tholian ships out there, he was certain of it. Saru squinted at the darkness outside, peering through the debris from the battle a few hours earlier, as if he might be able to pick out some sign of the glittering crystal ships from his vantage point.

The lieutenant couldn't see them, but the disruption of his attempts to contact the *Shenzhou* meant only one thing. The Tholians were broadcasting a scattering field throughout the system, blocking outgoing subspace radio signals and fogging long-range sensors. Three spinner ships would not be enough to do that, and he lost himself in contemplation of what size of flotilla the Assembly might have sent to the sanctuary system. *Five ships? Ten?* How many combat craft did a cargo vessel and a warship merit by the standards of the Tholian military?

"I have the unpleasant certainty that we're going to find out, sir," said a voice behind him.

Saru jolted with surprise and twisted in the seat to see Petty Officer Yashae climbing into the *Yang*'s rear compartment. He had been so deep in his own thoughts that he hadn't heard her cat-footed approach. "Was I speaking aloud?"

"Yes, sir." She managed a halfhearted smile. "Don't worry, I won't tell anyone." Yashae's milk-pale face and her blue uniform jumpsuit were blackened with smoke and grease, but she seemed unfazed by it.

"Report," said Saru, giving her his complete attention. If they made it through all this, the Kelpien was going to enter commendations in the log for Yashae, Zoxom, and the rest of the rescue party. Under the petty officer's guidance, they had evacuated the unconscious Saladin Johar and the rest of the people being held in the mess hall when the freighter's fire-suppression system had failed during the Tholian attack. The Vok'sha woman explained it all in a plain, matter-of-fact manner, but it was clear to Saru that she had deliberately put herself in danger several times in order to get the team and several of Nathal's crew to safety.

"The chief engineer is in the medical bay," she concluded. "Zoxom is there now with Subin. Last I saw, he was complaining about the Peliar doc-bots and patching up whoever needed it."

"You did well," said Saru.

She frowned. "I'm sorry we couldn't get to you, Lieutenant. I know you could have used more hands on deck up there."

He nodded. "We made do."

Yashae jutted her chin toward the communication panel. "Any luck reaching the *Shenzhou*?"

Saru met her gaze. He saw no point in being anything less than honest. "We are on our own."

"Can we warp out of here?"

He shook his head. "There is extensive damage to the engineering deck."

Yashae made a soft, spitting noise in her throat, a sound that Saru knew was a Vok'sha curse word. "All that work we did to get this ship up and running, undone in a matter of minutes. Johar is going to be really pissed off when he wakes up."

"He will be." For a second, Saru flashed back to what Ensign Weeton had previously suggested—that someone else be in command of this sorry situation—and contemplated how it would feel to give up the burden of this responsibility to an officer of superior rank.

Saru gave a faint shake of the head, dismissing the traitorous thought. The Kelpien had been in charge of personnel before, in training at the Academy, sometimes in task groups aboard the *Shenzhou*. But never like this. Never in a state where so many lives hung in the balance, where sentient beings would either survive or surely perish based on the choices he was making. Saru knew himself well enough to recognize that he could be arrogant at times, but this wasn't one of them. A good commander needed to be many things, to show strength when it was required, along with humility and compassion. He had never thought it would be so hard to strike a balance between those things, but now here he was, learning that lesson the hard way. Burnham had once spoken to him of a human axiom, something about being careful what you wished for, and now he saw the truth of it.

How does Captain Georgiou make this look so effortless? Saru wondered. He resolved to ask her.

If you live to see her again, said the faithless inner voice.

His communicator beeped, interrupting his train of thought. He snatched it up from his belt, flicking it open. "Saru here."

"Lieutenant, this is Weeton on the command tier." The ensign's voice was tense. *"Sir, you better get back up here. War is about to break out!"*

Saru thought he heard the sound of raised, angry voices in the background. "Have the Tholians returned?"

"Negative," said Weeton. *"It's the Gorlans and the Peliars. They're not listening to anything I say, and I think fists are gonna start flying any second!"*

"On my way." Saru snapped the communicator shut and vaulted out of the pilot's chair, toward the hatch in the floor.

"What should I do, sir?" said Yashae.

Saru gave her a *follow me* gesture. "I think I will need all the support I can muster."

"You are going to do the Tholians' work for them!" spat Nathal, cutting at the air in front of the Gorlans with the blade of her hand. "This will make things worse!"

"Do not speak to us like we are fools," snapped Madoh. He cast around, indicating the additional Gorlans who had arrived from the lower decks to fill the empty operator stations on the freighter's bridge. "You need us to fly this barge if there is any hope of evading the Tholian counterattack!"

"Everybody just calm down," said Weeton, trying to interpose himself between the two groups. "Madoh's right. With the Gorlans rounding out the numbers up here, we can pilot this ship properly. React faster, maybe get through this in one piece."

Nathal growled, looking to her second-in-command for support. "I agreed to accept help, but not from inexperienced neophytes. Has any one of them ever crewed a ship of this tonnage?"

"These men are former colony-ship crew," insisted Kijoh, her voice rising. "They can handle themselves."

"I do not share your confidence, Gorlan. We'll be killed by their incompetence before the Tholians fire a shot!"

Weeton didn't respond to Nathal's retort, partly because—if he was honest—he agreed with her. Twice already, the Gorlans had accidentally set off potentially lethal system conflicts in the big ship's control matrix by working the consoles incorrectly, and the ensign was afraid that when the shooting started again, any such mistake would prove fatal.

"Then get your own people to fly this Creator-forsaken hulk!" spat Vetch. "That's if your doting father will allow it!"

That was exactly the wrong *thing to say*, thought Weeton, and he saw Nathal's expression turn stony. "Commander, listen . . ."

She looked right through him, glaring at the Gorlan speaker. "The crew of the carrier have their own repairs to address. Their ship was hit much harder than this one." Nathal advanced on Vetch. "But as for my father, do you wish to prove him right? Gorlans are obstinate and primitive. Is that true? Are you too dense to be told what to do?"

All four of Vetch's hands came up to jab at Nathal. "Arrogant Peliar—"

"Stop right now!" Weeton turned to see a gangly figure emerge from the elevator, pointing his hand at them. The ensign had never heard Lieutenant Saru yell at anyone before, and his voice had a whip-crack edge to it that was hard to ignore.

Saru strode into the middle of the command deck with Yashae a couple of steps behind him, scanning the room with a hawkish glare. When the Kelpien unfolded to his full height, his hairless scalp was almost touching the ceiling of the compartment, and Weeton realized that all this time Saru had been purposefully slouching in order to bring himself closer to everyone else's eye level. Not so now; now Saru wanted all attention on him.

"As fascinating as it is to see sentients bickering in their natural habitat, it does not solve any of our current problems," he snapped, and Weeton thought he heard an echo of the *Shenzhou*'s captain in the lieutenant's delivery. "The fact that we are standing here proves that you are capable of working together in the face of a greater crisis! Like it or not, we are in an alliance. Starfleet, Gorlan, and Peliar. The Tholian Assembly considers *all* of us to be alien intruders. Division now will result in our destruction."

A weighty silence fell across the bridge in the wake of his words, and Saru let the moment stretch, let them all dwell on the harsh truth behind what he had said. For Nathal and Hekan and the other Peliars, there was only their individual sense of the fear that simmered beneath the surface; but for Saru, the undercurrent of *anger-terror-frustration* was raw and real and present. He could feel it in the dissonant aura-fields being projected by every one of the Gorlans. The ghostly sensation of their emotional states made the spiracles in his skin itch. He felt their dread prickling the air, akin to the pressure of a far-off thunderstorm. Saru was the only non-Gorlan who could consciously sense it.

The Peliars might pick up on it in some subliminal way, unknowingly reacting in opposition and feeding the negativity, but they could never know it as he did. The intimacy of it, the sense of creeping doom that would sustain itself if they let it.

The fragile coalition that had formed in the face of the Tholian threat was in danger of crumbling. That could not be allowed to happen.

"I do not doubt the commitment of the Gorlans," said Nathal, reeling in her earlier irritation. "But I am afraid this task may be beyond them." Kijoh was about to answer, and Nathal pressed on. "You are all civilian spacers. You are not battle trained, as Peliar Zel crews are. This ship may be a transport vessel, but every one of my people aboard it is a graduate of our military college."

"We are not warriors, this is true," admitted Madoh. "But Gorlans are *fighters*. If the Creator had not made us so, then we would not have lived to carve out colonies on dozens of unyielding worlds."

A thought formed in Saru's mind, and he took a deep breath, preparing himself. All through this ill-fated mission, the Kelpien had been struggling against the tide of events, trying time and again to find the right path, to do the right thing—and each time he found himself trying to convince others to go against their innate natures. *Can I make them see?* The question weighed heavily on him. *Do I have a choice?*

"Madoh. Kijoh." He looked down at the Gorlans. "Nathal is right, and as much as I wish it were so, no amount of sheer will is going to suffice. There needs to be unity here. Your people need to work as one, not as individuals."

"No . . ." Madoh raised his arms. He already knew what

was coming. "You cannot ask that of us. Do not say the words, Saru. *Do not!*"

But he did. "You must bring Ejah up here. You must bring the hub to this place and let her do what she does best. Unify the will of the Gorlans."

"No!" Madoh's rage flared crimson in his cheeks, and he gestured with the red bands around his wrists flashing. "You know what this means, don't you? I protect her! I will not put her in harm's way!"

"We are all in harm's way," Saru replied, keeping his voice level. "And we will all die, the hub along with us, if the Tholians are not driven off. You know this." He looked to Kijoh. "I know you can sense my aura just as I can sense yours. Does it shade toward duplicity? Do you believe that I am lying to you?"

"You do not lie," said Kijoh at length, sighing deeply. "But what you ask . . . Ejah is our most precious gift."

"I know." Saru's head bobbed in a nod. "But you need her here more than you need her to be isolated away in some hidden chamber down below." He spread his hands, tipping back his head a few degrees. For a Kelpien, this was the ultimate gesture of submission, of openness, showing his naked throat and offering no defense against an outsider. "Ejah can help us all. Her abilities . . ." Saru struggled to find the right words. "They'll give us an edge against the Tholians."

"She is holy to us," Madoh retorted. "She is a living link to the Creator. She must not be sullied by such things!"

Two of Kijoh's hands reached up and touched her comrade's shoulder. "You have sacrificed so much for our people, brother. Have you done so only for us to die here, in this nameless place? Saru is right. This is a matter of life and death for our colony, and for the Peliars and these Starfleet officers."

Madoh angrily shook her off. "I will not permit it!" One of his hands dropped to the hilt of a knife in his belt, and he retreated backward. Other Gorlans, most of them red-bands, instinctively moved to his side. "Find another way!"

"What would Ejah say if you asked her?" Saru stepped forward to block Madoh's path. He was very aware that if the Gorlan drew his blade, there would be little he could do to stop him from plunging it into his chest. "Do you have the right to make this choice for her?"

Make him see, said a voice in his head. It sounded like Michael Burnham.

"You are afraid," Saru went on. "I feel it radiating out of you like heat from a fire. I know that sensation. I live with it every day. But I overcome. I adapt. I ask you to do the same."

"I will not risk her life!" Madoh shouted the words in his face, and Saru saw the silver crescent of the curved knife flash as it emerged from its sheath.

It is not your place to decide. The soft, unspoken voice was suddenly there in Saru's thoughts.

Every one of the Gorlans froze, and Madoh's blade slipped from his fingers, clattering to the deck by Saru's hoofed boots. "Ejah," he breathed.

Saru *felt* her before he saw her, even as he turned back to the open elevator at the rear of the compartment. It was as if a breeze of cool, soothing air had passed across him, pushing away the coiling, heavy smoke of all the doubts and the fears.

The hub stood in her shabby white robes on the threshold of the command tier, looking around with open interest. A pair of muscular red-bands were escorting her, but they seemed uneasy, as if they were caught between the compulsion to obey her and the desire to grab Ejah and rush her back to a place of security. Moving with difficulty on her withered leg, she advanced into the room and her gaze briefly found Saru's. She smiled at him, then sought out Madoh. "Kindred, what are you doing?"

Her words broke the spell holding Madoh in place, and the Gorlan pushed past Saru, rushing to Ejah's side. "You cannot be here! You must go below, where it is safer—"

"Is it safer there?" she said, cutting across his words. "There are new dead and new wounded in the cargo modules, lives lost and others forever changed by that first attack." Ejah glanced at Saru. "I called them to crowd into the most forward pods, the ones closest to the sections of the ship where the hull is thickest, and abandon the other modules. Better that we cluster together in this than face adversity without community."

"Who brought you?" Madoh turned his ire on the two escorts. "Who told you to bring her up here?"

"She told them," said Saru, seeing the moment unfold as if he had been there. "I am right, aren't I? She knew this was going to come to pass. The hub saw it coming."

Ejah's head bobbed. "Sometimes the path is clearest when there is darkness all around. I go where I am needed."

"I beg you," Madoh was imploring her, his eyes shining. "Please, Ejah. Return to the others. They need you!"

"I will not!" The hub spoke sharply, drawing herself up. Saru saw that one of her hands was freshly bandaged, possibly from a burn, but she showed no signs of distress. "I am not made of spun glass, Madoh, I will not break beneath the slightest pressure! The ones who need me most are in this room." She limped across to where Saru and Nathal were standing and gave them both a nod. "Show me what to do. And be swift." Her gaze briefly lost focus and turned inward. "They're coming. In greater numbers. In all the possible paths, I see them coming."

"How can she help the Gorlans to better fly and fight?" said Nathal, studying the slight female with open dismay. "I don't understand."

"I am the hub," Ejah said simply.

"She will give her people focus and unity," Saru explained.

"We could all use some of that," muttered Weeton.

"And she has other talents." Saru frowned. Now that he was about to say it aloud, he realized how it would sound. *I believe she can see the future.* "Ejah possesses a latent precognitive sense. A telepathic ability."

Nathal's incredulity showed on her face. "You want us to put our trust in a *seer*?" She made the last word an insult.

Ejah leaned close to the Peliar commander and spoke quietly. Saru barely caught the exchange between them. "You love your father, yes? Despite everything he has said and done."

"Yes . . ."

"You will regret it if you do not tell him." The hub's words struck Nathal silent.

A strident chiming issued out from a vacant console, and Yashae stepped up to it. She visibly balked at what she read on the display there. "Lieutenant! I have a message coming in from Adjutant Craea on the warship. He says their sensors are picking up objects moving through the edge of the scattering field. Tholian ships, four of them this time."

"Confirmed," added Hekan, bringing up a holographic projection. "All four vessels are vectoring straight toward the Peliar warship. It's the same pair that attacked them before, this time with reinforcements."

"Makes sense," said Weeton. "They're going to concentrate their firepower on the warship, take it out of play first. Then it'll be our turn."

Saru felt a tug on his sleeve, and he looked down to see Ejah at his side. She pointed at Hekan's holograph. "I need to see that."

He blinked, unsure what she meant. "You are seeing it."

"Not with these." Ejah pointed at her eyes, then took Saru's hand and pressed it to her forehead. "With this." He felt a strange tingling in his palm and abruptly he realized he was touching the Gorlan sense organ that generated their aura-fields. "Do you understand? I can only help if I see the way this ship sees."

She wants me to connect her to the star-freighter's sensors. Saru's thoughts unspooled in a sudden rush. It was possible, of course. He could reprogram his tricorder to interpret the scanner outputs and render them not as text or images, but as a mild electromagnetic field. "I can do that. There's just one thing. It will be painful for you."

Ejah nodded. "I know. I trust you, Saru."

He took a deep breath and set to work. "Prepare yourself."

The Tholians were not ones to allow a mistake to stand.

On their first engagement with the intruder craft, they had determined that the vessels of the Peliar Zel were, at best, a minor risk to their forces, and dispatched a flight of warcraft commensurate with the threat represented by the aliens.

The Tholians had engaged ships from the Peliar moons on several occasions in the past, and in every incident it had been the carbon-based forms that had perished in their entirety. The Tholians were very good at making sure the aggressor races surrounding their territory remained afraid of them, ensuring that no distress calls were ever sent by their targets, and no wreckage was ever found of the ships they destroyed. The remains of any intruder craft were spirited back to Tholia encased in energy webs, where they could be picked apart and analyzed. In this way, the Assembly grew stronger and more knowledgeable about its enemies, while the outsiders could only become more fearful of them and puzzle over the disappearances of their ships and crews.

The Tholian Assembly considered the Peliars a low-level threat. A minor local power, lacking the skill or resources of larger aggressor states like the Federation. Thus, when two Peliar craft had not only driven off a flight of spinner ships but actually *crippled* one of them, there was an immediate reevaluation of the tactical scenario. An error of judgment had been made. It would immediately be rectified.

Four spinners powered in at maximum sublight velocity toward the craft identified earlier as a military fighter-carrier. The Peliars were still in the process of recovery operations for their inert drones, and they were caught off guard by the second assault wave.

This time, rather than deploy the power-hungry energy-dampening weapon for a primary strike, the Tholians went for a split-pincer attack pattern, their tight approach coming open in a spiraling starburst that spread them across the defense zone. Guns on the carrier opened up with desultory bursts, but the swift crystal arrowheads spun out of the firing line. In return, they sent back lashes of crimson particles, beams cutting through the blackness, revealing the deflector shield perimeters as the strikes hit home and battered the protective energy envelopes.

The carrier was a dedicated combat vessel, and it was built to withstand a sustained attack, but the Tholians fathomed its weaknesses and struck at them. Shield emitters, pushed to their limits by one direct hit after another, buckled and finally failed.

Shots from the dancing spinner ships slammed into the unprotected hull and the Peliar vessel trembled up and down the length of its curved fuselage. Atmospheric gas and sparking discharges from severed power trains bled into the vacuum. Robbed of its defenses, unable to launch its fighter drones, the carrier was a slow, heavy target waiting to be carved apart by the Tholian attackers.

"They're going to destroy it," said Kijoh, aghast at the ruthless efficiency with which the Tholians were assaulting the Peliar carrier. "Like carrion birds tearing at a wounded herd beast."

Saru looked to Nathal, and he saw doubt in the brusque Peliar woman's expression. "Commander?" he prompted.

She took a step closer, her voice dropping. "The initial attack . . . that was my first taste of real, open battle. I confess it has left me challenged." Nathal frowned, angry at her own words, but she quickly smothered the reaction. "Lieutenant Saru, I would welcome your input."

Flee. The impulse came from somewhere deep, dark, and primal in him. The Kelpien resisted the urge to say the word and stiffened. "We must disrupt the Tholian attack on the carrier."

"Agreed, but the range of our weapons is limited," she noted. "We would need to close to almost point-blank range."

Saru dwelled on Kijoh's description of the attack—*the carrion birds and the herd beast*—and he recalled something from his homeworld, a sight he had seen with his own eyes as a youth. The *ba'ul* would drive away packs of scavengers from their kills with shows of aggression. Perhaps the same could be done with the Tholians.

"Indeed," he said. "But we should use the other weapon at our disposal. *This ship.*"

"You want to *charge* them?" Kijoh understood immediately. "That's a bold move."

"It's one we can accomplish," said Nathal, regaining

some of her earlier steel. She shot Ejah a look. "Can you make them work together, Gorlan? I need to know."

"I can," said the hub. Her hands were trembling as she gripped Saru's tricorder. "We can."

"We can," repeated Madoh. "We will."

"All sublight drives to full power!" Nathal gave the order and the star-freighter lurched forward. "Saru, I am ceding helm control to you. Don't make me regret trusting you."

"Commander." He accepted the order and splayed his hands out over the podium. Saru's throat turned arid, and all of a sudden the collar of his uniform felt tight and restricting, but he buried those distractions.

"Power curve is stable," said Kijoh.

Madoh nodded. "Thrust matrix, stable."

"Together," whispered Ejah, and somehow her soft voice carried across the compartment. "We move together."

The hub's soothing aura washed over Saru and the tension in him ebbed. He had to resist the urge to look down at her, to wonder how it was she was able to do this. Before, the subtle electroemotional fields shared by the Gorlans were a dissonant clash of conflicting fears and doubts. Now they were meshing like the cogs of an invisible machine, the calm and the focus extending out to touch each one in turn.

Ejah breathed in and out in long, slow gasps, and as Saru watched, every Gorlan on the command deck fell into the exact same rhythm. *It was working.*

"Lieutenant Saru, take us in," said Nathal. "We will follow your lead."

He nodded and stared into the depths of the main viewer. "Turret guns, fire at will. Our aim is to interrupt their attack pattern, not to destroy them."

"Sir, do you want to try that tractor beam trick again?" asked Weeton.

"They won't fall for it a second time, Ensign," Saru

replied. "Put all available power to forward shields and the inertial dampers. Make sure the refugees in the cargo modules are protected!"

"Working on it," came the reply.

The big transport ship was moving swiftly now, gathering momentum. On the screen, the mass of the Peliar carrier and its attackers loomed large. The first of the Tholian spinners reacted to the oncoming juggernaut and broke off from its attack pattern, drawing back toward its fellows.

"They see us," said Yashae. "Reading increased transmissions between all Tholian vessels."

"They're wondering what we are doing," said Madoh. "Perhaps they think we are going to run."

"They will fire . . ." Ejah tugged on Saru's sleeve, and he heard the pain in her voice. "I see it." Her eyes screwed tightly shut, she reached out another hand and pointed at an area on Saru's vector screen. "There."

"Tholians are locking weapons on us!" shouted Weeton.

"Brace yourselves!" Saru thumbed a lateral thruster control and the freighter listed sharply to port—just as a lance of searing crimson fire issued from the prow of a Tholian ship and cut through the space where Ejah had indicated.

"Here," she said, touching a different place. Saru felt her aura surround him. She was trying to bring him into the unity, guide him just as the hub was guiding all her kindred.

Saru silenced a jolt of panic and allowed it to happen. They moved in coordination, weaving the giant ship back and forth through the oncoming torrent of beam fire. Glancing shots flared off the deflectors but still the bulky freighter's reaction was too swift for the Tholians to concentrate their firepower for more than a few seconds at a time.

The spinners were drawing back, and Saru wondered if they had decided to deploy the energy dampeners after all. The weapon would upset all their plans if it was triggered.

We must ensure it is not, he told himself, and he dragged the big ship's vector around to aim it right at the heart of the Tholian squadron's formation.

"Give me maximum thrust," said Saru. "And hold fast!"

The star-freighter bulled its way through the debris field left by the earlier engagement and into a headlong course toward the spinner ships. At the last second, the Tholian craft broke away in four different directions, forced to disengage and fall back from their attack on the wounded carrier or risk a collision.

Saru glimpsed one of the dagger-shaped ships barely avoid clashing its shields with the freighter's, and he saw the red blur of its engine grids as it came about, pivoting to track them.

"It worked!" called Weeton. "They've stopped shooting at the Peliars!" He gave a wild grin and words spilled out of him. "I could have made a crack about *playing chicken* there and I didn't—"

"Look sharp, talk less!" Saru retorted, channeling Captain Georgiou once more. "Perhaps if we live through this, you can explain to me the connection between Terran poultry animals and keeping one's nerve . . . but not now!"

"They're coming after us," whispered Ejah, but Saru didn't need her to tell him. He could see the Tholian craft following their leader, extending into a skirmish line to pursue the transport ship. "You've angered them."

"Good," said Nathal. "They're reacting instead of thinking; we need to exploit that." She looked to Saru. "The aft cargo modules are all vacated now, yes?"

"Yes," Ejah answered for him. The strain in her reply was clear.

Nathal turned to her second-in-command. "Hekan, give the Tholians something else to think about, keep them off balance. Release the empty modules into our impulse wake."

"Complying," said the engineer.

Saru felt the tremor run along the deck and up through his hooves. On a secondary viewer, he saw a dozen huge metallic cubes suddenly detach from the freighter's flanks and tumble away. The lead Tholian ship was too close, and as it whirled into a punishing thruster turn, one of the large container pods slammed into it, becoming a cloud of steel splinters. The spinner ship fell into an uncontrolled tumble, and Saru saw it drop off the bottom of the viewscreen, captured by the powerful gravity well of the nearby planet.

In response to this act, the remaining three Tholians opened fire as one, spraying the rear of the star-freighter with high-energy blasts.

"Weeton!" Saru called out to the junior officer. "Can you vent the warp plasma from our drive nacelles?"

The question took the ensign off guard. "I guess I could . . . but we, well, we need that for warp drive."

Saru's eyes narrowed. "I am aware of how the technology works."

"What are you thinking, Kelpien?" demanded Madoh. "Your man is right. Release that plasma and we lose the ability to go to warp."

"It would take hours to replenish," agreed Hekan.

"Does anyone here truly believe the Tholians will allow us to run?" Saru asked the question of all of them, and it seemed strange to hear the words coming from his own lips. "A trapped animal's reaction is always *fight or flight.* I believe only the former option is open to us."

"You want them to catch us?" Madoh pressed, his irritation flaring.

"Kindred," said Ejah, silencing him with a word. "We trust Saru. Let him proceed."

Nathal gave a reluctant nod. "Agreed."

"Venting warp plasma . . . *now.*" Weeton tapped out

a command string on his panel, and the secondary viewer fogged as a mass of shimmering white-gray vapor ejected from the ring of engine nacelles around the hull of the star-freighter. At the same moment, Saru deliberately put the ship into an off-kilter spin, simulating a loss of control at the helm.

"The Tholians have ceased fire," reported Yashae. "They must think we took a hit to our guidance systems."

"Let's not give them time to consider the question," said Saru. His voice was on the verge of cracking, but he kept on. "All turret guns, aim aft." Saru's hands were trembling, and he placed them flat on the panel in front of him to try and halt the reaction.

"You want me to point the guns right at the cloud of highly unstable plasma?" Weeton's expression shifted as he spoke. "Oh. *Okay.*"

"Tholian ships are changing course," called Yashae. "Sir, they're onto us!"

"Fire!" Saru shouted out the order, hating how desperate he sounded. "All turrets!"

A stream of energy bolts spat from the transport ship's meager weapons array, streaking past the Tholians and into the mass of the swiftly dissipating plasmatic fog. Where the blasts passed through the gaseous matter, an uncontrolled energetic reaction lit off, and sheets of fire exploded into being, spreading in flash-burn surges across the star-freighter's wake.

Empty cargo modules tumbling through the haze were caught by the effect and torn apart, adding to the chaos. Bright jags of thermic discharge whipped across, raking over the Tholian spinners as they desperately tried to get away from the brief, fierce inferno.

On the far side of the plasma cloud, the wounded Peliar carrier seized the opportunity to add its firepower to the surprise attack. The carrier sent a spread of merculite rockets from its missile tubes to put up a wall of detonations behind the Tholian attackers. Without warning, the spinners found themselves trapped in a hell storm of plasmatic flame.

The sensors registered massive secondary surges of ignition, and Saru's gut lurched as he realized he was looking at the Tholian ships being destroyed. He felt sick inside. *But they left you no choice*, said the Burnham voice in his mind.

A single wounded Tholian spinner burst out of the fire as it dissolved, scored black with damage and trailing pieces of itself. The craft bolted away at maximum impulse and raced toward the edge of sensor range.

The gathered collective on the transport ship's bridge let out a ragged cheer as they watched the attacker flee, but Saru couldn't summon the emotion to join with them in their shared victory. He felt hollowed out and heavy with fatigue, as if he had aged months in the blink of an eye.

"Incoming signal from the carrier," called Yashae. "Adjutant Craea passes on a message from Admiral Tauh. He wants his daughter to know that the Cohort will be impressed by her conduct."

"Tell him our allies deserve the credit," said Nathal.

Saru barely registered the conversation as he and Ejah watched the viewscreen and the shrinking dot of the surviving Tholian, while all around them Federation, Gorlan, and Peliar citizens clapped each other on the back and exchanged words of thanks.

Ejah looked away, toward the secondary screen showing the wreckage left behind by the brief battle. "Creator, absolve them," she said to herself. "This is violence done out of necessity, not desire."

"You give an entreaty for those that would have destroyed you," said the Kelpien.

"It is for you as well as them," she said, looking up at him. "I know you, Saru. I know the will to go to this extreme comes hard for a being of your kind."

He gave a brief, bitter smile. "A timid recreant, you mean?"

Ejah reached out and touched his hand. "I mean one who knows what it is to see the face of death. You went against your nature to fight for us."

"I could do nothing else," he said, and found he meant every word. Saru released a gasp of air, as if he had been holding it in all along. "At least we can breathe now."

"Not yet." His blood ran cold at the note of soft reproach in the hub's voice. "It isn't over."

"Lieutenant?" Something in Weeton's tone rang a warning in Saru's mind, and the Kelpien briefly abandoned his station, racing across to the ensign's side in three quick strides.

"Tell me," he said.

Weeton couldn't find the words, so he just pointed. The tactical scan visible on his screen showed a segment of the star system, the curve of the orbit of the sanctuary planet and indicator sigils for the Peliar ships. As Weeton manipulated the graphic to zoom out and show a larger area, the icon designating the fleeing Tholian appeared on the edge of sensor range, and beyond it the fuzzy boundary of the scattering field the aliens had deployed earlier.

Two new icons resolved at the scan's perimeter. One was another of the spinner ships, identical in mass and configuration to the craft that had been dogging them for the last few hours. The other was at least eight times the size of the smaller vessel, and even at this distance the freighter's sensor pallet was reading power outputs comparable to one of Starfleet's newer *Constitution*-class ships or a Klingon D10 battle cruiser.

Saru couldn't stop himself from looking up, across to where the hub was standing. Ejah was staring right at him, a terrible kind of knowing in her eyes.

It isn't over. She silently repeated the ominous statement.

"They're moving to regroup with the survivor." Weeton found his voice at last. "Lieutenant, I've never even *heard* of a Tholian ship of that type before."

"I believe that is because no one who has seen one has lived to speak of it," Saru replied.

"That's not very encouraging, sir," said Weeton.

"When you have faced death as often as I have, you tend to develop a clear-eyed perception of the reality of things, Ensign." Saru stepped away from the console and walked back toward his own panel.

The elation that had spread through the group was gone, and in its place a darker mood was settling. Against her better judgment, Ejah's bleak foreknowledge was bleeding into the unity of the Gorlans, silencing them, and the Peliars quickly picked up on the shifting temper around them.

"What is wrong?" said Nathal.

"It seems our respite will be brief, Commander," Saru told her. "The Tholians are regrouping for another attack. I don't know if we can resist them a third time." It cut him like a blade to admit it, and that inward voice of his cried out in defiance of the fate he knew they were going to face.

A flurry of possibilities rose and fell in his thoughts. Could they evacuate the refugees back to the sanctuary planet, perhaps even land the freighter? Would they be any safer down there than up here in orbit? Would the Tholians even entertain the thought of accepting a surrender after the blood that had been shed? Was there something he was missing, some shred of hope that he could grasp, some tactic he could employ to stave off destruction for just a little longer?

In Saru's darkest nightmares, he would feel the hot breath of a *ba'ul* upon the bare flesh of his neck, hear the rumble of its massive beating heart, and smell the stinking raw-meat odor of its exhalations. In the dream, in the blackness of it, the moment would never end. The terrible fear in the instant before the hulking predator struck, stretched out into infinity. *Death reaching for him, shrouded in the certainty that it was inescapable.*

He felt that now, shaded by a great sorrow. Saru had always believed he would perish alone, but it would not be so. Ejah and the Gorlans, Nathal and her people, Weeton and Yashae, and everyone else who had put their faith in Saru, they would all follow him to the end. *I am sorry*, he wanted to say. *This is all my fault.*

"I'm getting a new hail," said Yashae, breaking the grim hush.

"The Tholians?" Kijoh's voice had a brief note of hopefulness, perhaps that they might still find a way out of this—but the Vok'sha shook her head.

"Not Tholian . . ." Her brow furrowed as she tried to lock down the transmission. "The scattering field is making it hard to read. It's not a Peliar Zel signal either, I don't . . ."

"Let me hear it," ordered the lieutenant.

Yashae did as she was ordered, but the sound issuing from the command deck's speakers was thick with distortion and grating echo effects.

Saru pulled up a repeater panel and saw the incoming subspace wavebands. The pattern wasn't alien. It was *familiar*. "This is a . . . a Starfleet frequency!"

"Sensor contact!" called Weeton. "Another ship, emerging from behind the planet's magnetosphere!"

"Attention," said a voice. It was roughened by static and interference, but to Saru's ears, it was as clear as a bolt from the blue. *"This is Captain Philippa Georgiou of the* Starship Shenzhou. *We stand ready to assist."*

13

"We've cleared the planet's mass shadow," reported Detmer at the helm.

"Red alert, shields up!" called Commander ch'Theloh, shouldering forward over his control station. "Be ready for anything."

Michael Burnham looked past the Andorian, out through the ports of the *Shenzhou*'s bridge, and into a scene of chaos. "Are we too late?"

"Detecting a large debris field in close proximity to the Peliar ships," said Ensign Troke, the Tulian's face shading toward azure as he spoke. "Decay particles from sustained weapon fire, traces of excited warp plasma, tritanium, and cytocrystalline fragments . . ." He trailed off. "It's a war zone."

Only minutes earlier, the *Shenzhou*'s sensors had tracked a large energy surge on the far side of the sanctuary world, but their stealthy approach keeping the planet between them and their target had rendered them unable to directly monitor the event. Now Burnham realized that what they had seen was the wake of a destructive act of desperation. She looked down at her own panel.

"Admiral Tauh's carrier is at two-five-two mark three," Burnham noted. "The Peliar freighter is five thousand kilometers off our starboard bow. Both ships have suffered major damage."

Captain Georgiou acknowledged Burnham's words with a terse nod. "Mister Gant, where are the Tholians?"

"Holding at three-zero-eight mark zero," said the tactical officer. "Three vessels. One rather large one."

Georgiou twisted in the command chair, shooting a look toward the communications station. "Ensign Fan, any reply to our messages?"

The young woman nodded. "I have a response. It's Lieutenant Saru!"

"Give me holographic," snapped the captain, and she rose up out of her seat as a shimmering, hazy image of the Kelpien formed out of the air in the middle of the bridge.

Burnham couldn't help herself and stepped forward to get a better look at the errant officer. Saru seemed pale and worn out, but still he stood stiffly to attention as he realized his commander was addressing him. *"Captain. I am very pleased to see you."*

"You may come to think otherwise, Lieutenant," Georgiou said tersely. "Let's cut straight to the heart of this. What the hell happened out here?"

Saru opened and closed his mouth, then launched into an explanation. *"Some of the Gorlans compelled us to assist them in hijacking this transport ship. We recovered their people from the planet below, then regained control of the vessel from them shortly before Peliar reinforcements arrived . . . and so did the Tholians. We have been attempting to resist them."*

"So, you go off book and start a war with the Tholian Assembly?" Georgiou shook her head. "I'll say this for you, Saru, you don't aim low."

Saru looked chastened. *"Actually, they opened fire first."*

"I'm sure there's a lot more to it than that," said ch'Theloh.

"There is," admitted Saru, *"which I will cover in a de-*

tailed report if we survive the next few minutes. The Tholians are massing for another attack."

"He's right," said Burnham, watching the sensor feed on her screen. "The spinners are moving into battle posture."

"Fan, any contact from the Tholians?" said the captain.

"Negative," replied the communications officer. "I'm hailing them on all general frequencies, but they're ignoring us."

Georgiou gave her exec a nod, and ch'Theloh ordered Gant to power up the *Shenzhou*'s weapons systems. "All right, Mister Saru. You've done enough for one day, I think." The captain waved him aside. "Get that ship and those people away from the conflict zone. We'll cover your retreat."

"Retreat to where, Captain?" said Saru. *"There's nowhere we can escape to."*

"Detmer, put us between the Tholian approach and the star-freighter!" Georgiou grimaced as Burnham saw the same harsh truth behind Saru's words that the captain had. "Gant, pick your targets!"

Saru was still speaking. He leaned forward, imploring them. *"We can still help you!"*

"How?" said Burnham.

The Kelpien shot a nervous look off to the right, beyond the range of the holographic pickup. *"Let us just say the Gorlans have a unique predictive advantage."*

Georgiou hesitated, and Burnham touched her arm. "Captain, we're seriously outmatched here. Any additional edge has to be useful."

"Agreed," said Georgiou, after a moment. "Saru, tie in with Lieutenant Gant and feed him whatever information you have."

"Aye, Captain."

"Tholian ships are accelerating to attack speed!" called

Januzzi from the ops console. "Two spinner-type vessels, one unknown cruiser-scale craft."

"Reading prefire emissions from multiple particle-beam weapons," added Troke.

"One last try," muttered the captain, and she made a gesture to Ensign Fan. "Mary, open a channel." Georgiou took a breath as the long, skeletal mass of the Peliar freighter slipped by beneath the *Shenzhou*'s bridge. "Attention, Tholian vessels. We have no desire to escalate this situation any further. Deactivate your weapons and fall back, and we will do the same. We can discuss—"

"They're going to fire, break off!" shouted Saru. His hologram crackled and abruptly vanished.

Burnham's hand came up to shield her eyes as a savage burst of red light flashed across the *Shenzhou*'s bow.

"Hard to port!" Ch'Theloh barked out the command and Detmer complied, veering off as a punishing salvo of energy bolts crashed through the space that the starship had just occupied.

A glancing strike clipped the deflectors along the bottom of the engine nacelles as the *Shenzhou* banked like a starfighter, straining the ship's inertial dampers to the limit. Burnham grabbed at her console to steady herself as the vessel shuddered.

Through a port in the deck of the bridge, she saw a silvery shape streak past as the leading ship—one of the arrow-like spinners—crossed their course in a swift, jousting pass. More pulses of crimson light flashed, and Detmer hauled the ship around to avoid them.

"So much for talking," growled ch'Theloh.

Georgiou nodded grimly. "Fire aft torpedo!"

"Torpedo away!" Gant stabbed at a control and released a glowing missile into the *Shenzhou*'s wake, sending the photon warhead streaking after the spinner.

Burnham saw the detonation as the torpedo crashed against the Tholian ship's deflectors, knocking it off course but doing only minimal damage.

"Bring us around and pursue." The first officer stalked across to Detmer's station. "They'll find we're not so easy a target as some bulk hauler."

The view through the forward screens swung around as the *Shenzhou* pivoted and brought its bow to bear on the spinner. "He's trying to shake us off," said Burnham. She read the frantic jolts of thrust from the Tholian's impulse drives as the vessel's crew attempted to extend away from the Starfleet vessel.

Ch'Theloh was right. Up until now, the Tholians had only engaged the heavy, slow Peliar craft in combat. Facing off against a Federation ship of the line, even an aging boat like a *Walker* class, was a very different matter.

"Target phasers on his engine coils and fire!" Georgiou called the order and Gant obeyed, but the shots went wide as the Tholian suddenly rolled out from target lock.

"They're trying to pull us away from the main engagement." Burnham saw the tactic unfolding in her thoughts and spoke without thinking. "Divide our forces."

"All the more reason to disable him quickly," said ch'Theloh.

"Captain Georgiou!" Saru's hologram reappeared across the bridge as the interrupted communications link was reestablished. *"Your target will bank to port, then snap starboard . . . in ten seconds!"*

"Where is he getting this?" said the Andorian.

"Does it matter, sir?" Burnham shot back. "It was right before."

"Good point," agreed the captain. "Tactical! Photon torpedoes, proximity detonation, narrow spread, starboard quadrant!" She pointed out through the viewer. "On the mark!"

"Burnham, sound the count," said ch'Theloh.

"Seven. Six. Five." She called out the numbers, and on cue, the Tholian spinner made a sudden, sharp banking motion across the blackness.

"Target going hard to port!" called Detmer.

"Four. Three. Two." Burnham's breath caught in her throat as the Tholian veered back in the direction it had come, tumbling wildly to starboard. "He's reversing course!"

Gant didn't need to hear the order again. "Torpedo spread away!"

This time, three streaks of light burst from the launch tubes beneath the *Shenzhou*'s primary hull, seemingly aimed straight at empty space. But the fleeing spinner ship turned straight into the path of the photon torpedoes and their detonation surge as the warheads lit off in a fire chain.

"Direct hit!" Troke punched the air with a balled fist.

The Tholian craft lost its shields and then its power as the antimatter blast ripped into its engines and crippled the alien warship. It spun off into an end-over-end tumble.

"They're out of play," Georgiou said briskly. "Helm, bring us about. We still have work to do."

Burnham went to her station as the *Shenzhou* turned back into the fight, pulling up the sensor feed to track the other two Tholians. The second spinner was swinging wide of the engagement and moving slowly, likely because of damage sustained in an earlier exchange of fire, but the larger cruiser was homing in on the wounded warship.

The Peliar warship launched what was left of its autonomous fighters, but the Tholians picked them off almost as soon as they left their silos. The Tholian cruiser was a triad of great jagged talons, with a primary hull formed from an elongated tetrahedron and two arching claws rising and falling from its dorsal and ventral surfaces. Hard, blue-white glows gathered at their tips, throbbing as they emitted lethal threads of phased energy. A light brushed over the length of the warship, seeding a line of orange fireballs behind it.

"Fire on that ship," ordered the captain. "Give them something else to think about."

Shenzhou's phasers sent out a barrage, but at this range the Tholian cruiser shrugged it off and kept on pummeling the Peliar warship. Burnham saw the survivability numbers spiraling down and down on her readout as the carrier's hull integrity dropped by the second. "They're not going to make it," she breathed.

"Captain." Saru's image was wavering in and out, but his voice was still clear. *"We are bringing the freighter closer. Can you distract the cruiser's attention and give us cover fire?"*

"I thought I gave you an order to stay out of trouble, Lieutenant," said Georgiou.

"Respectfully, Captain, the vessel I am aboard is under Commander Nathal's authority, not yours."

"Done," said the captain, unwilling to argue the point. "Try not to get yourself killed, Saru."

"That is my intention every day of my life," said Saru, slightly confused by the statement. *"Good luck."* His image faded away again and Burnham looked up, catching Ensign Troke's eye.

"Scanners are picking up energy fluctuations in the starfreighter's systems," said the Tulian. "They're diverting power to their transporter grid."

"Saru's going to try to beam the survivors off the carrier," said Burnham.

"He'd better hurry," snapped ch'Theloh. "Their warp core is destabilizing."

"Let's give the lieutenant what he needs," Georgiou broke in. "Detmer, put us on an attack course with the Tholian cruiser. We're going to pick a fight with the bigger kid."

The *Shenzhou* flashed past on the command deck's main monitor, and Saru shared a fearful silence with Weeton and Yashae as the three of them watched their ship race into danger.

Saru felt strangely abstracted from events. Part of him felt like he should be over there, on the bridge with Captain Georgiou. He had a sudden, terrible vision of the *Shenzhou* battered by enemy fire, her hull raked by beam weapons as a rain of escape pods jetted away.

Two of Ejah's hands clasped around his wrist, and he had to pull himself away from the viewscreen to look at her. "Not today," she told him with a weak smile. "Not if we follow the path."

"Yes." He shook off the frightening mental image and concentrated on the controls. "Hekan, Kijoh. Can we activate the transporters in a single sweep?"

The Peliar and the Gorlan exchanged a wary look. "There will be a risk to those we beam up," said Hekan.

Kijoh nodded. "A staged-phase transport would be better."

"How much longer would it take?" Saru asked.

"Lieutenant, I can compensate for any phase drift!" Ensign Weeton broke into the conversation. "I've tied us into the computer core on board the *Yang*, see, the shuttlecraft's duotronic matrix can process twice as fast as this ship's—"

"Do it!" Saru interrupted.

"We need to be close," said Nathal.

Saru nodded, manipulating the helm controls. "One pass over the length of the carrier . . . I hope it will be enough." He was going to say more, but a flurry of brilliant lances cut through the darkness on the main screen, briefly silencing him as the *Shenzhou* and the Tholian cruiser traded fire.

"The Starfleet ship has drawn their attention," said Madoh with a frown. "I suggest we not waste the opportunity."

"Together," breathed Ejah. "We can succeed together."

"I'm taking us in." Saru applied power to the starfreighter's impulse engines and the big ship barreled toward the mauled carrier, vectoring into an approach that would pass within hundreds of meters of the warship's splintered, battered hull.

"Locking on to life signs," said Madoh. Despite the tension, he still maintained the same calm focus as before. The hub's centering influence remained firm. "Ready to transport."

"Signal from Adjutant Craea," called Yashae. "His crew are ready to evacuate."

Another flare of silent detonation flashed off in the distance, a miniature star glittering as a photon torpedo struck the Tholian cruiser. Blinding spars of light crackled back and the *Shenzhou* veered into them, taking hits that could have struck the other vessels.

Once again, Saru forced himself to look away from the unfolding melee, and he threw Nathal a sharp nod. "Ready, Commander."

"Hekan . . ." Nathal gestured to her second. "Bring them aboard!"

"Energizing," said the other Peliar, turning a pair of virtual dials to their maximum range as the freighter made its pass. Every system on the command tier briefly lost power as the energy shunt took place, lights fading, then returning.

"We've got them!" Weeton broke out in a grin as a

train of blue indicator lights illuminated across his screen. "Transporter cycle is active, pattern buffers holding!"

"Shunt the survivors into the cargo modules along with the Gorlan refugees," ordered Nathal. "The wounded will be safer there."

"I don't think any of Tauh's crew were expecting to end their day being rescued by us," noted Kijoh.

"Lieutenant, the adjutant wants to be beamed directly to the command deck." Yashae shot Saru a look.

"Ensign Weeton?" Saru looked to the other officer, who nodded back at him.

"Diverting his pattern . . . now."

A column of emerald light formed on a pad in the far corner of the compartment as the freighter completed its run and moved away into open space. On a secondary screen, Saru saw the view aft as the damaged carrier fell away behind them. Orange fire glowed in the wounded vessel's thruster grids, and it began to move of its own accord.

Saru turned back as the hum of the transporter effect faded and saw the Peliar officer Craea standing on the deck. His ornate headdress was gone, and the fine tailoring of his uniform was marred by burn marks and ragged tears along one arm. Coughing, the adjutant stepped forward, patting himself as if to check that his body was still intact.

Craea looked up and met Nathal's questioning gaze. Saru saw the look that passed between them and watched the commander's face fall. "My father . . . ? The admiral . . . ?"

"He chose another path," the adjutant said sadly, coming forward to put a hand on Nathal's shoulder. "Rather than return to Peliar Zel in disgrace, he chose service." He nodded toward the screen, where the carrier was gathering momentum for an attack run.

"No!" Nathal took a half step away from her station, then halted, turning rigid.

Saru felt a stab of empathy for her. She was in command, and she had a responsibility to her crew and everyone on board her ship. But she was also Tauh's daughter, and despite his behavior, it was clear she still cared deeply for him.

"I warned her," whispered Ejah.

In that instant, Saru glimpsed a fraction of the burden that Nathal was carrying. *The price of being a captain*, he told himself. It was a sobering thought.

"Do we have all the remaining survivors?" said Nathal, her voice almost catching.

Weeton gave a nod. "Confirmed."

"Then we must give the admiral the fighting room he needs," she replied, turning to look toward Saru. Her moment of fragility was gone.

Saru accepted the order with a solemn nod and vectored the star-freighter onto a new course, putting distance between them and the engagement.

On the screen, the crescent-shaped carrier fell into a wall of fire spitting from the Tholian cruiser's cannons.

"He's still coming!" shouted Januzzi. "Captain, the Peliars mean to ram them!"

"Kayla, get us clear!" Georgiou gave the order, but Detmer was already doing it, putting the *Shenzhou* into a climbing impulse turn that sent them out of the Tholian cruiser's fire corridor.

Burnham's hand went to her mouth in shock. She couldn't look away as the Peliar carrier threw itself headlong into the heaviest concentration of energy bolts and began to crumple. She blinked away the smoke issuing from the bridge's overloaded EPS conduits, ignored the wail of the starship's alert sirens, and watched the carrier meet its end.

The two warships collided with a flash of uncontrolled

discharge, and the claws of the Tholian cruiser seemed to close around the arc of the Peliar carrier's hull. Then Tauh's ship was breaking apart into two great severed chunks of burning metal, flaring and combusting against the blackness.

The metallic-crystalline form of the Tholian ship skidded through space, unable to absorb the full force of the collision. The cruiser's deflectors collapsed in a flash of radiation, and cascading shock damage became visible all along the dorsal and ventral surfaces. But still, the vessel's weapons glowed with their fierce, diamond-sharp fire. The warship's sacrifice had been a body blow, that much was certain, but it was not enough to end the fight.

"There's still another operable spinner out there," said Ensign Troke, as if he was reading Burnham's thoughts. "And that one we hit earlier."

"Captain, the Tholian cruiser's shields are down across the board," reported Gant. "They're defenseless."

"We can end this right now," said ch'Theloh, rounding on Georgiou. "Hit them with everything we have before they get their systems back up." The Andorian's antennae reeled back across his scalp. "We can send the Tholian Assembly a message they won't soon forget."

"Lieutenant Gant, charge all forward phasers and load photon torpedo tubes." Georgiou drew herself up, her manner becoming cold and clinical.

"Captain?" The word slipped from Burnham's lips. This wasn't what she expected from the woman she considered her mentor. Even in the face of such naked aggression from the Tholians, the thought of landing a killing blow here and now struck Burnham as a step too far.

Georgiou held up a hand to silence her. "Michael . . . when you pull a weapon, you have to be ready to use it." She looked toward Ensign Fan's station. "Mary, give me ship to ship. I think they'll listen to us now."

Fan gave a nod. "You're on, Captain."

"Attention, Tholian vessels, this is Captain Georgiou aboard the Federation *Starship Shenzhou*. You were warned not to turn this into a fight, but you ignored us. You violated nonaligned space with military intent. You deliberately provoked this situation by sabotaging a Federation monitor buoy, assaulting a Gorlan colony world, and firing on Peliar Zel starships. There is no doubt in my mind that you have done this in order to justify the expansion of your borders, and sow chaos among your neighbors. This will not go unanswered." She glanced at Gant. "Lieutenant, lock all weapons on the Tholian cruiser and prepare to fire."

Burnham's breath caught in her throat. *She's actually going to do it.*

And then Georgiou caught her eye, and there was something there that said otherwise. "I give you notice," continued the captain. "The colonies of the Gorlan and the people of the Peliar Zel Cohort have the protection of Starfleet and the United Federation of Planets, whether they ask for it or not, whether they are members or not. Unwarranted attacks on them will not be permitted." She took a step forward, knowing that her image was being projected directly onto the bridge of the Tholian craft. "If you don't back off, then you will be fully responsible for what happens next. This skirmish can end here . . . or the next shots fired will be the first salvo in a Tholian-Federation war. The decision is yours." Georgiou made a throat-cutting gesture, and Fan closed the channel.

Every voice on the *Shenzhou*'s bridge was stilled. Only the steady bleating of the red alert continued to sound, marking out the seconds as they passed. Finally, ch'Theloh spoke. "Burnham, you're the xenoanthropologist. Tell me, how well do Tholians respond to threats?"

"In all honesty, Commander?" She shook her head. "I don't know."

"Good," said the captain, "then this will be educational for everyone."

A chime sounded from the communications console. "They're hailing us," said Fan.

"Let's hear it."

The ensign touched a control on her panel, and a faceted shape appeared, projected in midair over the deck. The Tholian's strange, gemlike form studied them with a withering, fiery glare. *"Your ship crossed our borders in order to reach this location. That is a violation of treaty agreement."* The screeching voice was like nails dragged across a blackboard.

"You broke the rules first," noted ch'Theloh. "And we are on a rescue mission. What's your excuse?"

The Tholian concentrated its attention on the captain. *"We do not desire open war. But we will aggressively defend our borders. We will discourage all those who seek to encroach upon the Assembly's territories."* The alien paused, and Burnham sensed it was holding back a more belligerent response. *"Know this. If our sovereignty is violated again by Federation vessels, or those of any other species, those craft and all aboard them will be considered prisoners of the Tholian Assembly. If you test this resolve, then it shall be war."*

There was no wait for a reply. The hologram winked out as the Tholian's grating warning rang around the bridge.

"Detecting power spikes in their engine core," said Troke. "The cruiser is moving off, back toward the border."

"Confirming that," noted Detmer. "Looks like that other spinner is tractoring the damaged one out as well."

"Give them some space," said the captain, and then she blew out a breath. "But . . . let's just keep a bead on them until they're out of weapons range."

Georgiou looked back, and Burnham met her gaze. "Would you have done it?" she asked quietly as the bridge crew got back to work. "Crossed that line?"

Burnham's mentor was quiet before she found her reply. "Michael, I am very glad that is a question I did not have to answer today. I hope I can reach the end of my career and never have to find out."

Yashae was waiting for Saru at the foot of the ladder leading up to the airlock in the ceiling, where the shuttle *Yang* was still docked. Weeton's head peeked out from the open hatch and he gave a nod, before retreating back inside.

"Everyone's accounted for, sir," she told him. "Zoxom beamed back to the *Shenzhou* with Lieutenant Commander Johar and the other casualties. Subin is already on board."

Saru nodded, and hesitated. Now that the time had come for him to leave, it felt hard to let go. The Kelpien had the unpleasant sensation that when he departed, the delicate peace he had helped to create would start to crumble.

"We will take it from here," said Nathal, standing a few meters away, picking up on his reluctance. "Thank you, Lieutenant Saru, for all you have done." The commander's hard-edged manner had been blunted by her recent experiences and her losses. She was still finding her way back, he realized, and once more Saru was struck by the sense of what she had to be feeling.

Too often we think our leaders have all the answers, that nothing can affect them, he reflected. But Saru had been thrust into that role over the past few days, and he had learned the hard way how untrue that was. *I knew it would be challenging, but not like this.*

"Our people thank you also." At Nathal's side, Ejah stood with the Gorlan engineer Kijoh, and the hub inclined her head to him. "You should know that Madoh has promised to surrender himself to the Cohort's authorities. He will take full responsibility for his actions against the Peliar Zel and accept their justice. His crimes were fueled by desperation, but they were not the deeds of all Gorlans." Ejah glanced at Nathal. "I hope we can take steps to heal the divide between our species, Commander."

"We have each transgressed against the other," Nathal said with a rueful nod. "No more."

"The Federation will be glad to offer any help it can, to both your peoples," said Saru. He managed a brief smile. "In the meantime, I have some actions of my own to take responsibility for." He took a step toward the shuttle, but that reluctance to leave pulled hard on him and he halted again. "Forgive me," he began again, "but I cannot depart in good conscience without saying something."

Saru drew himself up and took a breath, surveying the faces of the Gorlans and the Peliar. All of them were so unlike one another, not just by nature of their outward appearance but by their cultures, their upbringing, and their beliefs. The idea of such disparate beings putting aside these things to find common cause seemed like an unclimbable mountain, at best an alliance of convenience that would fall apart once the threat that forced it into existence was gone. He had to show them that there was more at stake.

"These facts are undeniable. The galaxy is a dangerous place, and there are threats out there that you cannot anticipate. The next time, your enemies will not simply turn around and leave." Saru blinked, seeing dismay on their faces. He pressed on. "The Tholians endure. The Assembly continues to test its limits, as the Gorlan colony learned, and you must have no doubt that the moons of Peliar Zel are in their sights." He paused, trying to find the right words. "Don't allow yourselves to be driven by fear. Fear of them, fear of us, fear of each other." Saru gestured at the group. "I have lived a life of dread and I have learned that it cannot be dispelled if you are alone. Unity brings light. And light pushes back the dark."

He turned away and moved to follow Yashae up the ladder, but once more Saru felt that now-familiar tug on his sleeve and the ghostly presence of Ejah's aura pressing at his senses.

"Saru," she said, speaking quietly so no one else could hear her. "I want to tell you something, before you go."

He halted. "Yes?"

All four of her hands clasped around his, and her gentle serenity washed over him. "Don't struggle so," she said, meeting his gaze. "Don't push so hard against what you are. Embrace it."

"I . . . I don't understand."

Ejah nodded. "I know. Just . . . don't try to seek out a place without fear. It's a part of you, and you mustn't deny it. One day, you will find that, and it won't be real. Accept what you are, Saru. That's where your peace is." She withdrew and limped away, leaving him speechless.

"Lieutenant?" He looked up to see Yashae standing over him. "In your own time, sir."

He nodded and climbed aboard. "We're done here."

The *Yang* detached from the star-freighter's hull and fell away, turning nimbly about its axis to aim back toward the *Shenzhou*.

Saru slipped into the copilot's chair next to Ensign Weeton as the junior officer worked the controls, guiding them through the sea of wreckage that was still settling into an orbital band above the abandoned sanctuary planet.

"Wow," offered the ensign, glancing down at the transport ship's exterior hull. "Looks *way* worse from out here."

Saru had to admit Weeton was right. The big vessel had

weathered damage that a ship of its kind should never have been subjected to. It would take weeks for the craft to become fully spaceworthy again, and there was some irony in the fact that the *Shenzhou*'s engineering crews would once more be helping out with the repairs.

"With all due respect," said Subin, "somebody else can go over there and do the work this time. I want to get back to my own ship for a while." She smiled wistfully. "I really need a sonic shower."

"You really do," Yashae added dryly.

"And a decent meal," said Weeton, with feeling. "And after that I'm going to put in a request to remove my name from the landing party rotation for a few months."

"Agreed," said Saru.

Weeton gave him an odd look as he altered course to avoid a large chunk of broken hull metal. "Pardon me, Lieutenant, but is the captain going to be happy to see you?" He went on before Saru could answer. "I mean, let's be honest here, you are in pretty big trouble, sir. Captain Georgiou is reasonable, but do you really think she'll be—?"

Saru spoke over him. "Yes, thank you for reminding me, *Ensign*." He put hard emphasis on Weeton's rank. "Your tact is as nuanced as ever."

"Oh. Sorry, sir." The human shifted in his seat and brought the shuttle around, lining them up with an open bay on the *Shenzhou*'s primary hull. "I was just trying to be supportive, you know? And we're, ah, coming in to land."

"I trust you'll handle that with more finesse." Saru resisted the temptation to fold his arms defensively across his chest as he watched the bay grow larger through the canopy. The fact that Weeton was undoubtedly right did nothing to improve the Kelpien's mood.

The *Yang* slowed as it pushed through the force field holding the shuttlebay's atmosphere in place, and the craft turned gently as it settled to the deck. A pair of uniformed figures were waiting for them on the landing apron, both standing at attention. *Captain Georgiou and Lieutenant Burnham.*

"Y'know," offered Weeton, seeing them too, "on second thought? It, uh, probably won't be as bad as all that."

I am not going to wait to find out. The instant the shuttle's skids bumped to a halt on the deck, Saru was rising from his chair and marching back down the cabin, reaching the hatch at the rear before it had even finished sliding open. He strode straight toward the captain and ignored the look Burnham was giving him, refusing to flinch away from Georgiou's hard-eyed gaze.

Only a few days earlier, he had been in this exact spot, expecting a very similar conversation. The entire scenario felt unpleasantly familiar *and* ten times worse.

"Lieutenant Saru and landing party, reporting in," he said stiffly. "Mission accomplished."

"Oh, I'll be the judge of that," said the captain, and she turned her back on him, beckoning with one finger. "With me, Mister Saru. You've got quite a bit of explaining to do."

As he trailed after her, Saru couldn't stop himself from giving Burnham a sideways look. The human woman displayed a very Vulcan raised eyebrow, and an expression that said *Good luck; you're going to need it.*

The turbolift ride down to the bridge was exactly as uncomfortable as Georgiou wanted it to be, and she imagined that for the errant lieutenant it appeared to last for hours.

When the doors opened to deposit them on the *Shenzhou*'s bridge deck, she walked straight across to her ready room without waiting to see if Saru was following her, but from the corner of her eye the captain saw the sober look that her first officer gave the Kelpien. *Good. I want Saru to sweat this a little.*

She took the seat behind her desk and didn't offer him one. "Privacy," she said to the air, and the ready room's transparent doors turned frost white and opaque.

Standing at attention, Saru reminded her of a Terran greyhound she had seen as a child. Ropy and long of limb, he couldn't hide the nervous energy that was running through him even if he wanted to. She didn't need to tell him what mistakes he had made; he already knew. But for the record, it would have to be said.

"You're out of uniform," she began, noting that his delta-shield insignia was missing.

"I'm afraid so," he replied. "I apologize."

"From where I'm standing, that's the least of your infractions, mister. Start from the beginning," Georgiou told him, "from the point where you decided to follow your own initiative instead of Starfleet protocol."

Saru colored slightly, but he gave a small nod and cleared his throat. She listened in silence for the next ten minutes, taking in everything he said without interrupting or requesting clarification. If anything, that seemed to unnerve the lieutenant even more.

He talked about his good intentions toward the situation with the Gorlan refugees, the unexpected hijacking, and the guilt that weighed upon him from the troubling choices he had been forced to make in collusion with Madoh's plans. He talked about the Peliar captain Nathal and her people, and the discovery he had made among the Gorlans. Saru dwelled on the subject of the hub—the girl called Ejah—and the gift she had, and suddenly Georgiou understood what the lieutenant had meant about "Gorlan predictive abilities." It was a fascinating insight, one she intended to follow up at a later date, but for now she let it pass.

Saru went on, explaining how they had managed to regain control of the freighter after the rescue of the other Gorlans from the sanctuary world, and the new tensions that event had brought forth. Then there was Admiral Tauh and his warship, and she could guess at how the rest of it played out with the intervention of the Tholians. Part of Georgiou felt a silent dread as she realized how close the *Shenzhou* had come to arriving too late. She pushed away all thought of what might have awaited them had the ship been delayed.

The lieutenant's replay of events petered out. "You know the rest, Captain." He took a breath. "I am ready to accept whatever penalty you see fit."

She decided not to address the questions that were no doubt uppermost in the Kelpien's mind, not right away. "I spoke to Doctor Nambue just before you returned to the ship. He's quite busy with the patients you brought him. We've had to convert cargo bay one into a temporary hospital ward for the Gorlan and Peliar wounded. But in a way, I think it will be good for them. There's nothing like a hardship shared to bridge the gulf between two peoples. And you'll be glad to know that Lieutenant Commander Johar is already awake. I understand he's annoyed he missed out on all the excitement." She leaned back in her chair. "I am sure he'll have opinions on how he would have handled things over there."

"Better than I," Saru said, frowning and staring at the deck.

Georgiou shook her head. "Don't wallow in self-pity, Lieutenant. You're better than that."

Saru's head snapped up. It wasn't the response he had expected. "I made a lot of mistakes," he added.

"Yes, you did," she agreed. "What did you learn from them?"

"I am . . . uncertain . . ." He faltered. Saru was trying to figure out the right thing to say, the thing he thought Georgiou wanted to hear, and she shook her head.

"What did you learn?" She sounded out each word. "Something of value, I hope. That at least would be a saving grace for this whole incident."

The captain was deliberately pushing him, and he responded with a barely concealed flash of anger. "Perhaps if Lieutenant Burnham had been on that ship instead of me—"

Georgiou didn't let him finish. "You think I would be going easier on her?" When Saru hesitated to give an answer, she didn't relent. "Speak freely, Mister Saru. I won't have it any other way."

"Yes." He bit out the word. "Yes, Captain, I believe you would. I believe you favor her over me."

This is what I wanted. The truth. Georgiou wanted to smile but she didn't; instead, keeping her tone level, she said, "I do not play favorites with my crew, Lieutenant. I might stimulate competition among them, but that's all. I never meant you to think that . . ." She paused. "If you feel you're slipping behind another officer's performance, that's on you, not her."

His annoyance faded. "I tried to be more like Burnham, but that was the wrong thing to do."

"Of course it was," Georgiou said, not unkindly. "I don't need two Michael Burnhams on my ship. I need a Burnham and I need a Saru." She stood up and walked around the desk. "I am convinced both of you have the makings of excellent officers, perhaps even captains one day. But you're not there yet, not by a long shot. You need tempering, both of you." She let that lie, then went on. "If we are being brutally honest . . ."

"I would prefer it," Saru said meekly.

"You and Lieutenant Burnham are far more alike than either of you wants to admit." She gestured toward the door leading back to the bridge. "Michael is strong willed, opinionated, and intelligent . . . but that Vulcan upbringing of hers, the very thing that granted her all that, is also her weakness. She's strong, but she's brittle. Burnham needs to reconnect with her human side. And she's getting there." Georgiou met Saru's pale blue eyes. "As for you? Well, you're just as willful, emphatic, and smart, but you're in conflict with your innate Kelpien nature. You want to be aloof, but you want to please. You have an ego, but you are willing to subsume it for the greater good." The captain wandered past him, to the ready room's port, and looked out at the starscape. "Saru, I want you to find the path amid those points. I want you to learn to walk the line between who you *were* and who you *can be*. If you don't, you will never achieve your full potential."

"It is not easy for me," he admitted, moving to stand next to her. "I thought I was ready to make those kind of command decisions. I was . . . mistaken."

"Really?" Georgiou smiled slightly. "Lieutenant, you always think you are ready right up until you're not. The difference is, when confronted with that reality, the poor officers sink and the good ones swim. You kept swimming. You found solutions. Against every setback, you did not waver. You strove to make the nonviolent choice every time." She prodded him in the chest. "Not because of weakness, but because of strength."

"I did what I thought was right," he offered.

The captain lost herself in the view outside, seeing the distant starlight flash of the wreckage from the battle in orbit. "Violent responses are the quick and easy reaction, the refuge of the belligerent, like the Tholians. Starfleet will answer that in kind when we have to, but we always, *always* seek the other path if we can. That's the oath we swore to uphold when we put on these colors." She ran a hand over her collar. "You upheld that oath. But I won't lie, Saru, the way you got there was . . . shall we be generous and say *unconventional*?" His color deepened as she went on. "But you still did it. Thousands of people are alive now because of that. And perhaps hundreds of thousands more on the Peliar moons will rethink their attitudes to the Gorlans because of an example you set."

She waited for Saru to find his way to a reply. "I admit, the experience of being isolated from my own kind drove me in this. I know what it is to feel lost. I know how it feels to need the charity of others in order to survive."

Georgiou nodded but said nothing. She knew some of the story of how the Kelpien had come to leave his homeworld, of the Starfleet officers who had given Saru a chance when his own kind had turned their backs on him.

"I saw something of myself in the Gorlans," he explained. "And the Peliars too. I have seen how fears can divide people. But they can also be overcome, they can be a force with which to unite." A reluctant smile pulled at his thin lips. "And no one understands the nature of fear better than a Kelpien."

The captain gave him a nod. "It's a mess out here, Lieutenant. But that's how it goes. On the edge of Federation space, things are never as clean-cut as they seem in an Academy class. We find our way through and we move forward." She reached out and touched him on his shoulder. Saru's eyes widened. He was slowly catching up to the realization that Georgiou *wasn't* going to put him in the brig and demand his resignation. "I am standing you down for the next twenty-four hours, along with Weeton and all the others. Take a rest, you've earned it. And then I recommend you write a full and most highly detailed report."

"And Starfleet Command . . . ?"

"I'll speak with Admiral Terral. I'll explain it to him . . . logically." She jutted her chin toward the door. "You're dismissed, Lieutenant."

He nodded gratefully and walked away.

"Saru," she called as the doors hissed open. "Despite what you may think, you did well," she offered.

"Thank you, Captain." He nodded again. "I'll do better next time."

"I know you will."

Saru very carefully made certain not to make eye contact with anyone on the bridge in the short walk to the turbolift, and when the doors closed he managed to call out his deck in a low sigh before slumping against the wall.

His heart was still racing when he got back to his cabin and into the cool, quiet embrace of his personal space. It was odd how something as seemingly simple as a conversation with another sentient being could strike him with the same near panic as being chased by a predator—but then, Captain Philippa Georgiou was equally formidable in her own unique way.

"Waking from standby mode," said a familiar, artificial female voice. *"Do you wish to reset?"*

"No!" Saru said, with more force than he expected. "In fact, suspend all use of simulation program until otherwise ordered!"

"Confirmed." The computer gave an answering beep.

He took a deep breath, using it to center himself—and immediately Saru sensed something was *wrong*. It wasn't the same creeping discomfort he'd experienced back when the holographic simulator had been populating his cabin with unexpected dangers; this was a more subtle sense of something *not quite right*.

He turned in place, taking in the room, and then he had it. "Someone has been in here while I was gone," Saru said aloud. He scowled and moved toward the shelf where his personal effects lay, his eyes drawn first to the three-dimensional chess board in one corner. The pieces were still where he had left them, in the positions of a classic el-Mitra Exchange opening.

Saru was reaching for them when the door chimed, and he froze. "Who's there?"

"It's me," said a woman's voice through the closed door, and Saru immediately knew exactly who it was that had invaded his privacy.

"Enter," he snapped, turning to Burnham as she took a cautious step into the room.

"Saru," she said, by way of a greeting. She halted on the threshold, looking around warily, and then the Kelpien was certain his instinct had been correct.

"Do come in," he said, with a sniff. "*Again*."

"Is that hologram going to attack me if I do?"

"I turned it off." Still, she hesitated. "*Now* you're reluctant to enter? Please make up your mind, Lieutenant."

She stepped all the way in, and the door closed behind her. "I came to apologize, Saru, for what you have obviously already figured out. I suppose I should have known—"

"That Kelpiens have an unerring sense for the invasion of their personal spaces? Yes, you should. Perhaps you can add that to whatever report you are writing on me!" He said the last half mockingly, but then, off the expression on the human's face, he realized how close he was to the truth. "You *are* writing a report on me?"

"No," insisted Burnham. She gave an exasperated sigh. "It's not like that. It's just, after the freighter was hijacked and the *Shenzhou* was attacked, there were questions that came up. About you."

He stiffened, torn between a sudden need to ask what those questions had been and the fear of knowing the answers. "You can rest assured," Saru began, "that I have taken full responsibility for the damage inflicted on this vessel."

"Commander ch'Theloh wanted to make sure there was no question of you being under any kind of outside influence or suffering from any mental impairment," insisted Burnham. "Believe me, he would have had this place dismantled down to the bulkheads."

"Let me guess. You intervened? You offered to search my quarters and violate my privacy for him? How generous of you."

"I'm sorry I had to do it," she countered. "And perhaps the order was questionable, but I came here because I wanted to protect you!" Burnham came closer. "You can't be surprised that it happened. You never open up to your crewmates, Saru. You're standoffish, and people see that as unfriendly. No one knows what to think about you, and that can breed suspicion in someone like ch'Theloh."

He faltered. "It's not . . ." He stopped and tried again. "I am not a people person."

Burnham's expression softened. "Saru, I know you think like me. I know you want to get ahead in Starfleet, but to do that you'll have to meet people halfway. You know, actually try to make some friends?"

"I have friends," he replied hotly. But then his face fell as he considered the veracity of his own statement. "Well. Colleagues. Crewmates, really." The explanation seemed weak. He wanted to reject what Burnham had said, but in that damning moment he knew she was right.

"Sure," Burnham replied, without weight. She seemed to realize that she had overstepped, and gave a nod. "I should go. I'm sure you need to rest. Again, I apologize. I hope it won't negatively impact our working together in the future."

An uncommon thought occurred to Saru. *Has Burnham just tried to open a door, only for me to close it in her face?* He remembered what he had said to Captain Georgiou, about asking for and accepting help from others.

The idea that he and Michael Burnham might actually become friends instead of challengers seemed as distant as the stars outside his cabin, but then Saru found himself wondering if there was another way they could connect—a way they might be able to test each other that didn't involve disagreeing over every little thing.

"I am too—I believe the correct word is—*wired* to rest, Lieutenant," he told her, glancing at the chess set. "You play, I assume?"

Burnham bristled, as if the answer was obvious. "Of course. Vulcan children are masters of the game from a very early age. I used to play against Captain Georgiou until she got tired of me winning all the time."

"Of course," repeated Saru, and instead he went to the rectangular box of dark, carved wood placed on the center of the shelf. "Then perhaps you would be interested in a different challenge?" He tapped the long lid and it flipped around, opening out into a small playing board. "These are the only things I kept when I left my homeworld. These small items are precious to me." Once he began to explain it, he didn't want to stop. "Carved charms. Stones, and the like." He held one up for her to see, a faceted piece of black volcanic glass. "If one of us perishes, those who knew them well may take an item as a way to remember the lost. In that way, it connects us to our past and our present." Saru carried the box to a nearby table and took a seat, centering it before him.

"And this is a game as well?" Burnham came closer, clearly fascinated. She studied the board. "It bears a resemblance to one from an ancient Earth culture, the Royal

Game of Ur. The Boslics also have a similar thing, but it involves tethered birds and a board several hundred meters long."

"Indeed?" said Saru. He reached into the box and removed a handful of playing pieces and a number of tetrahedral dice. "The Kelpien name is *Kaasad*. The word means *memory*."

Saru saw a rare smile cross Burnham's face, and he shared it. He could see she was intrigued, not only by the concept of the game, but also by the insight it could provide into him and his species.

Before today, Saru might have felt like that would be inviting the discovery of something personal, but his experience out on the Peliar ship and with the Gorlans now made that thought seem trivial and foolish.

"I've grown bored beating the ship's computer each time I wish to play," Saru told her. "I could do with a better opponent."

Burnham gave a nod and took the seat opposite him. "Show me. I promise I'll try not to win too quickly."

Saru gave a low mutter of dry amusement and set up the pieces. In the starlight from the window, they glittered like secrets.

Acknowledgments

First and foremost, I have to thank Kirsten Beyer for inviting me to join the new voyage that is *Star Trek: Discovery*, and for the opportunity to help shape the backstory of a key member of the *Discovery*'s crew. I'm honored to be able to contribute to this new incarnation of the *Star Trek* saga, and working closely with Kirsten has been—as always—a great experience.

I also want to extend my appreciation to Lisa Randolph, Ted Sullivan, Bo Yeon Kim, Erika Lippoldt, Sean Cochran, Chris Silvestri, and Aaron Harberts for accommodating me and my numerous questions in the *Star Trek: Discovery* writers' room; thanks for enlightenment, enthusiasm, and the grilled cheese sandwich.

Salutes to Doug Jones, Sonequa Martin-Green, Michelle Yeoh, and the rest of the *Shenzhou* crew for performances that helped me anchor my narrative with a cast of compelling characters.

Tips of the hat must go to my sterling cohorts David Mack and Dayton Ward, for their collaboration, and their novels *Desperate Hours* and *Drastic Measures,* which set the pace for me to follow. Special thanks also to Margaret Clark, for her tireless work in making sure this novel happened, and Ed Schlesinger and John Van Citters.

My gratitude to Franz Joseph, Michael Okuda, Denise Okuda, and Debbie Mirek for their invaluable works of reference in the form of the *Star Fleet Technical Manual* and

Star Trek Encyclopedia, both essential tomes on my resource bookshelf for all things Final Frontier; and to my friends and fellow writers Peter J. Evans and Lisa Smith, MSc, for their insights into theoretical xenobiology.

And as always, much love to Mandy Mills.

About the Author

James Swallow is a BAFTA nominee, a *New York Times* and *Sunday Times* bestseller, and proud to be the only British writer to have worked on a *Star Trek* television series, creating the original story concepts for the *Star Trek: Voyager* episodes "One" and "Memorial."

His *Star Trek* writing includes the novels *The Latter Fire*, *Sight Unseen*, *The Poisoned Chalice*, *Cast No Shadow*, *Synthesis*, the Scribe Award winner *Day of the Vipers*; the novellas *The Stuff of Dreams* and *Myriad Universes: Seeds of Dissent*; the short stories "The Slow Knife," "The Black Flag," "Ordinary Days," and "Closure" for the anthologies *Seven Deadly Sins*, *Shards and Shadows*, *The Sky's the Limit*, and *Distant Shores*; scripting the videogame *Star Trek Invasion*; and over four hundred articles in thirteen different *Star Trek* magazines around the world.

Swallow is the award-winning author of the internationally bestselling "Marc Dane" thrillers *Nomad*, *Exile*, and *Ghost*; the *Sundowners* steampunk westerns; and novels from the worlds of *24*, *Doctor Who*, *Warhammer 40000*, *Stargate*, *2000AD*, and more.

His other credits include scripts for videogames and audio dramas, including *Ghost Recon Wildlands*, the *Deus Ex* series, *Disney Infinity*, *No Man's Sky*, *Fable: The Journey*, *Battlestar Galactica*, *Blake's 7*, and *Space 1889*.

He lives in London and is currently working on his next book.